C000127922

AERIETI CHRONICLES OF THE FALL

Roa Seeks

Independently published

Copyright © 2020 Electra M Nanou

All rights reserved. No part of this publication may be re-produced, stored in a retrieval system, or transmitted in any form or by any means, electronic, mechanical, photo-copying, recording, or otherwise, without the prior per-mission of both the copyright owner and publisher.

ISBN: 9798603421513

This book is a work of fiction. All characters, places, and incidents are either products of the author's imagination or used fictitiously. Any resemblance to actual persons, living or dead, events, or locales is entirely coincidental.

Interior design and illustrations: Natalia Junqueira

Table of Contents

Dear reader

It has fallen to me to translate the Aerieti Chronicles of The Fall into English. Our numbers are, of course, still stretched thin. And, of course, this is most important and honourable work. There is indeed nothing more shameful than to shirk duties related to such grave milestones of our order. And I am certain my fellow agents who also call my world home and were just seen releasing birds into the Archive were busy awaiting punishment for rejecting the grand honour that has been bestowed upon me. Alaron Phaere, my friend, my sorrowful thoughts art with thee.

As for the text to follow, the scarcity of written accounts to accompany our mnemonic sources has led to certain gaps in how the Key evaded our immediate grasp. Our scholars, however, are quite satisfied with the accuracy of the events compiled thus far. Future insights shalt be promptly inserted for thy convenience. Furthermore, while Luimari and Aerieti speech has been adapted from third-party translations, my fluency in Therean human permitted a loyal transcription of the varied accents and dialects encountered in the memories. To those wishing to discuss Itanian matters further, I humbly put my field of expertise at thy disposal.

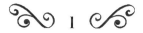

Prologue

It sounded like justice. The waters crashed with such sharp force into the basin. She closed her eyes and let the roiling rhythm echo through her. She leaned over the well's stone to feel more of the divine waters' spray. How soothing it was. *Perhaps only demons are affected by it.* If only she had a vial with her, she could take some to study. Her mistress would not need to know. It could even help her work.

'Parda.'

She stiffened. Her mistress could not read thoughts, as far as she knew. She straightened casually and turned to face the cloaked figure. The moons' light reflected off the waters to cast an enchanting glow over her mistress's grim form. Still, none of her features were visible.

The voice emerged again from beneath the hood. 'Hast thou begun?'

Parda nodded and stepped closer. 'I've a fresh collection of creatures. Each trial is proving more exciting than the last. You won't be disappointed.'

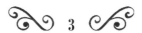

'Good.' The figure lowered her head while she reached into her robes. 'I have faith in thy skills, my friend. I believe thou canst make use of this.'

She produced a cylindrical glass case with what looked like flowers inside. Parda squinted as she took the container and brought it to the light. The blooms were an exquisite shade of purple dotted with red.

'Nightshade?' she asked.

'From the Dragon Fens,' the woman responded, chuckling softly at Parda's overwhelmed expression.

Parda's hands shook. For fear of dropping it, she clutched the case to her chest like a baby. There was no greater gift, nothing more precious to an alchemist. Nature growing from the bones of dragons.

'Mistress, I can't—I'm so—'

A slender finger silenced her.

'Those came to me at a great price. Do not waste them. Thank me with results, the best thou canst. Our time is shorter than we had thought.'

Parda curtsied deeply and watched the dark figure glide back into the shadows. She stroked the glass, dreaming of the things she could do. Her eyes wandered back to the glimmering water, still coveting just a few drops from it. But her mistress had been so kind. *It would be shameful to anger her.* When she succeeded she could ask for some. Yes, her greatest creation for an ounce of liquid divinity. And she was close. She turned her back to the well and made for the stables.

Chapter 1

T*he sun is my wine.* Meecha lifted his goblet to the sky. He covered the sun with the chalice so the rays could penetrate the glass, already tinted orange and crimson from bowl to stem. Tiny, embedded diamonds sparkled like stars against glorious fire. Radiance spilt from the glass and enveloped his hand. *Could that ever be possible, to drink the sun?* If it were caught and liquefied, perhaps. He would shrivel like a prune with sunlight in his belly. It would drink him.

Meecha placed the goblet on the windowsill behind his right shoulder. He looked over the stone roofs of Dadral, dull compared to dawn's blue, pink, and lilac. The male luima were emerging from their hovels with pickaxes, shovels, and hammers in hand. Their small forms trudged along the pebbled streets on their way to the mines and construction sites. Although luima himself, Meecha had always veered from the 'proper ways'. Crafting gadgets and playing with pretty precious gems did have their appeal, but spending day after day hacking and heaving at rocks,

metal, or another's shield had always seemed like a waste of time and intellect. Only the business of the tradesman and desk-minion had proven duller. Greater things were to be his – thus he had known many failed careers before his true calling opened its interdimensional doors to him.

He looked down from the window ledge. A precarious height, but not the gravest danger he had ever been in. His buttocks were getting numb, however, from hours of sitting on hard stone. He gathered his legs against his chest and put his back to the wall. With his feet perched on the edge of the ledge, he pushed upwards, cautiously inching onto the wooden shutter. As he neared his full height, he heard a strange sound – metal grinding against metal. Meecha, looking curiously around, leant forward, and felt the shutter tilt in the same direction. His eyes bulged when he realised what had happened: the shutter had slid off its hinges.

The weight made him teeter towards the edge. With a strangled gasp, he let the shutter drop to the side, hoping that it would simply land on the other end of the ledge. It did not. It rebounded and plummeted towards the street below.

'Watch out!' he screamed in Luimari.

Meecha recognised a passer-by, who looked up with a start and jumped out of the shutter's way. Its splintering crash echoed through the town. Curious heads turned to the sound.

'Roa!' Grek Rydon barked from below in the same tongue. 'Your father will hear of this.'

'I'm truly sorry,' Meecha groaned as the crusty miner stalked away, muttering to himself.

Meecha cursed his sour luck. He turned to the window, picked up the goblet from the sill, and climbed into

the attic, empty but for the top landing of a staircase on the far side. He bounded down two flights of stairs, rested the goblet on a step, and rushed to the front door, which he opened timidly and peered out. There was no one in the street, so Meecha made for the mangled shutter, quick and quiet. He had already brought most if it inside, when, as if waiting in ambush, two luima ladies, both mothers of orderly families, wandered past with a pointed look at the shutter and a tut. Meecha rolled his eyes as he dragged the last bit of wood into the hall and closed the door behind him, a little concerned about what those wilting gazes signified: if they knew, so would his father soon.

Meecha broke the shutter into even smaller pieces and piled them by the fireplace. Then he picked up the goblet – and a bag lying forlorn on the living room floor – before entering the kitchen, whistling. He carried his chirpy tune past the dusty dining table to the farthest corner between a lamp mounted on the wall and a gargantuan set of drawers, gifted to him by his late grandmother. He halted before the blank corner and, while still whistling, put the goblet on the drawers so he could shift the bag's strap to a more comfortable angle across his shoulder. Like a conductor, he concluded the song with a twirl of his fingers and watched as the floor's stone tiles magically dissolve to reveal a staircase below.

Down the secret passage he went, each of the five steps lighting up a misty white beneath his feet. With every descending tread, he traced a letter on either wall with each hand. Except for the fifth step. There Meecha stopped and leant in towards the sealed stone door. His lips barely brushed against the dark grey surface when he whispered the final password. The ancient, lazy door swung open.

Meecha was greeted by the musky sweet scent of dried flowers gathered into a basket hanging beside the door. He dumped his bag onto the large table in the centre of the chamber, unfastened the straps and flipped the flap, loosened the cord and undid the zipper.

A thin, no-longer-white cloak bulged through the opening, stains of yellow, brown, and haunting red unravelling with the garment. Meecha removed it from its confines and put it in a tub. The scalding water and ruthless soaps would come later. Next he pulled out a pair of tattered sandals that could be of use again with some leather and glue. They joined the racks of shoes to be repaired. An object in a round leather case the size of his palm was immediately locked in the heavily enchanted arvadeir safe in the stone wall behind the sink's mirror. When Meecha returned to the bag and pulled out a tiny pouch of seeds from its depths he gasped excitedly. He clasped it with care and lifted it onto the shelf lined with other pouches that would one day wreathe his house in blooms majestic and strange. Glancing back into the bag, he found a shell and black marbles strewn at the bottom. The coiled shell of gold and green luminescence was given a home on one of the numerous square shelves displaying souvenirs. A jar accommodated the marbles – the currency would come in handy if he ever returned to Uiedre.

Meecha looked up from the now empty bag to gaze around the room. A thin layer of dust coated the bookcases. His crafting and alchemy benches needed tidying. Coloured bottles, scraps of metal, screws, and tools lay exactly as he had left them when he had dashed out of the house a few weeks before, only to return late the previous night.

A jingle jolted Meecha half out of his skin before he realised that it was the visitor alarm. He raced up the staircase and through the house to pause for several heartbeats behind the door. He opened it slowly and saw his brother's broad back as he was about to walk away.

'Mern!' Meecha called, relaxing slightly.

The luima turned, his short ponytail quivering at the nape of his neck. He had a black-curled head, just like their father's, but with the soft chestnut eyes of their mother, the only feature he and Meecha had in common.

'So it's true,' Mern said curtly in Luimari, shoving his hands into the pockets of his frayed ankle-length breeches. 'You have returned.'

Meecha's smile was half a grimace. 'How angry are they?'

'About you vanishing again or dropping a window on old Grek's head?' Mern gave a gravelly chuckle as Meecha slapped his forehead and groaned. 'They're not thrilled,' he added.

'It was a shutter,' Meecha fired back, yanking the door wider, 'not a window. And it fell off me. And it only almost hit him.'

Amusement lifted Mern's brow, a cheeky smirk already curling his lips. Meecha noticed his brother's demeanour, always kinder than the other male members of his family, and then the sun glaring down at him. A pang of love and guilt moved Meecha to stand aside.

'Want to come in for some water? That's all I have.'

Mern shrugged, 'Why not?'

He lumbered into the hall, pausing at the arched door to the living room where he passed a casual look over the room, unfurnished but for three wall lights, one with a blue dream-catcher hanging from it. With a subtle quirk of his

mouth, Mern moved on to the kitchen, his hands still in his pockets.

Meecha strode past him to the steel pitcher on the kitchen counter and opened a cupboard overhead to find one tall glass and one mug. He glanced over his shoulder at Mern, but his brother, stretched out in Meecha's usual chair at the table, was making a show of straining his neck to give this room a far more diligent inspection. Meecha grabbed the glass, slammed the cupboard shut, and started pouring the water, when Mern suddenly broke the long, awkward silence.

'What's that?' he said and left his seat in the direction of the house's most important corner, a partition against the kitchen blocking it from Meecha's sight.

'What! What're you doing?' Meecha exclaimed.

He dumped the pitcher on the counter with a clang and rushed after Mern. Skin crawling with fright, he found his brother standing with his back to the solid, innocuous corner and holding up the beautiful goblet. Meecha had forgotten all about it.

'Where do you get this stuff?' Mern, distracted by the wealth in his hands, failed to see Meecha sag with relief. 'Treasure after treasure you bring and this place is still as bare as when you bought it.'

'I told you,' Meecha replied, drifting back to the kitchen and bringing the glass of water to where Mern had been seated. 'I'm gone so often that thieves make it more of a home than I do. Anything they've left is too heavy or worthless to carry away. And I suspect nobody's doing much to stop them.'

Mern lowered himself into the chair again, placing the goblet in the middle of the table. He sipped his water and eyed Meecha.

'That's one of my questions answered,' he said sombrely.

Meecha tilted his head and squinted. 'Actually, that was more of a statement.'

Mern, irritated, stuck his tongue over his teeth, but was amiable when he asked, 'Where did you get that?' He pointed at the goblet.

'I was given it.'

'By whom?'

'A man.'

'What man?'

'A friend.'

'Who?'

'Noneof.'

'Family name?' Mern's hand shot up to stop Meecha from responding. 'Let me guess… Yourbusiness?'

Meecha gasped, 'You know him!' and grinned.

Mern glared. He admitted defeat by gulping his water, allowing the silence to build up again.

'How's Mother?' Meecha hesitated to ask.

'Worried,' his brother grumbled. He took a few moments to put his empty glass down and then relented, 'but still holding the house up.'

Meecha nodded with a pleased yet remorseful little smile. 'And the others?'

'Father was promoted to Chief Overseer of the mines. Been strutting through town like he owns it. Well, he does, in a way. Jaika remains Champion of Dadral. I swear our big brother will wed that axe of his in the end.'

Meecha chortled at the thought of the weapon wrapped in white and pink ribbons and a veil, swishing in Jaika's arms, his shield the best man – none could claim Jaika's trust like that wall of arvadeir.

Subduing his own mirth, Mern continued, 'and Finkin's Finkin. Chasing the girls and a good laugh. He's no Meecha Roa, though.' He sounded almost proud as he winked at his youngest brother, who shrugged nonchalantly while lifting his chin an inch higher. 'You can see them all for yourself. We're having family breakfast tomorrow.'

Meecha's long moan rose in volume with every word Mern uttered. 'Mother's desperate to see you. I promised to persuade you to come. She's clearing the food stalls as we speak. Quit your whinging and come see us.'

Meecha ran out of breath.

'For Mother's sake,' his brother snuck in solemnly, ignoring the indignant stare directed at him.

Meecha ground his teeth, but soon conceded. 'Fine.' His miserable mumble barely left his lips.

'Promise,' Mern pressed him. 'Promise not to take off again.'

Meecha tutted and averted his eyes. 'I promise.'

'Great,' Mern gave the table a smug tap and smiled broadly. 'We'll see you in the morning then. I'd get a good night's sleep, if I were you. You look like a corpse struck by lightning.'

Chapter 2

After his brother had left, Meecha approached the nearest mirror to behold his extraordinary state. Curly ginger hair sticking out in every direction, except for the single dreadlock pointing down, skin drained of colour by sleeplessness, eyes bloodshot and sagging, dirt and dust smeared all over his face virtually black as soot. The scalding bath that had followed proved insufficient to beat the grime.

I'll have another in the morning, Meecha resolved as he sprawled himself across the mattress, bedding unnecessary.

Steam drifting up from his scoured body, muscles previously cramped now melted to sweet, stiff inertness, he sank into sleep. Exhaustion shrouded him in darkness and he floated there, light and peaceful.

Dreams visited him, his latest adventures fresh in his mind. He swayed once more upon the back of a giant insect as it crossed scorching deserts and seas

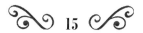

of sapphire-blue on long stilt-like legs and membranous wings. The goblet was back in his hand, but being clinked by others of equal splendour, these held by his benefactors. The sentient creatures, their diamond hearts pulsing white through bodies of shifting golden sand, showered him with grateful smiles and toasted their precious water in his name.

His father's thunderous voice ripped through the festivities, scolding Meecha for dropping a full bucket of water. How dare he waste their water, Yanga Roa demanded through chapped, sputtering lips. His black beard was all Meecha could see as he gawked up at that flushed face proclaiming the virtues of a 'real male': strong, disciplined, hard-working. Meecha's small hands took hold of the bucket's handle to swing the whole thing against the well, where it bounced and returned to whack Yanga's ankle. Meecha's vision blurred from the force of his father's roar and slap. Like a scarlet sandstorm, it swept him off his feet and lifted him above the stone houses, pain and fear driving him higher and higher, until the dreamless void reclaimed him.

Meecha hovered for a while, heart racing. No image or sound shook his rest, save his blood throbbing in his ears. Only when he was calm again did he look down to find a magnificent world open up beneath him, like a picture book spreading its pages. A luscious landscape of ancient forests, mountains, and oceans — the earth still ruled here. Meecha could feel the planet's pulse, her power, her magic, her will.

He neared the ground. He picked a plush valley to land in. It was filled with white and red flowers. As he flew closer, he saw a person carving a path through *them. It was a girl's face that turned up to meet his eagle eyes. The black of her hair matched the night, but golden ribbons illuminated her locks. Their sheen was the last thing he could make out as the dream dissipated. The sun streamed in through Meecha's window to gently stroke his eyelids.*

Stray thoughts of wonder accompanied his stretching limbs. *Who was that girl?* If she was someone from his past, he had had too few encounters with humans to remember her. He rolled over the cosy mattress, groaning with glee, flexing his fingers and toes and muscles, gradually pulling himself into a sitting position, where he slouched and gazed out the window at the early morning.

The family awaits, he mused, heart sinking.

His second soaking session was a leisurely process. He took the time to appreciate the luxury of a grithewood-scented bubble bath. Half-affected by his dreams and half-reluctant to begin the long walk to breakfast, he emerged from the tub only when his fingertips were wrinkled and his skin pristine as polished marble. He slowly pulled on a pale green shirt and grey breeches, brushed his hair, twisted his dreadlock, inspected his shadow of burgundy stubble, and made his way downstairs. At the bottom step he sat to lace up his shoes, shook his head at their loose feel, undid and re-laced them carefully. With a sigh, Meecha stood and approached the two items hanging from hooks by the door: his keys and his hat.

'I'll need you,' he told the hat – black with a bow on one side over a single little feather, reddish-brown and blotchy – and donned it.

He squeezed the keys in his hand as he stepped out into the warm street and locked the door behind him. Sauntering along, he kept his head and eyes low. Houses of solid grey stone towered over him on both sides, but Meecha did not look up. He turned into an alley, where he slowed down to take in the delicious scent of pie drifting out from a window. His childhood self would have crawled through it and snatched the pie without a second thought. Resisting that urge, he hurried to the end of the alleyway and into the square.

A hexagonal tower stood in the centre, made of the same stone as all the other buildings in Dadral, but this one had been mixed with emerald dust to make it gleam silvery green. Hombar Karkoo, the Head of Hammer and Stone, had his centre of operations there. A large gold bell glinted at the top, its sound long forgotten. Meecha crossed the square at an uneasy trot. His innumerable visits to the tower, each one logged into an actual black book of miscreants, had earned him a spot of red wax next to his name, marking him among the town's most infamous delinquents.

On the broad street on the opposite side of the square, row upon row of shaded stalls occupied most of the marketplace. Merchants had laid out their wares and were anticipating their customers. White, blue, and yellow lean-tos flanked Meecha's path as he dragged his every step, eyes fixed on the greyish-green door lying in wait at the street's end. The closer he got the more his heart tightened, the more his brow furrowed, the firmer his teeth gripped his lip. He halted to grimace at the house, top to bottom. Taking a deep shuddering breath, he finally braved the steps up to the door. He gave it a timid knock.

Heavy steps were heard, each one shrinking him further into a ball. The door opened and there was Finkin, his face instantly breaking into a wry grin.

'Someone's in trouble!' he chimed, jovial as ever.

'Who is it?' The house shuddered with their father's rumble.

A quiver started up Meecha's legs.

'The window flinger!' his brother hollered in return.

Meecha cursed under his breath and stepped inside. As soon as the door closed behind him, his father's growl shook the house – and him – once more. 'Meecha! Get in here!'

Consternation screwed his face as he slunk towards the doorway on his left. He hastily removed his hat and clasped it against his chest. He put his head round the door. His father sat in his chair glaring down at his hands, fingertips the size of plums pressed against each other. His pursed lips were barely visible beneath that beard, swathing the lower half of his face. His piercing grey eyes snapped up at Meecha, whose quivering had moved up his legs and was now churning his stomach. The hat spun in his hands.

'You threw a shutter at Grek Rydon.'

A statement, not a question.

'I didn't throw it.' Meecha gritted his teeth.

His father's chunky fists banged against the chair's arms. He opened his mouth, nostrils flaring, and was about to start an earthquake when his wife came to the rescue, her voice slicing through the heated atmosphere. 'My baby!'

Meecha swirled around. A flash of red hair was all he saw before her powerful arms locked him in her embrace.

Her pale yellow dress was silky to the touch and smelt of a meadow in spring.

Namoya Roa released her son and grasped his cheeks. 'You need food. Look at you, you're skin and bone. Mommy has just what you need.'

She winked and escorted him to the kitchen. His father came out of the living room behind them.

'I'm not done talking to him, Moya,' he grumbled.

'When are you ever done?' she retorted. 'All these years, and you still think that angry words will fix him.'

'I'm not broken,' Meecha whined.

'Hush,' his mother silenced him as they entered the kitchen, where his brothers were seated in tall-backed chairs around the dining table, three times the size of his own pitiful one.

'There he is,' Finkin announced, as if the rest had not seen him.

Meecha hung his hat on the back of a chair beside Mern, who observed his every move with a smug smirk. Jaika, the eldest Roa son, sitting on Meecha's right with his back to the door, barely acknowledged his presence but for a passing glance of distaste.

Jaika was in his prime, and bigger, stronger, and handsomer than most luima his age – in Dadral, that is. There was not a single girl who would not walk on fire for a chance to win his affections, and many of them had. When Meecha had looked into his family's ancestry, he had discovered that the Roas had been one of the bloodlines to produce the first dwarves. Jaika's impressiveness had suddenly made frustrating sense.

Mern clapped Meecha on the back as he sat. 'I have to say, little brother, the way you attract mayhem, they should put you in the mines instead of explosives.'

'I can just imagine poor Grek with a shutter round his neck,' Finkin guffawed. 'Him walking down the street,' his index and middle finger turned into Grek strolling along the table top, 'and wham!' his left hand thudded onto his right, flattening it. He barked a hearty laugh, while Meecha scowled at them both.

'It was an accident!' Finkin's cackles drowned out his voice. 'I was sitting on the ledge outside my window. As I was getting up, the shutter came off. I'd have fallen if I hadn't dropped it. I could have been killed!'

They all blinked at him. Finkin's chin wobbled, his mouth pursed tight. He snorted, and Meecha's eyes narrowed. His brother slowly raised his hands before him, right palm over the back of his left hand, and abruptly banged them onto the table top.

'Wham!'

Everyone fell about laughing. Even Jaika and father Roa cracked a sneer.

'Oh, stop teasing him,' Namoya scolded Finkin through teary eyes and kissed Meecha on the forehead.

She picked up a platter covered with a white cloth from the kitchen counter. She removed the cloth to reveal an assortment of food: poached eggs, sliced meat, fruit and – Meecha was happy to see – pie! She placed the platter in the middle of the table and proceeded to lay out plates, knives and forks, glasses, and a pitcher of water.

'What were you doing on the ledge, sweetheart?' Namoya asked with a concerned frown, just as Mern stabbed an egg with his fork.

'I couldn't sleep, so I waited for the sun to rise.'

Finkin chortled. 'Why?'

'Because the sun rising and setting is one of the most beautiful things to behold.' Meecha raised his chin.

'Indeed it is,' Namoya agreed. 'The colours are lovely.'

He turned to her. 'Did you know that the different colours you see are caused not solely by the sun but also by its angle and the planet's atmosphere?'

'Incredible.' Her delighted smile made her warm eyes gleam. 'Oh, how I've missed my clever boy,' she said, giving his cheek an affectionate pinch.

Yanga waved a knife at Meecha and growled from across the table, 'I should've sent you to your grandfather!'

As always, the Luima tongue sounded the harshest coming from his father's mouth.

'Put that down, Yanga!' Namoya barked – and her husband recoiled. 'Eat!' she commanded them all, and they snapped to, digging zealously into their breakfast.

It did not take long for every scrap of food to disappear. The largest part of the pie was demolished by Meecha alone. Of course, he spared the others the reason behind his sudden appetite for pie. They cleared the table but for the glasses and pitcher. A grumbling Finkin hugging a basin was sent to bring water from the pump outside so Namoya could wash the dishes. Mern left the room without a word, while Meecha, Jaika, and Yanga sat back in their chairs with guts bulging and happy. Jaika belched, the only sound he had made thus far.

'By the way,' their father said levelly, 'Grek demanded compensation.'

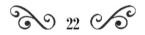

'What?!' both Meecha and his mother exclaimed. 'What for?' he added, and Yanga raised an eyebrow.

'To silence him,' Jaika finally spoke, clamping his jaw tight behind pressed lips. 'You've disgraced our name for the last time. It's only fair that from now on you pay for your own 'accidents'.'

'But I didn't mean to—'

'Oh, certainly not,' Jaika's comeback droned with derision. 'Just like you didn't mean to steal from our neighbours or drill holes in their roofs or paint Karkoo's hammer pink...'

'I was a child then!'

'And you think you're all grown up now?'

'I am!'

'Having your own empty house and playing at adventurer makes you an adult, does it?'

'No! It makes me free! Not a buffed-up puppet that can't function without his pa telling him what to do!'

'Be quiet!' Yanga bellowed and punched the table – it was sturdy enough to take the hit without a crack. Namoya had bought it specially.

Meecha seethed, struggling to stop himself from telling them exactly what he did for a living. He imagined their gawking faces flushing with shame. Finkin dashed into the kitchen, the tub sloshing in his arms. He looked around in alarm and, quiet as a mouse, made for Namoya. Meecha slid his glass closer and grabbed the pitcher. He lifted it with both hands to keep his furious shaking from spilling its contents. Pouring himself a full glass of water, he put the pitcher aside and took a few sips, while glaring at his father and brother from over the glass's rim.

Jaika's arms were folded like a tightly pressed spring. Yanga shook his head, too grimly for Meecha's liking. The silence was suffocating. He could barely swallow. He lowered his gaze to the rippling water. And this was when he saw them, inches from his nose: a pair of ghostly green eyes staring up at him.

His gurgled shriek ripped the silence as he flung the glass away. Imminent doom flashed before his eyes as he watched the glass fly towards Jaika's head. His brother ducked and the glass shattered against the doorframe behind him. Silence returned for a few precious seconds before Jaika roared like a bear.

'I'm sorry!' Meecha yelped.

He bounced to his feet and grabbed his hat just as Jaika's boot kicked his chair. Finkin and Namoya leapt onto the counter before the chair smacked into a cabinet. Yanga scrambled onto the table. The house rang with shouts and screams as Meecha dashed round and round the table with his brother hot on his heels.

'Please, stop!' their mother shrieked, hands gripping her teary face. 'Jaika, stop it!'

Meecha lunged out the kitchen, made a hard turn, and sprinted towards the the front door. When he reached for the handle, an air-borne Mern streaked out of the living room and tackled Jaika.

'Run!' he shouted. And Meecha found himself fleeing his home once more.

A small crowd had gathered outside. Meecha caught a few snide comments before he turned into an alley and hurtled through it. The dusty air stung his eyes. A bruise hindered his hip where a corner must have nicked him. But he did not pause. He did not even slow down to dodge the luima in his wake. Only when his front door slammed behind him did he stop. And breathe.

Eyes squeezed shut, lungs heaving, Meecha slumped back against the hard wood. His left hand, still clutching the hat, brushed his cheek. He frowned at his damp knuckles. The puffiness of his eyes and his runny nose told him that it was not just sweat.

Meecha shoved himself off the door. There was no time for tears; his caller was probably waiting for him. He ran up the staircase, into the bedroom, and, dropping the hat onto the bed, took his place before the oval mirror. In a chipped copper frame, it reflected him and the room, as it was supposed to. But when the right words were uttered…

'Ernath'a Isha,' he said, loud and clear. *I seek the Light.*

The glass shimmered—it alone bore the enchantment, to be cut and mounted however he wished. Flecks of light came to life in the mirror's depths, merging and growing into a uniform white sheet. A woman's face pushed through the glow, her pale skin barely discernible against the bright background. Her features rippled and flowed like the dancing flame of a candle, strands of pale hair occasionally coming into view. Her eyes found Meecha, and a breezy voice emerged from her plump, pallid lips.

'Agent Roa?' she asked in the tongue of humans.

He bowed slightly.

'Thine assistance is needed,' she continued. 'Thou're to journey to Therea, a kingdom of Itania. The quest may be long an' perilous. Prepare accordingly an' meet me at the crater at dawn. I shall explain further.'

Her dialect piqued his curiosity, but he felt awkward mimicking it.

'Certainly. I'll be there,' Meecha assured her in Oparu English.

She nodded. In the blink of an eye, the face in the mirror vanished, lights fading into a haze before dissipating altogether.

Barely a day's rest and he would be off again. It was the fastest summons he had yet had. And the first from a human, not his usual masters, the aerieti. A faint twist in his stomach warned of the unusualness of the situation. Something was afoot in Itania, a world of magic, tragedy, and war.

Chapter 3

No steam was twirling up from his cup by the time Meecha remembered it. He detached his eyes from the neat black writing and took a sip of the now tepid tea. The book's thick leather binding rested against his crossed legs, the pages yellowed but intact, full of lore and art related to one subject: Itania. The tome, written in Aerieti, was vast, heavy with the collective knowledge of his masters and their agents, historical, cultural, and environmental accounts spanning back long before the elves—or thaelil—had ruled, when the planet was wild and dragons roamed free. Wild it remained, but much had changed.

Thaelil were known as peaceful folk of unmatched beauty and power, also displaying a superiority complex of varied intensities. They tried to hide their hatred for humans, who had stripped them of their sovereignty about sixty and four years—cycles—past. But some of the thaelil's most revered kindred had been killed in the Rift War; they called it Is'mara Grae, the War of Embers. Their grudge still held strong. Meecha would have given anything to go back in time and watch those legendary battles between elf and human unfold. The other species was just as prejudiced towards its rival, but tolerated its rare visitations. They never spoke a word of Thaelil though—at least not in 'civilised' human cities. Cursing someone was considered worse if done in the language of their former oppressors. The tongue they did possess was an often mangled variant of Elizabethan English. How this particular Oparu dialect found its way into Itania was puzzling, since no one could simply stumble into another world. The fact that the same species occupied two different planets could not be a coincidence either. Vague primary sources from a few years leading up to The Rift mentioned well-dressed human visitors making a stir among their own species in the thaelil capital, now a charred ruin simply referred to as Old Anvadore.

Prior to the Rift had come the invasion of Arak Sildrax, the demon warlord from the abyssal world of Crantil. Meecha could only imagine the scene: the scarlet fiend stepping through the portal into Therea surrounded by his army of monsters and traitors; commanded by the mighty thaelil, the legions of defenders fighting and dying for their home; the dragons swooping in at the last moment to bring Arak to his knees. The Sildrax had fled back to Crantil, leaving only his severed hand and some demon stragglers behind. A note at the end of this chapter stated, 'Itania's salvation has been credited in part to aerieti intervention. The honoured agents have chosen to remain anonymous.'

Meecha scoffed. Everyone knew who they were. He sat back in his armchair, tapping the arms. Dragons, elves, humans, not to mention a formidable source of arcane energies—he could not predict how this mission might unfold, but he could prepare for the basics. The climate of Therea was predominantly warm with the occasional strong storm to counteract the heat and produce its glorious landscapes. The precise city or region he would be visiting was unknown, whether on the mainland, coast, or islands.

Among the many removable maps available in the tome, Meecha had already put Therea's aside for the journey, atop a booklet on Itania's flora, their properties and applications. He closed the tome and returned it to its shelf, tracing his finger down its spine before picking up the map and booklet from the end table and adding them to the items laid out on the central counter: a good arvadeir dagger, a set of lockpicks in a leather case, a water bottle, a tooth brush, a blanket, and the round leather case, retrieved from the safe. Five tubes stood in a line above them. Three contained salves: one disinfected and healed wounds, another warmed the body, and another chilled it. The fourth tube had toothpaste and the fifth, slightly larger than the rest, was full of rolled-up poultices for blisters. There was one more thing he needed.

He left the room and the house, gloomily avoiding other luima by sticking to the shadows and alleys. The glaring late afternoon sun was gradually scattering the busy marketplace, but it was still too crowded for Meecha's liking – too many eyes judging him, too many tongues flapping about the black sheep of the Roas. They had to be faced, though, just to the meat stall and back.

Meecha took a breath and exhaled sharply before strolling into their midst, feigning blinkers. It did not work. He noticed a few heads turn to either shake disapprovingly or whisper to each other, but he spotted the bloody haunches hanging from a rail and made straight for them. He reached the stall and gave the merchant a steadfast glare, which caused the luima to recoil a little.

'Easy there, boy,' Mr Traj chuckled in Luimari, showing his palms in surrender. 'What will it be?'

Abashed, Meecha softened his face and smiled thinly. 'Salt-cured desert boar strips, please.'

'Ah, travelling again, are we? How much do you need?'

Mr Traj's meat had kept Meecha alive on many a trip and the merchant, being no fool, had made the connection early on that Meecha would disappear shortly after buying preserved foods from him.

'I'm not sure. Give me a generous portion,' Meecha replied.

He moved to the edge of the counter as the monger laid out a piece of paper. He reached into a box to pull out several slices of salted meat and slap them onto the parchment. Meecha's mouth watered, while he counted out some coins. He glanced up and saw Mr Traj adding some liver to the pile before wrapping it all tight. Meecha opened his mouth to protest, but the luima spoke over him.

'Just an extra taster of what you're missing when on the road. You'll not find such fine stuff anywhere but home,' the merchant proclaimed in his smug sing-songy way and handed the parcel to Meecha. 'That's three silvers.'

Two more coins were rebuffed by Mr Traj, only accepting a heartfelt, 'Thank you.'

Home. Meecha pondered the word on his winding path through the crowd. A home was where you felt safe and welcome, loved or surrounded by things you love. Dadral had never felt that way – rarely, at least. Even as a boy, Meecha sat on the edge of luima culture, resisting every oddity imposed on him, testing the rigidity of all the rules and norms he could not understand. What he found was that many of them where hollow, susceptible to change, if such a thing was desired. The whole planet of Durkai, its stone-dry deserts dotted with miraculous oases and only yielding to stretches of grass and snow-tipped hills on its cool poles, was reflected in its people: set in their ways despite their potential for greatness.

Something brushed through the gap between his left arm and his side. He started and looked down to find an arm looped around his elbow. His mother was attached to it.

'Are you going home?' she asked softly. Meecha nodded. 'I'll walk with you.'

The stares were less judgemental and more pitying. Namoya smiled them down as she strolled along with her son.

'Don't mind them, sweetheart,' she whispered. 'Gossip is their favourite pastime after trying to outshine each other on who has the most and best fake plants. Useless,' Namoya hissed through the sweetest crocodile grin.

Meecha hunched, chortling. He lifted his right hand to cover his sneer, but jerked it back down to keep the parcel out of sight. Namoya had not noticed.

'You're still not part of that competition, I see,' he said, referring to the perpetual lack of greenery, false or real, in the family house.

His mother cocked her head. 'If I wanted plants, I'd make the two-week journey to Pilto and get some real ones. And then spend half my time and fortune trying to keep them alive in a place they were never meant for. Lamenting what you can't have – or be – is energy better spent making the best of what fate gives you.'

'Mother,' Meecha sighed.

'Strength of character comes from acknowledging and embracing the good and the bad of one's self,' she went on. 'Forcing your nature to change only leads to misery. Of course, you can adapt to situations, but for how long? Your mind, my boy, is like the rarest of gems and it should be no less treasured than the stone in your blood.'

Meecha gave her a sidelong look. 'Mother, you fit four wise-liners in two breaths.'

'I'm that good at them,' Namoya retorted with a snide arching of her brow. 'And their quantity does not negate their truth.'

Meecha smirked, rolling his eyes to the dimming sky. 'You scare me sometimes.'

'That's precisely what your grandfather used to say.'

'What about now?'

'Now, your father says it.'

Meecha halted mid-stride to bark a laugh. His mother circled around to face him.

'I suspect pa neglected to warn him that going into business with a Roa is far easier than being married to one,' Namoya told her son nonchalantly and then leant in to whisper, 'That armour Yanga has on a pedestal and never wears? The helmet's not the original. The first time he seriously disrespected me, I melted that down and made knitting needles.'

Meecha doubled over, cackling, but his mother was not done.

'Only when he fell to his knees to apologise did I make him a new one. And you can be certain as the rise and fall of the sun that it was superior to that first piece of scrap metal.'

'Stop, please,' Meecha exclaimed, clutching his stomach, its cramps tugging him to a squat. He straightened up to find that they were in front of the Hammer and Stone headquarters. He gently nudged his mother towards the alley. 'What's your point?'

'My point, sweetheart, is that you're more of a Roa than you know.' She hung from his elbow once more. 'Wealth, valour, ancestors of dwarves – qualities our name is associated with. Or what some Luima choose to remember. You see, not only has 'troublemaker' been attached to many a Roa before you, but also our chronicles of battle prowess and heroism are mostly glossed over accounts of hot-blooded, reckless rabble-rousers picking fights and overthrowing authorities that didn't agree with them.'

'Is there a compliment somewhere in there?' Meecha mumbled.

Namoya tutted as they turned the corner into the street his house was on. He could see the window above the ledge, the brown form of its single shutter overwhelmed by the harsh greyness that surrounded it. 'What I mean is that independence is in your blood. I can't tell you how proud I've been to watch your every defiant step – worried, so very worried, but excited too to be able to say, 'That's my son and he is already shaping the world around him'.'

I should paint the walls, Meecha instantly thought. *Colourful leaves and birds on brown and gold branches growing from the shutter.*

He glanced at his mother, tears swelling behind his eye-lids, which he quickly blinked away before hastening his stride towards the front door. Up the steps he went, while searching his pocket for the key, feeling Namoya's eyes on his back. He heard her inhale, as if wanting to speak, but it took a few moments for her words to emerge.

'But Meecha,' she muttered, 'you can't change a world you run from.'

The door clicked open, yet Meecha did not move. His left hand was on the handle – the right gave the parcel a squeeze. He looked down at it and then over his shoulder at his mother. She too was staring at the wrapped up meat. She knew what it signified.

'Meecha, please stay.'

His agitated sigh urged him through the door and her to follow. He turned to block the entrance.

'When are you leaving?' Namoya demanded.

'Soon.'

'You don't have to.'

'Yes, mother, I do,' Meecha stated levelly.

'If you fear your father or brother, I'll have another word with them—'

'I'm not afraid!' Meecha pulled himself short, his lips peeling into a snarl. He instead pursed them over gritted teeth and shut his eyes tight in an effort to calm his rage. 'I simply have things to do.'

'What things? Why won't you tell me? You used to tell me everything and now you disappear for vast lengths of

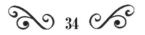

time and refuse to say why. I'm terrified that one day you'll leave and never return.'

'I'm sorry, mother, but this is something I have to keep to myself, for your sake and mine. Besides, I always come back. Yanga won't be rid of me that easily.' He immediately regretted the ill-timed joke when Namoya burst into tears.

In a panic, Meecha pulled her inside, peering up and down the street for onlookers. The living room could not contain the tense atmosphere, its four walls closing in on Meecha. He escaped for a few moments to the kitchen, where he left the parcel. Reluctantly, he then returned to his mother, who had done her best to dry her face, but its wrinkles and dimples suddenly seemed deeper, her tanned and plump features resembling rolling, earthy plains. Her hair, a scarlet of a brighter and wilder hue than his own with a few silver strands glistening throughout her messy bun of untameable curls, again added to Meecha's enduring notion that his mother was an embodiment of nature in summer. Love, anger, anxiety, whatever the passion, Namoya Roa's expression was that of scalding zeal, except for those rare times – becoming more frequent with age – when her fire was dampened by cool logic. Meecha was relieved to find that this was one such instance.

'No amount of pleading will change your mind. I know that. Whatever it is you're up to, I've never seen you so dedicated. Just tell me you're safe, that it's not as dangerous as you make it sound.' The last few words were emphasised by a sharp, wavering breath.

Meecha strolled to the other side of the room, step by calculated step, his eyes drifting up to the ceiling.

'Risk really is relative to skill and I can say that I'm safe in my own abilities.' *Mostly.* 'I'm not alone.' *Completely.* 'And, as I said, I always make it back.' *A little worse for wear, but alive. Not every agent can say as much.*

Namoya's squint and pressed lips showed her dissatisfaction.

'You better,' she warned. 'The longest you've been away is two months.' She pointed a finger at her son. 'You take longer than that and I'm coming to find you. Just to ground you for the rest of your life.'

When Meecha's bemused eyebrows rose almost to his hairline, the finger jabbed the air, as if shooting a bolt at his chest.

'That was not a jest,' Namoya snapped and Meecha's smirk was gone.

'Please, don't do that.' He was worried for a moment before realising, 'You won't be able to find me anyway.'

His mother stood to her full stature – a few fingers shorter than him, but fearsome.

'This is the Roa you came from, boy,' she barked. Meecha cowered back into his thirteen-year-old self. 'I gave you the brains you carry, but don't think for a moment that I've lost any of mine. Test me any further and you'll rue your doubting tongue.'

'Sorry, mother.'

Namoya softened her stance and approached Meecha. She cupped his face gently and spoke with hushed sincerity.

'Even as a baby, you possessed a rare combination of playfulness, cunning, and disarming kindness. Seeing that spirit still there gives me hope, because no matter what challenges you face, your heart will carry you through, I'm sure of it. You'll be back,' she stroked his cheek, while biting her trembling lip. She smiled thinly, 'You'll be back. You will.'

They embraced. Meecha let her squeeze him as much as she liked. He patted her on the back and was about to pull away, when she released him first. It was startling how abruptly she turned on her heels and made for the living room doorway. There she paused. Her head moved a fraction, as if stopping herself from looking back.

'I love you, sweetheart.'

Meecha cleared his throat and responded, 'I love you too, mama.'

The door slammed behind her. Namoya Roa's soft but swift footsteps grew fainter, until the street outside was quiet once more. Nightfall had come and the time for final preparations, but a lingering pang of guilt followed him to the secret chamber, stalling his hands as they tidied up and repacked his bag. His legs felt almost too heavy to climb the steps to the kitchen, where he set the backpack on the table and added the packet of meat to its contents, wrapped in an extra cloth. Fastening all the straps and pockets, Meecha leant against the table. *That's it.* He was ready for another journey. *Mission number twelve.* He placed his hat beside the bag and jogged up to the bedroom for an early sleep. Of course, as soon as he relaxed into his pillow, Namoya and Mern returned to scold him for running away. To plead for him to stay and somehow change the centuries-old luima custom of cruel, stubborn backward thinking that had nested like a pit of snakes in the skulls of his father and lummox of a brother. Unsurprisingly, his slumber was far from restful, but in this line of work you took what you could get.

Chapter 4

Meecha tried to grasp the bars of his cage, but they were covered in thorns. The sky was a peculiar faded orange, like rust, and everything else around him seemed discoloured. He glanced into the adjacent cage. The mound of deep brown fur, verging on black, rose and fell with sleep.

'What do thou think it is?' a voice asked on the other side of Meecha.

He turned to find the girl from the red and white field. She was squatting in the cage with him, looking out into the camp. The golden ribbons were as faded as everything else, and her hair was sodden, hanging limp around her shoulders. She looked warily at the animal.

'It could be a wolf,' she said in answer to her own question.

Meecha needed a moment to collect his wits before asking, 'Who are you?'

The girl gave him a perplexed frown.

'That must have been some blow to the head, Meecha. Stop playing games, now. We need to escape.'

Canvas flapped, and he looked beyond the thorned bars to a large tent. Something stepped out, tall, dark, and long of limb. It had horns, wings, and a spiked tail. Glowing red eyes fixed on Meecha. It showed dagger teeth in an evil grin, tongue lashing out and licking its chops. Meecha remembered seeing this creature in a book, but he could not bring to mind which one. The book doesn't matter. This is a demon.

It approached the cages with lithe motions. Meecha and the girl crawled back from the bars just as the wolf awoke. It snarled at the demon closing in and rose. The glint of its fangs was almost as mesmerising as the silver burning in its eyes. The demon chittered to the wolf, its manner showing anger. The animal hunched and reduced its snarling to a quiet rumble echoing from the pit of its stomach. Then both predators turned to face Meecha's cage. They attacked the bars with such vehemence that the whole world seemed to shake. With tooth and claw, they tore through the barbed metal as if it were wood.

The girl shrieked. She curled up against Meecha, gripping his arm and crying. While her wide eyes were on the beasts, he closed his and squeezed her delicate fingers, conjuring the field where they first met. He visualised himself in the midst of the red and white flowers, commanding the dream to take them there. Wolf and demon were still growling, but they instantly sounded quieter. The snapping of the bars was like a distant popping of bubbles. The world became still, muted, tranquil, and Meecha opened his eyes. The valley's splendid colours greeted him, alone. The girl had not returned with him. She was nowhere to be seen.

The dream echoed in Meecha's head. He busied himself with the straps of his pack, adjusting them. He straightened his hat and hefted the small satchel in his hand as he arrived at the shadowed alleyway behind his family house, a tunnel dug into the rock to create a corridor large enough to accommodate the households' tin bins and perhaps two adult luima walking abreast. A water pump stuck out of the ground every fifty feet or so.

Only one of the wall lamps was lit, fortunately not at the door he was tip-toeing towards. He halted behind it to listen. There was no sound from within. Carefully resting the satchel at the foot of the door, he started sneaking backwards, slowly turning to face the way he had come. But then the door jerked open.

'Meecha?'

A shiver ran down his spine. He looked up at Mern sheepishly.

'What're you doing?' his brother whispered.

Meecha straightened. He shifted from foot to foot, anxious to be off, but also wishing to say goodbye.

'You're leaving again,' Mern said flatly.

Meecha bit the inside of his cheek. 'Yes.'

'That explains mother storming about all day.' His brother's hiss was interrupted by the sight of the satchel.

He picked it up and opened the flap to find the dazzling goblet lying within. His eyebrows shot up, and then furrowed inquiringly at Meecha.

'It's to pay off Grek,' he explained. 'I must get going now. Fare—"

'Wait, don't move," Mern said. He dashed into the house only to re-emerge a few moments later, gently pulling the door ajar behind him. 'Take this.'

He held an open hand out to Meecha, who reached over and picked up the circular box-like object of gold perched in his brother's palm. It was cold to the touch, with no embellishments. He found a tiny button and pressed it. The lid clicked open. He lifted it further and realised that this was no box but a compass. Red, delicately painted patterns lined the interior beneath the glass, and its black needle quivered as it pointed to Meecha's left. That was wrong. Durkai's north was ahead of him. The needle wavered lazily back and forth as he moved. It was broken. Then the underside of the lid drew his attention, where a black figure was depicted, but that he could not quite make out.

'I was looking through grandpa Roa's trinkets,' Mern explained. 'I found that compass, and I thought of you. I was going to give it to you yesterday, but, well... I didn't get the chance.'

Meecha was flabbergasted and half offended by being associated with a compass that could not find its bearing. 'Thank you.' He cleared his throat. 'And for saving me from Jaika.'

Mern crossed his arms and tried to look impassive.

'Take care, little brother,' he said and stomped back into the house.

Meecha stood alone in silence, the compass clutched in his hands. He numbly turned and meandered back down the corridor, staring at the shape on the lid. The sunlight brightened the closer he came to the corridor's mouth. When he reached the adjoining street, the image finally became clear. It was a lizard, its curved tail turning into a hammer before its chest. The drawing was plain, and the paint slightly chipped, but of a remarkable concoction to have survived time and the elements so well.

Shoving the compass into one of his coat's inner pockets, he took off down the street, away from the square and away from Dadral. He ran until there were no more houses, only grey rocks and desert yet to be inhabited. He started to climb a rise, the earth crumbling beneath his hands and soft-soled boots. He reached the top of what might be presumed to be a hill, but was in fact the rim of a vast crater. Meecha held his hat in place as he descended the ridged slope.

There was no sign of anyone at the bottom. *I'm too late.* He slid down the last few feet and jumped onto the crater's floor, almost falling flat on his face when the solid granite unearthed by the meteor jarred his legs. Sweat streamed down his face. He trotted the rest of the stretch towards the centre of the impressive bowl. He had seen it before from above, but being inside it was a different experience. It could contain the whole of Dadral – twofold. He twirled a few times to take in its magnitude, but stopped suddenly when a figure materialised.

She was draped in a tunic of dazzling white light. Her ethereal skin glowed, as did her mane of white-blonde hair. Her green eyes were on Meecha, while her shape shimmered translucent, her face bearing a sad determination.

'Meecha...' Her gentle voice fluctuated. She seemed to be testing the utterance of his name.

He brushed his hair with his fingers and tossed the dreadlock over his shoulder, forcing a smile.

She looked him over before saying in human, 'Agent Roa. Thy name an' feats are on many lips in Athmae.'

He blushed. He clasped his hands behind his back and coughed with embarrassment.

'Thank you, my lady. I do my best.' He hoped his knowledge of Oparu English would serve well enough among Itanian humans.

'Do I unnerve thee?' she inquired curiously.

His eyes widened. 'N—no, my lady. I'm simply not used to being summoned by anything other than aerieti. I mean, I rarely get to work for... eh... um...'

'Ghosts?'

He shrugged. 'Well, yes.'

'Imagine my alarm when I foun' me dead,' she said forlornly.

He bit his lip and muttered, 'I'm sorry, my lady.'

'Thou needn' apologise. Thou didn' kill me. But my murderers are the reason thou're here. I'm to seek thy help, Master Roa. My life was but a piece of a greater puzzle. That may now threaten my world an' the balance of others.' Meecha hunched under the gravity of her words. 'The world of Crantil is on the prowl.'

Meecha blinked for a few shocked seconds, recalling his latest dream. 'Demons!' he gasped.

The woman noticed his quizzical frown. 'They're formidable foes, I know, but, if thy record holds true, thou can outwit them.'

'But,' Meecha tried to put his concerns in order, 'you need more than wit to face fiends of the hells. They're

bloodthirsty and cruel and monstrous. You need muscle and long legs to run with.' Out of all the agents that had encountered an abyssal creature, two had emerged with their lives: one a warrior, the other a mystic and legendary strategist. 'I don't stand a chance on my own.'

His assurance to his mother that he would return suddenly felt hollow. And then there was the dream. If there was anything to be read from it, it was that this mission could mean his death.

'Succeed an' thou shall be far from alone,' the ghost lady said. 'I shallna lie, the peril's considerable, but has tha' no' been a part of every quest thou've mastered?'

Meecha started to fidget. 'True, but one must be mindful of how far one's fate is tempted. I think I'm quite ready for a long time off.'

'We don' have that luxury,' the woman replied sternly. Her arms were crossed and her serene features hardened. 'Since Arak invaded, Itania's been infested with these creatures. They skulked in the shadows, made trouble from time ta time, but avoided too much attention. Something's differen' now. Small moves. You'd scarcely notice them, but they've become bold an' organised. An' tight-lipped. Whatever it be, it isn' for good. My guess? That which has driv'n their kind since life began. Dominion.'

A strange situation, being trapped between duty and family. It was a newfound mixture of emotions for Meecha, whose frail bond with home and kin had never interfered with his work before. Now, something had indeed changed. A faint hope of closure made him look back at the vast ridge blocking Dadral from view.

'If Itania's taken, her power in the hands of our enemy, what's to stop their sights from turning to other worlds?' the woman suggested, her voice softer. 'Thy Durkai could be next, one of many to fall because we didn' act in time.'

'Why me?' Meecha asked with more force than he had intended. 'There're hundreds of agents better suited to tackle demons. I can't possibly be your best and only option.'

With a sigh, she tilted her head and gave him a long pitying stare. He averted his eyes and removed his hat to run a brisk hand through his hair.

'What's a demon's favourite game?' the ghost finally asked.

Meecha frowned. 'Torture?'

'What kind of torture, physical or emotional?'

He thought for a few moments. 'Both, I suppose.'

'Correct. Trickery, manipulation, subterfuge, the foremost elements in their ploys to weaken prey before confronting them. So, Agent Roa, what skills would best face such an opponent?'

He indulged her. 'Similar to theirs. Guile, strategy, adaptability – if they take you by surprise you should be able to think on your feet. Unpredictability. Getting to know how they think would open ways to surprise them. Yes, an inconspicuous approach would be best, one they wouldn't anticipate.'

'What would be a wrong thing to do?' The ghost's hands were clasped calmly behind her.

'Underestimate them,' Meecha immediately replied. 'Seeing them as mindless monsters can give you a false sense of superiority, which they could easily exploit.' He noticed her coy smile and stopped.

'Still find thee the wrong person for this?' She lifted a hand and counted fingers. 'Thou're small, invisible to those awaiting aerieti brawn. Thou're gifted an' undaunted by unconventional routes. Thy reluctance an' understanding of demons' complexities promises caution – an' survival, as opposed to one who'd foolishly rush into this situation without thought or restraint. But the most important part of thee's thy heart. Demons thrive in darkness. They feed off pain an' despair, which thou've shown resilience to. There's a light in thee far more valuable in fighting Crantil fiends than any sword or spell, an' that I've come to find quite catching. Meecha, thou're a beacon of hope an' glee.'

'Please, please, enough.' One side of his head was a mess from the furious awkward rubbing. 'I'll do it. Just, please, stop.'

'Excellent,' she declared, when her white form almost completely dissolved. 'Shall we step onto the bridge?' Her request sounded urgent, breathless. 'I don' have the power to sustain myself for long in material worlds.'

'Certainly, my lady. Lead the way.'

The spirit turned her back and reached out a slim finger to touch the air a few inches higher than her head. Ripples appeared around her fingertip, and with an abrupt vertical motion, she ripped the air. The world's fabric crackled apart like paper to reveal blackness beyond.

The first time Meecha had been introduced to a 'gate' like this one, he had walked around it to find that the rip was not visible from any other angle. If one faced the back of the rip, one could see the landscape unscathed. If two people stood on either side of it – in front and behind – they were hidden from each other.

One last time, Meecha glanced back in the direction of Dadral. *Forgive me, mother.* It was not the oath he swore to the aerieti that moved him now towards the gate. It was the duty attached to his position. He was an agent of the celestial protectors and creators of worlds, masters of destinies, champions of all that was good in the multiverse. If Itania and its people were in peril, if Meecha had the potential to thwart the creatures that threatened it, then he would do his very best. He stepped into the void.

A prickling sensation like tiny shocks of static excited his skin. A clean, crisp smell flooded his nostrils to remind him of snow, a substance whose treacherous beauty always surprised him anew. The place he was entering was just as cold, the Space Between. The planetary worlds dotted its endless blackness, the farthest ones sparkling from the depths of the universe.

A reverberating groan came from above. He looked up to find a gargantuan, scaly head covered in horns and eyes descending towards him and the ghost lady. The Sentinel. The dread of standing on an invisible pathway like this one, with the void beneath stretching into infinity, was nothing compared to the terror of seeing one of the Sentinel's heads for the first time. It was heavily debated among agents whether the heads encountered on every trip were the same ones or but a few of the millions that guarded the worlds. One would think that the rest of the Sentinel's body was at the centre of the void, if there even was a centre. What if there was no boundary to the Space Between, some had wondered, and the Sentinel was one gigantic mess of necks and heads?

Meecha stared shyly at his own feet, while the current Sentinel's head regarded them both quietly. It gave a loud sniff and finally lifted away to allow them passage.

'Come, Meecha.' The ghost lady now looked solid and not as luminous as she had in Durkai. Even her hair, though still pretty, was subdued to a normal flaxen colour.

She walked along the bridge with Meecha in tow. A glyph embedded in his bones held him on the invisible path and allowed him to breathe normally. One misstep, however, and there would be nothing to stop him from floating through space for eternity.

'The first part of thy mission is to find a rogue elf, Azare Rynir.' The woman's breezy voice sounded like a bell in the void's absolute silence. 'He's a skilled warrior, experienced in hunting demons. He shall be invaluable against Crantil, but first he has his own journey to complete. Thou must assist him an' be my conduit. But,' she turned her head while walking so Meecha could see her firm expression, 'don' tell him of our involvement.'

Meecha nodded.

'What does he look like?' he inquired. 'Where will I find him?'

'He's tall, black of hair, with skin-drawings on his forehead. Handsome.' She shook her head. 'Thou shall know him on sight.'

Meecha raised an eyebrow but said nothing.

'The gate shall place thee in the kingdom of Therea. Start thy search at his cabin at the base of the mountains northwest of Crove, near the coast. I fear we don' know his precise location for he's on a hunt of his own.'

'Anything else I should know, like who or what he hunts?'

The woman stopped and swirled gracefully around to face him. She considered his question for a while, her brow furrowing as she stared into space.

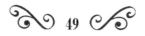

'They're two. A man an' woman. They raided his house an' stole from him. They seek something – a pendant.' She paused, seeming at a loss for words. Her mouth tightened, and she looked down at Meecha. 'That's all.'

He clapped his hands together and wrung them excitedly. 'I love a good treasure hunt!'

The woman's sombreness instantly lifted. Her sweet chuckle filled the hushed universe.

'Thou shouldn' treat this as a game, Meecha,' she reproached him half-heartedly. 'For the time being, thou're alone. I shall watch an' help as best I can, but the dangers of Itania grow with each passing day, an' my power is yet limited.'

He swallowed uneasily. The lady stretched out a finger and ripped the air like before. A bright blue sky appeared beyond the opening, and a vast green valley overlooking rolling hills and trees and the edge of a sea.

A loud grunt jolted Meecha out of his skin. He spun around to come face to face with the Sentinel, the massive head resting upon the bridge, it seemed. Meecha scowled and inched away from the jutting teeth. He lifted a hesitant hand and waved before scuttling towards the rip.

'Good luck.' The ghost's blessing made him touch his hat.

The prickling transition quickly passed, and soft grass squished beneath his boots. The fresh smell of dew was a delightful change. He inhaled deeply as the rip mended behind him.

Chapter 5

The bonfire blazed through the night. There was more grace to be found in the flames than in the people dancing around it, sloshing their drinks and grinding against each other. The female dancers relished the caresses their curves and guiles earned them. Koro's eyes watered from the heat, light, and smoke. He sat back in his chair, one hand on his cup of bitter wine and the other tucked in his pocket. He chose this corner for its clear view of the square without having to worry about his back. He glanced at the shadowy figures inhabiting other tables. They all looked alike – hard, shifty eyes, mischievous half-smiles, and grubby, hairy faces. How many daggers were hidden beneath those layers of clothing? Each one waiting to be plunged into someone's gut. This was Crove, the city of thieves, murderers, pleasures. The firelight caught movement on the eaves of a building across the square. Koro spotted a cloaked man crouching on the roof just beyond the light's border. *A lookout.*

Wolf-whistles and rising voices drew Koro's attention. He looked to the bonfire and saw a striking woman striding

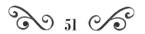

past it, scarlet braid swishing. A large man – an extremely unwise man – intercepted her. Koro groaned and left his seat. The woman scowled at the babbling drunkard and, with a roll of her eyes, tried to overtake him. He grabbed her arm and yanked her towards him. Koro cursed just as the woman took a retreating step and landed a kick to the man's stomach.

He cried out in shock. Dancers yelped and moved quickly away to watch him fall into the bonfire. Agonised screams brought the celebrations to a halt. They all stood, hushed statues, gaping at the man thrashing in the roaring logs. He rolled out of the fire, but the flames had sunk their teeth deep. He howled and flailed, his skin burning and crackling and melting like wax. None of the onlookers ran to his aid. Koro noted their expressions: alarm, confusion, a little guilt or pity, a disturbing degree of amusement. He was glad to hear the crack of a bowstring – the arrow found the man straight through the heart. *Good shot.* The human torch dropped dead.

A cruel smirk marred the woman's breath-taking beauty. Dressed all in black – jerkin, pants, and laced-up boots – she slouched like an abyssal cat ready to pounce and maul everyone around her. Even the other cold-blooded killers in the square now gave her a wide berth. Koro approached her, while the corpse was dragged away. The music started up again, the festivities rekindled.

'Was tha' necessary?'

She shrugged casually. 'No.'

'Thou an' fires,' he grumbled.

Her green eyes narrowed. 'What can I say? I'm homesick.'

They glared at each other, until Koro broke away, grinding his teeth. He glanced at their target.

'Thou are taking thy time,' she snarled, biting the words in her foreign accent.

'We need caution, Naya. We can' do this if we've half the thieves of Crove out for our heads. We get him alone. Discreetly!'

Naya glowered at 'Crab' Galob. The old man and his companions had returned to their boisterous drinking around three joined tables. There were others of less importance leaning against walls or perched on barrels listening in on the conversations, while keeping a watchful eye on their surroundings. The shrouded man on the roof had not moved from his place. Galob and his fellows eyed Naya and whispered to each other. They suddenly roared with laughter, banging the tables and clutching their bellies.

'Come on.' Koro started towards an alley, but Naya stepped in the opposite direction.

She ignored his curses as she made straight for the master thug. His minions took notice and drew blades. Two strapping men walled up the distance between her and their chief. She smirked at them.

'Do not worry,' she purred. 'I'm not here to harm.'

The men closed in, but Galob's courteous rasp stopped them. 'Let a through.'

They reluctantly moved aside and allowed Naya to stand before him, her arms crossed.

'Galob, the Crab.'

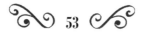

His greying brow furrowed and his wrinkled mouth quirked into a scornful smile.

'How 'bot thou give me thy name, ha?'

'My name is Naya. I want to join thy crew.'

The men hooted scathing remarks. The old man nearly toppled from his chair, laughing. She remained impassive, however, awaiting his response.

He coughed, cleared his throat. 'And what thou have t'offa?'

She chose to overlook the slyness in his query.

'I'm more capable than all thy men combined.'

His minions bristled. He tilted his head and raised an eyebrow.

'If I wished,' she went on icily, 'I could take your heads for trophies before you even remembered your blades. Just for the fun of proving how small man always is. I'm not shy of blood. I've shown this. Recruit me, and I shall paint the city red for thee.'

The gang had fallen silent. Many were leaning away from her or resting hands on hilts.

'An' why would thou want to join us, ha?' he inquired warily, now serious.

Naya shrugged. 'Yours is the most lucrative crew in Crove, is it not? And thou, Crab Galob, would be a fool to reject my talents. With thy competition, thou want me as an ally. Unless thou prefer to face me as a foe.'

He tapped his lips thoughtfully. His men seemed just as eager to hear his verdict. Some sour faces seemed to re-sent the idea of her joining. Others were likely considering the daunting prospect of her being taken by a rival crew.

The thief-master finally nodded his consent. 'Very well, blazer lass. I respect thy spirit, but thou mest prove thyself regardless. It's I who decides thy worth.'

Naya sniffed. Her nails tapped her thigh.

Chapter 6

The shirt was sticky with sweat. Meecha squirmed. His veins felt full of molten lava instead of blood, cooking him from the inside out. He trudged through the knee-high grass with the buttons of his sand-coloured linen shirt undone and his sleeves rolled up. He rubbed another layer of cooling salve on his chest and forearms, sighing as the pleasant chill sank and spread through his skin. But it would not last long.

He reached into his pocket and pulled out the compass. To his surprise, it was no longer idle. But, if the map was still accurate almost a decade after its creation, the black needle was pointing southeast. *The planet's magnetic forces must simply be different.* What intrigued Meecha more was that the compass was responding to this world and not Durkai. *Was it made here?*

To the south was Crove, a city buzzing with what a fellow agent described as 'pleasurable and immorally profitable activities.' A golden, fiery glow illuminated the central buildings. Music and festive voices carried all the way to the hill where Meecha had stopped to stare. The promise of an entertaining night was intriguing, but the dark cracked walls that encircled the tiled roofs loomed like a warning of the corruption that hid behind the city's jovial appearance.

He crossed the dirt-road leading into Crove and resumed his trek towards the northwestern mountain. As the ghost had described, a forest gently sloped down one side; past the other the ocean gleamed in the ample light of Itania's three moons. The coast ran southbound, until sea and land and sky came together on the horizon. Grasping the straps, Meecha hefted his backpack and strode on.

Four days it took him to reach the mountain and begin his ascent along an overgrown path. There were prints upon it from shoe, hoof, and paw. Meecha's water bottle was nearly empty, but he sipped a few drops. The morning sun was trying to break through the treetops overhead, but Meecha was well concealed, the path a decent distance to his right. Chirping birds followed his leisurely progress. Coming from a dry and inhospitable planet, he had always felt that a respectable traveller should hold breath and haste within such a forest. They should show it the silent reverence it deserved. This green realm, for instance, looked the same as any other Meecha had been in, but the energy it exuded was hair-raisingly unique.

He halted mid-stride, having spotted a strange mark on a trunk to his left. He wandered over and saw that the bark had been hacked by a blade. He peered around the tree, deeper into the forest. More of its companions bore similar cuts.

Curious, Meecha followed the trail to the last mark. From there he discerned a slight thinning of the trees, some of them blackened from a recent fire. It turned out to be a clearing with the remains of a small wooden structure in the middle. The once grassy earth surrounding the hut's charred skeleton was now dark and patchy. A deer lay on the ground nearby.

Meecha covered his wrinkled nose. The animal's corpse had been picked at by scavengers, but its head, only slightly scathed by the fire, was intact. A deep gash was visible across its throat, and its chest had a hole, from an arrow perhaps. This was someone's game. Perhaps Azare had returned from a hunt and discarded his prey when he found his house in flames. Meecha theorised that the elf had been confronted by the trespassers and a fight had ensued – that explained the trees, slashed in the heat of battle.

Meecha entered the structure through an opening that would have been the front door. He kicked dust and debris in search of buried clues. The wooden furniture had been reduced to ash. A few metallic items were strewn across the floor, most of them dented or melted. Nothing else. Absolutely no indication as to what happened – other than the fire and the fight – or who this Azare was. Meecha whirled slowly to take in his surroundings: overturned earth, the deer, wooden stumps of wall, a white flower, burnt trees...

He froze. He turned casually to face the back 'wall' and the blossom beyond it, growing right on the edge of the treeline. He stepped towards it. It was unlikely that such a delicate thing would have survived a fire that had burnt the trees around it. Azare must have planted it after the event – a rose-like blossom with a golden stem and stamen, and white petals. *An elven ritual?*

'Now what?' Meecha sighed aloud.

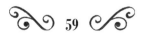

He decided to return to the path. Leaving the grim site behind, he tried to put himself in both parties' shoes. The thieves had just been caught having robbed and ransacked someone's home. They ran back to the road, while battling Azare, and managed to escape. *On horseback, perhaps?* The elf returned to his house to... plant a flower. Then he began his pursuit. He might have known where the thieves were going. The closest city to seek refuge – and presumably where they had come from – was Crove.

'Oh, no...'

Meecha's moaning continued as he dragged his feet back down the road.

'I'm off to Crove now,' he chimed. 'A full set of armour would be nice. Or invisibility magic. An army would be greatly appreciated.'

He never got a response, but talking aloud made his job a little less lonely. Sad, but true. Most importantly, his single-sided conversations also helped remind his busy employers of his existence. Aid might find him sooner or later, but usually when the aerieti deemed it suitable, his life not a priority in their evaluation. Indeed, dire cases had been known where they were required to sacrifice one life to save many. This was why all agents were warned from the start of their training that they must learn to depend on themselves for survival. The aerieti would not come to their rescue if it meant jeopardising an important mission.

'No pressure.' Meecha set his sight on Crove's menacing mass of stone, tile, and smoke.

Chapter 7

'Congratulations, Naya.' Koro's level voice was laced with derision. 'It took thee six days to become the greatest assassin in Crove and butcher thy own crew.'

Galob's headquarters, a three-storey warehouse lined with crates and barrels filled with weapons, equipment, and merchandise, was littered with mangled bodies. The floors and walls, even the ceiling, were covered in blood and gore.

'We shall have no-one hunting us, as thou requested.' Naya batted her eyelashes. 'And the other crews shall be too busy fighting each other for reign.'

'Don' thou know what discretion means? We weren' to draw attention to ourselves. Why 'n the abyss did thy declare thyself to them?'

Naya rounded on him, her tongue thickening with a ferocious snarl.

'We do not have time for discretion. There is nothing more important than the Key, and we have already been delayed too long. If I have to kill everyone in my way, I shall.' She leant in, green eyes darkening, 'And that includes thee.'

Koro swallowed hard. He knew how sincere her words were. She could cut him down right there and go on her merry way. She had no fear of being recognised. All she had to do was take another identity and she was Naya no more.

'Where is he?' Koro asked.

Naya straightened and gestured towards the staircase behind her. 'This way.'

She led him up the winding steps to the third floor. They walked down a hallway dimly lit by candles mounted on the walls. The scattered dead were fewer here, but the brutality of their demise was greater, if that were possible. Koro was not squeamish. He too had killed scores for the cause. But Naya's works of art made his skin crawl. This particular three-dimensional canvas bore fierce strokes and spatters of deep crimson sprung from the bodies – sculptures, here sitting, there hanging, carved and moulded to dramatic angles. He cringed all the way through what could be considered her masterpiece.

'Has he said anything?' Koro was trying to distract himself.

'I've not asked any questions yet,' she said slyly as they approached a closed door.

Creaking hinges announced their entrance. A window lay open across the room, presumably overlooking one of the alleys that surrounded the warehouse. The night breeze filled the little chamber and made the window's glass-paned sashes knock against the wall. The second thing Koro noticed was how dark it was. A candle in a clay holder, barely visible by moonlight, sat on a table near the window.

'Light that,' he commanded Naya.

She turned her back to the window, and her face was instantly dipped in shadow. 'As much as I love fire,' she said with scorn, 'I cannot breathe it.'

Koro sighed and charged past her to the man seated in the centre of the room, his hands bound behind his back. Koro grabbed the chair by its legs and pulled it round until it faced the window. Galob's face was battered bloody.

'Had fun?' Koro's sharp tone could cut stone.

Naya smiled defiantly. 'Much.'

He looked down at the Crab. The old man could barely keep his eyes open.

'Galob.'

There was a twitch, but no response. Koro called his name again, gave him a shove, and the thief-master shuddered awake. He groaned, while Koro lowered himself so he could stare straight into the man's teary eyes.

'Did she hurt thee?' Koro asked, soft and gentle.

Galob frowned. He pursed his lips and nodded hesitantly.

'I'm going t' ask some questions,' Koro explained. 'If thou don' feel like answering, I leave thee to her mercy. Course, she has none. Agreed?'

Galob's bulging eyes and brisk nod confirmed that it did.

'Good.' Koro straightened up. 'Thine old partner, Inan.'

The Crab blinked with surprise.

'Ye were friends for years, yes?'

Galob's mouth tightened as he dipped his head in affirmation.

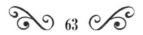

'Thou know 'bout an item he possessed? Like a claw? It was small and of a substance the colour of amber but harder than any metal. It had carvings on it.' Koro stopped when he noticed those bloodshot eyes widen slightly. A smile inched across his face. 'Know what I speak of?'

The thief-master glanced up apprehensively and bit the inside of his cheek.

'Oh, come,' Koro coaxed. 'It's too late to remember what loyalty feels like. Thou betrayed him once before. Thou can do it again. He shalln' care once we find him.'

Galob's face, sagging and inflamed, scrunched up into a scowl. His jaw clenched.

One word was forced out through red, chipped teeth. 'No.'

Koro glanced over their captive's head. Light approaching footfalls shook the once stalwart Crab. Her hair tickled the back of his neck. He cringed, whimpered, and suddenly gasped when her claws dug into his skin, just below the right shoulder-blade, worming their way through flesh and muscle. The room rang with his shrieks. He jerked violently, fists clenched, face drenched in tears and sweat.

Koro's bark could barely be heard through the old man's howls. 'Changed thy mind yet?'

'Yes!' Galob screamed, but Naya's hand continued to carve its way towards bone. 'P—please!' he sobbed. 'Make her stop!'

'Naya!' Koro snapped.

She tightened her grip on Galob's flesh and twisted. The thief-master's piercing scream deepened her euphoric expression. Koro cursed and punched her in the face. Naya staggered back with a hiss, releasing Galob. She gave her head a fierce shake before peeling back her lips and snarling at Koro. He stiffened, but his rage was too great to allow himself to cower.

'We can kill each other *after* we finish our damned job. Why thou think they paired us in the first place, thou brainless harpy? Thou're reckless. A hazard. Thou can' be trusted. Now, hold thy tongue, so we can end this.'

Naya was speechless and incensed by this outburst. Her intense desire to leave Crove was perhaps the only thing keeping her from tearing his head from his shoulders. She cocked her head and folded her arms as a sign of a temporary truce. Her cold glare followed Koro as he bent down as before to catch Galob's eye. The man was quivering in his chair when he was asked where the Key was.

Galob rasped, 'Inan... used ta wear a chain 'round his neck. Only once did I see what hung from it. It was that claw.' He wet his lips and went on, 'He wouldn' tell me 'bout it. But he never took it off. After... after I turned on him, he left for New Anvadore an' took it with him. That's the last I saw of it.'

Koro's face turned grim. 'Why'd he go there?'

'He had family. A wife and... and a child.'

'Did he have a house?'

Galob nodded. 'Yes... but I don' know where.'

The thief-master sighed. His head drooped. He was exhausted, bleeding out.

'Stay awake.' Koro slapped him and he hauled his head back up with a cough. 'Is the family still there?'

Galob groaned, 'The wife died. The daughter... I don' know.'

'What was her name?'

'Whose?'

'The daughter's!'

The Crab grimaced and his head swung limply from side to side as he whined, 'I don' know. He rarely spoke of her. It was something like... like Jude or June. Dune?'

Koro bolted upright. Fury rolled his eyes in their sockets. His grinding teeth threatened to shatter. He took a deep, shaky breath.

'Rune?' he asked in a voice as deep and ominous as the ground's rumble before an earthquake.

'Yes!' Galob gasped, 'that was it. Rune.'

Naya hunched. For the first time, she was afraid of Koro, who grabbed the candlestick and hurled it at her. She ducked with a hiss. It streaked over her head and smashed against the wall.

'Thou pleased?' He stormed towards her. 'I told thee she was hiding something! She knew more an' thou killed her! I should just drag thee back to be flayed!'

'How was I to know she was his daughter?' Naya fired back.

'If thou'd done as I instructed, she'd have told us!'

Naya scowled without a retort – another first.

'We go to New Anvadore. We track his moves and maybe – if we're lucky – they lead us to the Key.' Koro cupped his face in despair. He rubbed it fiercely and ran his hands through his greasy hair. His nostrils flared as he addressed Naya once more. 'From now on, thou do what I say. Am I clear?'

Her lips twisted with disgust.

'Am I clear!'

The answer came in the form of an imperceptible nod.

'Good. Now, let us finish off here,' Koro said, just as Naya's brow furrowed.

Her startled gaze was on the ceiling. She hissed, and Koro turned around to see something stir between the wooden beams above his head. The form retracted arms and legs, and dropped down, barely making a sound as its feet met the floor. It rose from a near crouch to its full six-foot height between Galob and them. Were it not for the moon's radiance streaming in through the window, the man would have been completely invisible, his gender sur-mised only from the outline of his broad shoulders above the slender curves of the rest of his body. Koro recalled his hooded shape perched on that roof on Bonfire Night. Even without the darkness to conceal him, his stealth was worthy of praise. He must have snuck in while Naya was fetching Koro and listened in on their conversation without being detected by her keen senses.

'Thy master's of no further use to us.' Koro spread his hands in a reassuring gesture. 'Thou can have him back.'

A voice emerged from beneath the hood, deep and harsh, but noble. 'I have no master.'

Naya muttered into Koro's ear, 'He's thaelil.'

He shied a step back. 'We have no quarrel with thee, elf. We shall leave quietly. We have what we came for.'

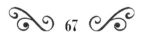

The stranger reached over his shoulders and pulled out two swords, steel resounding as they slid from their scabbards. Moonlight glided upon their smooth sides. The long, single-edged blades were slightly curved, edges razor-sharp.

'So have I,' the elf rumbled.

Koro unsheathed his own sword just in time to deflect an incoming swing. The force of the blow jarred his arm, however, and he stumbled back with a grunt. Naya sidestepped him, black claws extended. The elf's swords whistled towards her in consecutive arcs, but she dodged them, agile as a cat. At the first chance, she swiped a hand towards his chin. Her claws would have sliced off his face, if the elf had not, in the blink of an eye, leant back and under her extended arm, swinging his left sword towards her knees. Naya jumped into the air, legs gathered tight beneath her. The blade passed under her, only to return with its twin. Before she could be hacked into three pieces, Koro lunged into her and threw them both out of the swords' range. They rolled across the floor, scrambled to their feet, and made for the window. Without a backward glance, Koro dove through the opening with Naya beside him. He flew through the air and into the earth's pull. These were the moments he hated the most, when he had no choice but to leave his life in Naya's hands.

Chapter 8

Crove welcomed Meecha with open gates, their oak surface gnarled by age and weather. Even before he had stepped onto the first flagstones, the smell of filth and decay had given him pause. He stepped cautiously around puddles of stagnant water, blood, and excrement. Stooped, Meecha scanned his surroundings, the rim of his hat low. He avoided eye contact with the humans that crossed his path. Sinister and dismal, they wasted nought on him but a sneer or mocking jab. He did not feel as bad picking their pockets—a bit of coin would surely come in handy.

A new scent was added to the blend. A distinct putridity, mild at first, but thickening the further Meecha went. His suspicion was confirmed when he reached a large square. People with wheelbarrows piled with corpses were trundling about. Scarves and cloths covered their faces, but judging by the frowns, the stench was just too strong.

The square held nothing of interest. The half Meecha stood in was lined with unkempt stores, while a sizea-

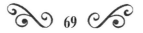

ble inn and dozens of tables strewn before its great doors took up most of the other side. The blazing midday sun bestowed some lustre to the city, but not as much as to the polished silver armour of three soldiers glowering at everyone from a corner of the square. The white bird on their crimson capes enveloped each of them with its wings as they turned now and then to talk to passers-by. There was little the sun could do about the streets' broken slabs of stone, the packs of shifty-eyed thieves—some children—clustered against walls, the beggars slumped in shady corners, and, of course, the dead bodies streaming out of a lane to the far left of the square.

Meecha strode down it to find a vast building from where another cadaver was being removed. A quick glimpse at the wounds suggested that the poor fellow may have been the victim of an exceptionally vicious predator. Meecha quickly crossed to the corner opposite. There were two men in plate armour arguing before the main doors, shadowed by two others in studded leather and helmets. The smell wafting out of the edifice twisted their scowls and tempers further, the yelling steadily rising. By the guards' faces, constantly pressed against their bracers, they were close to abandoning their posts.

'I can' believe not an eye saw what happened,' the shortest of the squabblers was saying. Meecha turned his ear in their direction and paid closer attention to the strange dialect. 'Coin has thee false. Thou in league with the crooks.'

The taller fellow was staring him down, brawny arms crossed. 'Thou know what I see? A mountain of dead. What did that I don' wanta cross. I have a family. And thou know what else I see? All those dead are crooks. I'm at peace to let the matter be.'

That man, apparently a member of the city's law enforcement, left the scene, leaving his three colleagues to guard the doors. Meecha heard a clatter and turned to see the other officer standing over a toppled barrel, its white powdery contents—soap perhaps—spilt into the street. His hunched shoulders rose and fell, his massive chest moving with his sigh.

'When the last body's out, go,' he growled at the guards, who cursed but stayed put, while he stormed off further away from the square, stepping through the soap, its bubbles turning brown in the stagnant muck. Meecha strode after him.

'Should we save the soap?' he heard one guard ask from behind a fist as he passed them by.

'What the use?' his partner responded before Meecha was out of earshot.

'Excuse me!' he called after the armoured officer.

The man barely glanced over his shoulder. 'To th'abyss with thee, girl. I don' have time for thee.'

Meecha faltered mid-gait, but then skipped faster to the human's side, where he scowled up at him.

'I'm not a girl, sir. Nor a child. I want to offer my assistance.'

The officer scoffed. 'Thou?' He studied Meecha from head to toe and his weary features twisted with disgust. 'Cease pestering me, jester.'

'No, not a jester either,' Meecha retorted light-heartedly, 'but I do like stories. And there seems to be one brewing in your city. Now, I'm just a visitor, a stranger to you, but something you should know about me is how much ruffian ingrates anger me.' The officer's face was pinched by frustration, his chin giving an authoritative jerk. 'I overheard about the lack of support you have from your own men, so I'm offering my services.'

'Send a manling as thee into the pits o' Crove? Thou must wish to join the dead. Why so eager?' The officer almost sounded concerned, yet his brown downturned eyes looked suspicious of Meecha.

'Call me curious and very good at my job.'

'Which be?' the human finally stopped walking and crossed his arms, glowering at Meecha like a father questioning his naughty child.

'Investigating the impossible. Give me what crumbs you have and I'll follow them as far as I can go. I ask for no reward, so you have only to gain from this arrangement: more information, if not the truth. And don't you worry, I have full awareness of my limitations, as well as my advantages. Like not being a guard. What say you?'

The officer stared at him long and hard. He then glanced back at the warehouse, where two workers had salvaged what was left of the soap and were carrying the barrel inside to start washing. He rubbed his close-cropped hair all the way to the back of his neck and left his hand there, clutching the tense, taut muscles. He snapped his eyes back to Meecha and nodded, giving his hand.

Meecha shook it as the human spoke, 'Very well, sir. Don' say thee not warned. Follow me.'

They continued down the same street, Meecha virtually skipping with joy and trying to keep up with the human. The only way he could find out where Azare had gone was by asking around. And whose better brains to pick than the lawman's and the crook's? Acquiring names of interest from the first would focus and speed up his search for answers.

'When did this… incident happen?' Meecha inquired, unable to restrain his curiosity.

They had already turned a few corners and were now crossing a street with distinctly less grime underfoot. The air was less pungent too. It was laced instead with the smell of freshly baked bread and flowers. Some of the cramped houses had a blooming pot or two out front, if not a garden, tiny but loved. The officer must have noticed him staring.

'Crove's known for rogues and murderers. But that not all it be.'

Meecha studied the brick of the buildings. There was more red than grey to be found. And more wood. And sun, strangely enough. Everything looked warmer, more… civilised.

'And who gets to live on the nice side of Crove?' Meecha's derision escaped his control.

The officer sniffed, but did not reply immediately. He eyed either side of the street, looking for words or a distraction.

'There's good folk in the poor parts. They want and deserve better living. But of them that find it, few do so without suffering.'

He suddenly grabbed Meecha by the scruff and barked, 'Move faster! Or I have thy thieving hide for a banner.'

Meecha blanched and tried to break the man's grip on his shirt. He was about to kick him in the shin or groin when he noticed people coming down the street towards them. He relaxed a little and played along.

'Yes, sir,' he whimpered and stumbled forward when the officer shoved him.

It was a couple, a man and a woman, that passed them by first, then an elderly woman lugging a sack over her shoulder. All three stuck their noses up at Meecha, thinking he was the city guard's prisoner. He lumbered on, hands in pockets, wearing the most dejected face he could muster: mouth downturned, bottom lip stuck forward, eyes downcast and hooded.

At some point, another street intersected with theirs from the right. That next block was one large slab of a building with two reinforced double doors. A sign over the first read, 'Crove City Guard.' Apart from that and the doors, there was no other hint of wood. It was made entirely of stone. It even had arrow slits and crenellations, no windows. The barracks was a castle. The way it huddled and glared at the surrounding buildings contradicted the welcoming sign.

Meecha felt a rough hand on his shoulder that urged him towards it. The officer's other hand pushed the right-hand door open—they looked like oak, also bearing hefty ring handles of iron. A waft of closed space and tobacco wriggled up Meecha's nostrils. He rubbed his nose as he stepped inside to be faced with a rectangular room about fifteen feet wide and thirty long, illuminated by oil lamps mounted high on the walls. The right wall was covered with notices, sketches, and wanted posters. At the far end of the room, past tables, chairs, benches, and strewn bits of arms and armour, a shield here, a gauntlet there, was a single door. There were two arches on the left side, both seeming to lead into an adjacent room; perhaps the second set of doors outside belonged to it. A practice dummy was visible through one opening—grunts and thumping sounds suggested the existence of more—and racks of swords and helmets through the other.

Leather creaked. Shuffling of feet. Meecha turned to see a guard leap up to attention from a bench, thumping his left shoulder in salute. No, it was a woman. Tall and lanky, but muscular. Her light brown tight curls were short, a few fingers in length, plaited back a little from her forehead. Her big honey-coloured eyes were on the officer just as the cloud of smoke she had exhaled a moment before drifted up to smother her. She batted the air, dropped her pipe, hurled a stream of curses, and proceeded to stamp out the smouldering leaves that had tipped onto the stone floor. It was dirty to begin with.

'Guard Namael.' The man's stern voice made her bolt upright, the pipe back in hand.

'Captain! Forgive me, Captain,' she blurted, her bronze cheeks hiding any blushing.

He gave a low snarl behind pressed lips, then said curtly, 'Enjoying protecting the barracks, are we?'

Meecha followed the Captain—as it turned out—past the guard to a door at the back. The young woman was watching them with great interest, unconcerned about her superior now that his back was turned.

'Come,' the Captain said, as the lock clicked open.

Once an oil lamp was lit and the office door shut, the human grabbed a black bottle from the top of his desk and took a swig before plopping into his chair, exhausted. The lamp shone and shaded his face; hills, slopes, and grooves of a dark earthy brown mapped his age. He was older than his stout demeanour and hairless, rounded face indicated.

'So what do I call thee, little man?'

'Meecha, sir. And do I call you Captain?'

The human swallowed another sip of spirit and put the bottle aside.

'Captain Namael,' he said, leaning forward to rest his elbows on the desk and fix his guest with a flat look.

Meecha's eyebrows shot up. He opened his mouth to inquire, but instead just pointed a thumb at the door.

'My niece.' The man gave the word a soft bite. The way he tilted his head down made Meecha wonder what else the girl had done wrong. He did not have a chance to ask, as Captain Namael changed the subject. 'We found the state of the warehouse from the smell. Early dawn this day. They must have been cooking for two days. Maybe. It was Galob's place, so no surprise none saw nothing.'

'Galob?' Meecha piped in.

Namael nodded. 'One of the crew leaders. The big one. So now the two dogs left are scrapping to get on top. That's Parda and Lazlo.'

While Meecha made a mental note of these names, the Captain lit a second lantern and retrieved a map of the city from a cabinet in the desk. He spread the scroll on the top, picked up a stick of charcoal from a drawer, and they spent the best part of an hour poring over where each crew's base was located, where valuable information might be found, and which areas to avoid. Namael even produced sketches of the leaders, just in case Meecha bumped into them. He hoped he would not need to delve so deep into Crove's underworld, but an agent must always be prepared for any scenario. Finally, the Captain rolled up the marked map and handed it to Meecha.

'Thou find anything, bring it to me,' the human instructed, while circling the desk to the door.

Once the scroll was secure in Meecha's bag, he looked up at the old warrior. 'Yes, sir.'

Captain Namael's eyes narrowed. 'I must be desperate. Truly. But thou prove a cheat and my threat in the alley shall come true.' He yanked the door open and strode out.

Meecha once again suppressed his terror of the man. When he too stepped out into the hall's ample light, he found several more people in it. Some guards sat around rolling bread and spirits in their mouths. Others stood near the office, presumably waiting to speak to their Captain. Young Namael was among them, hands on hips, eyes and ears focused on her colleagues. Her uncle passed orders for continued questioning of the locals regarding the massacre. The woman asked to join the effort, but she was rebuffed with a wave of the Captain's hand. She seethed for a few moments and then stormed off into the training room. As Meecha was passing him by, Namael senior turned with a grimace, as if he had just spotted a rat crawling towards him.

'I said, get thy wretched hide out of my barracks,' he snapped. All the guards sneered. 'Jesters have no place in the Guard.' Meecha caught some amused whispers, but he did not wait to make out what they were saying.

The castle door thudded behind him.

Chapter 9

It stung. He said it to throw dust in his guards' eyes, but Meecha's head still rang with Captain Namael's last words. His hat's rim was low over his frown as he made his way towards the northern parts of Crove, occasionally stepping aside to discreetly peruse the map. He was heading to a tavern by the name of the Brass Raven, where the infamous were said to lurk. How would he broach the subject of the warehouse, though? Would they be suspicious of a fellow scoundrel visiting the city in search of opportunity and wondering about the dead pouring out of a large building in the centre of Crove? That felt like a safe way to start. If no witnesses could be unearthed, he would ask about potential work and hopefully become acquainted with better-informed individuals. He would give himself until noon the next day to work out which way Azare had gone—if he had even been here. That was a daunting possibility. If Meecha came out with nothing, he would contact the aerieti for assistance.

A hand latched itself around his neck, tore him off his feet, and into an alley. He barely had a moment to yelp when he was slammed into the wall, his hat flopping onto the ground. He gurgled and gawked up at his attacker, whose hand was now squeezing his throat. Just enough to make him light-headed.

'Who are thee?' the blurry face growled. 'What thy business with the Captain?'

Meecha focused his sight and finally saw her curly hair and brownish eyes, her dark heart-shaped face and long limbs. Young Namael had the most vicious expression of anger blazing down at him.

'Am—Am helping—For answers—Warehouse.' Meecha just croaked key words until the guard finally loosened her grip. A little. Just enough for him to be able to speak.

'Helping? How?'

Meecha was apprehensive about sharing too much. Even if she was an officer of the law, she could be corrupt. But she shook him so hard the words jumped out of their own accord. 'I'm going to pretend to be one of them. To get their trust. And what they know about what happened.' He sighed. 'I'm to report back to the Captain when—if—I find anything.'

The woman's glare softened from life-threatening to curious. 'Thou no guard. No warrior even. Thou some mercenary? What thou paid to do this?'

Meecha licked his lips. She would never believe that he was helping for free and that would mean more time wasted in questioning. 'A small amount, true. But it's hard times. One can't be picky. Will you let me go, now? So I can do my job?'

Her nostrils flared at his tone, but she released him nonetheless. She crossed her arms over her leather-clad chest as he straightened his shirt and picked up his dusty hat. Once shaken out and returned to his head, Meecha looked up at the guard with what was left of his dignity.

'Was there anything else?'

'Yes,' she said. 'I'm coming along.'

Meecha groaned louder than he had intended, causing her ire to swell again. He did not care. 'I can play the crook. You can't. You'll get us both killed.'

Namael fired back, 'Thou shall die without me any-how. Thou need a bodyguard and I need true guard work or I shall lose my mind.' Her clenched teeth stopped the deluge of spit and gripe.

Meecha's mouth hung open for a moment or two, while he processed a realisation. 'Your uncle won't let you work?' Reluctantly, she nodded. 'Because you're family?' Eyes rolled, mouth tightened, her head swayed in a yes-and-no manner. 'And because you're a woman?' She glowered right at him, throat and jaw atremble. He blew a heavy sigh at his boots and conceded. 'Very well, Guard Namael. My back could use the protection. But how likely are you to be recognised?'

'I've lived in Crove for a year or so, but, as I say, I've done little real work. My face shouldn' be known.'

'Still, can you look less… high and mighty and more… world-weary thug?' Meecha asked as politely as possible, to which she glanced down at herself in puzzlement.

Back straight, legs slightly apart, she looked accustomed to standing in military lines. Awkwardly, she stood at ease, unbound her arms, and slouched with them dangling by her side. She even made a dumb face—lazy eyes, loose mouth, slight sideways tilt to the head. The gangly creature had Meecha in stitches. At least her clothes were nondescript enough: dark brown leather breastplate over a black short-sleeved shirt, leather wrist cuffs, black baggy trousers under leather thigh armour and boots. A short sword hung from her left hip, a buckler from her back. As a precaution, she pulled up her shirt's hood, black and covering her head down to the brow. Perfect.

'Let's be off, then,' Meecha declared excitedly and they hastened along the street he had been on earlier.

He had to admit, he felt safer having a human battering ram prowling alongside him. On their way to the Brass Raven, he offered her his name and found out that hers was Marilli. She grew up with three brothers; they valued her roughhousing talent early on, even if her mother did not; they taught her to fight with fist and sword; their father had died a few months before she was born; her uncle— her father's brother—had reluctantly accepted her into the guard; he always said she had the skill and grit to do some good in the world, but he was too protective, among other things. Meecha had to cut her off when he saw the sign over the tavern's ramshackle door.

'Are you ready?' he whispered, mindful of the shady figures at every corner.

'Are thee?' she chuckled and sauntered over to the entrance.

Meecha shrugged under his pack as he followed her to the slab of unremarkable wood, which, on closer inspection, was reinforced with strips and bolts of metal. Against the wall above their heads perched a large carving of a raven in flight with a beak painted in the orange-gold colours of brass. It even had little bolts on it, bright enough to still be seen in the dimming sunlight.

The door did not budge to Meecha's first push. Before he could put his shoulder to it, Marilli had shoved it open with one hand. He rolled his eyes at her smug smirk and raised a foot through the opening.

'Watch thy step,' she said without breaking eye contact, cool and sweet.

Meecha looked ahead. His foot was hovering over empty air, the start of a steep staircase. He gave an indignant puff and stomped down it stiffly. The sounds and smells did not register until he was standing on the other side of a second door at the base of the stairs. Was it the room's lighting that froze him—various shades of red emitted by wall lamps? The haunting cloud of tobacco smoke, its scent mingled with sweat and bile? No, it was the eyes. They snapped towards him, all of them, seeking, judging, hating. A fiddle was playing somewhere nearby, seducing his skittish heartstrings with its titillating tune. Then the malevolent looks changed. Some raised eyebrows, others turned away completely. A whistle or two accompanied the fiddle.

Meecha turned to find tall, strapping, hooded Marilli looming over him. She put a protective hand on his shoulder and all the evil in the world could no longer touch him. He gave her a thin, grateful smile and made for the bar to their left, his composure reclaimed. He dumped his bag under a stool and clambered on top of it. Marilli perched on the edge of the next seat, facing the room. She crossed her stretched-out legs and produced her pipe from a small bag on her belt. While she filled and lit it, the bartender, a balding human in a dirty shirt and overalls, strolled over.

'Yeah?' he said with a lazy simplicity that almost made Meecha overlook the calculating squint.

He responded in a weary yet jovial manner, 'What's your cheapest spirit, friend?'

A half-smile creased the bartender's mouth. 'The cheapest? That be piss.'

'You even charge for that?' Meecha grimaced. 'I should have come to Crove sooner.'

The human snorted.

'I'll have the cheapest drink that doesn't come from a being, if you don't mind.'

He watched the man turn to the first of a line of barrels set on their sides along the back of the bar. Meecha could see a group of people clustered at the far end, with the fiddler busking away behind them. The rest of the place was occupied by tables and people of different types and sizes. Masculine and feminine, round and angular, long and short, polished and popular, grimy and stuck to the shadowy walls. None matched the sketches Captain Namael had showed him.

A clay mug was placed on the counter in front of Meecha's folded arms.

'Old Mafter's ale,' the bartender said and opened his palm. 'Three coppers' worth of a bad head.'

Meecha gave the man his coins from the little he had filched from Crove pockets. He looked at Marilli, chin resting on his left shoulder.

'Aren't you having anything?'

She slowly removed the pipe's stem from her mouth, followed by a billow of smoke. When she turned to him, head and hood, he could just about see up to her eyes.

'It be best I stay alert,' she muttered.

Meecha shrugged and risked a sip of his ale. A convulsion in his throat tried to push it up his nose instead. He clapped the counter as he forced the liquid into his stomach, gasping and coughing. Both Marilli and the bartender laughed at him—others too. He was not making a good impression as a hardened mercenary.

'What are thee doing in Crove, little man?' a stranger asked two stools down.

Meecha studied him through teary eyes. A cloak hid everything except his head, which was gaunt, bearded, and topped with short-cropped black hair. A little black twirl was inked into his left temple.

'We're just passing through, really. Hoping for a bit of work. If not, moving on.'

'Work? What kind of work?' The human's pale stare narrowed.

'Oh, nothing complicated.' Meecha unconsciously lifted his mug to drink, but put it straight back down. 'Mostly obtaining hard-to-get merchandise of interest to certain markets. Perhaps offer some help with… shop-keeping.' The man's head was bobbing up and down. So was the bartender's. 'Although, this whole warehouse butchery business makes me rethink our stay.'

Teeth were sucked from multiple directions. Their conversation was drawing attention. The dark-haired customer glugged the last of his drink and scowled.

'That was a sick thing, brother.' He hiccupped that last word.

'What happened?' Meecha pressed with a whisper and then allowed his voice to rise—slowly and unintentionally, of course. 'I don't mean to pry, but I heard some strange things. Some shout assassin; others demon. A fool even spoke of elves.'

'Elves?' both men exclaimed at the same time. It was the bartender who continued.

'Fables… Galob bothered many, but elves?'

Meecha gave him a blank look. He then directed it at the other human. Neither was prompted to elaborate, so he threw another bone. 'Who's Galob?'

They exchanged cagey squints until the cloaked fellow shrugged and shifted one stool closer to Meecha. He leaned in. Meecha thought he felt something brush against his other elbow, perhaps Marilli trying to listen in.

'Galob was chief in Crove. It was him an' his men that got gutted.'

Meecha raised his eyebrows in awe. 'So the top gang here was murdered? All of them?'

The human shook his head. 'No. Just them that were there.'

'Could one of the other gangs be involved?'

He received an uneasy shrug before the men scanned the room for watchers.

'I heard something 'bout a woman,' Marilli's voice drifted out from under her hood, flat, nonchalant.

'Oh, yeah, her.' The bartender shivered just as the other man mumbled into his mug. 'Scary wench.'

Meecha frowned at his bodyguard. Why had she not mentioned this earlier?

'Do tell,' he prodded all three humans.

The bartender grumbled, 'A red-haired woman came through an' joined Galob a few days 'fore they all died. Vicious one. She wasn' among the dead an' word is she was a hired killer. Too many tales 'round to know for true. She had a companion too, but he kept to himself.'

Two suspects. *Azare's targets?*

'And nobody actually saw anything?' Meecha did not want to sound too persistent, but he had to ask.

The men's heads shook from side to side. Not that they knew of, they said. Meecha managed to swallow another mouthful of his ale. It went down easier. What to do? Would the woman have stuck around after such a deed? That would not be wise.

'She still in the city?' He heard his question emerge from Marilli's smoky lips.

'Why? Eager to meet her?' the bartender replied.

The guard set a hard stare on him. 'One woman rends an army limb from limb an' walks? Shake her hand, I shall.'

Meecha jumped in. 'Now, now, my friend. No need for such talk.'

He gave her arm a nervous pat and the men a sheepish smile.

'None've seen her, anyhow,' the bartender said as he walked away to serve another customer.

Another sip of ale and Meecha's head tingled pleasantly. He decided to put the warehouse matter aside for now.

'So you wouldn't know of any work, would you?' he asked his cloaked neighbour.

'There's much, brother. If thou know where to look.'

'And do you?'

The human smirked. 'Why tell thee?'

Meecha looked offended. 'Because we're brothers.'

A scornful puff of rank breath met him. 'Croven brothers sell each other regular. What else thee offerin'?'

Meecha only had six coppers left, nothing to please a discerning gentleman such as this. He felt movement behind him and Marilli's leather-clad arm reached between them to leave a gold coin on the counter beneath the man's nose. A flash of pale, scrawny fingers from under his cloak and the golden glint vanished from the bar.

'Talk,' Marilli snarled.

The way the man cowered made Meecha regret bribing him at all. She could have bullied the information out of him. In any case, he uttered two final words to Meecha.

'The fiddler.' His eyes flitted up at Marilli to see if she was pacified. She still glared at him with disgust, so he hunched over his ale and spoke no more.

Marilli gestured with her head for Meecha to follow and meandered around the bar towards the source of the music. He hopped off the stool, grabbed his things, and trotted after her, leaving his drink behind—nothing good would come of finishing it.

Chapter 10

The fiddler was a sliver of a man, his movements fluid, in complete harmony with the rhythm of his tune. His long, silken hair was pale blond—almost white—and tied at the nape of the neck with a dark blue cord. His skin was a rich, flawless brown, ageless. Brow high over closed eyes, he looked serene. A vest of the same shade of blue covered a grey shirt, the sleeves of which stopped at the elbows, just before the man's forearms. They were adorned with vine-like tattoos. The buttons at his knees, where his black breeches stopped, glimmered blue, as if made of sapphires. He wore stockings, dark grey, and black shoes with silver buckles. What odd fashion to find in Itania, let alone a seedy tavern? Meecha ceased his wondering and returned to the man's face. His piercing stare was brown and violet. It was no trick of the light. One eye was dark chocolate, the other like an amethyst.

The bow continued to caress the strings of the beautiful instrument, reddish-brown and engraved at the neck. But the fiddler said nothing. He just played and stared at Mee-

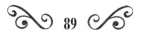

cha, who found his throat dry. He coughed, licked his lips, and advanced.

'Excuse the interruption, but… umm… I was told you might know about… ah… work.'

The fiddler lifted an eyebrow, the edges of his sealed lips quirking upwards. A chill ran down Meecha's spine, while the human performed a little bow, still playing. The melody ebbed and flowed like waves.

'Right. Good. Can you tell us about it?'

With a smooth downward arc, the man used the instrument's neck to direct Meecha's attention to the hat at his feet. Meecha tutted and glanced at Marilli. She was gripping the pommel of her sword. The fiddler's wolfish sneer taunted her, drawing her closer. Meecha grabbed her forearm, but she tore it away. The instrument and its master danced an impish, jittery tune as the hooded guard towered over them. She stood there for a moment or two and then staggered back a little, thrusting her hand into her pocket and tossing a gold coin into the man's hat. Meecha released his breath.

The fiddler's song instantly changed to a high-pitched screech that made the whole Raven squirm. But then a mellow seduction, like that which first greeted Meecha, put them at ease. It appeared they were going to have to wait for the enigmatic artist to finish his act, which Marilli did not look happy about. Meecha could just discern her pursed mouth beneath the hood. Her arms were crossed, her buckler resembling a tortoise shell over her hunched back. Meecha went and stood beside her.

'Don't fret,' he said, while the group of men at the bar behind them roared with laughter. He grimaced and had to talk louder to Marilli. 'We're doing well. We'll get more answers soon enough.'

She shook her head before leaning towards him. 'That's not what bothers me.'

'What then?'

She glanced at the fiddler, but quickly averted her eyes. 'My head… He got in my head… His music.'

Meecha frowned. The musician's eyes were closed once more, a crease barely breaking his brow. There was something eerie about him—there was no doubt about it. Could it, in fact, be magic?

'Are you well now?' Meecha asked.

She nodded—a bit too vigorously. The music and voices grew louder again, so Marilli shouted into his ear. 'We shall find the truth an' my uncle shall swallow his tongue. I'm not returning to the barracks—'

A sudden dip in the fiddler's tune cut her words short. Meecha's stomach clenched. He looked around for any sign that they had been found out, but luck was with them. Both he and Marilli glowered at the fiddler, whose eyes had opened to slits, just enough for their evil glint to shine through. The rowdy bunch of rogues jostled Meecha, wearing his patience further. It was not unlikely that they were being fooled, discovered even and waiting for a trap to snap around them.

A table was vacated. Its two occupants, women both, walked past Marilli. One of them, a girl with freckles and black hair, braided and threaded with orange ribbons, lifted her gaze to meet Marilli's—and the guard forgot her rage all of a sudden. As she tried to look at the girl better, the hood slipped back a few inches, but she caught it before it left her head entirely. She bowed to study her boots tapping the floor, a smirk dimpling her cheek. Meecha grinned and gave her side a playful poke. She retaliated with a fake pout and a shove to his shoulder. It was gentle. Had it not been, he would have barrelled through the whole group of men instead of into the back of one.

Meecha's shoulders bounced off the stranger's buttocks before the sound of something breaking caught his ears. He turned to look at the human's feet. A clay mug lay, its fragments rocking, in a spreading pool of what Meecha assumed was ale. His wide eyes snapped up to the man's face, while his neck shrunk into his shoulders and his feet carried him slowly away. What had started as an affronted scowl quickly transformed the drunken rogue's face into a snarling mask of fury. He lunged with both great hands to grab Meecha, but the edge of Marilli's shield cracked into his wrists. A chair was thrown at her. She skipped out of its way, deflecting a leg with her shield, and drew her sword. Meecha's dagger was already in his hand. The thug's five friends tore into them, while the rest of the Brass Raven's customers flew to the walls and door.

Meecha lured his two attackers away from Marilli and between the tables. One man jabbed his short sword at Meecha's stomach, but he leapt sideways behind a chair. Stepping backwards, he led the human further into the labyrinth of furniture. He ducked under a swipe of the sword and immediately lunged forward with his dagger, burying its blade into his foe's upper arm—that was as far as he could reach before stepping away again. It was enough for the human to drop his weapon, though, and let his friend take over.

That one was cautious now, his own two daggers held hilts forward and blades parallel to the wrists, their serrated edges facing Meecha. The thug kicked. Meecha blocked with crossed wrists and dropped to his back. His skull had almost been skewered by those nasty knives. A grunt escaped Meecha as he rolled aside and up beside another table. As he snatched a bottle from the top—it was hefty with spirit—he glimpsed Marilli's shield smashing a head and her sword goring a paunch. Meecha flung the bottle at his attacker's chest. Caught between tables, the human had nowhere to go, so the bottle hit its target, but only doused him a little and thumped to the floor, intact and spilling its guts onto his boots. Meecha cursed and dashed towards a bench against the wall. Everyone, even the bartender, had abandoned the building by now.

Meecha heard his foe behind him. The bench was too heavy for him to lift and swing. But the lantern above was another matter. He jumped onto the wood, grabbing the lamp from its hook, and whirled around, hurling the thing as hard as he could. Unlike the bottle, this smashed. Oil and spirit caught the flame, which latched onto the man's right arm and leg. Small flickers flared stronger and ran along the paths of fuel to his chest and neck. Weapons abandoned, he cried out and batted himself. Meecha did not let him suffer long. He flipped his dagger, caught it by the blade, and launched it at the rogue's throat. It struck home, slicing his scream to silence. Quickly, Meecha found an abandoned coat and threw it over the flaming corpse and floor. A few more stamps and it was out. In that moment of precious quiet, Meecha caught his breath, barely sensing motion behind him. He swirled just in time to see Marilli catch his first attacker in a headlock and snap his neck with a sharp, blood-curdling crack. Now it was over.

The Brass Raven was littered with bodies, broken cutlery and chairs. And blood. The aftermath of Marilli's battle was far more impressive. But it was not smoking like his. He retrieved his hat from between the tables. *There is no glory in killing,* he scolded himself. The aerieti accepted the occasional necessity of it, but did not condone it, especially if it could be avoided. Meecha's introspection was interrupted by the realisation that they were no longer alone. Three gaping people were at the door.

'What th' abyss is this?' the man in front barked. 'Those my men!'

The face matched one of the Captain's posters. Lazlo.

'Ah,' Meecha began, but the gnarled human was having none of it.

He raised his broad chin and pushed a thin bottom lip forward. His longsword, fine steel gleaming, slid out of its sheath.

'Wait, you don't want this! Let me explain,' Meecha pleaded. He was not eager to get into another fight so soon. 'They attacked us.'

Lazlo's nostrils flared, making the silver nose-ring between them quiver. 'I don' care. I needed 'em for a job and ye—Ye go' all six of 'em?'

'Do you see anyone else here?' Meecha fired back and then continued calmer. 'But let me offer an alternative to killing us.' He wondered if the fiddler had done something after all. 'You say you wanted these men for work, but clearly they were a waste of money. Since we owe you, and have proven our skill, why not let us take their place? We pay you back with our service and perhaps make a little profit for ourselves. How's that?'

The human sucked his cheeks in thought—his face was gaunt enough. Short black hair framed his features from scalp to jaw.

Meecha risked another nudge. 'The job's tonight, I take it. That's why you're here? You must have use for two talented strangers. Our faces aren't known as part of your company and won't draw suspicion. My friend is an exceptional warrior, and I'm adept with a blade, but even better in the sneaking and thieving trade. We have references.'

'Enough,' Lazlo snapped.

From beneath thick eyebrows, his grey glare took them both in, weighing their worth, no doubt. Meecha noticed that Marilli's hood had fallen during her struggle. She was not drawing any negative reactions, however.

'Fine,' the man grumbled. 'This night was long coming. Keep yer mouths shut and do everything ye're told. Ye hear?'

Meecha nodded. An irritated sigh left Marilli before she relaxed the guard-posture she had unconsciously taken and followed his example. Lazlo was desperate indeed if he allowed them in so quickly.

'What're we doing exactly?' Meecha inquired, his new employer's first rule already forgotten.

As Lazlo made his way back to the staircase, he barked over his shoulder, 'We're taking the city.'

Meecha recovered quickly from the shock of those words and trotted after the two other men. Marilli was behind him. When he looked back, he saw her deep frown, but could say nothing to ease her fear.

The cool evening air made him gasp. He had grown too accustomed to the tavern's stench. He spotted the bartender leaning against the wall on the opposite side of the street.

'Hey, where you two going? You paying for yer damage.'

Meecha was going to try and explain the situation somehow, but Lazlo was in no mood to wait.

'Stuff it, Graz. We got bigger business.'

No matter how sorry Meecha felt for the Raven's owner, it was true. More important things were afoot and there was little time to deal with mishaps. A high-pitched sound reached Meecha's ears. He halted and focused. A plucking of strings, like rain trickling on tin rooftops. It was the fiddle, somewhere far yet close enough to tickle his nerves.

Chapter 11

The bottles clinked in his arms. The bag they were stuffed into was too shallow, so the top half of each glass vessel threatened to keel overboard.

'Abyss take the cheap wretches,' Meecha cried. 'Filthy, clueless, rabid… dogs.'

He was stomping alongside a long row of attached houses. The streetlamps were lit and shed their yellow glow intermittently across his path. The topmost edge of the next beam touched the side of a barrel standing in front of a door. He continued to rant and drag his feet along the flagstones. When he reached the barrel, one of the bottles of wine finally escaped his embrace and smashed on the ground. Meecha groaned at the sky, cursed his luck, and gave the barrel a mighty kick. It was empty and easy to send thudding onto the door. He turned his back to the house, while lamenting the loss of his bottle.

A column of light rushed over him, pinning his shadow onto the wall he was facing.

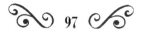

'What 'n blazes are thee up to, boy?' a rough voice behind him demanded.

Meecha spun on his heels with a horrified expression. 'Forgive me, sirs. My temper got the better of me. I didn't mean to—'

'Who are thee?' the man towering over him growled. The light from the house was on his back, so Meecha could not see his face.

'I—I'm a merchant, good sir. I—I sell fine wines,' Meecha stuttered and shied back, while a second man stepped out to peer around the shoulder of the first.

'A merchant?' that one asked. 'Thou don' look like a merchant. What thee doing here?'

Meecha clutched his precious bottles. 'I mean no trouble. I'm just coming from a bad deal. A customer wanted all these wines and then refused to pay me. I was just passing by and kicked that barrel and—I'm sorry to disturb you.'

'What kind of wines?' the first human asked, which earned a shove and a scowl from the second.

'Good ones, sir.' Meecha's face broke into a hopeful smile. 'Would you like to buy some?'

One man snapped, 'No,' while the other hummed thoughtfully. Two more joined them.

'He has wine,' the interested man informed the newcomers.

'For sale,' Meecha piped in, but seeing how sceptical they still were, he added, 'You can try one for free. See if you like it.'

He carefully removed a bottle and presented it to them. It was snatched from his grasp, despite their friend's continued protests. Three of the four sipped and sipped. Round the bottle went.

'Interested in buying the rest?' Meecha ventured.

One of the drinkers passed his fellows and prowled towards him.

'Better idea,' he said. 'I gut thee an' we take 'em all free.'

Meecha gasped and retreated, while they spread out before him. They were moving further and further away from their open door. He was nearing the alley's opposite wall.

He whimpered, 'Take them. Take them. Spare me, I beg you.'

They obliged, but as soon as the last bottle was out of his hands and into theirs Meecha edged around them and sprinted towards the house, pressing his hat to his head. They were too busy opening the bottles to pay attention to what he was doing, except for the one man with an ounce of intelligence.

'Hey, where thee going?' he roared.

Meecha leapt through the entrance and found himself in what could be called a kitchen and dining room. A square rickety table and four chairs stood close to a small fireplace with a cooking pot boiling next to it. More of Parda's crew were inside, both just rising from the straw beds laid out beyond a set of opened curtains. The smart human came in behind Meecha, who reached into his pocket.

'Damn my head, I've taken a wrong turn again,' he told them, hand on chest, and hurled a small jar at the floor between them.

Before it smashed and spewed its smoke, Meecha had covered his face with a protective mask—glass lined with sponge. The same was worn by Lazlo's rogues and Marilli as they charged into the house, some through the door, others crashing through a square, boarded-up window above the beds. They made short work of their rivals, already weakened by the fumes.

They did not wait for the milky mist to subside before one of the rogues started feeling the brittle grey wall on the left. Meecha glanced out the front door at the street. The sleep mixture in the wine had knocked out the three sentries and they would remain that way for a few hours, Lazlo had assured him. At least they would get to live. The aerieti would be pleased.

He heard a grinding sound. The rogue had found the secret passage to the next house and was pushing the wooden panel that had been painted to look like stone. He vanished for a short while, scouting ahead for traps and enemies. When he returned, he confirmed the existence of hidden wires—now neutralised—and five armed guards beyond, his voice muffled but audible from behind the mask. The humans hunched through two by two, six total. Meecha walked straight and proud at the rear.

They paused in the short dank passage, a moment's silence to collect themselves, before a slit of light appeared at their feet accompanied by rustling. A panel made of canvas, Meecha guessed—he could not see well from there. A match flared. A fuse sparked. A jar rolled into the next room. What returned were surprised shouts, a bang and an orange flash, a billow of smoke that blew the canvas like a sail. Then they charged, except for Meecha. He stayed at the edge of the passage and watched. Six against five was already unfair.

Dark-clad shapes of men and women writhed through the mist. Punch, dodge, parry, thrust, sword, dagger, Marilli's shield. While waiting for the battle to wane, Meecha noted the beds, tables, dartboard, and crates of food and spirit. This house—or section of Parda's lair—served as a place for her crew to recuperate. Then his eyes fell on a familiar red cape hanging over the back of a chair. Some new red blotches studded the white bird's tail.

The last of Parda's minions fell.

'Thou not helping, little man?' Lazlo panted at Meecha, the glass of his mask steaming. He yanked it off so hard the string holding it in place snapped.

'You have it all sorted, I think. I'd be in the way.'

Lazlo's nose wrinkled and he stalked away towards the panel at the other end of the room. Marilli approached Meecha.

'What happens when this is done?' she whispered as close to him as she could get while walking.

He knew what she was worried about. Did Lazlo's plan of taking the city include the barracks?

'We can go back. To warn... them,' he suggested.

She sighed, a heavy but relieved sound. Her eyes narrowed with renewed determination.

An explosion sounded somewhere ahead.

'That be the rest,' one of Lazlo's minions said.

Their leader had reached the panel and, with blade poised, pulled it aside. A glass-faced, blood-spattered

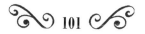

throng was trickling towards them. Three were in the hallway and more peered through the opening behind them. Menacing glares broke into grins of recognition.

Lazlo stepped into their passage and looked around. He stamped and pushed, but there was no secret entrance, apart from the two their groups came from.

'Search. A door. A lever. Something,' he growled.

They scattered, touching and examining what they found. Meecha walked back towards the canvas they had come from, using his eyes more than his hands. Dust lay everywhere, except on wiped surfaces or parts of the floor worn by shuffling feet. There were no suspicious wires or strings. No trapdoor below or above. The ceiling was low and made of cheap wood. One plank against the wall to his right looked rotten and bent. He stood beneath it.

'Is there another floor?' he asked and pointed up.

Lazlo shook his head. 'No.' One black eyebrow rose. 'But there may be crawl spaces.'

'Want to give me a lift?'

Lazlo gestured to the tallest of his men—of a height with Marilli. Meecha removed his hat and bag. He reluctantly stuffed the first into the latter and turned to her.

'Could you watch these for me?' he requested, his hushed tone showing how important their safety was.

The guard seemed taken aback, but nodded nonetheless. She shouldered his possessions as he returned to the mound of a human, all leather and muscle, who readied his palms for Meecha to step into. Once he did, he was launched at the ceiling so fast he stifled a yelp. His hand stopped his head from hitting the wood. Cursing under his breath, he pulled out his dagger and pried the plank from its fitting. It cracked loose easily and gave to his push. He put the weapon down on the floor of the black passage and hoisted himself into it, elbows, hips, knees wriggling between the opened plank. A groan was pushed out of his belly when he slumped onto the filthy boards. The space was barely large enough for him. None of Parda's crew he had seen so far could have fit in there.

A cobweb tickled his forehead, but he could not see it. The only thing he could see was a sliver of lamplight from outside sneaking in through a crack in the roof further ahead. He picked up the dagger and crawled towards the light, while his eyes adjusted to the darkness. Eventually, he could make out a corner. He moved faster, jumping when his hand brushed something furry—little feet ran away from him. With an uneasy grumble, Meecha reached the corner that turned left into another long crawl space.

He estimated that he was creeping over the secret passage he and his team had used. Looking forward, his eyes fairly adapted now, he thought he could make out a square of deeper darkness, a hole perhaps, in the floor of the next corner. Meecha perked up. Lizard-like, he rushed for it, the passage creaking around him, lifting dusk, clicking. Halfway through, he passed by another opening that presumably led to the sentries' room. Its darkness shifted. He froze. It hissed. Stomach clenching, limbs numb, Meecha turned slowly to look.

Spider-eyes gleamed. Hook teeth gnashed. A clawed paw touched the border of their passages, the brawny canine leg it was attached to flexing as it brought the rest of its body forward. Meecha tightened his grip on his dagger and gradually shifted his torso to face the beast, while preparing to slink in retreat. No time. It pounced. He screamed.

Meecha slammed his left hand into its neck to keep it at bay, only to have his palm stabbed by needle-fur. He cried out as one of its monstrous fangs nicked his eyebrow and its paws latched onto his shoulders. He shoved and stabbed it, but it only snarled and pushed harder.

He had never been so happy to hear wood splinter. The planks under them snapped. A heart-wrenching rush and…

Chapter 12

He was waist deep in tar. A flat grassy plain was almost within reach. The more he tried to move, the further he sank. Its pungent odour burned his nostrils. He felt faint, light-headed. Meecha reached out a hand and tried to take another slow step towards dry land. He did get a little closer, but, at the same time, the tar came up to his chest with a disgusting gurgle. If he moved again, it would touch his chin. In two steps, he would be completely submerged. There was no way out without help.

The tar rippled, and a black bulge broke the surface beside him. He watched it emerge, soon realising that it was a head, then a neck and shoulders. The tar miraculously slid down the face to reveal skin, smooth and fair, and a familiar pair of blue eyes.

'You!' Meecha gasped.

The girl's hair was so black and sleek—he mistakenly thought it still had tar on it. But the sticky substance slipped off her as if it were water. She smiled at him, the top of her gleaming golden dress appearing through the blackness,

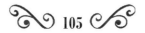

and her hand took his. The garment too escaped the tar unmarked. She gracefully pulled him out of the sludge and back onto his feet. He sighed and tried to shake himself off, but the stuff stuck to him like a second skin.

The girl suddenly leapt into the air and flew off. Without thinking twice, Meecha shot after her. He fancied himself a sparrow speeding through the air, the horrible tar replaced by feathers. In an instant, the girl's golden form had changed to white. He discerned long tail feathers as he closed the distance between them. When he finally swooped in beside her, she had transformed into something like a peacock. It was smaller and lacked the characteristic plumes but not the majesty. A phoenix! She's a white phoenix!

She opened her beak and let out a trumpeting cry. The joyful, triumphant sound lingered long in his ears, until it changed. It became urgent, intermittent; angry, even. It formed his name. Meecha. Meecha.

'Meecha!' Marilli shouted into his face and slapped him.

He groaned loudly and covered his head. He was still in a daze, but his memory of the monster jolted him upright.

'Where is it? Is it gone? Is it dead?' he sputtered, searching the room.

Marilli told him to calm down, while Lazlo kicked a large crate under a thick mattress that his burly minion was sitting on, legs spread so he could peer down at a gap in the box. The spider-dog was trying to bite and claw and wrestle its way to freedom.

'Nasty beast,' Lazlo's fellow grinned.

Meecha had no doubt it would break out eventually. Frustration puffed his cheeks. Adrenaline subsiding, he remembered something else. The hole in the ceiling he fell from was above him, so he pointed at the corner to his right.

'There's something behind there.'

Lazlo commanded his men to break down the wall, and Meecha finally felt the pain in his shoulders, brow, and left hand. The last was bleeding from several pinpricks. He grimaced. Retrieving his pack from Marilli, he applied a thin layer of his healing salve on every wound. Marilli ripped some strips from a sheet and proceeded to bandage him up.

The corner of the room was being battered with hand hammers, boots, and a shovel someone discovered. There was probably a latch somewhere to open the passage, but Lazlo was frothing at the mouth to get to Parda. Finally, the bricks crumbled and a vertical laddered tunnel was revealed.

Three men were told to stay and guard the exits—and their grisly captive. The tall rogue was replaced. He followed his comrades down the ladder, one at a time. Bag returned to its rightful back, Meecha soon descended the metal rungs himself. The lighter circle at the bottom was tiny, meaning the next stage of their adventure was a fair distance underground. Slow and steady, though, all thirteen of them reached it, the start of a much larger tunnel. It was not a sewer, but the smell was not far off. Torches blazed along the walls.

'Well,' Lazlo's voice bounced off them. He cringed and spoke softer. 'Eyes sharp. Parda knows our presence, for certain.'

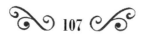

They spread out, sticking to either side of the tunnel, which opened into additional corridors. Their party moved straight and true, weapons at the ready. Did Lazlo know where he was going? Meecha suspected that the human's hatred for his rival had provoked a rather impulsive attack. Sloppy, unprepared, he was putting his people at risk.

Once they had passed two cross-sections, running footsteps resounded around them. Blade-wielding foes poured out of the corridors ahead and behind. There was no evading this battle. Meecha and his allies were outnumbered this time, but Marilli and the male giant hefting two hand-axes quickly cut a few down. Meecha danced with his opponents, punching groins, kicking knees and shins, trying to knock them down without bloodying his blade. It did not always work. Lazlo showed no such hesitation. Whether slicing men or the air, that longsword flowed from one formation to another, smooth, graceful, pitiless. The other rogues were no less adept. All their attackers were soon no more, leaving only minor injuries as payment. Meecha caught himself feeling proud. *You're an agent of goodness, not shadow.*

They were running again, Lazlo leading the way to the end of the tunnel. There they halted, so he could study a red drawing on the wall. It showed a horseshoe shape resembling the body of a snake, but the tip of either end curved outwards to form a bestial head: a dragon and a demon, if Meecha was not mistaken. He had refilled his lungs sufficiently before Lazlo grabbed a torch from its sconce and dashed into the corridor on their right, the direction in which the demon was baring its teeth. On second glance, Meecha thought the horseshoe might be a chalice.

Once more, the party was trotting down a tunnel, following Lazlo's light. Meecha ran alongside Marilli and two others close behind their leader. They were reaching an open space. Lazlo stepped into it, but then tripped and staggered forward a little. He swirled around, searching for what had caused his loss of balance—a sunken square of floor. He then looked past their heads into the tunnel. Meecha saw terror break Lazlo's stone-hard face for the first time.

'Run! Run back!' he screamed.

Behind the five that had emerged safely, a row of metal spikes had sprung out of the floor. Two rogues were just backing away from it, when a second row stabbed and slammed them into the ceiling. The fourth row caught another man. The deadly wave chased the remaining crew back to the main tunnel, killing one more. Marilli stared at the poor skewered sods in front of her—the giant was among them. Their blood cascaded over the blades, tainting their sheen. Meecha tried peering between them all.

'Three survived, I think,' he said aloud. 'But they can't come this way again.'

Lazlo cupped his hands around his mouth and shouted to them. 'Go back. Keep watch with the others.'

'We going on?' one of his remaining rogues, a young woman, exclaimed. 'We donnot know what be ahead.'

'That bitch is ahead,' Lazlo roared.

The space and its three adjoining tunnels rang with his fury. His cheeks, his neck, his eyeballs were flushed. The woman shied back, exchanging worried looks with her partner, and let Lazlo choose the next stage of their journey.

But he looked frustrated. Confused. Lost. His glare darted from tunnel to tunnel and the strips of wall between them. All around. Meecha and the other three kept their lips sealed tight. If they were not staring awkwardly at nothing, they were following his gaze. Several minutes later, they were still standing there.

Meecha checked his hands. The bloodied bandages suggested greater damage than there actually was. The puncture wounds were nicely sealed and numbed by the ointment. The blood of their comrades, however, had pooled and trickled into the space, making the survivors veer away from it. Lazlo watched it miserably. It streamed towards the central tunnel. Then it changed course. The scarlet line curved to the left. And the man's face lit up.

'Of course,' he nearly howled. 'This way.'

Meecha grimaced at Marilli. She looked just as mystified. They shadowed him nonetheless into the tunnel indicated by the blood.

'Forgive me, but I must ask,' Meecha blurted. 'How do you know where to go?'

Lazlo pursed his lips. He remained silent for a few steps, but then spoke with his eyes set on the strange flickering straight ahead. 'The fiddler showed me.'

Meecha paused mid-stride—Marilli nearly trampled him.

'How?' he called as he picked up speed again.

He realised that the flickering was water, cascading over the tunnel's end, an opening gaping into a vast, deep cistern. The party of five looked past the curtain of water. There were other tunnels emptying their bowels into the vat. Meecha could not tell if it was rainwater or sewage. The smell was tolerable at least. But there was no way forward, except by jumping. The bottom was so far down, however, and only partly submerged. It would be suicide.

Lazlo's arms rose and fell twice, as if asking the waters for an explanation. He grasped his head, fingers entwined

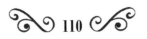

against the top of his skull, elbows angled forward, flanking his disbelieving face. Nobody dared say a word.

Meecha looked all around the tunnel's mouth, walked back the way they came, examined the stones on either side for marks or switches. He was surprised at how dry the stones were, despite the rumbling waterfall. And the scents he was detecting were odd. Mixed with that of stagnant water were floral traces. No, they smelled almost creamy, cottony, soapy. The sharper tang of disinfectant shocked him. He turned. They were definitely coming from the waterfall. He wondered if it was not what it seemed. As that idea came, the scent of stagnation left his nostrils entirely.

Meecha lost hold of his jaw. It began to drop open before his broad smile stretched it out instead. His eyes were bulging too when Marilli noticed his ghastly beam.

'What's wrong with thee?' She looked repulsed.

'I know what it is,' he heard himself bay like a sheep, but he was too absorbed by his thoughts to care.

Illusion magic was cunning. According to aerieti lore, a wielder of this craft could project an image from their own consciousness. The more skilled they were, the more detailed and convincing the image could be. But the cleverer spell involved projecting the image through their target's mind. In their current case, each of them was seeing a cistern; a dead end. Their senses were being fooled into embellishing the illusion with smells, sounds, and textures. It was real as long as they believed it was.

Meecha strode straight for the waterfall, gasping at every failure of the spell. The din of rushing water weakened, dulled, and vanished to leave the echo of his own footfalls. Streaks of water rolled their last and were no more. The light of the cistern's open space dimmed—a candle snuffed

out by lack of air. Little black dots punched through the image of the tunnel's circular mouth, multiplying, spreading, erasing the projection. Warnings and curses were hurled at him just as he stepped through where the water used to be. He found a metal door at the corridor's real dark end.

He spun around and chuckled at his companion's shocked expressions. They were still seeing the illusion. In truth, they stood in the middle of a corridor no different than the others. He stuck his head towards them. Lazlo's rogues jumped, while their leader and Marilli twitched and blinked.

'Are you coming?' Meecha asked sweetly and pulled his head back.

He leaned against the wall beside the door and waited. It took several minutes for the first, Lazlo, to make what they saw as a plunge. Not expecting his feet to find floor so soon, he wobbled, arms outstretched, but the next moment he bolted upright, stiff and awkward. His eyes latched onto the door and he stepped towards it slowly. The last three of their diminished party leapt into reality, one by one, clenching and whimpering. Meecha could not get enough of their awestricken gasps and backward glances.

Lazlo's palm was on the door, sliding down to the handle. Determination compressed his features, lips pursed, eyes narrowed, brow deeply furrowed. The nose ring quivered in tandem with his tense body.

'Why do you want her so much?' Meecha asked quietly.

Lazlo's response was curt, but it tripped over a lump in his throat. 'Thou shall see.'

The door whined open.

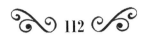

Chapter 13

This was the origin of the disinfectant smell. A laboratory. A grotesque museum. Two long benches ran to the far end of the chamber. Pots and burners and books and vessels of various shapes sat atop them. Along parts of the walls were brimming bookshelves and racks displaying skulls and things in jars, twisted, bizarre, dismembered. Sturdy metal doors were in the walls themselves, dozens of them. Ample lantern light flickered golden-red, giving her skin an amber, almost healthy, shade. Even so, Parda's porcelain paleness was a striking contrast to the light burgundy of her garment that flowed to her feet. The loose fabric shook against her back. Her bare arms moved with the effort of whatever her hands were doing in that far left corner. Curls like spun strawberry gold were heaped at the top of her head. A few escaped ringlets bounced against her long neck.

'Come in. Please, come in,' a silky voice glided through the room, a gentle breeze of winter's chill. 'I apologise for the poor hospitality, but I don't get many visitors.'

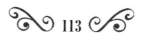

Parda straightened as she spoke, turning slowly. Her toes peeked from under the garment's hem as she floated to the right and came to stand at the head of the two counters. She held her palms up just as Meecha's mother would when covered in juices. Parda's hands were stained dark purple. Her face was even more youthful than Captain Namael's poster had suggested. She looked seventeen at most. But the feature that truly intimidated him was her eyes. They were white. She looked as if she had been entirely carved from pearl marble, dressed, and topped with a blonde wig.

'We shall be thy last, wench.' Lazlo's vehemence made Meecha cringe and slink aside.

The man had already drawn his sword and was making for Parda. She set her bored face on him.

'Lazlo, be quiet,' she sighed. 'And still.'

She thrust an open palm in his direction. He recoiled as if hitting a wall, staggered, nearly fell. He peeled his lips back to snarl, but Parda's fingers snapped together and Lazlo's mouth mimicked the motion. In his panic to unseal it, he dropped his sword. Then a knife whizzed through the air towards Parda—it originated from the female rogue behind Meecha. As soon as his eyes fell on her, an unseen force tossed her against one of the metal doors with a clang. A violent bang answered her, rattling the hinges. Her male comrade, Marilli, and Meecha were wise enough not to move, except to retreat from the heaving door.

'Interesting companions, Lazlo,' Parda said, passing an inquisitive stare over them all. 'You were hardly stealthy, I must say, but the lot of you made it this far. You must be worth something.'

Lazlo, sword back in his grip, the struggle with his mouth abandoned, was groaning at her furiously, but refrained from charging straight on again. Even without colour in her eyes, Meecha could tell that she was rolling them.

'Very well, Lazlo. I may come to miss your inane presence. Say what you must, but do make your last words count.'

Where are her thees and thous? Meecha squinted suspiciously as the witch flicked her wrist and Lazlo's roar exploded. 'Crove isn' thy playground. Our people—our children—aren' fodder for thy tricks. This is my city an' I'm ending thee.'

Parda stared at him. A few more silent moments and she spoke, breezy tone flat and scornful. 'How… pointless. You really are a fool, Lazlo Talza.'

Her hand flicked. The door to the chamber slammed shut. She lifted her other hand and clapped. At first blink, a black and purple cloud burst from her palms. Meecha blinked again. And he was alone in a dark swirling haze. Metal whined and clanged. *The doors.* His thought was answered by two screams. One was human. The other was not. Its guttural shriek rooted him to the ground. He managed to unsheathe his dagger—what good it would do him remained to be seen.

'Meecha?' Marilli's voice came from somewhere not far to his left.

He also thought it was the right-hand doors that had resounded, so he shuffled quickly in her direction.

'I'm here,' he hissed, not wanting to make too much noise.

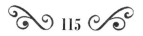

Shapes and gusts shook the fog. He could not tell if they were illusions. The blackness itself was real—disbelieving it was not its solution. Meecha bumped into something, jumped. There were bookcases in that corner, but this was not one of them. Its surface looked woody—more like bark. He wanted to touch it, but his urgency convinced him to keep moving. He bypassed it, looking over his shoulder. It was strange how quiet everything was. Parda's magic must have also dulled sounds. His breath was knocked out of him when he walked straight into something else, his arms automatically wrapping around it. So it was not the wall. And it flexed.

A repulsed whimper came out of him as he leapt back, clutching his chest. The bark-like thing had a hand at the bottom. It was an abnormally large arm—long fingers, long forearm, long bicep. Another whimper escaped him when hair tickled his forehead. His knees buckled as his eyes continued to rise. He fell to a squat and gaped, now mute with horror, at the face above him. The features had once been feminine, but no longer. She was more tree than woman, skin brown and cracked, mouth gagged with vines, long black hair turning green and sparse, almond-shaped eyes like black walnuts.

She lifted her other hand and was going to crush him with it, but Meecha's feet woke just in time to propel him sideways, screaming. His shoulder slammed into a leg—a table's leg—as the floor trembled from its impact with the tree-woman's fist. He was against one of the counters. Immediately, he crawled under it on hands and knees. He felt her fingers brush against his ankle, but she failed to get a hold. She reached for him from the side. He stabbed and stabbed at the wooden hand. He kicked and punched to no avail. It caught him, its cruel grip spanning from his armpit to his neck, and dragged him into the open. Once beneath its emotionless gaze again, it began to put its weight into Meecha's back, squeezing the air out of him. The last of his howl emerged as a squawk.

The black cloud broke and out clattered Lazlo's boots. That was all Meecha could see of the man, who recoiled, presumably at the sight of the monster. Its pressure on Meecha lessened slightly—the newcomer distracted it. Lazlo's foot shifted and the wooden hand was gone, momentarily replaced by the falling force of her severed arm. The sound Meecha made was a gasp and groan combined. His lungs filled up, while Lazlo vanished into darkness again in pursuit of the retreating tree-woman.

Meecha rose to his knees, coughing, and brought his pack before him. Opening it, he unpinned the little feather from his hat. He closed and shouldered the bag, and hauled himself to his feet, using the counter for support. He estimated that he was almost halfway to where Parda had been mixing her magic dust. Dagger in the right hand, feather in the left, Meecha advanced.

The metal doors on his left were all closed and silent. Nothing came out of them. But, since the tree-woman had no mouth, there was still the question of what made that initial screech. He reached the end of the counter, black tendrils rolling around him, with no other sign of life, friend or foe. He found the witch's little stone table, where a bowl full of the purple substance sat along with other paraphernalia.

He was turning the corner of the long counter when his lonely pocket of misty existence was broken into again.

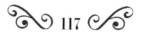 117

Marilli streaked across it with the other monster latched around her stomach—it must have just rammed into her. This creature too was a blend of humanoid and natural—or unnatural—characteristics. In this case, its thin, masculine body was pure white and completely hairless. Static sparked from its azure eyes and fingertips. Its terrible shriek crackled, like lightning through howling winds. A collar of bluish-black metal was around its neck and fresh red scars were visible on its shoulders and back where its rags did not reach.

Meecha followed where they fell. The creature battered Marilli with its fists, too fast for her to mount a counterattack. All she could do was block with her arms—her sword and shield were gone. Meecha tried to stab the beast in the back, but it leaned sideways, out of the dagger's path. It punched his stomach, catapulting him backwards out of their bubble. Meecha gripped the feather, if not the dagger, as he hit the floor. Stunned, he watched the black tendrils gather above him. He clutched his abdomen, waiting for the pain to pass, and then crawled onto his feet again. He limped forward.

The scene had changed. Marilli was up and wrestling the creature. Its swift reflexes were impossible to match, but she did her best, blocking incoming blows and trying to wear it out; disarm it somehow. Nose bleeding, temple bruised and swelling, she was slowly forcing it into the corner where the alchemy table stood. A few more fists and kicks were exchanged before she gave a growl and heaved him hard against the table and wall. The stone counter was not damaged, but tools, vessels, oils, and the bowl of dust flew in every direction around the struggling pair.

Marilli got her hands around the creature's neck above the collar and, snarling, flung it against the adjacent wall and back again. Its senses were being choked and jarred. It was trying to break her grip, but she was putting all the force she could muster into it, her muscles bulging. Then the creature's eyes flared brighter. Its hands crackled with white energy, while its collar began to glow. It shrieked, slammed its palms into Marilli's chest, and a crack of lightning launched her backwards, all the way to the opposite wall. Before Meecha rushed to check on Marilli, he noticed pain flash across the monster's face, its collar vibrating.

Marilli was unconscious. Her leather breastplate had a huge black burn with smoke rising from it. But she was breathing, despite the twitching limbs and curls standing on end—they shocked him when he tried to touch them. Meecha glanced behind him and realised that the magic mist was slow to refill the space the lightning had cleared. He also noted that the creature was no longer interested in them. It was glaring at something not far to Meecha's left, along the long wall where its cell was.

Its palm jerked up and hurled another thunderbolt in that direction. Its collar glowed and vibrated again, seeming to cause it painful spasms. There was a cloud still blocking Meecha's view of the creature's target. It moved between the central counters and fired again. It gasped and tore at its scalp, while the nerves in its neck tensed beneath the punishing collar. It stamped and roared and clasped its hands together. Meecha felt sorry for it. Lazlo had spoken of tricks. *Experiments?* Was this what it was? A human turned monster?

Its connected hands emitted a white and blue radiance, which sputtered and grew into a ball of lightning. Bearing the pain, shaking its throbbing head, the creature continued to feed the sphere. Its agonised howl reached an ear-split-

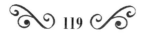

ting pitch. When the ball would expand no more, the creature threw its arms wide and lightning flooded the chamber, striking everything. Meecha flung himself over Marilli and covered his head with his arms. Chunks of stone rained down as bolts struck the wall. Wood splintered, metal rang several more times, the creature's cry finally surpassing the lightning's chaotic crackle. As suddenly as it had begun, the storm retreated, leaving behind only debris and dusty, sharp-scented air. The fog was gone.

Its eyes stared at the ceiling, lifeless, sparkless. While Marilli stirred, Meecha approached the creature's body, sprawled on the floor. Blood trickled from its eyes and ears, but its—his—gaze was flat, peaceful even, obscuring the suffering he had endured and died of. Meecha looked along the side of the room the human storm had been so interested in and found Parda panting and seething in a corner.

'Why would you do this to people?' Meecha cried.

She just sneered. Lazlo was not far from her, so he lunged with his sword. The tree-woman lay behind him, hacked to bits. Meecha could not take his eyes off her wooden stare, blank yet melancholy. He heard Lazlo growl. Parda had transported herself before her alchemy table. Seeing it in ruins, she swirled in a rage to face them.

'Were you responsible for the warehouse?' Meecha demanded.

'Oh, no,' she hissed. 'That was someone worse.'

She knew. She had his answers, but her attention was drawn to a tottering Marilli. The witch flicked her hand and the guard was lifted from the floor and dropped back down. Parda vanished and reappeared in the corner where the tree-woman was, aiming for the door. Lazlo beat her to it. Again she transported herself to another corner and another and another. Lazlo and Marilli ran back and forth, until she had nowhere to go but the middle.

Parda landed before Meecha, her failed experiment between them. Some of her curls still held stubbornly to her scalp, but the rest were in disarray. Her skin and garment were smeared black and purple. Their glares met.

'At the warehouse. Who was it?' he asked firmly.

Her violet hands rose as she snapped at him, 'A friend. I'm not alone, see. My death will achieve nothing.'

Marilli was sneaking up behind her when Meecha presented the feather to the witch. He held it up before her open palms. She looked perplexed, then infuriated at his jest. She clapped like before, but this time emitted a powerful pulse. Marilli was tossed like a doll once more. The corpse at Meecha's feet nearly swept his legs from under him—he skipped over it. Lazlo cursed loudly behind him. But Meecha himself was unaffected. A small white nimbus surrounded the feather. It was resisting Parda's magic, shielding him. She gaped and her hands separated in shock, the wave of energy disrupted—Meecha's chance. His blade sank into her stomach. She screamed, grasped his hand that gripped the hilt, her mouth wide and gasping. He gritted his teeth and shoved the dagger deeper. Parda gave a strangled grunt and, finally, slid to the floor. *One less evil in the world. That's what it achieves.*

Meecha watched her blood pool around her. Friend, she had said. Human, demon, or something else? He had already wasted too much time and killed the one person who could point him in the right direction, willingly or no.

'Well done, my friend!' Lazlo exclaimed as he dashed passed him to search Parda's body.

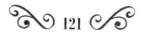

Soon a keyring jingled from Lazlo's index finger, accommodating a great number of keys. Marilli had joined them by now, lugging her battered body. She nodded and smiled at Meecha with approval, perhaps even admiration. He tried to hide his hot cheeks by busying himself with re-attaching the feather to his hat, which he left in the safety of his pack for a little while longer.

Lazlo made for the first metal door on the chamber's left side. Meecha noticed the bodies of the other rogues. Victims of the creatures, judging by the broken bones. Their chief knocked on the door. There was no aggressive response, so he started trying the keys on its lock. Marilli hunted for her weapons, while Meecha checked the main door. With Parda's magic lifted, it opened easily. The cell Lazlo unlocked turned out to be empty, so he moved to the next one, starting again with a knock. Marilli came closer, blade returned to her hip, buckler to her back. As soon as that cell's door creaked open, a gruff voice rushed out.

'Do—Don' hurt us. What the abyss happened?'

The room was a sizeable rectangle of bland stone and darkness. Crouched within it were four men, filthy and scared. Lazlo peered at them.

'Ye're free, friends. Helder, that thee?'

The acquaintances clapped each other on the shoulder, while the other three scampered to the exit.

'You might want to wait,' Meecha suggested. 'The tunnel we came through is blocked. We can find another way out together.'

The beleaguered fellows eyed the corridor outside with unease and eagerness both. Reluctantly, they nodded and skulked by the door.

The next two cells were empty, but the third, once opened, rang with the cries of children. Meecha and Marilli rushed to help. Five boys whimpered in the back of the room. It took some calming and coaxing to earn their trust, Marilli's guard-and-protector aura going a long way. Lazlo continued opening cells. Another five children were found—girls—who needed even more of Marilli's charm to emerge. Two of the last cells on that side contained women, seven in total. Lazlo handed Meecha the keys, so he could inspect the cells opposite, while the rogue and Marilli spoke to the now large group. All Meecha found was a variety of marks—scorches, cracks, scratches—and traces of substances, like soil, ash, and what seemed to be tar. Parda must have held creatures on this side. Captured, created, or both? He would never know.

Meecha turned to find the group waiting for him. Some women had children in their arms or timidly clutching their hands and clothes. Lazlo took the lead once more, Marilli the rear, and the rest clustered between. At the end of the tunnel, Meecha noticed that the illusion of the cistern was gone. All of Parda's magic had died with her. When he looked ahead again, they were standing in front of the blade-obstructed passage. Attempts were made to shield the children's eyes from the bodies and congealed blood. Meecha had a moment to spot that one black-haired woman's clothing differed from the rest. It was no less ragged, but it was a riding dress and seemed to be made of fine blue silk rather than plain cotton like the others' garments. He could only see her back as she huddled against another woman. Meecha's curiosity was shoved aside by Lazlo's semi-confident choice of an alternative tunnel. There was little else to do but follow.

Chapter 14

The night was cool and quiet. The clear air quickly banished the musty dungeon smell. After traipsing the underground passages for another long while before finding a circuitous route back to the main tunnel and then clambering back to the surface, Meecha now strolled lazily in the three moons' mystical light with his hat back on his head, following Lazlo and his four surviving rogues to their safe house. The few that had stood guard above the tunnels ran ahead with the spider-dog temporarily secured inside a sealed crate. Most of the prisoners had bolted as soon as their feet had touched the street. The children were taken to safety. The black-haired woman left with three others before Meecha had a chance to find out more about her. Only Lazlo's friend stayed with them, hoisted up by two rogues.

Marilli and Meecha listened intently to the conversation.

'Galob and Parda're dead. Their people shall scatter, no?' a woman was saying.

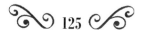

Another responded, 'They might seek revenge.'

'Enough of us're left to deal with them and recruit new blood,' Lazlo said, his attention straight ahead. His stride had purpose.

Meecha decided to join in. 'So that's it? The city's yours?'

'Almost.' The flat sing-song of Lazlo's tone was disturbing.

Marilli responded, 'We done with thee? I think our debt is paid.'

The rogue halted and turned with a curious, almost hurt, expression. Arms crossed, he squinted and raised his chin at the guard.

'Why leave? We the winning crew. Riches an' power be our future now. You two have more than earned a slice. Stay with us.'

From his coy little smile and softening eyes, Meecha wondered if Lazlo was developing a crush. At least two heads taller than the rogue, Marilli frowned down at him.

Meecha took over. 'It depends on what you plan to do. And what we would be risking for a cause that isn't ours.'

Lazlo sucked his teeth. He leaned in. 'The Guard is useless. We all make business under their noses for cycles, an' what they do for Crove? Get in our pockets, is what.'

Marilli had so far remained impassive, but out of the corner of his eye Meecha saw her forearm twitch, her fingers drum her belt.

'Don't tell me you mean to attack the Guard?' he scoffed.

Lazlo cocked his head. 'They have failed. We take care of ourselves.'

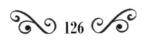

'You just admitted to preying on Crove for years – cycles.' Meecha's scorn was genuine. 'And now you want to protect it? Explain yourself.'

Taken aback by his bluntness, Lazlo rounded on him. He pointed a finger at his face and growled, 'Galob and Parda rotted this city. Once, we had fun… an' balance… spirit! Then Galob's greed ate 'im a path to the top. He slaughtered countless to get there. And then that worm crawled into the sewers to steal our own an' spew her filth. And the Guard? They barely scraped a boot, while those two reigned an' we all suffered. We still suffer! We wan' Crove back. No, no… a new Crove. That none can harm again.'

Meecha risked a glance at Marilli, long enough to catch her fiery eyes and downturned mouth.

'And how in the abyss do you plan to defeat a host of trained soldiers?' he countered. 'You've a handful of people and, judging by what happened in the tunnels, you aren't ready for something like this. Forgive me, but we're not risking ourselves for your reckless rebellion, at the expense of your own people, no less.'

Some eyes fell to the flagstones. Others' hands toyed with buckles or hilts. Lazlo picked up on the rustles and shuffles, the sudden tension from his comrades. A sliver of guilt rankled Meecha for planting dissent, but a clash with the Guard was something he could not allow.

'What thou know?' Lazlo snarled. 'Thou think the hounds patrol the streets in threes because they like the company or because they need the protection?' He turned on his heels and barked them onwards.

The street sounded again with their steps. Nobody else was out but them. Doors and shutters were closed, blind to what was on the cusp of happening. Meecha thought wildly. He and Marilli could go to the barracks as originally planned. Or they could slay Lazlo and his lackeys then and there. Or knock them out and drag Lazlo to the barracks. With the last of the crew leaders out of the game everything should calm down. A playful whistling reached him from somewhere nearby and made his ploys feel less distasteful. His only loyalty was to the aerieti, but these dastardly fellows were starting to grow on him. Did he like them more than the guards? The memory of the upstanding warriors jeering at him did not help the issue.

The whistling seemed closer as they turned a corner into another street. It was not coming from one of the people around him. Meecha peered between them and straight ahead. A figure leaning against the right-hand wall was outlined by a streetlamp. Its hand was waving and flicking back and forth to the rhythm of the tune emerging from its puckered lips. The rogues veered left into the next alley. Meecha stumbled after them with his head twisted back, his eyes fixed on the mysterious twittering shadow. It finally turned towards the lamp's dim radiance and the person's pale hair glistened like moonlight beneath a hat. The fiddler! The instrument and its bow were dangling from his left hand.

Without thinking, Meecha trotted towards him, ignoring Marilli's questioning calls. The whistling did not cease, nor the dancing hand. The fiddler seemed completely entranced by his own music. The man's closed eyelids did not even quiver. Meecha slowed down to a tiptoe so as not to disturb him, until he came to a stand before him. He did not know if he should speak, cough, or tug at his sleeve.

Fortunately, Marilli solved the problem by hissing at Meecha's back.

'What thee doing? There's no time for this.'

The fiddler pressed his lips shut, dropped his hand, and slowly set an icy glare on her. She recoiled a little, while Meecha cleared his throat.

'I need your help again,' he began and the fiddler's hard mouth relaxed into a smirk as he laid his black and pale gaze on him. 'You found us work and, apparently, guided us to Parda. I don't know who... or what... you are, but I've none other to turn to, so...'

With a flourish, the man presented him with the underside of his hat. Meecha cringed. The idea of pleading Marilli for more coin had barely brushed his mind when her voice stabbed his ear.

'No, Meecha. My pockets are near dry.'

He smiled sweetly at the fiddler. 'You wouldn't do it for free, would you?'

Another flourish and the hat was back on the man's head, this shaking indignantly. His eyebrows were arched almost to his hairline. Meecha sighed and turned to leave. The rogues had not waited for them. They were already at the other end of the street. He wondered if he had anything of value he could part with, in exchange for the fiddler's aid. He had no jewels of any kind. The compass? It was fairly useless, but it was an heirloom. He could not give that away. The dagger? He swirled back around.

'My dagger's made of pure arvadeir. Hard, rare, and valuable.'

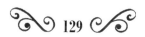

The fiddler pursed his lips and puffed a plummeting tune. It probably meant, 'No.' The man slowly took the bow from his left hand and pointed it at Meecha. Higher than Meecha. At Meecha's hat.

'No!' he shouted, putting a protective hand over it. 'You aren't having my hat.'

The fiddler rolled his eyes and moved the end of the bow closer, until Meecha, cringing, heard the faintest of rustlings. His jaw dropped.

'How did you…?' his question trailed off as he brought the hat before him and eyed the special little blotchy feather.

Marilli was giving the fiddler a sidelong scowl, while Meecha pondered his chances of survival in Itania without some protection from magic. They were not grand, but he had to move on from Crove. He would simply have to take additional care from then on. Exhaling heavily, he unpinned the feather and surrendered it to the fiddler.

'This is rarer than the dagger,' he warned the smug human, whose strange eyes gleamed.

As soon as it left his palm, Meecha felt naked, vulnerable. He pouted as it was pinned onto its new owner's lapel, who then gave a deep, exaggerated curtsy, arms outstretched, bow held in one hand, the instrument in the other. He lifted his piercing gaze to Meecha, awaiting his request. The fiddler's trustworthiness was uncertain, but he seemed to be no friend of Parda and, by extension, her potentially demonic friend. And, if Meecha dawdled any longer, Azare's trail would grow cold.

He shuffled forward to whisper in the fiddler's ear— warm whiffs of coal and sweet-scented wood made Meecha think of a bonfire, freshly lit and aromatic. 'Three people may have come through Crove, an elf on the hunt for two thieves, one of whom may have been a red-haired woman, who may also have killed Galob and his crew. I need to know where they all went.'

Meecha inhaled through his teeth, feeling both panic—he had perhaps revealed too much—and relief for having got his frustration off his chest. The fiddler showed no emotion, however. Instead, he snapped up into position, abrupt as a clockwork toy, placing the fiddle's base beneath his chin and slowly bringing the bow down to meet it. His face was screwed with concentration. When the strings finally met, a moment's silence followed. It stretched and held Meecha's breath.

A jolt passed through him—heart, skin, hair—at the violence with which the fiddler broke into a ferocious melody. It whipped between low and high notes at varying speeds. A long bass tone would whine into a sequence of almost metallic clashes. The music then jittered a little, like a buzzing bee, before this rhythm opened into a set successive pattern. It paused with a squeak and dipped into a gentle seduction. Goose pimples made Meecha shiver, as if the delectable trills were whooshing over his flesh. So sweet and spirited. So rich yet tender. Even his tongue tingled, as if encountering a crisp, juicy fruit. A berry. Scarlet bliss bursting in his mouth.

Fierce shaking yanked Meecha out of his trance. He yelped into Marilli's face, blinked a few times, and looked around. The music was gone and so was the fiddler.

'What...?' he gasped. 'Where'd he go?'

'He left. Thou been gawping at the wall. I should have left thee too. Thou don' hear that?'

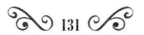

Meecha frowned. 'What? What's happening?'

It only then registered that there were sounds coming from where Lazlo and his group had been headed—battle sounds. It took a moment for his senses to reassert themselves. Meecha leapt into motion, sprinting along the street, soon to be overtaken by Marilli. They reached the next corner and cut round it. The bashing noises were closer, coming from an alley further down. Marilli took the lead to its mouth, but, as soon as she reached it, she skidded to a halt, eyes wide. Meecha stepped up behind her—she was drawing her sword and shield—to see a tangle of rogues and guards, the latter discernible against the brink of dawn by their helmets and better armour.

The ground was already littered with blood and bodies, one rogue, two guards. Lazlo was being assailed by a massive man's battle-axe, barely managing to keep his limbs from being lopped off. A female rogue manoeuvred the field to his opponent's back. The next time he lifted his axe, she drove a knife into his armpit. He convulsed, bleeding profusely, and his elbow hit her in the head. While she crumpled, Lazlo sliced through the guard's thick neck. The beheaded corpse was still falling to the floor when the rogue chief turned to meet another foe, smaller than the last, but stout and wielding a longsword and shield.

Marilli's hesitation dissolved. She rushed in as the two blades clanged. The combatants' agile circling brought Lazlo's back to her. As he was swinging with both hands for his opponent's right shoulder, already being shielded, Marilli slapped the side of his neck with her cold steel. He froze, quivering with blood-rage and disbelief.

'Stop, Lazlo,' Marilli barked, turning her sword so its edge was now against his skin, not the flat side.

Meecha crept closer. Men and women stood poised to resume. Lazlo's people looked shaken, however. Their eyes kept darting to their leader.

'Marilli?' his opponent snapped from beneath the helmet, a familiar rumble. He pointed his own weapon at the rogue's neck.

'Captain,' she greeted her uncle through gritted teeth and averted her hard stare from Lazlo, who was cautiously turning his head.

'Thou a guard?' His booming voice filled the neighbourhood. He was flushed with anger. 'Two-faced wench!'

Captain Namael spotted Meecha skirting the alley.

'Well, rip my eyes,' he chuckled, passing an inquisitive look between him and Marilli. 'I had thee for dead.'

'No, still alive and very busy,' Meecha replied, earning his own suspicious glare from Lazlo.

Young Namael eagerly took charge of the narration. 'Parda's dead, Captain. She was taking innocent people an' turning them into monsters. We freed them after we… after Meecha defeated the mage.'

The Captain gaped at him, sceptical. 'Thou?'

Meecha shrugged. 'I gave the final blow, but it was a team effort. In truth, none of it would have been possible without Lazlo and his crew. They fought bravely—lost many—to end Parda's evil and free your people from her clutches. Men, women, children.'

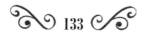

'I can confirm that,' Marilli interjected, exchanging hopeful glances with Meecha.

Lazlo's bewilderment kept him mute. Chin raised above the blades around his throat, he scowled at everyone. The Captain was experiencing a similar confusion.

'An' thou suggest what? That we let these dogs go?' he asked sarcastically.

Marilli hardened again. She may have thought the same as Meecha. Even if Lazlo was shown mercy, there was no certainty that he would not carry out his scheme, now or in the future.

Their deadlock was disturbed by the sound of voices and footfalls. Both sides tensed and wavered, not knowing on whose side the newcomers would be. The shattering of glass answered them.

Smoke-jars flew from windows on either side of the street. Meecha no longer had his mask; nor did Marilli. He covered his mouth with his sleeve, while the acrid fumes spread and battle erupted once more. Lazlo, taking advantage of the mayhem, slithered out from between the Namaels and dashed into a side alley, past his fellow glass-faced shades emerging with blades thirsting. Before disappearing, their leader shouted a final command.

'Bring me those traitors' heads!'

Meecha gulped hard and gripped his dagger firmer. He coughed into his arm as Marilli's choked voice cried for him to run. He wanted to stay, to fight with the Guard, but the smoke was overwhelming, the violent flurry of dark and glistening figures. His legs seemed to move of their own accord, retreating back the way they had come, away from two rogues who were now running towards him. Before he knew it, Meecha was sprinting, hands holding his hat in place. He clattered along, cut the corner on his right, and made full speed for the end of the street.

'Get him!' The rogues had become three and were gaining on him.

Meecha zigzagged from alley to alley and through narrow spaces between buildings. Twice he thought he had lost his pursuers, but, knowing Crove's hiding nooks and crannies, they would split up and sniff him out. Eventually, he reached the square, his backpack jingling, his feet lifting a trail of dust behind him. There were people out along with the sun's early haze. Still clutching his hat, Meecha pushed through them. He darted towards the great inn, where Crove's denizens were having their morning brews. Without decelerating, he dove under a table. Shouts and curses were heard from its occupants as his pack bumped the underside of the table, spilling their drinks. He hastily crawled under the next table and the next and the next—chairs, bottles, crockery, and a few people toppled in his wake.

Through the confusion, Meecha spotted the mouth of a narrow lane and scampered through it on all fours. He stood and swerved into another passage on his left, skidding on slimy stones. He turned right and hurtled out of the shadows. Blinded by terror, he failed to notice a large purple-gowned woman standing before him. The wind was knocked out of him as he rebounded off her cushiony bulk to land on his backside.

'Oi! Watch thy step,' the woman barked.

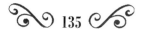

Meecha tried to catch his breath while rubbing his squished nose. He felt a strange lightness to his scalp.

'My hat!' he yelped.

He looked around frantically, but it was nowhere to be seen. His heart pounded in his chest, and his eyes began to water. He sprang onto hands and knees, and scrambled about, searching in corners, on benches, under feet and dresses. Gasps and giggles trailed him. He looked up with imploring eyes at the women who had gathered around him.

"Have you seen my hat? Please! I need to find my hat!"

Sympathetic gazes of blues, greens, greys, and browns met his. Long eyelashes fluttered at him on a range of pretty faces, some painted and some not. Their luscious lips curved into pouts and sweet smiles.

'Have you seen it?' he asked softly.

The women's expressions started to change. Puzzled frowns framed their mesmerising eyes. One of them, a shapely brunette in a blue low-cut dress, clasped her hands over her mouth. Her kohl-lined eyes of hazel widened.

''Tis him!'

Gasps and excited chattering made Meecha draw himself in.

'The little man...'

'His hair...'

'I recognise him.'

'I too.'

He interrupted their ravings with a polite, 'Excuse me...'

Silence fell like a boulder.

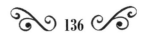

He cleared his throat and continued in the same timid tone, 'Who do you think I am?'

The babble started up again, denying him any coherence. As abruptly as it had commenced, it was cut short. Angry male voices were heard from somewhere down the street. Meecha peered between the dresses to find his three hunters bounding in their direction. He jumped to his feet.

'Save me!'

The burly lady he had collided with grasped him by the shoulders and lifted him up. He was carried past the wall of gaudy frocks and dumped back onto his feet. He wobbled a little, while the woman approached a broken chair and yanked one of its legs off with a crack. Her friends followed her lead. They grabbed anything they could use as a weapon—knives, sticks, brooms—and turned to face the oncoming men. The matron made her way to the front, tapping her club on her left palm. The rogues halted before the glaring courtesans, a sight they were surely unaccustomed to.

'Ge' ot the way!' one man demanded.

Meecha's large defender retorted coldly, 'Make me.'

'That an enemy o' Lazlo. You protect 'im, you pay 'n tears.'

She hefted her bulk and tossed her head.

'I hear you rats were crushed by that fiend, Parda,' she sneered. 'Lazlo can play gutter-king all he wishes now, but Crove be done with the likes of him. We don' fear him any more than we fear you.'

The men exchanged uneasy looks. They were reluctant to admit defeat, yet they dared not advance. The foreman cocked his head assertively.

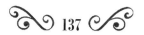 137

'This not the end,' he spat. Chewing on his fury, he prowled away with his indignant fellows in tow.

Meecha grinned at his fierce and beautiful saviours as they twirled around, dropping their weapons. A blonde woman in a red cotton dress walked over to an overturned crate. She bent down and, to Meecha's delight, picked up his hat. She dusted it off with a few graceful strokes and approached him.

'A lovely hat,' she said and returned it to his head.

He pushed it down into place happily. 'That couldn't be more true, my lady.'

She blushed and giggled. It was a pleasant livening of such a weary face, cheeks gaunt, eyes deep set and pink from crying. Meecha was soon surrounded by women again. He let them escort him to a two-storey building further along the street, red and lilac drapes hanging from its eaves, partially concealing the front of the house. A mouth-watering aroma escaped its open door and untangled the anxious knot in Meecha's belly—it promptly gave a loud growl.

Chapter 15

Meecha moaned heartily, grease dripping from his chin. With a firm grip on the rib, he dug his teeth into the succulent meat. He had not realised how hungry he was until he took the first bite. In that instant, he had forsaken his fork and every bit of his manners. He stopped his gnawing for a moment to take a breath and acknowledge his audience with a guilty smile. The flabbergasted ladies were still watching him, some chortling behind cupped hands. One of them had been kind enough to move his hat to a safer distance.

'Forgive me.' He hiccoughed, causing another wave of affectionate coos and giggles. 'I haven't eaten in a while.'

Remae, the voluptuous matron, clapped him on the back. She sat in the chair next to him. Her mass of chestnut curls, previously gathered into an intricate bun, flowed over her shoulders.

'Don' mind,' she said. 'Fill that starved belly of thine.'

He started nibbling on the bone again, his legs swinging from the chair about a foot off the floor.

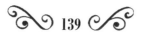

'It's not that bad, honest,' he mumbled while chewing. Blushing, he swallowed. 'My kind processes food so slowly we can go for days without eating.'

He licked the juicy remnants off the bone, and dropped it onto the brass plate, proceeding to suck his fingers clean.

'Go wash off an' thou can tell us all abou' thy kind,' Remae prompted him.

Meecha climbed down from the chair, and picked up his plate. He walked through the opening between two burgundy curtains and into the kitchen. Two women—one young and fair-haired, the other older and ginger—dressed in plain cotton dresses were whispering beside a counter lined with cupboards and crockery. They paused when they saw Meecha enter, but then the girl darted to him, wearing a warm smile beneath her quizzical frown. He gave them the plate before hopping onto a stool to reach a basin filled with hot water. He scrubbed himself clean of gravy and grime, and dried his hands on a towel beside the washbasin, which he neatly folded and replaced. He thanked them and returned to the dining area.

Remae and her ladies had seated themselves around the table and on the steps of a staircase leading to the floor above. Their excitement was palpable. The front door was shut, muffling the noises from outside. Meecha suddenly felt very self-conscious. He returned to his place, eyes darting between their eager faces and the floor. He clambered onto the chair. It creaked—loudly. He paused, one buttock still in the air. He glanced around and, wincing, eased the rest of the way into the seat.

'What're thee?' someone blurted, shattering the terrible silence. It was the blonde, the one who had returned his hat.

'A dwarf?' another woman interjected.

'What's thy name?' a third asked before Remae cut in.

'Quit jabbering! Let the poor boy speak!' She then shouted at the curtain, 'An' make some blasted tea!'

A ruckus came from the kitchen, while Meecha prepared to answer their questions.

'Well,' he began, directing his attention at the respective people, 'my name's Meecha Roa. No, I'm not a dwarf, although our races are related. And I'm not a boy. In human years I'd be about... twenty.'

Childlike smiles were exchanged. Before they could ask anything more, he uttered his own query.

'As grateful as I am of your rescue, I can't help but wonder why. How is it you know me?'

All faces lit up, but it was Remae who spoke.

'We dreamt of thee,' she whispered, and her eyes, dark as coffee, gleamed.

Meecha frowned suspiciously. 'All of you?'

Remae nodded.

'What did you see?'

'A woman,' a redhead said from across the table.

'A ghost!' exclaimed the blonde, and pieces of the puzzle fell into place.

'She showed us thy face an' told us to protect thee,' Remae explained.

A scrawny girl with brown hair spoke next, curled up on the staircase behind him, 'She said thee presha... peshious... The world mus' na lose thee.'

'When we knew the same dream came to us all, we didn' know what to think,' Remae shrugged, 'until thee appeared.'

The curtains parted, and the ginger woman emerged from the kitchen. She was carrying a tray containing a steaming kettle and a handful of mugs. Her friend appeared behind her, bearing another tray of cups. Everyone assisted in handing out the beverages, until they all sat quietly sipping on hot black tea, plain or with an added sweet substance—not honey, but similar. It tasted fruity. Meecha stopped himself from asking about it. The scene was too tranquil, too precious, to disrupt.

He felt like he has just stepped into a painting. The courtesans were pleasing to look at. Some were sweeter or handsomer or more exotic than others, but what interested him most was this: they unconsciously huddled together. And beneath the pretty gazes, the silky skin, the vibrant shrouds and plumes was a dull, hardened sadness and a warning of swift claws. They were a pack in a city of predators.

He harrumphed softly before finally intruding in his companions' reflection. 'Maybe you can help me with something else.'

They regarded him curiously.

'I'm looking for an elf who may have come through Crove.'

Remae chuckled, 'An elf? I never seen un since I was a mite.'

Her cohorts shrugged and shook their heads.

'What about the warehouse? Do you know what happened there?'

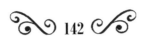

Remae motioned towards the blonde woman, 'Berry should tell thee. She was there that night.'

Berry. The fiddler's music! Had it guided Meecha to her? Had it predicted or incited his path—the fighting, running, and encountering of these women? Then another realisation hit him as he studied Berry's face.

'I know you!' he gasped. 'You were one of the prisoners.'

Her haggard appearance now made sense. Who knew how long she had been in that dungeon. She shivered. Her fingers picked at her dress. One of her friends embraced her from behind, rubbing her arms for comfort.

Berry lifted a timid, tearful gaze to Meecha. 'Thank thee... For saving us... I don' know how much longer I...' Her fragile voice broke and she folded herself into her friend.

The staircase creaked. Soft rustling feet descended the steps. All Meecha could see were those sitting on them shifting to let someone pass.

A gentle question was directed at their group. 'What is wrong? Is something amiss?'

'One of yer heroes be here,' the brown-haired girl replied and looked back down at Meecha.

With a motherly smile, Remae invited the new presence to join them, and a girl appeared from around the banister. Her black hair was familiar to Meecha from the tunnels. And so were her blue eyes, pale complexion, and small pointed nose, but from a different place, a different realm entirely: his dreams. It was her. She was real and standing in front him, smiling thinly.

'Greetings,' she said and curtsied.

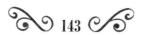 143

No longer in the tattered riding dress, she wore a grey nightgown under a dark green woollen shawl, which she pulled tighter around her shoulders. She was not as thin as Berry, but the dark hollowness of her eyes betrayed the girl's ordeal. She looked only a little older than the child on the stairs.

'Greetings,' Meecha finally echoed.

He casually returned to his tea and sipped, while she accepted a mug of her own and sank into a chair. His mind, however, was ringing. Who was she? Another Ward—a person to be guided—like Azare? But Meecha's dreams had started before he received this mission.

'Thou wanted to know about the warehouse,' a voice drew him out of his deep thoughts.

It was Berry. She had composed herself, but was still frowning.

'Tha' was Crab Galob's place,' she grimaced. 'I was crossin' the square when I 'eard a scream. I followed, bu' I didna want to go too close. It stopped an' I waited to see what 'ould happen. There was fighting. Then two people jumped out the window! I was sure they were falling to their deaths, bu' one of them... changed! It was a woman an' then a beast—huge, hairy. It landed in the street, caught the man, an' ran away with 'im on its back. Then another came out the window—a man, I think—an' onto the roof opposite! He was gone quick. I never seen none move like that!' After a few moments of bewildered silence, Berry shrugged. 'Then I ran. If anyone found me, they might've thought I was meddled!'

'Thou coulda said something,' the redhead complained. 'It woulda saved Crove stinkin' up.'

Berry sulked at her hands folded on the tabletop.

'The bodies were roasted well in this heat,' Remae made a face and downed the last of her tea. 'When they were found, they were already melting. Hideous.'

Meecha sighed. One of the thieves was a shape-shifter and Azare was still after them. They were two days ahead.

'Did they leave Crove? Which way did they go?'

The women looked at each other.

'We donna know,' Berry replied. 'None others saw them.'

Meecha puffed with frustration. Even if he departed immediately, where would he go? His tracking skills were not good enough to pursue them solely by footprint. He studied his murky tea. His breath formed ripples. He had to consult the aerieti without delay, for which he needed privacy. Then he would have to go where either their instruction or his best guess directed him. At present, all he had was confirmation that his targets had been there and dreams that were possibly more than they seemed. And if this girl was important, he could not simply leave her behind. He was also worried about Marilli and her uncle. If anyone could have survived that battle, it was them, but he needed to know for certain. Meecha turned to Remae.

'I'm grateful for your help and hospitality, but I must get myself some rest. Is there an inn you'd suggest?'

'Nonsense,' she boomed. 'We have a bed for thee. A clean bed. Stay as long as thee wish. Anything thou need, let Mama 'Mae know.'

It was clear she would not abide contradiction, so Meecha accepted her invitation. A few hours' sleep would do

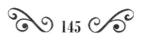

him and his strained mind some good. Before he could make a move to stand, however, more tea and food—scraps of bread, cheese, meat, cake—were brought to the table. He tried to resist, but laughter, song, and dance were quickly bringing the house to life. Before Meecha knew it, he was frolicking amid lurid gowns with a bright green shawl of his own swirling over his head. Even the mysterious girl—Delia was her name—was soon up and prancing alongside him. The kitchen curtains were left open to make more room. The house was small, but it managed to accommodate all their merry company. An occasional customer would knock on the door or try to peer through the filthy windows, only to scurry away at Remae's growl.

It was nearing dawn when their exhaustion struck home and their numbers dwindled. Meecha was shown to a little cot—it could have been a child's bed—in a tiny room upstairs. There was barely enough space for the bed, let alone the door, but to him it was luxury. Meecha placed his candle and cup of water on the windowsill before sitting cross-legged on the bed with his bag before him. He rummaged through it until he found what he was looking for: the round leather case. He undid the zipper and pulled out a pocket mirror no larger than his palm. He crafted it out of arvadeir and painted it so as to resemble a grey rock when closed. Meecha opened the lid and looked at the glass, a small part of the larger enchanted slab provided to all agents. The mirror in his bedroom used up a greater portion.

'Ernath'a Isha.'

The glass glistened orange-gold from the reflected candlelight.

'Are you there?'

No response.

He spoke quietly to avoid being overheard. 'I've found Azare and the thieves' last whereabouts, but their direction keeps evading me. One of the thieves is also a shape-shifter. And something… strange has happened.'

At last, a light burst forth from the mirror. Meecha squeezed his smarting eyes shut. When he opened them again, the glass had settled to a subtle white glow. From its shimmering vicinity the ghost lady was smirking up at him.

'Is thine army to thy liking?' she asked.

Meecha chuckled. 'They've been very gracious, thank you, but I need help again, I fear.'

Her smile shrunk. 'I heard thee an' I have information to offer. Galob's spirit is still… disorientated, bu' I got some words from 'im, including 'Anvadore'. I doubt the thieves intend to dig up the old city, thus they must be making for New Anvadore.'

Something about that revelation unnerved him. He ruminated its significance, while the ghost lady continued. 'As for the shapeshifter, it could be a mage. Or a demon. Be wary.'

Meecha nodded absent-mindedly and licked his lips. 'There was something else.'

Her eyes narrowed.

'New Anvadore's colours are white and red, aren't they?' Meecha inquired. 'And the phoenix is its emblem?' He sighed when she concurred. 'I started having dreams before we met, before I took the mission. Two dreams had these signs and in all three there was also a girl. And I just met her. And my path seems to lead where the dreams hinted.'

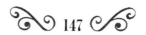

The lady's eyebrows shot up. 'Visions. Not normal for thee, I take it.'

Meecha shook his head with vigour. 'No. Not in the slightest. If the aerieti aren't behind them, I can't say who is. Or what.'

'Visions aren' familiar to me,' she admitted. 'While I ask our friends up high, I suggest thou keep note of what thou see. It feels important. In the meantime, make for the capital.'

Meecha nodded, sucking in his nervous belly.

'Oh,' the ghost lady exclaimed softly, 'an' I salute thee for Parda. Most impressive. Thou are doing well, my friend.'

She twinkled out of existence, leaving Meecha in a hunched heap of relief and concern. He carefully placed the mirror back in its pouch and into his pack. He extracted his toothbrush, dipped it into the cup of water, and scraped some toothpaste out of its tube. While he cleaned his teeth, a realisation flickered behind his eyes. The ghost lady's speech had a Crovian tang.

Chapter 16

Meecha found Remae in the kitchen counting coins with a knotted brow. He told her about his lady's instructions, and the matron assented without hesitation. After separating her bounty into two piles and scooping them into two pouches, she disappeared through a side door. Meecha scratched his thickening stubble until she returned clutching only one of the purses and a bulging cloth, bound at the top. She handed Meecha the latter. It contained two apples, chunks of cheese and meat, and some bread. He protested. He had rations to last him several days. But it was not just for him, she explained. There was another who needed to get to Anvadore.

Delia soon descended the stairs with a dark grey cloak over her blue riding dress. The garment had been washed, though no amount of scrubbing could get the meaner stains—or the rips—out. Meecha and she looked at each other curiously.

'Thou have company in the caravan,' Remae announced to the girl, who actually smiled.

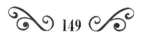

'I shall be glad for it,' she replied graciously and bowed her head to Meecha, a long braid sliding off her shoulder and onto her chest.

He returned the gesture, suddenly conscious of his own dreary dreadlock. He turned to Remae.

'Have you heard any news around the city? About Lazlo or the Guard?'

She shrugged. 'Nothing great. Same old enemies. Same old scuffles.'

It was not enough. 'Is there time for me to run to the barracks? I can meet the caravan after.'

Remae shook her head. 'The un scheduled for this morning is leaving soon. Thou miss it, thou wait two days for the next.'

'Is there anyone who can run over with a message? Now?' Meecha asked sheepishly.

The matron's shout brought the mouse-haired girl clattering down the stairs, while Remae found parchment and charcoal. It was the shortest, messiest letter Meecha had ever written, but it got the message across with what Itanian he could put into writing.

'Dear Marilli, I pray thou live. It was honour to know thee. I go to New Anvadore on the karavan. I wish thee luck and prosperity. Thy frend, Meecha Roa.'

He blew some of the excess charcoal away, but was still reluctant to fold the parchment. He handed it to the girl, Etta, with the two ends between his fingers, the rest of the letter simply curved into a tear-shape. She took it carefully, imitating his pinch.

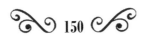

'Put this in the hands of Marilli—Marilli Namael—at the barracks. There's a chance that she was killed last night.' His throat clenched. 'But if she lives I'd be very happy if this reached her as soon as possible.'

Etta's smiling nod exuded confidence. She bolted out the front door, the hems of her dark trousers lifting to reveal bony calves. Meecha only had time to say farewell to the women in the dining area—eating, patching up clothes, grooming hair—before Remae ushered Delia and him outside. They trotted behind the burly woman, who was swift on her feet, but also imposing enough to make crowds part before her.

Meecha almost felt sad to leave the glum, reeking streets behind, the rundown buildings and sneering Crovians. He had hoped to resolve the situation with Lazlo, help the guards come to a peaceful solution. He had also wanted to reimburse the Raven's owner. It seemed, however, that his time there had come to an end. Parda was vanquished, at least. Her prisoners were freed, her creatures put out of their misery. Marilli would earn respect in the Guard. Her uncle should breathe easier too with only Lazlo to contend with. What that would lead to was a matter for Crove's protectors to handle. Meecha blinked with surprise when the nose-ringed scoundrel popped into his head before Captain Namael. He smirked to himself as they reached the eastern gates, where four wagons were waiting, their goods concealed by grey canvas.

The animals strapped in and ready to lug them all the way to New Anvadore looked like horses. Large and brawny, it was as if the animal from Oparu was bred with a native Itanian creature that produced a heftier mount with a longer head and a multi-coloured spotted coat. The wag-

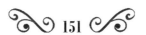

on drivers, gruff men in light clothes, boots, and gloves, were leaning against their vehicles, smoking and grumbling about a delay.

Remae approached the least rumpled of the lot. He stood beside the second wagon, a stern, wrinkled man with grey streaks in his black ponytail and beard. He scowled at Remae's request to take Meecha and Delia as passengers, but reconsidered when she jingled the pouch of coins in his face. She concluded the negotiations with a threat of disembowelment if any harm came to them. With the driver's tense promise that the 'lad and lady' would be delivered to New Anvadore in one piece, she left the man to count his coins and came to tower over Meecha with her fists on her hips. Delia, previously inspecting the wagon, inched closer and thanked Remae for her kindness.

'It be our pleasure to do our humble duty. Don' forget us if thou visit again. And stay brave, girl, but 'ware it don' turn to folly,' the matron said, squeezing Delia's hand before tucking a black lock behind her ear.

Remae informed them that New Anvadore was almost a ten-day journey, but the drivers would press for speed. Meecha conceded that it was the best he could hope for. He was expressing his gratitude to Remae when the thundering of feet interrupted him. They were coming from a street behind him. He backed away from the tall figure, armoured and helmeted, charging out of the passage, skidding to a halt before him. That sword and shield—he knew them. He beamed, close to tears, as Marilli, heaving for breath, pulled off her helmet, held it under her armpit, and grinned in return. For a moment or two, neither uttered a word. They just smiled at each other. Then Meecha shuffled forward and wrapped his arms around her waist. She bent over him, engulfing his little self in a cavern of leather and metal—she took care not to disturb his hat too much. Still they were silent, until Marilli patted his back and they separated, sniffing and harrumphing.

'Will you be well?' Meecha's question emerged gruff as he tried to harden his quivering voice.

Marilli nodded. 'Lazlo escaped, but the Captain knows about his ambitions and the Guard is preparing. We can face him. Before I forget,' she reached into a pocket while speaking, 'this is for thee.'

A hefty pouch clinked into Meecha's open palms. He gawked at it.

'Uncle said thou asked for nought, but we both agree thou deserve this and more,' Marilli explained and hushed him when he tried to protest or repay her the gold she had spent. 'Thou did more for this city in a night than a guard does in a week. Thine example shall be changing much here.'

Meecha's driver barked at him and Delia to board the wagon. Marilli walked over with him, shaking hands with Remae in the process, who lifted awed eyebrows at the guard. Delia climbed onto the wagon's lowered door and helped Meecha in after her. Remae took her leave with a final wave, but Marilli hovered a while longer. She stood at ease, one hand on her sword's hilt, the other around her back. The afternoon sun turned her hair a fiery tawny. She bowed her head and stepped out of sight, out of the next horse's way, while Meecha crawled to the front of his vehicle.

To his relief it contained heaps of furs—of what animals, he could not tell. As soon as he had made himself comfortable, with Delia facing him on the other side, he heard trotting horses approach the wagons followed by exasperated

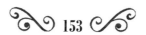

cries and curses. When he peered through the loose flap behind the driver's seat, he saw riders in padded armour circling the wagon. The driver appeared round the back to close the door. He gave Meecha a brisk nod before pulling a strap loose from the rolled-up length of canvas above his head. The curtain fell with a snap and the driver tied it to the door by a pair of cords. Meecha and Delia were plunged into gloom. The man climbed into his seat as the first wagon rumbled towards the open gates. Their driver cracked his whip and the wagon jerked into motion.

Chapter 17

Running she could handle. Craven horses too. The creatures annoyed Naya more than water, but they did not cling to her or chill her to the core. Except their stink. Yes, that smell of horse-sweat and filth sickened her more than the thaelil's scent—he was no longer in the air. Naya caught herself sigh as she trudged away from the riverbank, hair plastered to her face, clothes sodden and heavy. Koro staggered out of the water after her.

'Did we lose him?' he gasped.

'For now,' she grumbled.

They made for the trees in what the human supposed was south, but neither of them was in a hurry. Even she had to submit to her weariness. Two days of fleeing and hiding and riding had brought them to the river. And still he followed—their hunter seemed to care for nought but their trail. In desperation, they had jumped into the torrent. This was their chance for some rest. Naya approached a boulder next to a vast tree—plenty of cover. She plopped down against the stone.

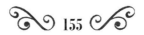

'We can' stop here. He could be close. An' we must reach Anvadore.' Koro leaned against his knees, still panting.

Naya growled, 'I need sleep. Food. Make thyself useful. I carried thee half the way.'

He grimaced and squatted before her. He glanced this way and that, said he could catch them some fish or bush-creature. As he pulled out his knife and prepared to prowl, his uneasy stare settled on Naya.

'What is it?' she snapped.

He licked his lips. 'Thou true think he hunts us for Galob? Could he be with the aerieti?'

Naya shrugged. 'Thaelil are thaelil. Few know what they want or do for true.' She stretched her legs, angrily pushing a pebble with her heel. 'But he hates us. He smells of death.'

They glared at each other, yet it was fear she sniffed in him. She snarled him into motion. He left to catch their dinner, but if he were kin, he would have laughed in her face, for her terror far exceeded his. He did not know. Ignorant human fool. Staying there or fleeing further made no difference. There was no escaping a thaelil hunter.

Chapter 18

Delia's leg dangled over the edge of the wagon's lowered door. Her other was at an angle under her dress, which created a kind of safety net for the bits of parchment and wood to fall into. Meecha watched her busy fingers turn and fold and cut the paper, while she glanced around now and then at the bustle of people preparing to set off again. It was dawn. Above the bags of food covering their faces, the horses' ears flicked towards the morning birds chirping from the sparse trees flanking the road. Meecha stood beneath one and watched the inspection process for the vehicles. It involved a variation of kicks to the wheels and tugging of the covers and harnesses. The caravan's armed escort, five male mercenaries, was already mounted and smoking impatiently. Delia was the only woman there. Meecha had already let his dagger shine at a few leers. Their driver's sharp grumbles also helped to keep them at a distance.

Meecha gave the horse behind their wagon a pat on the shoulder—he could not reach higher—and climbed back in to sit opposite Delia, not without some ungainly effort.

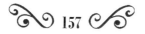

'So what is it?' he asked for the tenth time.

Delia tutted. 'I said, thou shalt see. If I do it correctly.'

The paper was taking shape, but there were others beside her, strips and folded forms, as well as a thin piece of twig about five fingers long. Meecha had learned much about his companion over the last day. She was born in New Anvadore. She had three older siblings she was not very fond of. Apparently, her sister was mean to her and her brothers ignored or looked down at her. That was why she would often sneak out and visit her friends in the city. Her parents would scold her for that, but she did not care. She loved New Anvadore. She had beamed with pride at that statement. When Meecha had asked how she had ended up a prisoner in Crove, the girl had looked embarrassed. She tried to stop some men from hurting one of her friends from the orphanage, she had said. Her friend escaped, but she was captured instead and taken to Crove, sold to Parda. Her friend had been spared, at least. Meecha admired the genuine relief and happiness she expressed about that. There was no resentment regarding her own fate.

'I've never been able to make creative things. At least, not well. I'm too impatient,' he admitted in a low voice so as not to distract Delia.

She replied in the same tone. 'A friend teaches me how to craft toys. Simple things of what materials are at hand. We take them to the orphanage and gift them to the children. It makes them happy.'

'You do that often?'

Delia's fingers paused. They quickly resumed, but her brow remained slightly wrinkled.

'I suppose,' she muttered. 'I feel sad for them. And others in need in New Anvadore. Their lives could be better, but… I wonder sometimes… If they care at all.'

Meecha frowns. 'If who cares?'

The girl lowered her creation into her lap as she looked up at him, truly looked, searching. She appeared keen to speak and then uncertain. Her lips tightened. She smiled politely.

'Do not mind me,' she finally said and picked up the parchment figure again. It was a bird, or shaping into one. There was the head, beak, chest. She started working a separate piece of paper into the first, folding, weaving, twisting. Meecha was mesmerised.

'Thank you,' her little voice drifted towards him.

He was confused. 'For what?'

Delia shrugged. 'Everything. Saving me.' Her eyes lifted to the driver of the next wagon, who was climbing into his seat. 'For being here,' she whispered timidly.

Meecha glanced around. The feeders were off the horses and he saw the owner of the last vehicle hoist himself onto it. Meecha gestured to Delia to move further in, so he could lift the door closed. Just then, their driver appeared. He gave Meecha an approving half-smile before securing the door and bringing down the loose canvas. But he only let it drop halfway, leaving plenty of room for his passengers to see and breathe. He tied it into place and left.

'You're welcome,' Meecha told her, tipping his hat. He kept, 'It was destiny,' to himself. Less eerie that way.

She cupped the paper bird protectively as the wagon lurched forward. The wheels rumbled beneath them. She picked up the stick and put it in her lap, while she tried to continue with her work of art. Meecha scooted further in to

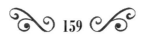

lie on some furs, leaving his hat beside him. They softened the ride. He assumed that there were about eight more days to their journey and his backside was already sore. He wondered what he would do when he reached Anvadore. Ask people if an elf had been sighted. Any kind of trouble? Anything strange? Delia clearly had connections he could make use of. *Maybe she really is a gift from the aerieti.*

A soft snarl came from the girl. Meecha turned to see the bird on the floor a couple of feet away from her. It was slowly unravelling and one of its wings was almost completely torn. Delia leaned her head back against the wooden wall and closed her eyes. Meecha felt more pity for the paper figurine than her—its form had broken into a jagged mountain range of a desert's creamy brown.

'Shame,' Meecha mumbled.

Delia flung the scraps from her dress and crawled onto the furs too, moving deeper into the wagon before sinking into a small heap of her own, facing Meecha.

'I crafted it wrong from the beginning. Nandil would have mocked me,' she sighed.

'It could still turn out beautiful,' Meecha replied. 'Flaws and all.'

'I suppose, but I lack the skill to make that happen.'

Meecha's fingers, entwined upon his stomach, rose and fell. 'The mended broken emerge more interesting than the perfect-born. In fact, I believe that perfection is a fabricated idea intended to hide imperfections.'

He heard Delia shift on her furs. 'Thou soundst like mother.' The sweet girl's wryness surprised him. He chuckled as she added, 'She says flawless people hide ugliness.'

Meecha squinted. 'Harsh, but not mistaken, if she

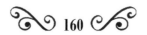

speaks of people who present themselves as flawless. But then there's my mother and her pajum pie. That's perfection to me.'

While a craving bloomed in him, Delia asked what a pajum was.

'Oh, it's a fruit,' he replied. 'Sweet and succulent. It only grows where I come from.'

'I do not mind sweet, but I enjoy savoury foods more. Cheese. Anything with cheese,' she moaned.

Meecha chuckled. 'Shall we stop talking about food?' He was developing an appetite, and so was she, judging by her fervent agreement.

They fell quiet. True silence was frightened away by heavy clopping hooves, wheels rolling over hard dirt, and the occasional clicking of the driver's tongue. They were almost hypnotising sounds, until the wagon rocked over a stone. Or a branch. Meecha could not tell from the jolt. He jumped all the same and grumbled his way onto a thicker pile of furs closer to the front. He and Delia formed a triangle behind the driver. There they lay for several more hours, dozing and talking and dozing some more.

They spoke of simple things, like the weather and the landscape, which Delia explained was generally quite flat and fertile, but lacked many farmers due to the limited protection from dangers descending from the mountains. Bandits, creatures, and such. There were more homes around the main road to Anvadore. The patrols were more regular. She asked Meecha if he had seen any soldiers in Crove and seemed puzzled when he answered, 'One or two'. The men in the red capes. They were the only fully armed people he had encountered besides guards.

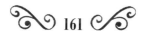

Then the conversation turned to Parda and her experiments. When Meecha expressed his sadness at the transformed people's fate, Delia revealed that a third creature had been there when she was brought to the mage—a water nymph, she said. She saw it while being dragged to her cell. It was hovering before Parda by magic. Its tail hung almost to its full length. It had a fin down the spine, skin a greyish-blue and covered along the back in small moving tentacles that two men on either side of the chamber had watched with unease. Before the cell door had been shut in Delia's face, the girl saw Parda thrust her hand into the nymph's chest. Delia shivered as she tried to describe the creature's cry, which penetrated the locked door. *Parda was playing with elements*, Meecha thought. Like the nymph, she must have found other living creatures that harnessed air and wood, taken their essences somehow, and tried to combine them with humans. She had succeeded to a certain degree.

Midday found them in a glum mood, so Meecha attempted to cheer Delia with cheese. It had a decent effect, as did the apple it was accompanied by and a slice of his own preserved meat that she wanted to try. He chortled at her expression, pleased yet perplexed astonishment. Meecha pulled the canvas behind the driver aside and offered the man some food. He accepted some bread and meat—the Itanian kind—and even smiled.

Meecha lay back feeling quite contented. He nibbled a small hunk of cheese and then bit into the second apple, the sweet juice mingling wonderfully with the lingering saltiness. But the wagon rolled over something hard again. The bump jammed the fruit against Meecha's teeth. He groaned before tearing off a chunk. While chewing, he stared through the open flap at the wagon ahead. A horse's tail flicked the air on its right-hand side—one of the caravan guards. The sky beyond was bright and warm.

Stiff limbs aside, and senses jiggled by the wagon's motion, Meecha was enjoying himself. He had good company, a new world to explore, and leads the aerieti would be most intrigued by, not to mention mysteries to keep his mind occupied. He nibbled his apple to the core, deciding to give the rest to the lovely chestnut bearing him to New Anvadore. He wondered what had happened to the old Anvadore. He could recall something about a king who went crazy some time after the Rift and burned down the city. Meecha put the core aside and re-tied the food bundle. It was smaller now.

'What th' abyss...?' their driver cried.

New sounds erupted around the wagon, shouts, thuds, startled cries, while Meecha stuffed the bundle into his bag. Horses screamed. Delia sat bolt upright, trembling. Meecha froze and listened to galloping hooves approach the right side of the wagon. The first vehicle swayed. Someone went flying off it. Another someone leapt onto the seat next to their driver. He gasped and a blade jutted out of his back to point at Meecha's cheek. Delia clapped a hand over her mouth as the wagon charged forward behind its panicked beast. Meecha's breath lodged itself in his throat. He shook, his stomach clenching and roiling violently, cold sweat breaking out all over his body. Blood dripped onto his clothes. The sword was slick with it. It was yanked out of the driver, and Meecha fell flat on his belly. Delia followed suit. The wagon skidded to a halt, horse still screaming and snorting. The momentum caused the largest pile of furs to fall on top of them, covering Meecha completely. From under the thick, stuffy pelts, Meecha could hear voices shouting to each other.

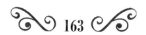

'Gather our horses!'

'Check the cargo!'

Meecha heard the canvas behind the driver's seat flap.

'Furs!' a brigand yelled.

'Iron!'

'Smoke!'

Meecha lay perfectly still. Delia must have been hidden just as well.

'Tie a horse behind each wagon!'

'Done!'

'Back to camp, then!'

The wagon started off again but soon turned and left the main road, its relatively even surface replaced by rockier terrain. Tossed up and down, back and forth, Meecha could swear his heart was getting bruised against his ribs. He had to escape. Creep under the furs to the back. Untie the horse attached to the wagon. Ride away.

Meecha's hand snaked under the furs until he felt open air on his fingertips. He lifted the edge of his cover to look. The flaps behind the driver's seat were fastened shut. He closed the peephole and his hands fumbled for Delia and his backpack. He caught the strap, but found no arm or leg, so he started to burrow through the furry mountain, dragging the bag along with him. The wagons were making such a racket that his crawling presence would not be noted. Finally, he felt motion to his left. He reached through and brushed against skin, which flinched but then revealed itself to be fingers that grabbed hold of his hand. Perhaps in vain, he pointed in the direction he was crawling in and gently pulled her as well. It seemed she understood as she began to move. Meecha retrieved his hand and continued.

The dense centre of the mass would not budge, so Meecha moved like a caterpillar around it. The heat generated was unbearable. He crawled and heaved and crawled and heaved. He must have been half way through, when the wagon dipped into a pothole. Meecha and the furs rose and fell, producing a muffled thud as they collided with the wood. A groan escaped him.

The canvas snapped. He held his breath. No voice or sound reached him, and the wagon was still in motion. The canvas rustled again, but he waited a few moments before resuming his escape plan. Crawl and heave. Crawl and heave. On he went, sweating profusely. *How much further?* The furs bore down, suffocating him. He had to get out. Crawl and heave. Shouts from outside. He did not care. He crawled several more feet before he realised. The wagon had stopped.

There were noises in front of him. It sounded like canvas... being rolled up! The door was unhinged. Meecha reached for Delia, possibly punched her in the shoulder. He drew her towards him, while closing the distance as carefully as he could. Her face finally appeared, fearful and soaked in sweat.

'Listen,' he whispered urgently. 'I'll distract them. When you have the chance, run.'

'No, Meecha,' she protested, squeezing his wrist.

He shushed her pleas. 'Don't worry about me. You get away.'

The wagon shivered. Someone was climbing in. Meecha shoved the girl back to her side and lay in wait.

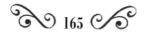

'Hand them down,' a man said.

There was a disturbance on top of him. They were removing the furs, and did not know he was there. This was good. One fur—Meecha slid his right knee up beneath him. Two—the left knee came up. Three—he gripped the backpack. Four—he braced himself. Five... Six... Seven!

Meecha bolted up with the wildest roar he could muster. The man leaning over him yelped and tripped backwards onto his two helpers, standing behind the wagon. They grunted with fright too before catching him and collapsing under his weight. Meecha leapt to his feet and, still howling, charged them. He jumped through the opening when a fourth man stepped in front of him. Meecha landed on his head and clung to it as they toppled.

'Get it off me!' the human screamed against his stomach.

Before they hit the ground, Meecha rolled off and onto his feet. The men were quick to stand up too, glaring. He pretended to hesitate until all four were moving towards him. Then he bolted to the left through two rows of tents. A glance behind confirmed that the men had left the back of the wagon to pursue him, shouting for his capture. He shouldered his pack and swerved into a narrow gap between two tents. A bulky man intercepted him with arms spread. Meecha ducked and punched the human in the groin. He turned back to the passage where more and more people were being drawn from their tents by the ruckus. He made for another gap but was stopped again. He ran for the next one. It was pointless.

Meecha darted right and left, dodging hands and blades and even arrows. People were laughing. They barked bets to each other. He passed some sitting and watching the show. He ducked under a two-wheeled cart loaded with barrels, and as soon as he reached the underbelly of the other end he shoved it upwards. The cart tipped. The barrels crashed down the passage and onto his pursuers. Meecha resumed his zigzag sprint.

The rows of tents opened up into a sort of courtyard. On the edge of his vision, he glimpsed a man emerge from a tent slightly larger than the rest. Meecha reached the centre of the opening, when the air around his legs pressed against them. It seemed to thicken and harden, like concrete, inhibiting them. Before he knew it, he was fixed in place, paralysed from his waist to his toes. His arms were still functional, however, waving around as he tried to fight the magic encasing him.

A host of men swarmed around him panting, cursing, and chuckling. The one Meecha had punched stalked up and walloped him across the face. Meecha grunted, swaying in an arc around his immobile legs. A burning, throbbing pain started up the left side of his face, and he could taste blood. The backpack was ripped from his shoulders. His assailant prepared to strike again but was halted by a booming voice.

'Hold!'

The man retreated grudgingly and joined his friends rummaging through the bag. Meecha looked over his shoulder. They were holding up the bundle of food.

'Thou're no dwarf.'

Meecha's attention turned to a human with eyes pale as ice. That piercing stare was curious. It beheld him from an angle. The man stood tall and lean yet slightly hunched, hands held casually behind his back. He had a long angular face, high cheekbones, a strong stubbly jaw, and messy light brown hair. People swooned for a man of his looks.

'Where thou from?' Grey-eyes inquired.

Meecha glanced behind him to find his compass in the filthy clutches of one man and the leather case in another's. They hungrily inspected the objects, when he suddenly remembered his hat. He had left it in the wagon.

'Please.' Meecha addressed Grey-eyes, for he appeared to be in charge. 'I'm a simple traveller. Please, let me go.'

The human shook his head solemnly. 'I cannot do that. Thou've seen our camp and—'

A deafening clap of lightning erupted behind Meecha, and a bluish-silver light washed over the tents. A charred body landed nearby with a thud. It belonged to the man who had tried to open the aerieti mirror. While everyone else shied away, their captain rushed past Meecha to inspect the scene. He knelt over the unzipped pouch but did not touch it. He emptied the food bundle and used the cloth to pick it up. Then he came to tower over Meecha.

'What is this?' Grey-eyes demanded, showing him the brown case with the mirror's stone-grey edge peering through the opening.

'It holds my medication. Pills.'

The man's eyes glimmered.

'Show me.'

'Look, it's expensive stuff. I had the case enchanted against thieves—'

'Open it.'

'My life depends on this medicine. If you drop it—'

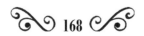

'Now!'

'No!'

'Let me guess what it contains,' Grey-eyes snarled. 'A mirror.'

Meecha stiffened.

'Thou're clearly not aerieti, which means thou're an agent,' the man inferred.

Meecha licked his lips. 'What's an air-yeti?' he managed.

'No tricks manling!' Grey-eyes roared. He immediately reined in his temper with a shake of his head, but his eyes still flashed like white steel in moonlight. 'I know thy masters. As thou know mine and what they shall do to thee for answers.'

He does serve the xalikai!

'Grak'a Isha!' Meecha blurted. *I break the light.* And the magic glass encased in arvadeir burst into flames, flaring out from the closed lid and scorching the case around it.

Grey-eyes cursed. He dropped the thing, but quickly hissed, 'Eza nin.' *No fire.* Thaelil magic.

The flames dwindled and puffed into smoke. But not fast enough. The human upended the charred case. The arvadeir frame—more like a piece of coal than stone—clattered to the ground and clicked open by a fraction. Ash poured out. All that was left of the aerieti glass. Meecha gulped. Such mirrors had once been manipulated by enemy spies, so a destruction spell was added to their creation. If compromised, the glass could be neutralised. But that now left Meecha on his own, truly and utterly alone, in the middle of a xalikai den.

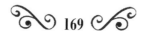

A shuffling of feet came from behind him.

'Let me go!' Delia's voice reached his ears before he turned to see her being dragged towards the clearing by one arm.

She hit and kicked her captor, but to no avail. Another man sneered and tried to stroke her cheek, but she lashed out, teeth bared, too fast for the old rat. A bite and a backhand with her free fist sent him staggering, shocked and outraged. Delia sneered back.

Chapter 19

'What's thy name?' Grey-eyes asked again, leaning against the cage.

Meecha remained as tight-lipped and tight-limbed as he had been all night. Hunched with arms folded, legs crossed, and a determined scowl on his face, he denied his interrogator a single word. Yet the human was unbothered. There were probably far graver measures he could take to make Meecha talk. The fact that he had not implemented them was almost an insult. If he thought that starvation and threats would break Meecha, he was mistaken.

'Which world're thou from?'

Meecha clenched his jaw.

'The aerieti must've truly low standards to recruit such a thing as thee,' Grey-eyes coolly observed. Meecha's eyes narrowed. 'What did they think thou could do? No more than a child, and they sent thee here to be slaughtered. Is that thy purpose? Do the aerieti mean to have thee sacrificed for some greater plan?'

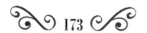

Dread pounded through Meecha. Could that be true? Was his death to be one more means to an end?

He bit a stubborn, 'No.'

Grey-eyes smirked. 'But there is a plan, yes?'

Meecha swallowed. He looked away at the surrounding camp. His and Delia's iron cage was located right next to the wizard's tent on one side of the circular clearing. Beyond the tents across from him, vast trees loomed, hiding the encampment and its spying eyes from the valley and the road below. More trees stood behind Meecha's cage and past them the stone face of the mountain range stretching east to west. His gaze fell on their neighbour slumbering in the adjacent coop. A mound of pure white fur rose and fell with the slow, steady breathing of sleep. He could not discern head from tail, except for two ears twitching to every sound.

'The dwarves,' Grey-eye's curt voice demanded his attention, but Meecha kept his eyes fixed on the animal, 'have thousands of symbols. Their tongue is one of the hardest to learn. They breed like rabbits and each rabbit walks under its own crest. Emblems rise and emblems are forgotten. All but one.'

He brought his left hand forward. Meecha caught a glint of gold. He heard a click and realised that it was his compass. He frowned at the human, who glanced down at the open device before turning it to face Meecha. The lizard and hammer were clearly visible against the golden shine.

'The symbol of the first dwarves,' Grey-eyes said.

Mystery solved.

'Their oldest chronicles tell of dwarves riding giant lizards and wielding splendid hammers of a metal and craftsmanship that no Itanian smith had seen before. They made

the mountains their home and have not moved since, even after their lizards died out at the hands of dragon-hunters. They weren't dragons, of course. No fire-breathing. No wings. They were no larger than a horse. They simply had the misfortune of resembling dragons, and that's all that mattered to the hunters.'

Meecha obliged him with a cautious reply. 'You seem to know a lot on the subject.'

'I know much about many things.'

'I bet I know more. And I don't feel like sharing.'

Grey-eye's face turned stern, but Meecha's new-found bravery kept his cutting words coming.

'You think yourself powerful, and yet you crawl before demons. I was *chosen* by the aerieti. Many have underestimated me before and, as you can see, I yet live. You think I fear you, wizard? I pity you. You've less spine than a kraken. And, yes, I've met one.'

The human turned to face the cage and clasped his hands behind his back. His stare was hard, and there was a cruel twist to his smile. That strange white shimmer resurfaced in his eyes. There was a low rumble, and Meecha turned to his neighbour to find her unblinking golden eyes fixed on their captor. Her ears were flat against her scalp as she snarled another warning. The human ignored her and spoke to Meecha, his voice sharp as a razor.

'If thou didn't reek of fear, I might have believed thee. Thou shall give us what thee knows, and I do wish thou would give it to me, if only to protect thyself from facing my masters. I promise thee. Thou shall not survive that.'

He stalked away and ducked into his tent. Meecha slumped. Azare was getting further and further away, while he was stuck yet again. Meecha's neighbour had set her silent attention on him, but the cat-creature soon flicked her ears and turned her great head away. A smaller bundle of fur squirmed and whimpered, seeking its mother's attention or perhaps crying for food that would not come. The sound woke Delia. She stirred behind Meecha, rising to one elbow, back against the bars. She yawned.

'We must escape,' he told her.

She lowered a dejected frown to the floor. Meecha grasped the bars of his prison, the metal chill against his palms. He shook them, testing their solidity. They were unyielding and too close together to allow him a squeezed passage. The lock seemed easy to pick, but without a wire of some sort the mere thought was moot. And he was stripped of all his belongings except for his shirt and trousers; the cool mountain air tingled his toes. Most importantly, where was his hat? Meecha nibbled his lip with worry. Even Delia was left with only her dress. She sat cross-legged and let the garment fall to her feet, covering them. Meecha gave the bars an angry shove. He got to his feet and paced, studying every inch of his confinement. Not a hole. Not a crack. There was not a single blemish he could make use of. That meant that the flaws outside his cage were his best and only option.

He glared at the grisly passers-by. Tall and short, young and grey, brawny and scrawny—they all walked with the same dark determination. Whether they were working, sitting about, or laughing with their friends, their hands rarely left the comfort of a loyal blade's hilt. And they all looked human. No xalikai in sight. But from what Greyeyes said, the demons were in touch with this camp. The atmosphere was taut and grim. Meecha suspected that if he plucked and poked enough it would snap, like a fiddle's over-tightened strings.

The stench of their lengthy inactivity reminded him of a stagnant bog. If he were in a more convenient position, Meecha would have snooped for information on why they were there. He got the impression that they were waiting for something. Grey-eyes's tent was surely ripe with answers. But at least one fact was obvious. They were gathering resources. This was perhaps not the only encampment hidden in the shadowy depths of Therea, and the demons would not be appeased by simply waylaying caravans. Other schemes would supply them with even more... what? Wealth? Power? For what purpose? War?

Meecha shuddered. His insides churned at the probability of war between Crantil and Itania, two worlds with the power to devour each other and drown this spot of the multiverse in blood and magic. The cataclysmic ripples of such an event would have unimaginable repercussions. The notion was horrifying, but destruction on a scale as grand as that was not beyond a demonic mind.

The cub's sudden mewling seemed to echo his fears. He glanced over and saw the mother cleaning her infant. The cub was whining now that it had her undivided attention, her large pink tongue covering half its body. Her massive paws had formed an impenetrable barrier around it. The cub tried to claw its way out of her embrace, squirming and snarling. Every time it neared escape, she picked it up by the scruff and placed it back in.

Meecha smiled, his previous dread almost forgotten. The value of his goal became clear again. He could not give up, if only to protect the lives of Itania worth saving. He peered at Delia. She was watching the creatures with fondness too, but fear was still in her eyes and hunched shoulders. It only then dawned on him that she was a prisoner for the second time, waiting, helpless, for whatever came. She spoke with a softness that worried him.

'I know what they are.'

Those words sparked Meecha's memory. He had been here before, in this cage. In the dream, a dark wolf had been in the creatures' place and Delia had asked him what it was. He could not begin to imagine what the differences between the vision and reality meant.

'White chanters,' Delia continued, speaking as if in a trance. 'Nandil has a picture of them in his store. They like to sing.'

A footfall and a jingling drew their attention. The gaoler approached the cage with a leg of some kind of poultry in his hand. His rotting teeth dug into the leg, while his pink eyes mocked Meecha and his neighbours. The animals stirred, salivating. The fat, misshapen man bared a crooked grin as the mother-cat growled at him and the cub whined, its moist tongue dangling.

'Hey, swine-guts,' Meecha called.

The gaoler responded to the taunt with a juicy grimace.

'Are you to be skewered next?'

'Me thinks thee fit nice in a pot,' the man grumbled, spittle flying through the bars of the cage. 'Them beasts can feast on dwarf stew.'

'That's all I'd be good for, I fear, but one leg of yours and the whole camp could be fed. Or poisoned.'

The gaoler wiggled his ravaged bird leg at Meecha, 'Thou keep talking, imp, and I carve the skin from thy back.'

He sucked the remaining meat off the bone and threw it into Meecha's cell.

'Breakfast.' The man sniggered and ambled away, keys chiming from the ring hooked onto his screeching belt.

Meecha made a face at the jointed leg-bones that glimmered with the man's slobber. He met Delia's disgusted expression before picking them up with two fingers and nearing the adjacent cage. Two pairs of hungry eyes watched him advance. He reached through the bars of his cell as far as his arm could go and tossed the bones into theirs.

They skipped twice along the floor and the mother snatched them up. The cub whined and pawed at her as she moved the leg around in her mouth, until one bone was hanging free. She bit down, crushing the joint, and let the loose bone drop to the floor. The cub pounced. It clamped its tiny jaws around the bone with wide-eyed excitement. It licked and nibbled on any scrap of meat that the human had left behind.

The mother's piece was already gone. Meecha met her emotionless stare while her cub wrestled with its meal. He marvelled at her thick snowy fur, adorned with streaks of gold by the rising sun. Her majestic head with its short muzzle, slit pupils, and round ears made her resemble a lioness in a wolf's pelt, but twice the size of either animal.

She sighed and looked down at her little one quietly gnawing one end of the bone to get to the marrow. She lifted her nose and sniffed the air. Her ears twitched backwards. Meecha looked through the bars at the pale blue sky. The white-clawed fingers of a grey cloud were reaching over the cage from the mountainous north. *And here comes the rain.* As if his fate were not cruel enough.

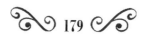

Chapter 20

The storm struck like a hammer. The swirling grey chaos threatened to drown them all or sweep them off the mountain. Meecha clung to the bars as the cage rocked and shuddered. Delia huddled against him, back to back. The cub hid under its mother, while she dug her claws into the floor to keep steady. Grey-eyes stood in the centre of the clearing with arms outstretched, casting a shield around the camp, but the rain battered through his defences. Men ran through the mud, securing anything they could from the thieving wind. It plucked tents and barrels, flung them in every direction. One or two humans clashed with a gust, tried to push against it, but could only manage to stay upright, if at an angle. The storm eventually died down, but not before the encampment had reached a great degree of disarray. Sodden shirt plastered to his skin, Meecha shuddered and watched the wizard's minions attempt to return the camp to order. Tents were re-erected, horses and poultry gathered, supplies retrieved, but Meecha could see it in their gnarled faces: their spirits were bent. And the soft drizzle that still pattered their backs

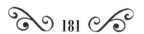

could only be nudging them further towards breaking. Did the storm have a mind of its own, a mind akin to Meecha's? Judging by the glares he was receiving, it was a common suspicion. True or not, even false hope that he was not abandoned was enough to boost his morale.

He glanced at his overturned surroundings. The cage remained intact, but the gale had delivered a shrub to the back of it. Nobody had noticed it leaning against their prison. It was a bush of dark green leaves veined with red on branches sharp as daggers and dotted with thorns—an ugly thing, but a perfect addition to his plan. He assigned Delia to keep watch while he crawled backwards until his shoulderblades found the bars. He pulled his right sleeve over his hand and carefully reached into the bush. Thorns tugged at his sleeve, only barely touching skin underneath. His hand found the stalk and then the base of one of the branches. He took a breath and, pinching the base, tried to twist the branch loose. Pain shot up his arm. A thorn from an adjacent limb had bit into him. He stifled a moan, breaking into cold sweat. Warm blood streamed down to his shaking hand, but he kept at it, twisting, yanking at the branch. Meecha gave it one final wrench and it snapped free. The thorn in his arm sliced him further on its way out. With a ragged sigh he retrieved his arm and laid the twig on the floor behind his back. He brought his hand before him and pulled down the red-blotched sleeve. He grimaced at the slash in his forearm. It brimmed with blood. A yowl came from the neighbouring cage. The cub was staring at him, tongue lolling. The mother was watching him just as intently.

'You're not having this,' he snapped, making Delia turn.

She gasped at the blood. Meecha pulled his sleeve over the wound and pressed down on it to staunch the bleeding. His captors were still too busy to notice anything. Three men walked by, a corpse slung over one's shoulder. The other two were hauling a second, larger, body by its legs. Both of the deceased were battered. The storm's doing, no doubt. They disappeared through the tents. Meecha's arm throbbed. The bleeding was stopping, so he kept the pressure on.

'Meecha,' Delia hissed.

He lifted his gaze and froze. Grey-eyes stood at the entrance to his tent, staring straight at them. Hunched and eerie, the man was more a spectre in that misty gloom with his dark cloak rippling around him. He sniffed the air and advanced. Like a hound, he seemed to be following a scent. He halted before their cage and scanned Meecha from top to bottom, steely eyes burning white. Delia shied away.

'Thou're bleeding,' he said and then snarled, 'Why?'

'I hurt my hand during the storm.'

Meecha held up his bloodied sleeve.

'Liar! I would have known.'

The wizard's gloved hand came up and grasped the air. Instantly, an unseen force encased Meecha's wrist. He tried in vain to squirm free. His sleeve was yanked down, forearm exposed. It was still covered in blood, making the wound indiscernible. With a wave of his fingers, Grey-eyes gathered the falling raindrops into a shimmering, flowing ball, both terrifying and astonishing. The sphere grew until it was large enough to envelop Meecha's arm. He could not help but sigh as the cool water soothed his skin. The dried blood dissolved and his gash was revealed. Grey-eyes frowned.

'Captain!'

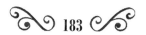

A man trotted up from the western flank of the camp. His soaked hair fell like rats' tails around his face. His bare upper body was slick with sweat and rain. He called again.

'What?' Grey-eyes barked over his shoulder.

The man slowed to a walk and gave Meecha a wary glance before responding, 'The... eh... package has arrived, my lord.'

The wizard's expression instantly changed. He looked alarmed or excited. He released his magical grip on Meecha's hand at the same moment that the bubble of water burst. Its contents splashed onto the floor of the cage. Grey-eyes walked off with the messenger.

Once safely alone, Meecha turned his back to the clearing. Gingerly, he picked a thorn off the thicker end of the branch. It felt a good enough weapon in his grip with a few bristles along its point, this almost the length of his hand.

'What is thy plan, precisely?' Delia sounded sceptical.

Meecha smirked at her. 'Patience. It'll take time.'

He crawled to the corner of the cage closest to the neighbouring cats, but farthest from the door and the bars facing the clearing. He hid the branch by sitting cross-legged before it. He took a deep breath and let his voice fly.

'Hey, how about some food,' he shouted. 'Can someone hear me? Where's that muttonhead? Hello! Hellooo!'

To Meecha's surprise, the cats took up the howl. The little one yowled as hard as it could, but the mother... Meecha's jaw dropped, goosebumps rising, as her deep, fluctuating croon filled the encampment. That was, indeed, what she was doing: singing. Lo and behold, the gaoler appeared. His big hands cupped his ears.

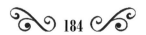

'Why making that noise? Stop!'

The mother snarled into silence. The cub, however, continued to meow and growl on its own, trying to match its mother's voice. Failing that, it yapped and wrestled with her head.

Meecha turned to the gaoler. 'There you are, you ugly dimwit.'

The gaoler lowered his wobbly arms and scowled at Meecha.

'What thee want, dwarf?'

Meecha heaved an exasperated sigh, 'Oh, let me see, rum-guts. Some food. A blanket. Water, maybe.'

The gaoler barked a laugh. 'I feed thee my fist.'

Meecha guffawed. 'As if you could. Tell me, why don't they send you on missions like the others? Why're you left here to watch us helpless prisoners?'

The gaoler's eyes shifted, and he ground his teeth.

'Let me tell you why,' Meecha offered in a flat, dry tone. 'Because you're a coward. A fat, worthless coward.'

The human grunted in outrage, his face turning red and blotchy. He lumbered up to the cage and thrust an arm through the bars. He heaved and stretched and whinged, but Meecha was out of reach. Delia watched this unfold from the far right-hand corner. The gaoler retrieved his arm and glanced uneasily at the white beast staring at him from Meecha's left. She licked her chops.

Then the wizard reappeared accompanied by three riders. Two were clad in padded leather jerkins. One had a bow slung across his back and a full quiver hanging from

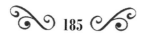

his saddle, while the other bore a sword and shield. The third man was beyond a doubt the one they were escorting. He was well-dressed—burgundy doublet over leather trousers and knee-high boots, a fine woollen black cloak hemmed with red and held by a brooch of gold. His shoulder-length brown hair framed a pinched, clean-shaven face that Meecha placed in its mid-thirties. The uptight posture and conceited expression suggested high birth. A longsword rested against his hip in a black sheath wreathed with golden scrollwork. His splendid charger was also black—to match his outfit.

The gaoler slunk away as the man in black dismounted and began to unstrap a square-shaped object from the back of his saddle concealed by a fur blanket. He finally flipped the cover aside to reveal an old metal box covered in dents and marks. He lifted it carefully from its perch and followed Grey-eyes into his tent. The horses were taken away, while the guards took up places on either side of the entrance. Meecha's agent-instincts tingled.

The hours dragged on with no sign of the gaoler or the two leaders. Rain still fell, a misty sheet, over the encampment, which was still recuperating from the storm. Boots made slurping, sucking sounds in the mud. Smoke drifted up from various parts of the camp. From Meecha's initial tear through the western lane, he recalled glimpsing a lean-to or two big enough to shelter five or six around a fire. How he wished he could light one too. He was safe from the rain, but the humidity and mountain air had chilled him to the bone. He envied the furball next door, barely visible against its mother's magnificent coat. The cub reached up its tiny paw to touch her nose. She leaned in and nuzzled it.

They both purred. The little one made an erratic wheezing sound compared to the mother's tranquil hum.

'This is him?' a bemused voice said, and Meecha snapped around to find Grey-eyes and his friend striding towards them.

Delia crept behind Meecha to the corner where the branch lay. The cub disappeared under its mother. She repositions herself into a crouch, her hackles high and her golden glare fixed on the approaching pair. The groomed gentleman chuckled as he stopped in front of Meecha's cage. His guards followed close behind.

'How underwhelming. I imagined the mighty aerieti agents quite differently,' he said to the wizard.

Meecha rolled his eyes. The man stood almost a head shorter than Grey-eyes. One could call him dark and handsome, but his attire was trying and failing to scream rich and powerful. The cloak was worn. The doublet had a sewn-up gash over his heart and had clearly been made for someone of a larger build. Meecha surprised them by straining his neck to glance down at the man's pants. They were slack.

'These aren't your clothes,' Meecha ventured. 'You stabbed their owner and stole them off his back. You're nothing but a scavenger.' His contempt could not be made more obvious.

The man flushed. Ire sparked in his eyes.

'Mind thy tongue, worm. Thou not know who thou speak to,' he proclaimed.

'Such bravado! *Almost* convincing. So you're supposed to be a lord or something? Is that your emblem?' Meecha

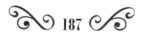

pointed at the brooch—it bore a fox-like animal with ruby eyes. 'Is that why you polish it every day?'

The human's jaw dropped. Denial squirmed up his body, but was never uttered. He glared at his smirking companions. The brooch had gleamed at Meecha through the bars as he had glimpsed the man's trousers. Only a pampered jewel would shine like that.

'Is that what the xalikai promised you? A title? You're dressed up, so whose boots do you mean to smack your lips on? The king's?' Meecha was overreaching his bait, but it was worth a try.

'Be quiet!' the man barked and drew a gilded dagger.

Grey-eyes seized his wrist, 'Fool. We need to question him.'

'He knows enough! Kill him now!'

Meecha's eyebrows shot up. The king it was. The xalikai were targeting him, but for what purpose? Assassination or manipulation? Whatever the case, the capital remained Meecha's destination.

Grey-eyes subdued the Scavenger. The dagger was sheathed, his imperious stature resumed. That malicious gaze abandoned Meecha and drifted past his shoulder to Delia.

'Who is the child?'

'We don't know yet, but it matters not,' the wizard replied. 'She can serve as an infiltrator.'

The other human continued to squint at her grimy face.

'Good luck finding blood,' he muttered, which caused Delia to shrink, hiding behind her gathered knees. *What blood? What for?*

 188

Then the Scavenger's attention found the cats.

'What have we here?' he exclaimed.

A rumble emerged from the mother's throat. She bared her teeth.

'A white chantress,' said the wizard. 'Our northern troops captured her with her cubs. Regrettably, only one survived.'

'That was her I heard when I arrived. How marvellous. A handsome prize. She could help me greatly.'

Meecha's heart clenched.

'We have other plans for her.' Grey-eyes' voice was tight.

'I want the cub then.'

'No!' Meecha and Delia gasped at the same time.

Their outburst was ignored. The wizard lifted a hand, and the huge cat suddenly hunched. She was agitated, her tail swishing. She gave a ferocious roar, twitched and jerked. Then she rose. The front half of her body was lifted from the floor. A mewling was heard from under her as she was pulled upright by magical ropes.

'Bring a box,' Grey-eyes shouted, and the gaoler appeared with a barred crate in his arms.

'No! Do not do this to her!' Delia cried.

The chantress yanked at her invisible bonds, tried to bite them, but there was nothing there to tear at. Her belly left the floor to reveal the squalling cub. It looked confused, frightened. It padded nervously from side to side before retreating towards its mother, who was now pinned upright against the bars.

'Open the door,' Grey-eyes commanded the gaoler.

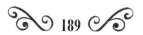

The fat man rushed to unlock it. The door whined open, and the chantress struggled with greater violence. The whole structure shook. Her mighty legs kicked and shoved and scratched the floor, the bars, the air. A few hours earlier the camp had been filled with her song. Now her shrill, anguished howls made the sky weep in torrents once more. The captain flicked his hand again. The cub's nails scraped the wood as it was dragged crying from its mother's side. The gaoler grabbed it by the scruff and lifted it out of the cage. One of the Scavenger's guards held the box open, while the gaoler stuffed the wriggling cub inside and secured the door with a sturdy padlock. He then closed the mother's cage and locked that too. While the wizard was lowering her back down, he muttered something under his breath. She jerked limply, her eyelids fluttering shut. Before she had even touched the floor, she had slipped into peaceful slumber. Grey-eyes dropped his arms with a sigh. His eyes closed. He seemed to savour the silence that had fallen so abruptly. It was soon broken by the Scavenger's cruel voice.

'Thou art most kind, my friend. I assure thee, it is to go to a very good home,' he said and walked off with his guards in tow, one cradling the imprisoned cub.

Meecha slumped against the bars, his reproachful glare trained on the wizard's downturned face. Insult upon insult swirled inside him, but Meecha was too crest-fallen to speak. The human met his tearful stare. The urge to spit into those pale eyes, to stab them with his stick and pluck them out one by one was almost too much to bear. But something stopped him. A startling thing. For a moment, just a second, Meecha found his sadness mirrored in the man's gaze. And what was that around his irises, like rings of moonlight?

Grey-eyes turned on his heels. His ghostly form glided through the rain, a misty glimmering sheet, to vanish from the world for several hours after.

Chapter 21

Meecha uncurled himself and stretched his limbs with a groan. Despite the conditions—cold, hard wood, stinging hand, blinding anger—he had fallen asleep fairly quickly, but his dreams made him wish he had not. The chantress's mournful song would echo in the background, while the terrible scene replayed over and over. Meecha tried different ways to rescue the cub, but he always failed. And the Scavenger always walked off to the unknown with that little ball of fur crying in his grip of stone.

This pointless cycle had triggered another memory that unexpectedly sprung from the depths of Meecha's mind. His own mother screaming at him. It had been after his very first mission. He had told his family that he was going on a camping trip with friends, who were in fact away visiting relatives. When Meecha had reappeared a few weeks later than he had predicted, his mother had been in hysterics. Simultaneously laughing and crying. In the dream as in real life, he was taken aback by her reaction.

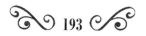

A soft moan came from the other cage. Meecha flipped onto his front to look and found the chantress still collapsed on the floor, too miserable to stand. It was some time since she had woken from the enchantment. Meecha would call to her and speak kind words, but she was deaf to the world. She lay and droned and slept. Her last living child had been snatched from her. Who could blame her for falling into such a wretched state?

'Don't lose hope,' Meecha whispered. 'Please, don't give up.'

Two slits of gold opened for him but only reached halfway before closing again. She heaved a sigh and rose from her prone position up to her elbows only to flop onto her side and sigh again. Her usually bright form was depressingly dimmed that moonless night.

Indeed, apart from the stars, a flickering lantern hanging from a pole nearby offered the scarce light that Meecha had to see by. His eyes had adjusted to the darkness, not that there was anything of interest to observe. The drizzle, glinting like shards of crystal as it fell through the orange light, pattered against the canvas and felt tents that wavered in the breeze. Snoring came from a few of them. A horse snorted now and then or stamped a hoof in its sleep. A bird hooted from the trees on the opposite side of the clearing. They looked like a black wall over which Meecha could see the southern mountaintops thousands of leagues away and the twinkling sky above. The rain's gentle rhythm lulled Meecha's eyelids shut. His head relaxed on his folded arms, and he started to drift back into sleep. He would worry about everything in the morning.

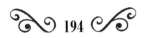

Clinkclinkclink. Meecha frowned. Clinkclink. The noise sounded familiar, but he could not quite place it. Squishing sounds arrived next. He opened his eyes, while a thought poked his brain with a hazy finger. Mud... Steps... Boots in mud! He bolted up and swirled onto his knees to see a round form shambling towards his cage. The gaoler halted when he noticed Meecha watching him, but sneered and continued to approach the cage's door. Meecha slapped Delia's shoulder and whispered, at the chantress as much as the girl.

'Wake up! Psst, wake up!'

They both stirred. The gaoler put the key in the lock, a malevolent grin still on his pudgy face. Meecha scuttled to the corner. With a quick glance over his shoulder, he grasped the branch-dagger in his left hand and waited. Delia squatted in the corner opposite, fists clenched over her dress as the door swung open. The gaoler passed a slobbery tongue over his lips. He replaced the keys onto his belt before clambering into the cage, making it rock like a boat.

'A coward, am I?' the man grumbled and closed the door behind him.

Meecha had a tight yet sweaty grip on the branch. He prayed it would be enough to fell the thick-skinned beast. The gaoler drew a crooked dagger and made for him, hunched to fit in the confined space. His bulk took up the whole breadth of the cage. Weapon held out of sight, Meecha moved into a crouch and watched the towering gaoler close in. With surprising speed, the scowling human swung for Meecha's neck, but he ducked under his arm and jabbed at his stomach. Layers of blubber rebuked his assault. The gaoler felt the prick nonetheless and yelped. He tried to jump away, but there was nowhere for him to go. His weight slamming into the side bars caused the cage to sway even harder. The wheels beneath them squealed, while Delia tried to keep steady by clinging to the bars. The gaoler regained his balance and prepared for a second strike, so Meecha sprung into a stabbing frenzy. The gasps and cries spurred him on as he skipped this way and that, thrusting and slashing at the man from every direction. The cage rocked and shook violently. The gaoler tried to shield himself with his arms—his own weapon lost in the struggle—but Meecha's dagger had already scratched them bloody. He pounced on the human with a growl, mustering all his might for one final stab.

'Meecha, no!'

Delia's scream froze the point inches from the man's eyeball. Meecha's confusion only lasted a moment. He gripped the branch and punched the gaoler between the eyes. Blood squirted from his nose, while he collapsed in a daze. Meecha snatched the keys from his belt. He flung the door open with a loud bang and jumped down. His knees were weak. They buckled, sending him sprawling into the mud. Delia's landing was marginally more graceful. Alarmed shouts filled his ears as he fought his way back up, the sludge sucking at his hands and feet. He ran around the cage to the chantress with Delia close behind, she trying not to trip over the hem of her dress, heavy with water and muck. The cat was up and looking very excited. He reached her door and shoved a key into the lock. Feet splashed towards him. The key did not fit. He tried the next one. No! The third...

'Stop!' a male voice shouted unnervingly close, just as Delia, hopping beside the cage, yelped for him to move faster.

Snap. The joyous sound rang in Meecha's ears. He yanked the door open and dove out of the way. A grander sight he had never seen. The massive chantress swooped down from her prison, snowy fur ablaze in the lantern's light, her terrible roar chilling his blood. The poor man who had tried to stop him only had time to scream before he was kissed by her jaws, embraced by her muscle and claws. Meecha stared in horror as the bereaved mother unleashed her vengeance, rending flesh, limb, and bone. Her fur was no longer pure—it dripped blood. And she had only just begun.

She bounded towards her next victim, Meecha and Delia luckily forgotten. Grey-eyes emerged from his tent in nothing but linen trousers and ran after the berserk creature. Meecha dropped the keys and darted towards the tent, ignoring Delia's protests. Men raced through the clearing, but the massacre that was taking place in the eastern wing kept them distracted. Meecha reached the open flap unnoticed and ducked inside.

Light and warmth washed over him. His body tingled happily as the chill was wiped away, but his arm burned and stiffened. He paused for a few stunned seconds, relishing, despite the pain, the heat that seemed to be coming from nowhere. Then Delia nearly knocked him over on her way in. They shuffled further in. At the back of the tent a vast carpet of grey and russet covered the earthen floor. Upon that was a second layer of grey and white fur along with pillows and a blanket that had been hastily flung aside. A wooden desk and a stool against the right side was the first thing that one met upon entering.

Meecha eyed Delia. 'The jailor wouldn't have spared us, you know, if our positions were reversed.'

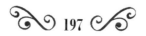

She was looking at the neat assortment of items spread across the desk when she responded sulkily, 'Only because thou taunted him. He was simple. Perhaps he was taught no other way to be. He did not deserve death.'

There was a black-feathered quill, an inkwell, and a small jar of pounce. Candles melted down to different lengths, parchments, maps, and, on the far edge of the table, Meecha's compass. A broad grin split his face in two. He grabbed the compass, clutched it reverently. Heart aflutter, he scanned the desk for anything that might offer insight into the xalikai's plans. The bits of paper were blank. The maps were of Therea, but they contained no markings or notations of any kind. He turned away from the table to find a massive, padlocked chest sitting against the opposite wall. Promising.

'We should go,' Delia whispered, touching his arm.

Meecha ignored her and moved closer. The wood was dark, heartwood perhaps, reinforced with steel patterned into silver flames that crossed the length of the chest like a zipper. The lock was fashioned into the likeness of a demon's head, the keyhole its snarling mouth. There was no key in sight, of course, nor any wire to pick the lock. Meecha wrenched at the lid. He grabbed a candlestick from the desk and tried to bash the lock. A few futile thunks later, he threw the candlestick away, infuriated. It pained him to think that he could be so close to answers, to Itania's salvation, only to be thwarted by a meagre obstacle of wood and metal. And magic, no doubt.

'Forgive me. I'll have to find this information another way,' he mumbled and made for the exit, stuffing the compass into his pocket, the only item of his possessions reclaimed.

The chantress was still roaring outside, men yelling. Meecha gasped when he stepped from the exquisite warmth into a curtain of icy wetness. Shivering, he and Delia sped past the cages. The gaoler's foot was protruding from between two bars, the rest of his body slumped on the bottom. He was clutching his face and whimpering. Delia's words suddenly struck home.

Into the shadows they went behind the tents on the left side of the eastern lane. Keeping low, they snuck through the undergrowth, barely outlined in the glow of stars and passing torches. Meecha held his hands before him as he picked his way through the shrubbery, hoping that his bare feet would not step on anything, thorn or snake. Both he and Delia hopped and cursed a few times. They should have gone the other way or across into the sloping woods, but he simply could not leave without knowing what happened to the chantress. Men with ropes and nets and even bows ran through the lane in the same direction as them. They had to hurry. He hastened their pace, making more noise than he would have liked, but the ruckus ahead could drown out a marching army. They were close. Through the undergrowth and cobwebs and roots jutting out to trip them up—most of them succeeding—they soon reached the edge of the camp.

There was another wide clearing bordered by tents and broken-down carts and rubble, some of it caused by that morning's storm, no doubt. The remains of a campfire in the centre were scattered throughout the circle—along with the pieces of several men. Meecha peered through the openings in the perimeter, and his breath caught at the sight of the carnage. Mangled bodies. Severed arms and legs, blood and entrails were everywhere. And prowling through them was she. Gore dripped from her darkened jaw. Her eyes were a bestial black. Her coat was a bristling bush of varied shades of fresh and dried blood. Not a spot of white remained. She was faced by a swarm of men armed with spears, longswords, bows, and a dozen heavy nets. Grey-eyes stood to one side hefting an axe but doing nothing. Why did she not jump through an opening? Perhaps the wizard was doing more than he seemed.

As Meecha skirted towards the easternmost side of the circle that touched the first of a dense mass of trees, he picked up a rock. He threw it at an opening between a tent and a cart. He was only half startled when sparks attacked the airborne rock. When it landed unnoticed on the other side, it was black and charred. The chantress would be cooked if she dared cross that barrier. Once Meecha and Delia reached the top of the circle directly opposite the mouth of the lane, they squatted behind a sizeable blue tent and searched the ground for more stones, a large one in particular. A roar came from the chantress, the snapping of wood, and then another man's agonised cry. She had devoured two more by the time Delia found what they sought. Into the gap between the blue tent and a neighbouring green Meecha rolled a melon-sized rock. Sparks flew and crackled, but the electrical current that fuelled the barrier did little more than blacken its hard exterior. Meecha grabbed one of the metal pegs the blue tent was tied to. He pulled it, wriggled it around, wrested it from the soil's grip. Delia was working on the second peg, her tongue sticking out of a puckish grin. She giggled when the spike finally slid out of its hole. The tent wavered for a few seconds and then began to lean towards Meecha. And the sparks vanished from around the rock. It worked! He's distracted!

Heartened by the success of his plan so far, Meecha and Delia popped up from their hiding place to revel in the surprised faces of the wizard and his men, even that of the chantress. Before anyone could react, Meecha drew upon his years of experience of pelting eggs at Luima to hurl his little round pebble at Grey-eyes. Delia threw a rock of her own. Meecha gave a hoot when both their projectiles found their mark, but it was the girl's that smacked into the man's pretty forehead. She gave Meecha a smug shove.

'Come on,' he yelled at the chantress, while the tent and the wizard collapsed simultaneously.

Meecha did not wait to see if she understood. He bolted in the opposite direction, sprinting through the trees as fast as his legs could carry him. Delia was faster, but did not go more than a few steps ahead. The murky light in the distance became their destination. His blood was pounding so loudly in his ears that he failed to hear the chantress until she had overtaken them. The huge feline shadow hurtled past them straight and fast as an arrow, lifting dust, mud, and leaves in her wake. The sounds of pursuit were not far behind and they were closing in fast. Meecha's legs ached, but he could not stop. He could not be captured again. Delia was clearly thinking the same thing—she hopped over a fallen branch and picked up speed. Their captors' angry voices drew nearer. Their legs were longer and stronger than Meecha's. There was no way he could outrun them. He prayed for some hope to be found beyond the trees. Clearly it would not be the chantress. She was long gone by now. He cursed his soft heart. But then a dark form took shape against the greying horizon, pacing up and down. She's come back for us! The closer he got, the clearer the chantress became. She kept growling in their direction, but

Meecha would trample her if need be, teeth and claws be damned. It was when they broke through the other end of the woods that he saw the truth of the matter. She was not waiting for them. There was just nowhere else to run to, for a few feet ahead the earth abruptly stopped where empty air began.

Meecha dug his heels in and Delia grabbed his shirt collar, but his momentum made him stagger five steps too many. The chantress watched them with hunched curiosity as they skidded to a halt on the lip of the cliff. A squeak left the girl. Meecha yelped, head spinning from looking down the perilous slope and into the churning river below. The wind howled, and a sudden gale swept over them and flung them onto their backs. With a gasp Meecha found his breath again, while his heart hammered on furiously. The cloud rolled over them, black against the dark blue night, before it started spitting great big droplets. Could it be? Could aerieti control the weather? Had they been watching over him all this time?

The only answer he got was the sound of running boots behind him and the chantress roaring at the trees. Meecha rose to his knees. A host of shadows emerged from the woods and surrounded them slowly. They did not approach. They still feared the chantress, despite their shining steel. The cloud rumbled and flashed above their heads, the momentary illumination revealing glares and grinding jaws on a wall of grisly faces. They promised pain, torture, and a slow, gruesome death. Then the middle of the throng parted for a single tall shadow. Another ear-splitting crack of thunder shook the skies and the mountain around them, followed by a brilliant blaze of lightning. And in its glare, Meecha saw something he had never seen before.

Grey-eye's frame, which had previously seemed fairly toned, was now double in size and muscle. His finely chiselled face was even more angular and seemed to protrude slightly in a way that made Meecha think of a wolf. The man's hair was darker and shaggier. The truly disturbing change, however, was not in his build or his looks. It was the long fangs he was so fiercely displaying and his hands that were now armed with black claws.

'A werewolf,' Meecha whispered, and the lights went out.

The wind whistled softly before a gruff, reverberating voice filled his ears.

'Thou could have lived, weakling. If only thou obeyed.'

Meecha shook himself and tried to sound fearless when he shouted back, 'Weakling? I escaped you, didn't I?'

The captain barked a raspy laugh. 'Thou're going back in thy cage. The masters want a word.'

'Well,' Meecha stepped backwards. 'They're not getting it.'

He took a deep reassuring breath and found himself calm and strong as he explained himself to the shadows. 'For the tiniest spark of light in the world, I'm willing to give my life. Is a single taint of darkness worth yours?'

He was pleased to hear the silence. Delia, on the other hand, kneeling beside him, begged him not to jump.

He inhaled and continued, 'Even in death, I'll still fight the xalikai.' Despite the bravado of his statement, it was sincere, and so was the next. 'I, Agent Roa, promise you that you'll fail! Itania will never be taken!'

A guttural roar answered him, and Grey-eyes attacked. The chantress rose onto her hind legs. The rain had been

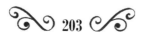

washing her blood-drenched fur. White strands had resurfaced. Her roar was long and brutal, her taunt to the wolf. The cloud cracked its whip a third time. The charging werewolf was halfway to them when a dazzling bolt of lightning tore the darkness asunder.

The ground quivered beneath Meecha's feet as he clutched his stinging eyes. Stray questions unfolded behind his eyelids. But they all dissolved, chased away by terror, when he lost the earth beneath him. His heart was wrenched from his chest. It fluttered wildly as he fell and fell and fell. His innards would have jumped out of his mouth, especially when his front—chest, stomach, knees—landed painfully on soil. Or so he thought. He bounced once and then started to slide. Through mud and rock and roots he glided faster and faster. Meecha wanted to scream, but the sludge running down with him kept his mouth and eyes shut. From head to toe he was battered, scraped, and caked. He could do nothing but ride it out and hope it did not kill him at the bottom. He was launched into the air again, when he finally screamed. His holler was quickly cut short, though, by icy water. The river, was his last thought before his senses abandoned him. And he sank and sank and sank.

Chapter 22

Meecha's consciousness floated back into his body. A dim throbbing sensation crept in with it. He felt light as a feather, drifting up towards a bright, warm glow. The sound of running water pierced his fuzzy awareness as if through cotton in his ears. A cool breeze eased him up through the final layers of haze, and he groaned, regretting his awakening.

The first thing he noticed was the heat in his right arm. His fingers were stiff, painful to move. He smacked his lips, suddenly realising how thirsty he was. He cracked an eye open and immediately closed it against the sun's glare. He turned his head to the left and tried again with both eyes. He blinked several times before his sight came into focus.

He lay on a riverbank, his head resting on grass and the rest of him on pebbly dirt. The river licked the soles of his feet. A short distance away the torrent was crowned by a stone bridge. His gaze lingered on the dark moss-laced structure as the shades of the previous night returned to

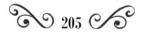

him. His flight through the woods. The werewolf. The lightning. Delia and the chantress.

He tried to lift his head, but a wave of dizziness dropped it back down. Stubbornly, Meecha pushed himself to his elbows, gasping at every cramp and pain. The front of his body was especially bad. Black and blue bruises, long cuts and scrapes were visible under his shredded clothes. He was fortunate that such a fall had left him with no more than superficial injuries, which was more than he could say about the thorn gash. The dirt must have done its damage—he could feel the inflammation pulsating in his forearm.

He grunted his way upright when something bumped against his thigh. He frowned, but then remembered the compass in his pocket. He reached into it with his good hand and plucked out the shiny instrument. He bit his lip nervously, fearing that the water had damaged it, but, when he opened the lid, it was pristine. The dwarven symbol was no more chipped than it had been before his dive. There were traces of moisture on the glass but none beneath it. The needle was still pointing southeast.

Pleased, he put the compass away and stretched his muscles, wishing he had a tub of scalding water he could jump into. Instead he stepped into the water's edge, not too far or the river would sweep him under. There he squatted and drank his fill, immediately seeing the water turn brown from the caked mud in his nose. He blew it, rinsed it. He washed his hands and arms, his face and feet. Meecha inspected his forearm. He grimaced at its rosiness and the slight swelling around the wound. He needed to find a healer before the infection worsened. His knowledge of Itania's medicinal plants was lost along with his belongings. If only he had studied those manuals while he had the chance.

Standing and shaking his dripping hands, he looked around at the countryside. It was lush, bright and colourful, nothing like the dreary grey of Durkai. He glanced upriver. On his side the plain was flat as a saucer, whereas on the other, a fair distance from the road, the earth rose. It reached for the mountain peaks but stopped abruptly. And somewhere among those trees up high the xalikai's bandits lurked, waiting for another caravan to loot. Meecha hoped from the bottom of his heart that the cliff had become Greyeyes' grave.

There was no sign of Delia or the cat. He sloshed out of the river and onto soft pasture, studying the ground for footprints and the length of the river for white or black hair, a green-dressed form perhaps. Nothing. He did not want to think the unthinkable. But he did. The fall was rough, the waters wild. It is likely that the child drowned. His heart clenched—he had to find her. She was important. He took a few steps and halted. His chin touched his chest as he sighed heavily. He could not linger any longer. The mission came first and that meant reaching New Anvadore as soon as possible. Delia was alive, he was certain. She was safe in the aerieti's gaze.

The road ran straight through a clear, rural area dotted with a handful of trees and shrubbery. He supposed that if he followed the road he would find civilisation sooner or later, so he set off through ankle-high grass, angling away from the road. Even though shelter seemed scarce throughout the valley, keeping off the well-worn track felt like a wise precaution. Now that the xalikai were aware of his presence, he would need to be doubly careful of spying eyes.

By midday he neared the first tree, an old being with a great shadow cast over a carpet of dead leaves. Meecha trotted the last few feet, eager to rest his sore legs in the shade. It was cool and permeated with a sweet, woody fragrance. He approached the thick trunk, but gasped when he trod on a hidden nut decaying in the leaves. He dragged his feet along the ground the rest of the way. He looked up at the canopy. It quivered in the wind. The sunlight twinkled through the foliage. And from the many timber arms, round furry morsels hung in clusters.

Licking his lips, Meecha pulled off his shirt and took hold of the nearest branch. His arm stung, but he was too hungry to care. HHe began to climb step by step, twig by twig, picking nuts along the way. Some time later he returned to earth, shirt bulging. He plopped himself down and unfolded the bundle between his legs. Using shaky hands and teeth to break through the outer shells, he munched on the little nuts within. His toes wiggled happily.

Once satisfied, Meecha wrapped up the remaining nuts, hoping they would last him to the nearest village. There he would get himself supplies, either by charm or sticky fingers, both of which largely depended on his right hand not having rotted and fallen off. *You're overreacting.* Yet his wound was unlikely to get better on its own.

'What do you think?' he asked the tree.

It rustled but had nothing meaningful to say. He laid his hand upon his knee and rested back against the bark, his eyes drifting over the road a short distance to the south. Not a soul had appeared thus far, man, horse, or carriage. They were all probably ambushed. Meecha urged himself upright, shouldered his bundle, and grudgingly left the shade. He would rest again when he found civilisation, whether a hovel or Anvadore itself.

Chapter 23

A zare pulled his hood up. The curtain walls of New Anvadore stood to the east as he stepped onto the fork where the road to Crove met the one bound west. He halted to scrutinise the immense grey fortification shining silver where the sun touched. The crowned white phoenix flapped its wings against its fiery sky—the banner of the Therean capital soared above the vast oaken gates. He had heard of this city that the humans had erected to replace the old. There were rumours, bitter whispers, of thaelil and other arcane arts being implemented in its construction. The wall was certain to have undergone a merging—a magical integration of the stones to form one solid, smooth barrier.

'Git out tha road,' a raspy voice growled behind him.

He turned calmly to face a bearded old man lugging a cart. Sacks of grain were piled high upon it, which explained the human's perspiration and heavy wheezing.

'That is a great weight thou carry.'

The hunched man released the cart's handles as he guffawed. 'Tha think, tha freakish oaf?'

Azare ignored the insult. 'I could help thee with it.'

The human's mocking expression melted into a suspicious scowl. 'Why?' he asked warily.

'Do people not help each other in times of need?'

'No.'

'I wish to assist thee, good man.'

'No, tha donna. Tha just wanta get inta tha city, donna tha?'

Azare was always astounded by the intelligence humans rarely exhibited.

'Yes,' he admitted and fished a gold nugget from his pocket.

The old man's squinting eyes brightened at the sight of gold, but he still seemed uncertain.

'Tha're not gonna cause trouble, are tha?'

Azare shook his hooded head. 'No. I swear I only search for someone. I mean no harm.'

The man's wrinkled mouth squirmed, but then he gave a hesitant nod.

'Me bones could use some rest,' he complained and stepped aside to let Azare take his place, the nugget quickly shoved into his pocket.

When Azare began to walk in the human's wake, he did not think his cargo weighed more than the baskets of feathers he carried as a boy. Yet again, Azare found himself wondering how the thaelil could have been defeated by the humans, so feeble they were.

'Tha best keep thyself as small as tha can when we reach tha gates,' the man advised.

Azare glowered at the hobbling elder's back, wondering if that would be this day or ten from now.

'Would thou like to ride with the grain, old man? We shall move faster.'

The human swivelled around in bewilderment.

'Tha mean that?'

Azare nodded. The man shrugged and scuttled past him to the back of the cart.

'Who am I to refuse?' he chuckled.

He clambered on with the sacks, his stumpy legs dangling over the edge. Azare set off again, barely feeling the cart's extra load. Silence prevailed as they crossed the dale at a good pace on thaelil-foot and wheels, until the man started to whistle. Amusement bloomed inside Azare at the sound of the shrill but jolly tune. Although the wordless melody springing from those craggy lips did give a liveliness to his stride, it was not as sweet as an iradi's song. The thought of Arhan and its birds, chanting amid the ancient trees of his birthwoods, darkened Azare's mood.

'Thou know many in the city?' he called over his shoulder.

The man abruptly ceased his chirping—he may have noticed the edge in Azare's voice. He replied amiably nonetheless.

'I may have a few friends. What of it?'

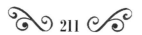 211

'What about a man called Inan? He had a daughter by the name of Rune. They have a house somewhere in the city.'

The old man was quiet. Azare glanced behind, but he could only see the human's back.

'Neva heard of 'em.'

Azare sighed. 'Thou need another nugget to remember?'

'Give me all the gold in Therea, an' those names shall still be strangers ta me.' The man added in a snide tone, 'Who're they to thee?'

Azare pursed his lips.

'This Rune thy lady? Tha going to steal her? Tha look the part, tha do.'

'There is no one to steal, old man,' Azare fired back. 'She is dead. She was murdered by the creatures I hunt, and they seek her former home in New Anvadore. Can thou help me find it or not?'

There was a timid pause before the elder replied, 'Aye, mayhap I can. Most of me friends are as old as I. They may be able to point thee the right way.'

'What are their names? And where do I find them?'

'Tha want to write this down? It be much to remember.'

'No. I have a good memory,' Azare said curtly.

'As tha wish. Who am I to judge a young lad's mind? Soon even me own name shall abandon me.'

Azare ground his teeth. *I am hundreds of years your senior, miserable ant.*

As the wall drew nearer, so did the queue of people seeking entry into the capital, a long procession of carriages and riders, farmers leading sheep and cattle, walkers lone or in groups. The irksome hubbub had already reached Azare's ears.

'The names, old man,' he demanded of the human, who was still babbling to himself.

'Alright, tha crank! No need to get upset with poor old Mell. Here be thy names. Alek Fell. He lives on Holden Street in the northwestern section of tha Ground District, tha twelfth house. Lorne Hithe has a shop in that district too...'

Azare walked and listened, creating a mental map of the information. Another flicker of hope appeared with each new name, until 'old Mell' stopped after the fifth. Azare hissed a curse. Five people. Five rotten humans were all he had to go on.

It was not long before they joined the end of the line shuffling into New Anvadore. His temper soured further still when Mell picked up his whistling again. It took every ounce of Azare's discipline to lower his head against the curious eyes, to keep walking, and not bull his way through the gates. *They are not your enemy. Not anymore.*

Chapter 24

'N o healer?' Meecha echoed in dismay.

'As I say,' the farmer sighed, 'they all gone to market in Anvadore, including the midwife. She may have helped thy hand, but…'

He continued to gape at the middle-aged woman. Her mane of greying black wire was held back from her thin face by a dull orange ribbon. The sun had kissed her cheeks and nose. She was dressed in a plain woollen dress of a brown that reminded Meecha of the leaves beneath that tree he had rested under. There was a white-pocketed apron around her waist smeared with grass and earth, drooping with the assortment of gardening tools it contained.

'Is there nothing you could offer me?' he pleaded, clutching his throbbing arm.

'I can break a fever or fix a cut, bu' that,' with disgust she pointed at the scarlet, pus-ridden tragedy that his forearm had become, 'is beyond my healing.'

He dropped his head, dejected. This was the last of fourteen houses that made up the nameless village. No matter how he smiled or tried to reason and beg with them he was shunned—awkward apologies, slamming doors, insults. The temptation of offering the compass in exchange for shelter was quelled in an instant. Such a treasure did not belong in the hands of some heartless human.

'Wait here,' the woman grumbled, and he smiled after her as she entered the house.

Meecha unconsciously held his breath, waiting for her to reappear with some kind of poultice or food. At least one of the villagers had been kind enough to give him a full water skin. Meecha had already drunk half of it. The woman emerged with something in her arms. It was clothes.

'Here. They were my son's,' she explained and handed them to Meecha.

A tattered grey shirt, brown breeches, and worn leather sandals—that was all she had to spare. *At least my corpse will be dressed*, Meecha thought bitterly, but gave the woman his thanks.

He stalked off down the road, wincing with every step his blistered feet took along the hard, rocky path. After a while, he approached the nearest tree and hid behind it. He stripped off his torn clothes and pulled on the new ones. He sat down to button up the shirt and strap on the sandals. Stretching his legs, he peered round at the road. Up and down he looked, but there was no sign of movement. So he clutched the water skin and got back to his feet. He skipped a little when he felt the blisters in his soles again. They throbbed and prickled, but the thin layer of leather between them and the earth was already offering some comfort. If only he had something to relieve his hunger as well. The nuts had all been devoured by the time the sun had turned the peach red of evening.

Bearing his wretchedness, Meecha trudged on alongside the road and dusk's now murky purple and orange radiance. The moons and stars were already watching from above. He kept glancing over his shoulder and at the vast grassland that surrounded him. If there was any danger, the darkness was hiding it. His fragile mental state was not helping either. Every effort his legs made sent warm pulses through his body—not a pleasant heat, but the uncomfortable feverish kind. He was certain that his festering arm was to blame, but there was nothing he could do. Nothing except keep walking. There was help to be found somewhere along the way. There had to be.

The night whispered by and so did Meecha, his steps soft and listless through the grass. It was blackened by the gloom yet it often twinkled with moonlight captured in its dew. The shimmering haze and the quiet had an enthralling effect on Meecha. They made his addled mind wander through times and worlds. He flew again upon the backs of giant dragonflies in the wilds of Ornaka. His lungs breathed the blue waters of Vadeira, where the mer-people had granted him gills and fins to traverse their oceanic kingdom. His nose recalled the stench of industry in machine-riddled Conzor. He still had difficulty understanding the laws of physics that made up Jeaji, the world where time and everything it encompassed moved backwards. He revisited all the souls he had rescued from ruin, all the moments of triumph when failure and death had been a certainty. Oparu immediately came to mind, its flamboyant America racing to the rhythm of jazz, a chapter in Meecha's life marked by both splendour and sorrow. He unconsciously tried to touch his hat, but it was not there. Tears filled his eyes. It made him sadder still to think that, after all those victories, he might fail the aerieti on the greatest mission of them all.

His thoughts returned home, to his family. If they knew where he was, if they knew he was in danger, would any of them come to his rescue? Or would they, like Jaika, think that he should face the consequences of his choices alone? Their ungratefulness infuriated Meecha, but then he remembered once again that they did not know. They would never know that the most disgraceful of Roas, their son and brother, was in fact a hero. And a soon-to-be martyr.

He removed the stopper from the water skin and took a swig. There was not much left. He would have to make it last, despite his terrible thirst. His fever sucked in seconds every drop he consumed, leaving him feeling dryer that before. Meecha plugged the skin and returned his attention to the horizon. The tips of trees were like black arrowheads poking at the starry, bruise-blue sky. One foot ahead of the other, through chill and dirt and jagged rocks, he followed the road. If he did not, he would surely lose his way to wander in an aimless stupor until, if not an animal or a blade, his ailment took him. He felt it in his swollen arm, the sickened blood flowing through and into the rest of his body. The pain would not cease no matter what Meecha did. At first it had felt as if burning foam was building up in his hand, gradually spreading and numbing its way to his shoulder. Now the pulsing foam was threatening to burst through his skin, rendering even the slightest motion of his fingers a torment.

His legs carried him of their own accord. He did not know how much time had passed before he reached the first of the trees. It was still dark and eerily hushed, but he thought nothing of it. There was no emotion left in him — no apprehension, no anger, no melancholy, only a blank longing for the grave. As he passed by the copse a breeze picked up. It crept under his clothing. He hunched in a frail attempt to hide from the ethereal fingers tickling his skin. They tugged at his breeches and sleeves as if urging him to turn to the trees, but he shrugged them off. So they pushed harder, until he surrendered to his need for shelter.

Meecha trotted into the grove, looking right and left, from canopy to floor. Branches clacked against each other like chattering teeth. The leaves made a good effort of keeping all celestial light out of their dwelling. The wind was even more unwelcome. Try as it might, only a faint draught touched Meecha now. He heaved a sigh and, when deep enough, plopped himself onto the ground. He cradled his arm and rocked gently from side to side. Closing his eyes, he took a shaky breath, held it, released it, and a flood of tears followed. It was not the fear of death that made him weep. It was not the loss of his hat or the pain in his hand. It was the helplessness, the feeling that he had proven all his slanderers right. He was too small for these big affairs. He was ill-suited for the mission, and what little worth the ghost lady had seen in him was false. All he had accomplished was to get himself lost and killed by a measly infection. He was no hero. Jaika was right — he was nothing but a miscreant, a good-for-nothing Roa.

He doubled over and lay in the soft grass. Perhaps, if his hat had still been with him, things would have happened differently. But did he deserve the hat? It was supposed to protect his soul, but his soul had already been marred before Oparu. He had been sent there to guide one more Ward to his destiny. Curiosity and his failing attempts to help this troubled human had led Meecha from bar to bar drinking spirits and listening to jazz. As usual, his size would draw fascinated—often mocking—glances, but he had soon found a friend in a wizened fellow, dark of skin and sharp of mind. His deep, god-like voice still reverberated in Meecha's memories. The man had told him all about that part of Oparu called the United States of America and the war that had recently shaken the world. Then the wise man had removed his hat and given it to Meecha.

'To shelter your soul,' he had said in a secretive manner.

The Ward had, eventually, found his way—five days before the old man was brutally murdered.

Dry leaves crackled nearby. Meecha's eyelids quivered. He peered through the slits. A huge black figure loomed over him, blotting out what little light there was. Gleaming eyes of white gold stared down at him. The last thing he felt before losing consciousness were jaws clamping shut around his shoulder.

Chapter 25

'Stop with the hissing,' Koro snapped as he and Naya approached the inn.

She snarled back, 'My head burns.'

The beacon of New Anvadore stood vigilant upon the lip of the cliff that dissected the city into the northeastern and southwestern halves. The latter, the district below the crag, was where the commoners resided, while the rich and significant lived in the city's high section. That was also where the castle was, a mighty monstrosity allegedly constructed by the brightest architectural minds in Therea. Rumour had it that one of them was personally invited by the king to oversee the construction of the beacon. Where this man had acquired the knowledge to create such a contraption was a frustrating mystery to the xalikai, for it supposedly had the ability to ward off demons. And it appeared to be working, judging by the reaction Naya had the moment she crossed the city's boundaries.

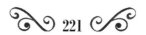 221

According to her, the gold and white light encased within the lantern-like device fixed to the top of the giant white column towering higher than the castle itself had grown brighter in her eyes, searing them. Even when she did not look at it, it pounded her head like a gong. It caused her concentration to slip, and Koro often saw the red snake eyes break through Naya's green. He wondered how much more she could bear before her xalikai form broke through the human.

'Focus an' keep thy head low. Try to behave normal.'

Koro entered the Watery Grave, a name partly inspired by the water duct trickling past its front door. They were assaulted by a boisterous din of people and cutlery. A pair of musicians in a corner played the lute and flute, adding to the cacophony. Naya's face was downturned, but Koro could still make out her scowl. He headed for the bar. From behind it, a tall strapping fellow was chatting to a customer clutching a large tankard. The bartender broke off when he saw Koro approach—and he eyed Naya curiously.

'What can I get you, friends?' The skin-drawings on his muscular arms writhed when he leant against the bar. He seemed amiable enough.

'We seek information about someone who used to live here,' Koro began.

'Name?'

'Inan. His family name is unknown to us, bu' he had a daughter, Rune.'

Both the bartender and the snooping customer wrinkled their noses.

'Never heard of 'em,' the stout man replied. The customer shook his head. 'But there's someone who may have known them.'

Koro allowed himself a smile, 'Who is he?'

The bartender hesitated, raising an eyebrow. 'I'd tell thee, if I liked thee.'

Koro's teeth clenched. 'Please, friend, thou've nought to fear from us. Information is all we seek.'

'Thy companion seems to have other plans.'

Koro glanced at Naya and beheld the murderous glare she had fixed on the bartender. He could almost hear her violent thoughts. He licked his lips as he turned back to the bar. 'How much is it worth to thee?'

The bartender straightened and folded his brawny arms. 'More than thou can afford.'

The customer seemed ready to leap from his stool at the slightest hint of violence, his fearful eyes darting from one man to the other, avoiding Naya entirely. Koro retreated, if only to avoid a massacre. They would have to track this lead another way.

With all haste they left the inn, but as soon as they stepped outside Naya gasped and cupped her ears. She snarled and panted like an animal. Koro dragged her into an alley. She thudded against the shadowy wall and started punching and tearing at it. She clawed at her scalp.

'Damn thee. Control thyself,' Koro groaned, looking up and down the street.

She ignored him, her hands and head bloodied from the frenzy. He was surprised and somewhat relieved that she was at least keeping her screams to herself.

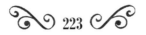

'Hey!' a hushed voice called.

Someone slunk towards them from the inn. Koro stuck his head into the alley. 'Someone comes. Be quiet.'

He turned to greet the stranger, who looked over his shoulder as he drew near, a hunched, shabby, middle-aged rascal. Koro knew why he had come even before the man uttered it.

'I...eh... heard thy words with Jackal. I can help thee. For a price.'

'Thou'll get thy fortune, my good man. What thou have for me?'

The stranger leant in and said, 'Nandil Hithe. He used to work in his grandfather's shop down here, bu' he made friends an' got himself a nice place with the nobility. He lives in the Sky District, over his new shop, Hithe's Fineries. He knows everyone in the city.'

'We're most grateful,' Koro responded with a courteous nod.

The man's leer wavered. 'Where's my money?'

'Thy fortune is right here.' Koro stepped back from the entrance to the alley and gestured towards it.

The man took his place, squinting into the darkness. He only had time to mumble a quizzical, 'What...' before Naya's black talons sprung out of the shadows to envelop his head. His terrified cry went unheard as he was snatched into hell's jaws.

Chapter 26

A sponge. It felt like a sponge. It sucked at his forearm, wet and coarse, and it stung. His fingers twitched with every twinge of pain. There was also a sense of heat coming from the slimy substance the sponge was leaving behind. It was almost soothing. Meecha swallowed and winced when his parched throat scratched him awake. He licked his cracked lips before remembering his waterskin. It still contained a few fingers of water. He opened his eyes to meet the sun's rays winking through the leaves above. He moved and tried to take his sticky arm with him, when something heavy pushed against his chest and forearm, pinning him back down.

He squirmed, but the weight only got greater. He was about to lift his head to see what had immobilised him, when a large object landed on his face. Meecha groaned into the soft leathery thing smothering him. His left hand grasped the furry... arm? He attempted to pull it off, but it would not budge. Instead, it gave him a firm shove into the ground. He struggled and kicked and moaned, until a series of sharp objects pressed into his right forearm. He stilled himself mid-punch. The sponge started to soak his forearm again. It lathered it with layers and layers of the substance. He could do nothing but huff and puff into the leather of his confinement. Fur tickled his face, and he had an excruciating urge to scratch it. Then, as suddenly as it had appeared, the weight was lifted, the thing on his face gone.

He bolted upright to face his assailant and froze, eyes and mouth wide with shock, when he beheld the grand form of the chantress sitting like a sphinx beside him. Her intelligent eyes bore into his skull. Meecha gulped and crawled backwards. His movement was slow and rigid as he warily retreated from the creature until he was stopped by the trunk of a tree. The chantress turned her head with indifference and sniffed the air. He stiffened when she stood, but all she did was approach another tree to stare past it with unnerving intensity. She seemed to be watching something. When he heard a horse whicker nearby, the reason for her hungry look was made clear. Why was *he* still alive and not in her belly?

He spotted the waterskin. He scrambled to his left, occasionally glancing towards the chantress—she still did not care about him. As soon as he reached the skin, he unplugged it and greedily downed the last of the water. It was far from enough to quench his thirst, but it soothed his throat. When his eyes fell on the empty vessel, he noticed his wounded arm.

It was not swollen. It did not hurt anymore, and the redness had gone down. He dropped the skin to inspect the gash. He was astounded to find it partially healed. Through the slimy substance it was covered in he could make out a thin scab. He flexed his fingers and then his whole arm, unhindered, and smiled broadly. He then realised that the substance was no mystery at all—it was saliva.

He looked up at the chantress, who had abandoned her longing for horse meat and was now sitting on her haunches staring at him. Her tongue dripped as it lolled from her open mouth. She panted heavily. It suddenly dawned on Meecha how tormenting the warm climate was for her. Her thick white coat was designed for the icy mountains of her homeland. He glanced down at the waterskin and a pang of guilt struck him. She had saved him and he had not spared a drop of water to help her in return.

'I'm sorry.'

The chantress lowered herself to the floor, crossed her front paws and rested her head upon them. Meecha took that as a gesture of disappointment. Shame washed over him. He had to make it up to her. There had to be another source of water somewhere nearby. Or food. That would surely cheer her up.

Looking at the sky through the treetops, he decided it was around midday. At sundown it would be cool enough for her to travel in the open. He resented the idea of wasting more precious time, but he could not leave her. What was his worth as an agent, as a person, if he abandoned those he was fighting for when they needed him most?

A branch quivered overhead. The chantress's head jerked up. Her pupils were dilated. She positioned herself, ready to jump. A branch moved again, and in that same moment she sprung up, her paws reaching past the branch, proof of her sheer length. She batted the leaves in pursuit of her prey before she decided to take the whole thing down. Meecha recoiled when the branch snapped free of the tree. Wood and leaves and animals came crashing to the floor. Squeaks could be heard between the chantress's frustrated roars. She darted and pounced and swivelled all over, until, finally, the inevitable happened. By the time the dust had settled, she was sitting again with paws crossed and licking her bloody chops, satisfaction drifting her eyes shut.

Meecha hoped that morsel would be enough to keep her teeth from sinking into him. With luck, another would come along before she became desperate. He too would need to find food of his own. He felt around his stomach and was horrified by the ease with which he could trace his ribcage. He stood slowly under the calm gaze of the chantress. His legs were shaky and his mind quite feeble, but he warily passed her by, until her claws emerged. He paused, but then realised that she was only stretching. She spread her front legs wide and gave a big yawn before flopping onto her side and shutting her eyes.

Meecha watched her smack her tongue lazily, while he strolled towards the edge of the copse. He stopped and looked out over the sunlit plain, the road a fair distance to the right. He sat on a comfortable spot on the ground and crossed his legs. He plucked a shoot of grass and chewed on it. The bitter taste mattered little, for his hunger was too great to care about flavour. He continued gnawing on grass as he watched time go by. He slept and daydreamed and grazed the noon away, always wondering if Delia had survived too. Surely she had.

Evening arrived, and the drop in temperature was noticeable. A cloud had covered the sun when Meecha got back to his feet. He heard movement from the trees behind him and turned to find the chantress loping towards him. It seemed that, not only did she have the same plan of travel, but she was also headed in the same direction. She passed him by without so much as a glance. He tapped the compass in his pocket and tightened his grip on the waterskin's neck before leaving the copse to resume the long journey to New Anvadore.

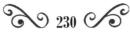

Chapter 27

'Hithe's Fineries,' Azare read under his breath.

The large building across the street was made of stone and red tile, while a rosewood sign written upon with an elegant hand hung over the front door, a slab of sturdy, finely carved oak. From the shadows of the grove the thaelil watched the humans bustle in and out of the shop; too many of them. Ladies favoured the establishment the most, strutting in gowns of the sweetest pink or peach to a black blacker than the abyss yet bedecked with diamonds and emeralds. But lords in silks and flowing capes honoured it with their presence too. The lane itself was busy with a steady flow of people, nobles and commoners alike, man-drawn carts, soldiers in heavy plate armour patrolling the streets in twos and threes. He noticed bands of white and blue-robed figures rush past, eyeing everyone in their path. Fortunately, none of them appeared to notice Azare kneeling among the trees. If he ventured

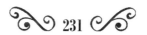

into the open, however, someone could get curious enough to guess his identity. He would have to wait until nightfall and try to get Hithe alone.

An almost pointless two-day affair it turned out to be, tracking down all the names given by the old man, Mell. The human had smuggled Azare through the gates under the pretence that he was his new helping hand from the Mountains of Qee, where its people lived within caverns due to their sensitivity to the sun. The explanation seemed to satisfy the guards' suspicion over Azare's hooded garb. Luckily, they already knew Mell by name and let him pass with a friendly pat on the back. The thaelil escorted him to his destination before thanking him with another gold nugget and kicking off his search for the man's elderly friends.

Naphe Crage, Alek Fell, and Evin Trand had all died — the first and the last in their beds. Master Fell managed to make a joke of himself when he fell into a cauldron of his favourite spiced wine and drowned. The fourth on the list was Lorne Hithe, but when Azare visited the place where his first shop used to be he found it barred and barren. Rori Bayben, the final name, was an old female rocking in her chair and rambling incoherently at the wall. Fortunately, her granddaughter was more than eager to answer his questions, once he made use of the realisation that the bubbly woman was blushing for him. It was she who informed him of Hithe's own grandchild's rise in standing and where his new shop could be found.

And there he was, squatting in the shadows of human aristocracy. He had to admit that he found himself impressed by New Anvadore's opulence, despite the dirt and smells. For one thing, the presence of the grove and the rays of water ducts spread throughout the city showed that humans were not as indifferent to nature as he once thought. The most extraordinary element of the capital, however, was its so-called Beacon. The moment he set foot in New Anvadore, Azare could sense the powerful magic emanating from the structure. When his search brought him to the edge of the city, he put a hand on the stone of the First Ring, the curtain walls encasing the entire city, and could feel an arcane pulse. It was in the water too.

At the base of the cliff, directly beneath the Beacon, was a vast flagstoned square. A well built into the rock face received the frothing waters of a waterfall springing from beneath the grand column. The water ducts of the Ground District originated from this well. Azare had looked into its waters and was amazed at how clear and pure they were. He saw people drinking from it with vessels of silver, brass, and gold chained to the well's marble exterior. None, he had realised, were using their hands. He took the vessel closest to him, a simple brass bowl, and scooped some water into it. Before he even brought it to his lips he could smell its crisp freshness. He drank solemnly, remembering the rivers of Arhan. And the lake. Just as in them, there was magic in the waters of New Anvadore. That pure, white magic was perhaps what kept it clean and safe from stagnation.

A suspicion grew in him while he sat beneath the trees, thinking. Water symbolised purity and goodness. Its spirits, although mischievous, were known to aid good causes when called upon. And Therea's history was marred by demonic hands. It could be that the king had had the common sense to prepare for the possibility of a second infiltration. If this was the case, and the city was somehow warded against demons, would that not have deterred his prey from entering? Perhaps only the human of the two had dared the venture.

Dusk found the street illuminated by lanterns and much less crowded. There could be no further delay. Azare stepped out of the trees. He approached the entrance and walked in reluctantly, allowing the door to close behind him. The shop had a pleasant air about it. The walls were panelled rosewood. Cream-coloured silks hung from corner to corner of the ceiling, and a candle chandelier dangled over the middle of the large room, its flames giving it a warm, golden luminescence. On his immediate left were wooden figures of women, like dolls, in dresses, hats, gloves, and shoes. Behind them the wall was mounted with rolls of fabrics. On the other side of the room were dolls of men clad in trousers, breeches, shirts, cloaks, and so many other strange things. Further along on either side were cabinets and shelves filled with all sorts of odds and ends. Most of them looked decorative: little figurines of animals and people, intricately shaped pieces of art made of metal or marble or crystal, pictures and embroideries of scenes—hunts, battles, dancers, fishermen. There were vases and plates and tea sets and toys. One peculiarity after another caught Azare's eye.

He reached the back of the room, where more cabinets stood filled with jewels, necklaces ranging from the simplest pendant to spider webs spun from gold and gems, rings with stones the size of his sword's pommel. Some of the earrings resembled the chandelier, and even the combs and hair ornaments were things of extravagant beauty. Brooches, little daggers, and belt buckles were available for the male customer, although his attention was most likely to be drawn to the weapons on display on the walls: swords of every type, axes, maces, bows, and shields. Azare wondered where Hithe acquired all his stock.

A door creaked open behind the jewellery case, and a man emerged. He was clean-shaven. His black curls were gathered back from his face, barely lined by maturity and toil. A burgundy waistcoat covered his white buttoned-up shirt. A pair of shiny, dark leather boots over cotton trousers of a red darker than the waistcoat completed his smart outfit.

'Master Hithe?'

The human's black smiling eyes greeted Azare.

'Nandil Hithe, here to please. Welcome, stranger, to my house of wonders. What can I help thee with this splendid evening?'

He was too nice. Azare hesitated. 'I... seek a name and a house that goes with it.'

'Oh?' Hithe raised an eyebrow. 'Who do thou seek? I know many names.'

'Inan Iridan.'

'Inan! 'Tis an age since I last saw that miserable face.'

'So thou knew him?'

'Yes, I knew him—Hold! What thou mean 'knew'? He's not gotten himself killed, has he?'

'I do not know. He has disappeared.'

The storekeeper shrugged. 'Inan disappears all the time. A common thing in his line of work. An' he's damn good at it. He gets the job done, Inan does. Abyss, he provided my grandpapa with half his goods.'

'Thou know where he lived?'

'Aye, I do.' Hithe leant over the cabinet. 'But what interest does an elf have in a master thief?'

Azare took a step back, ready to reach for his swords. The killing of a single man, however, could mark the end of his quest and his life.

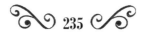

'Thou not the first pointy-ears to come sulking through my shop. Thy kind is pretty easy to spot, if thou know what to look for.'

'All I want is directions to Inan's house. Not trouble.'

'I believe thee. But, if thou're discovered, trouble shall find thee whether thou want it or not. An' if I help thee, that trouble may reach me. I need a very good reason to risk my reputation for thee.'

Azare worked his jaw. This human was his last chance. He had to play along.

'I understand,' he grudgingly admitted. 'I shall explain as best I can.'

Hithe locked the entrance. He returned and gestured towards the door behind the cabinet. 'Please, come.'

Azare followed him into the back room, which turned out to be an office with a staircase leading to the building's upper levels. Hithe offered him a seat at a table, picked up two tall-stemmed glasses from a shelf, and filled them with the red spirit the humans called 'wine'. He handed Azare a glass, who accepted it with a grimace. He glared into the red liquid, sniffed it. Its aroma was sweet and fruity. Hithe watched him with a fascinated expression. Azare finally took a sip and was taken aback by the flavours that invaded his tongue. It was sweet but slightly dry, and he thought he recognised a faint haze of blackberry in the concoction.

'Not bad, ha?' the irritating man said.

Azare responded with a vague bob of his head and put the glass aside.

'I'd feel a lot more comfortable if I could see thy face.'

His demands were picking at Azare's patience, but he obliged the human once more by pulling down his hood.

He smirked when he saw the storekeeper squirm at the sight of his marks, a series of small inverted arrow shapes – twenty and seven of them – starting from the edge of his hairline and running in a straight line to the tip his nose.

'A hunter.' Hithe nearly choked on a mouthful of wine.

Azare said nothing.

'Thou on a trail?'

'I am.'

The man inhaled sharply and swallowed the rest of his wine, wincing.

'A demon? Here?'

'I followed it from Crove. It travels with a human. They are after something that used to be in Inan's possession.'

Hithe stood to refill his glass. He drank half of it as soon as it was poured and then chuckled.

'That would explain the priests. Riling for days.'

'Priests?'

'Yes. 'Divine Architects' is the most accurate term— masons with magic tricks devoted to something called the Light. They designed the whole of New Anvadore before it was even built. Thou can't miss 'em. They swarm the streets as we speak. But if what thou say is true an' the priests are searching for a demon in our midst, then whatever you're all searching for must be damned important for the creature to dare enter the city.'

'This is why it is so urgent that I find Inan's house first.' Azare's clipped words put the human further on edge. 'He may have left clues as to where this object may be.'

'Thou know what it is?'

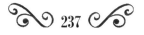

'All I know is that it looks like a claw made of amber. It is said that Inan was wearing it as a medallion the last time he came to New Anvadore. Look, Master Hithe, I have told thee all I can. Thou must see how urgent it is that I find this house.'

'Absolutely! In fact, I'll take thee myself.'

'That is not necessary,' Azare growled.

'I think it is. Thou came to me, so the demon may not be far behind. The way I see it, I shall be safer with thee. An' I know more about Inan than thee.'

Azare grunted and yanked his hood over his head. He rose to his feet. 'Shall we?'

'Let me get my coat,' Hithe said.

He did so before knocking back Azare's barely touched wine and pocketing the keys to the shop. As they made for the front door, he spoke again, sounding a bit light-headed.

'Please, call me Nandil. How rude of me! I didn' catch thy name.'

Azare mumbled, 'I did not give it.'

Chapter 28

They made a new friend. Whoever said that clouds were a bad omen had not met Meecha's cloud. It resembled the fluffy white frosting on a cake, but the sun trying to burn through it made it glow yellow. So far it had proven resilient to the assailing rays, and for the past two days had shielded him and the chantress. The shade made it easier to travel during the day, but the warmth seeping into the air and earth stalled them numerous times. The cloud was kind enough to provide them with a few drops of rain. They sat under it with mouths wide and tongues wiggling like pink slugs. Meecha had held out the waterskin as well, but it only accumulated perhaps a finger of water at a time. As soon as there was enough to make the slightest impact, he poured it into a hollowed rock he found and left it for the chantress.

Even though they had grown almost accustomed to each other's presence, they kept their distance. Whether

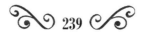

following, leading, or walking abreast, there was always a sizeable space between them. Once, he broke into an empty cottage and came out with a string of sausages, along with a loaf of stale bread and the waterskin freshly filled from a nearby well. He had to nibble on the bread and wait until he could cook his sausages, while she demolished hers on foot. But his gift of food clearly made an impression on her. When he finally gathered enough twigs to light a fire, he stopped to make his dinner, expecting her to keep going and leave him behind. He was touched, however, when she came and sat by the campfire—at a reasonable distance, of course, and after lengthy deliberation.

That night Meecha decided to find a name for his stoic companion. He shuffled options in his mind, resolving that only a godly name would do. He scoured his mythological knowledge of civilisations old and great that he had encountered in his travels. Mahath came to mind, the queen of the cat people in Ornaka, but he quickly dismissed her. A fierce, neurotic creature she was, who loved being pampered and adding to her mounds of jewels. The White Flower, Sacnite, was too sweet. And he had never liked the sound of Kirina, the war goddess of the Ba'shi, beings as harsh and unforgiving as the ice their citadels were built from. One by one he discarded them, petals from a flower, until only two remained: Freya, the mighty and beautiful goddess of the Vikings, and Chione, the Grecian nymph of the snow. Meecha could not decide which he liked best, so he put them to the test. He uttered them both—whichever the chantress responded to would be her new name.

On the first attempt, she did not even twitch an ear to either of them. He tried a second time with the same result. He persisted. 'Chione,' he called and then 'Freya!' Over and over he spoke them, until she finally moved, lifting her head to fix him with a flat, searching look. He pressed his mouth shut. Chione! Her name was Chione. For the rest of the journey Meecha tried to introduce her to the principle of name-calling by gesturing to his self and then her, while speaking their respective names. The activity did not last long, for they were soon standing on a rise, staring at the walls of New Anvadore.

'I made it,' he gasped in disbelief. He whooped and punched the air triumphantly. 'I made it!'

He gawked at the massive fortification looming black over the procession of people and caravans, their lanterns flickering before the gates. Under the light of numerous torches, he could make out four armed guards attending to a man driving a horse-drawn cage containing a bear-like creature. In the column behind him there were a few more imprisoned or chained animals: a large striped cat, a primate, an assortment of exotic birds, a rather large red lizard... Chione would fit right in.

He looked at her. 'Are you really going in there?'

She did not reply, but her sharp gaze was trained on the gates. Could it be that she followed her cub all this way? How did she know where to look? It may be that she had an uncanny sense of smell or that... *White chanters formed telepathic bonds with their children?* Whatever the explanation, it seemed Chione would storm those gates if she had to. She suddenly turned her golden eyes to Meecha. They lingered on his face for a moment, blinking once, before she loped off towards the procession.

'What're you doing?' he yelped when he realised where she was going.

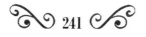

He ran after her, hoping to stop her, but the horses and other animals had already caught her scent and were getting rattled. The humans too became alarmed, even drew weapons. Chione ignored them all.

'She won't hurt you,' Meecha shouted to them, begging his luck for it to be true. 'She's harmless!'

The chantress angled towards the end of the line and halted behind a cart. When Meecha arrived, scarlet and breathless, he found two humans—*father and son?*—frozen in fear and staring at the panting cat, who quietly laid herself on the ground.

'Do forgive her,' Meecha pleaded through intakes of air. 'She forgets the effect she has on people.' The father gave him a perplexed look, and Meecha smiled innocently. 'Would you have a bowl by any chance?'

He received brisk nods from both humans. The boy handed him a tin saucer.

'Thank you.' Meecha placed it gently before Chione and filled it with water from the skin.

The chantress drank heartily, and so did he. When he lowered the skin from his mouth, he noticed the tiniest crack of a smile forming on the boy's lips. His father was still frowning at them with uncertainty.

'Is she for the festival?' the boy asked softly.

Meecha stared at him, the wheels of his brain working up an answer. 'Yes,' he chose to say. 'Are you?'

The boy giggled. 'No. I know no tricks. We sell fruit.' He pointed at the covered crates in the cart beside him. 'Does she do tricks?'

Meecha eyed Chione. She was staring aimlessly at the trees on the right side of the road.

'There's no better trickster in the whole realm,' he replied with a grand flourish.

'She dangerous?'

'Oh, yes!'

The child's smile vanished.

'You should never try to touch her,' Meecha said, his voice low and grave. 'She'll pounce on you.' The boy's unblinking stare was on him and his hands turning into claws gripping a little skull. 'She'll take your head in her paws.' He allowed the silence to stretch a little longer and then roared, 'And kiss you to death!'

The boy jumped and shrieked with laughter, drawing an amused look from his father. Chione turned at the noise and cocked her head curiously. The adorable sight caused the child to hoot even louder, which in turn made her yowl. Meecha and the father started to laugh as well, while the boy doubled over, clutching his belly. Their mirth grew in volume and turned some heads. Meecha thought it might just be possible to earn Chione a few more admirers and sweeten her way through the gates.

...

For the third time, his sleeve rubbed the brooch. He did not even look. Koro was laying out the plan and each of their roles, while the other human pretended to listen. *Arrogant slug.* She wanted to kill it. Crush it. Tear the meat from its bones. Koro's too. Paint the house with their blood. Paint the city. *Filthy, weak humans.* She hissed at the newcomer, who jumped at the sound. He had not sensed her standing in the shadowed corner of the room, watching them. His regal posture slumped into a cower as he beheld her true form. Koro smirked.

'Be calm,' he said. 'We're all on the same side.'

She convulsed in agony, the Beacon thrashing her mind to madness. She shook wildly, clenched her jaw in an effort to settle her body, but it would not obey. The only thing that seemed to work was surrendering to her rage, embracing her berserk nature. But she could not do that either. It would ruin everything.

'We need blood,' Koro informed her and picked up the small jar he had brought back from Hithe's store—the man had not been there.

In her native tongue, she demanded the reason. She was sick of their ways and games.

He responded in broken demon, 'We've a chance at the royals. The masters shall be pleased.'

'It is perfect,' the grovelling slug inserted in Therean. 'I knew not what I was looking at then, but we have another chance now, Naya. Give thy blood. We must hurry.'

Her rage burst. 'Thou dare make demands of me? Filth! Naya is no more. Thou speak to a Crantil slayer. I do not bow. I do not fear. I slaughter. Thou and all unworthy of my sight!'

Both humans recoiled, even reached for their swords. What could they do against her? Soft flesh hefting tooth-picks against pure Crantil fury. They would fall. *They all will.* Every one of these squeaking balls of slime. *In time. In time.* She had slunk and waited for so long. *Our time will come again.*

She stretched out her arm and put a claw to her wrist,

while Koro lunged for the jar in time to catch the first drops of blood. She glared into his downturned face, vowing to rip it off him when this business was all done. When the true sides were revealed.

A scent snapped her nose towards the shuttered window overlooking a dark alley. Thaelil.

Chapter 29

The echoes of their footfalls rebounded off the alley's sides. These walls belonged to houses long abandoned, left to crumble in everlasting shadow. The slums were cornered between the cliff and the First Ring, so the sun rarely saw them. There were faces in the windows. People or ghosts; Azare did not care to know. The houses' doors barely clung to their hinges. He could see figures walking about behind them against dim candlelight. A clowder of cats watched him from the rooftops as he passed by.

'We're almost there,' Nandil whispered over his shoulder.

Azare followed in silence, understanding the human's compulsion to speak in hushed tones. It felt as if they were walking through a graveyard, detached from the merriments that had begun in the main square.

'Ah! This is it.' Nandil approached one of many identical rundown buildings.

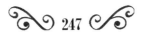

They stepped through the doorway, the door itself gone. Only a straw mat before a tiny fireplace and a small square dining table lying on its side were left to show that this was once a sitting room, perhaps attached to a kitchen. All other furniture had been taken. Nandil noticed Azare's troubled expression.

'Inan tried very hard to provide for his kin. When he saw that legal ways weren't paying off, he turned thief and mercenary. The coin's not bad, as long as thou have the stomach for it.'

Hithe turned his attention to two doors. He went for the one on the left, while Azare tried the other. A small room was revealed to him. A child-sized straw bed was all he could discern in the blackness. A light appeared behind him. Nandil walked in with a lit candle in hand.

'This should make things easier,' the human stated, while Azare gazed around the bare bedroom.

There were drawings on the wall beside the bed. When Nandil brought the candle closer, the charcoal stick figures of a woman, man, and girl came into view. They were surrounded by the outline of a castle and flanked by trees. Rune was ambitious. Azare could not blame her after seeing this place. It must have been hard growing up in the blind side of New Anvadore.

'I remember her,' Nandil said softly. 'Quiet girl. Clever. Whip of a tongue, though.'

Azare pulled away from the wall. 'Thou find anything?'

'Eh... no. His bedroom's been cleared as well. But...' Nandil scanned the walls and the corners, the floor and the ceiling, and stopped to add, 'If there's anywhere he'd stash something, it would be in here. Hold this.'

He passed the candle to Azare and reached up to the ceiling. He brushed a stone with his fingers—it had a cluster of tiny holes in it. He nudged it and found it loose. He tried to pry it out, but it was held in place. He pushed instead and it complied. Up a few inches into the ceiling it went, until there came a *click*. And the brick dropped into his palm.

'How thou know?' Azare demanded, and the man shrugged.

'He came into grandpapa's old shop one day with Rune an' I remember him telling her... How did he say it? We're all specks of dust an' it's up to us to find a wind to help us fly—or something of the sort. These holes reminded me of that. It was a guess, in truth.'

The brick was hollow; a piece of parchment was rolled up inside it. Azare snatched it from its nest and sat on the bed to read in the candle's light.

'What does it say?' Nandil asked excitedly.

'Pixie,' Azare began. 'I wrote this in the desperate hope that thou would return one day. Thou've suffered enough for my mistakes, but if thou seek our secret, go to the city's first rock, and thou'll find thy next step. I can say no more, in case other eyes read this before thee. I hope thou built thy palace, little one. Thou're always in my heart and my thoughts. Ride the wind.'

The old, dry paper crunched in Azare's fist.

Nandil was pensive. 'The claw object the demon is searching for—it could be this secret, yes? But what in the abyss is the city's first rock?'

Azare composed himself. 'Whether it is a riddle or the true first rock the city was built upon, the Architects are the ones to ask.'

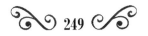

Disdain pinched the human's face, but he nodded. Azare held the parchment over the flame of the candle.

'Wait, what if Rune comes back?' Nandil exclaimed.

Azare watched it catch fire, the yellowish paper turning into black soot as the scarlet dancers consumed it and its message. He let it drop to the floor, where it scattered before it even touched the stone.

'She shall not.'

'Thou sound certain of that.'

Ignoring Nandil's suspicious words and frown, Azare put out the candle, placed it on the floor, and left the bed. He strode out of the house with the human in his wake; Nandil stopped short of coming abreast with him. Azare could feel his tension.

'Where is the Architects' temple?' he asked and glanced over his shoulder to meet Nandil's sharpened stare.

The human replied flatly. 'In the grove around the Beacon.'

They reached the eastern end of the alley where it met with the cliff. They turned left through a narrow passage and headed for the bright lights. On their way to Inan's house they had found stalls and tents being erected in rows throughout the square. It had already accommodated at least thirty visitors with enough space to fit hundreds more. Nandil had explained that it was the eve of the cyclic Market Festival, a ten-day celebration of the Therean Empire's abundant beauty. Merchants and farmers came from all across the realm to display their goods.

The smells of cook-fires—roasting meat, wood smoke— reached them when they stepped into the busy square once again. Some more merchants had arrived and were taking up places in the rows being formed around the well. They were doing their best to make the lines neat and spacious enough for people to walk comfortably between stalls, but it was all still shabby. No stock was being put out yet for fear of theft. Azare glared at the imprisoned animals on display—a gaaz was being carted in, its hairy mass barely fitting its cage. Children and women flocked around the creatures to point and shout and laugh at them as they prowled or cowered in their coops. There were groups of robed priests walking through the throngs as well, but they appeared more interested in people's faces than the festival.

Azare hunched as he and Nandil crossed the square, swerving around stalls and citizens on their way towards a road sloping up to the Sky District, the well not far to its left.

'Master Hithe.'

The human halted mid-stride to address the grinning elder ambling in their direction.

'Master Zill,' Nandil smiled broadly, but there was nothing friendly about this encounter.

'I thought I'd find thee here, remembering thy roots,' the other human said pointedly.

Nandil lifted an eyebrow, 'Looking for me, were thee? An' still trying to match the Hithe shadow? How's that going?'

He stalked off, leaving this Zill to grind his teeth. Azare caught up and received the explanation he did not ask for.

'That spineless swindler,' Nandil spat. 'He's always envied our success, even before I moved the shop. He an' grandpapa used to barter on the same street, see. He blamed him an' now me for his own incompetence. He simply doesn't possess the social gifts needed to thrive as an Anvadorian merchant. Success comes from what an' *who* thou know."

They had not taken five steps before another voice called, 'Nandil!'

Azare rounded on him. 'Thy social gifts are not wanted now.'

A young female crashed into the merchant's arms, her dress tattered, her black hair tangled, her too-big shoes full of holes.

'Delia?' Nandil exclaimed, holding the breathless child tightly. 'Thou're frozen. Where thou been? Thou smell, lass.' He pushed her off him, wrinkling his nose, yet kept hold of her shoulders.

Her fearful eyes flitted behind her, darting this way and that.

'Soldiers have been out looking for thee. What happened?'

She heaved little breaths. Azare followed her line of sight, but saw nothing noteworthy. Nandil gave her a gentle shake.

'What's the matter?' He glowered at the bruises and scratches on her face and arms. His voice grew tender, truly concerned. 'Who hurt thee?'

She nodded and muttered, teeth chattering, 'They tried to.' Nandil tested her clammy forehead and frowned deeper, while she stammered on, 'Taken. I—I was taken to Crove. We were rescued.' Tears burst from her eyes. 'Meecha. We fell. I think he—he drowned.'

Hithe embraced her again and rocked her like a baby. 'I heard Crove kept some of the men gone searching. But thou've returned. Thy friend might appear too. Don't fret.'

He hailed two guards patrolling the square. Azare hunched beneath his hood and turned his back to them. As they approached, lazy and annoyed at being summoned, Nandil showed them Delia. They stopped in their tracks, gawking, and made awkward bows.

'Thy Highness,' they mumbled as one.

Nandil charged them with taking the child to the castle and the healer.

Delia spun back to the merchant. 'Someone was following me,' she gasped, gripping his shirt's collar. 'He was going to take me back. To the cage. The monsters.' Fresh tears rushed out.

The more she wiped her eyes, the more she wept. But she let one of the soldiers guide her towards the ascending road. Nandil scanned the crowd around them for anyone suspicious. On the other hand, the delirious girl could have imagined it.

'Thou do have important friends,' Azare remarked.

The human dragged his hard eyes onto him. 'Delia, the royal pain in my life. One could say we grew up together. She'd sneak out of the castle an' straight into our store. Always underfoot. Always asking questions.' He sighed. 'Sweet child, but too impulsive an' keen for trouble. Not ideal for the king's youngest an' favourite daughter.' He started towards the well, declaring his need for a drink, while shaking his dismayed head. 'And she was snatched.'

'She has been missing long?' Azare asked.

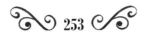

'Twenty days at least. That we know of! She often ran from her family only to be found hiding somewhere in the city. I wonder how long it was before they realised she was missing for true this time.'

They were almost at the large stone basin, its crystal waters sparkling, when a deep hum came from above. Azare looked up and noticed the light in the Beacon flare brighter. He was about to mention it to Nandil, when a dazzling white ray streaked down from it. Shrieks were heard from the crowd as everyone shielded their eyes. One howl, however, surpassed them all.

It was a shrill, agonised squeal. Azare wheeled round to search for its source under the cover of his hands. A cat thrashed on the ground a few feet away, clawing at its own skin. White and blue forms closed in on it, staves in hand, armed soldiers at their backs. Azare drew his own swords just as the cat began to change.

Chapter 30

Meecha walked down the street with Chione padding alongside him. The conspicuous, awed stares put him on edge. The sight of him, a man smaller than a dwarf, commanding a fully grown white chanter had dumbfounded even the guards. His supposed performance at the festival was eagerly anticipated, and once the white-cloaked man hovering at the gates had given his consent, Meecha and his pet were allowed entry. One thing he happily came to find was that he did not need to squeeze his way through the throngs swarming the main street. They parted before him like water for a boat. Even the figures in the shadows seemed less menacing—not that he had anything of value for them to steal. His compass and Chione were all he had left in this world. And no price would persuade them to dare cross her.

There were lights in the distance radiating from a cluster of tents and parked carriages. Music and jovial voices were carried to Meecha, as well as the smell of fires and roasting

meat. Chione smelt it too. Her mouth was watering. He pictured himself tearing into a tender leg of cattle or poultry. And a pie. *They must have pie.*

Meecha's daydreaming was cut short when a bolt of blinding light seared his eyeballs. He yelped and squeezed his eyelids shut, veering away from the beam. Shouts and gasps rippled around him.

'It's the Beacon,' someone warned.

'What's it doing?' another complained.

The beam finally dissolved, but something else was happening in the square ahead. At the first scream, everyone in the street went perfectly still. Their mouths hung open, forgotten in a moment of fearful confusion. All eyes were on the tents, from where sounds of battle were coming. Then a stampede of humans broke through shrieking, 'Demon!'

Meecha pushed Chione against the nearest wall and watched the humans flee. He looked at the chantress and gestured for her to follow. A clenching in his gut told him that whatever was occurring in the square had something to do with his quarry; thus he strode against the howling drove. By the time they reached the first row of stalls, the crowd had all but dwindled, leaving behind only curious fools and animals in cages. A guttural wail pierced the night, freezing the blood in Meecha's veins. Even Chione hunched a little, snarling with hackles high.

They jogged down a lane towards the sounds. They grew louder and more violent. Things were being wrecked amid the cries and grunts of people and... something else. Meecha turned into the next lane, but a barrier of felt, canvas, and wood blocked his path and sight. He sped along in search of another opening towards the square's centre. He found it and skidded through. He turned right and headed for a gap between two tents, when a man clattered through a cart and thudded onto the path before them. One look at the soldier's savaged chest, and it was clear that he would not be rising again.

Meecha peered through the new hole. The first thing his eyes locked onto was a monstrosity standing eight feet tall in the middle of a silver legion. Its skin, smooth as polished stone yet studded with patches of sharp scale, was a dark grey broken by random red patterns. Black horns protruded from its elbows and the rear joints of its dragon-like legs. Hands and feet were tipped with claws just as black, just as lethal. Its long narrow head had horns too, over its scalp and down the spine. Blazing red eyes glared at the circling soldiers, while razor fangs gnashed at them, threatening to rend more man-flesh.

The second figure to draw Meecha's attention stood out from the other cloaked and metal-clad defenders. He was clothed all in black, and even though he was perhaps three or four heads shorter than the demon, the two of them were quite alike in demeanour. Imposing. Deadly. Two strange but fine-looking swords were in his hands. *Azare?*

A flurry of action broke out. The two swords whistled towards the demon, but it dodged and hopped away, lithe as a snake. Two of the soldiers at its back drove a sneak attack. One succeeded in scratching the creature's leg before it spun on them. Its arm lashed out to slice one throat with an elbow-horn. Its talons then tore the second man's torso from navel to shoulder, his armour useless. The human ring enclosing the demon slackened, giving the creature the chance to bull through it, slashing and biting. It made for a road leading up the cliff, when a number of robed figures thrust their staves into the air. With an angry snarl, the demon was yanked back into the circle by a magical force. It landed on its back, splashing in pooled blood, but immediately pounced upright and wailed in fury at the elf.

Movement behind Meecha made him jerk around to see Chione stalk off towards the right side of the square. He trotted after her, his head kept low. She sniffed the air and her step hastened. She yowled, but the cries of imprisoned animals and the demon's incessant screeching were the only response she got. Chione called again. If by chance her cub was crying back, the racket was drowning it out. They continued through the lane with the chantress sniffing and yowling all the way, until she suddenly halted and pricked her ears. Meecha did not have long to rest before she broke into a headlong sprint. They rounded a corner. Three shapes were huddled before a far tent, two men and a woman. Meecha's first thought was that the poor people were paralysed with fear, but then he heard Chione's vicious snarl.

The woman kicked one assailant, while the other tried to force-feed her something in a jar. Meecha sped to the rescue, drawing their attention. She cried something and fought harder, but they easily overpowered her. Her voice rang out again, clearer this time.

'Meecha! Help me!'

He almost tripped over himself in shock, but then ran faster, shouting Delia's name.

'Get away from her!' he boomed, his panic greater than his rage.

The jar touched her lips. He was almost there. She sputtered and wriggled, shrieking, sobbing. Meecha prepared to bull into them, when a strange hum reverberated somewhere above, and the blinding beam whitened the world again. Meecha squeezed his eyes shut, leapt in the direction he knew the attackers to be, and sure enough thudded into two cursing masses and swept them aside, his fists already pounding blindly. A thunderous roar filled the air around them. *Not the chantress. Or the demon. Something greater.* Their world shuddered and exploded—a large being had crashed into it. Meecha rolled away. He huddled and shielded his head from flying debris, as the creature thrashed and smashed its way onto its terrible taloned feet.

Chapter 31

Azare picked himself up from the floor, blinking through the shimmering residue of the Beacon's beam. Struck in the shoulder, a newcomer had fallen from the sky, spinning like a dazed fly. He now rose from the wreckage on the right side of the square, one upper arm steaming. The humans shook in their boots, while the she-demon rushed to her saviour.

He was taller than her and built for butchery, with four arms and two great horns on his head. His wings were edged with talons, and his skin was jagged, its spikes as keen as obsidian blades. The last time Azare had faced one of these he had two brothers with him, and even then it was a challenge. He prayed for luck's favour, and it answered with a roar and a streak of white.

A huge feline creature—*a vijala!*—leapt from the rubble and bit into one of the demon's wings, twisting in the air, its weight dragging the monster aside. The she-demon moved to help her friend, but Azare intervened. Most of the humans targeted the larger beast, which was having trouble shaking off the cat—no matter how much he flapped and spun and pulled, the vijala's might had him stumbling backwards across the square. Spheres of light and lightning were flung at him from the priests' staves, even some containing water from the well, while the warriors jabbed and slashed at his legs, arms, and wings.

Azare swung a blade at the she-demon. She was too fast. The priests devoted to this fight used their magic to throw her off balance or distract her. It worked enough to give her a few cuts, but she cleverly kept her distance.

The ground shook as the male demon jumped and swerved in the air. The vijala and a number of soldiers went flying. The demon landed back down to charge at the priests. More corpses were added to the gory carpet before the cat resurfaced. It dashed behind the demon, hacked at his legs, and sped away before he could catch it. It prowled a bit and then charged again too fast for the bulky fiend to react while being showered with spells by the remaining priests. Azare glimpsed the fearless vijala land a blow to the demon's head. On the next attack it ripped into his wing. He howled and managed to bat his attacker away. The vijala hit the cliff face and slid unconscious to the ground. The seething demon advanced, a deep chittering laughter emerging from its throat. Azare could not help. He could not let the she-demon escape. The monster was almost upon the cat when a voice rose above the din.

'Leave her alone!'

A tiny man scuttled through the battlefield and flung something at the demon. An egg hit his head with a *splat*. He whirled around to glare at the dwarf, who threw something else. The demon's face was splattered with the red innards of a tomato. The dwarf's mockery seemed to enrage the beast more than anything else. It roared at the little man and rushed at him, horns first. The dwarf yelped and fled through an opening between tents. The demon uprooted them, but his target jumped out of another gap further down the line and flung another tomato. Azare was half inclined to stop fighting and watch the show, but the cowardly she-demon finally recovered her offence.

She hissed and slithered left and right, swiping at his ribs, hitting the mark twice. It was only skin she broke through his armour, but that was no excuse. *Focus.* Azare tried diagonal cuts from both sides, which she avoided by hopping backwards. He skipped forward and kicked her hard in the stomach. She fell. Azare lunged. Her left talons came up to strike his thigh, but he stepped back, twisted a blade, and took her whole hand. The she-demon squealed just before a third hum came from the Beacon and New Anvadore was again flooded with light. This time it was brighter, and the hum grew louder.

The two demons' wails were deafening. Azare dropped his swords to cover his ears. There was a clap of wings. A gust of air. The shrill cries were carried away, up and up to the sky. And they were gone. When the light dissipated for the last time, the square belonged to the humans once more—and a thaelil, a dwarf, and a vijala. The latter limped towards the ruins the winged demon had wrought when he fell. The little man jogged after it, and they both scrambled over splintered wood, iron, and shredded canvas of what used to be three separate stalls.

Once Azare had retrieved his swords, his curiosity drew him towards the peculiar pair. He found his way to them and saw the feline's backside wriggling out from beneath a collapsed tent covered by all sorts of debris. The dwarf was anxious. He leaned back and forth, as if wanting to dive in there himself. Azare was almost of a mind to help the vijala, when it suddenly bolted, upending everything that was on top of it. He noticed a white thing of fur dangling limply from its mouth.

The dwarf gasped and clutched his cheeks. The vijala—a female it seemed—set the cub between her paws, while her friend crawled closer and knelt beside her. Azare watched the mother nudge and sniff and lick her infant. The young dwarf—judging by the slightest of beards—wept quietly. Moments passed and the cub, bony and dishevelled, was still lying lifeless. Azare stepped forward. He could reach out to her, comfort her, make her understand that her child was gone. Tears had formed pale streaks down the dwarf's smudged cheeks. He looked up at Azare, his eyes imploring him to do something. But there was nothing more Azare could do. He was a warrior, not a mage. Humans seemed to think that all his kind could wield magic, which was not the truth.

A long heart-wrenching moan came from the mother. The dwarf sobbed harder at the sound of her grief. The woeful drone filled the square. It made all within hearing range grimace and bow their heads. They gazed in sorrow at their slain comrades.

Aaak. The weak squawk silenced the mother cat like a whip. She, the dwarf, and Azare snapped their heads towards the cub. It whined again and squirmed. A whoop escaped the dwarf. He laughed hysterically, gripping his temples. The vijala fussed over her child, until it turned onto its back, put both paws on her muzzle, and nibbled her nose. The dwarf bent down.

'You scared us, little guy,' he said and scratched the cub's ear.

The mother gave him a big wet lick across the face. The act seemed to take him by surprise. He gawked at her for a few breathless moments and then grinned stupidly.

'Halt there,' someone called from behind Azare.

Soldiers were climbing the debris towards them. The closest one had removed his helmet, which he had hooked under his arm. His hair was cropped very short, making every line, edge, and scar on his weathered face prominent. Two stern green eyes studied Azare closely.

'We're in your debt, strangers. But I must question the coincidence of two demons an' an elf appearing in New Anvadore at the same time.'

Azare suddenly remembered his hood. In his weariness and distraction, he had failed to feel its absence. He was now aware of the scrutinising stares coming from behind still donned helmets.

'Thou are correct. It is no chance. I have been hunting the female demon for over twenty and five days.'

The human inquired, 'Why?'

'For reasons best discussed with thy priests.'

The man agreed, if reluctantly, and turned his attention to the dwarf and his companions. The cub was now sound asleep, snuggled against its mother.

'And thou, lad? Where do thou fit in all this?'

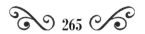

'I fit very closely, sir,' he responded cryptically. "But, I agree, it's a discussion best kept for the right ears.'

'There's someone under there,' a soldier broke in, pointing at a hand moving under the rubble.

The dwarf pounced towards it, suddenly manic. The men worked with him to clear the wreckage, until three bodies were revealed—one was the she-demon's companion.

'You!' gasped the dwarf, glaring at the second man, who was fighting for breath.

He was well dressed. A gold brooch gleamed from his cloak.

'Keep him alive,' the little man commanded. 'He's an ally of the demons.'

The soldiers moved in to take the male survivor, while his accuser peered solemnly at the third form sprawled nearby. Everything suddenly froze. The humans' eyes widened when they spotted the female. It took a moment for Azare to recognise her amid the dust and blood. Death glazed the beautiful blue eyes of the Anvadorian princess.

Chapter 32

All feeling drained from Meecha's body. How could he forget about her? His mind had left her, hooked by the cub's discovery. He had cried over that baby and not over her. Laughing, talking, forgetting her. She was crushed. The only broken bone Meecha could see was her collarbone pushing against the skin. Her eyes were wide. Afraid. Pale tear streaks marked her temples. Blood smeared the rest, out of her nose and mouth. Lips, teeth, chin, cheeks, all red, wrong. Meecha knelt beside her, staring. Her green dress was badly wrinkled, ripped, and caked in mud. She had survived the river. She had lived. Alone, she had made it home. And died here. *Alone. Terrified.*

A hand touched his shoulder. Meecha looked up to find the Captain of the Guard gesturing for him to move. Waveringly, he stood and tottered aside. He watched the human close Delia's eyes with tentative fingers before squatting beside her, head bowed, and pulling her into

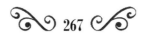

his arms. She offered no resistance. Like a string puppet, she slid towards him. When a splintered stick got caught and dragged by her dress, several of the nearest soldiers twitched, but one, a bearded bear of a man, beat them all to it. He carefully removed the wood, barely touching the fabric, and threw it away. Meecha heard his annoyed sniffle as he backed away.

The Captain rose. Her head rested against his shoulder, as if sleeping, her black locks, now a tangled and dirty mane, engulfing it. Meecha recalled the dream where the blackest tar would not stick to her. But this was reality. She was no mysterious, untouchable god-child. She was simply a child—a princess, it turned out—but still a young girl who cared and lived and feared. When the Captain started to move towards the climbing road, the crowd parting before him, one of her shoes fell off. Meecha picked it up. It was old, torn leather and several sizes too big for her. She may have found or been given them on her journey from the river. He could not take his eyes off it as he followed the procession.

Meecha, Azare, Chione, and her cub, riding upon her back, were ushered up the cliff by a wary fist of soldiers. Meecha noticed their suspicious glances, but he did not care. He remembered about the jar and mumbled to one of them about it, but his words were a rambling mess. The scowling soldier shook his head and turned way. They were led past the outskirts of the grove and Meecha noticed the Beacon for the first time. Normally, he would have been excited about its obvious and surprising origin, but the shoe was more important to him now. Through the Second Ring they went, the city's inner wall that surrounded the castle. The Ring itself was bordered by a deep moat filled with water from a river entering from the northeast. This moat then fed the waterfall dropping directly from the base of the Beacon.

Meecha could not help noticing the castle's interesting design. The night did not do it justice. But despite the lush gardens encircling it, the white peacocks strutting along the symmetrical pathways, the polished red granite walls mounted with huge pennants of the white phoenix, the majesty of its size and its towers, it was in fact a plain circle—smoothed, windowed, topped with crenulations and black-tiled conical roofs. It possessed a somewhat introverted character behind its flamboyant facade.

They were escorted up some steps and into the castle proper through a set of oak and steel doors. The huge galleries were carpeted in red and gold. Meecha gawked numbly at portraits of royal faces and landscapes in intricate frames made of wood and yet more gold. Vases of freshly plucked flowers stood in every corner, and crystal chandeliers hung from an impossibly high ceiling. How were the candles lit? He went where told in a near trance, until he found himself locked in a room with only the chanters and Azare for company.

The ghost lady had been right about the elf. Hooded, he stood out in a crowd, but what he hid beneath the cowl was more striking still. There was a subtle blue sheen to his black waist-long hair styled into something like a cockerel's plume with three small golden clasps holding it together. The hair on the once shaved sides had grown back a little and so had that on his jaw. Tiny black arrowhead tattoos streaked down his forehead to his nose, which was straight and perfect. His permanently furrowed eyebrows ran for his temples at an upward slant, as did his almond-shaped eyes, light brown and brooding. Even with that bitter twist to them, his lips were flawlessly plump. Meecha grew irrationally annoyed over how impeccable this fellow was. He cursed the injustice of being born a luima and not a six-foot, strapping elf. He smirked at the barely perceptible scars that marked Azare's copper skin. Their jagged lines were like streaks of lightning

'Sit down,' he complained.

Azare had been pacing since they were brought in.

'Burning a hole in the floor won't make them come any faster. Nor will getting on my nerves.'

The elf paused, 'I can put thee out of thy misery, if thou prefer.' And he started pacing again.

Meecha sighed loudly and decided to play with the cub, if only to distract his own disturbing thoughts. He took a long-stemmed flower from the vase next to his armchair and flicked it in front of the furball. Its pupils widened. It squatted between its mother's paws, shaking its rear as it prepared to pounce. The cub jumped out into the open and Meecha jerked the flower away. He dragged it across the floor, smiling at the little one scuttling after it. He lifted the flower over its head, made it hop and then run around some more. Its nails scraped the wood where the rug did not reach. It served their hosts right for abandoning them.

The stray thought made Meecha's concentration falter. He yelped when the cub's claws nicked his fingers, the flower snatched from his hand. He groaned and sucked on the scratches, but still chuckled at the cub obliviously playing with its trophy. Chione stood.

'It's fine,' he mumbled through a finger, but she sniffed closer.

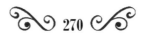

He abruptly considered that she might be more interested in the blood than his wellbeing. He stiffened worriedly. But she growled at him, and he submitted his hand. To his relief, she simply licked his wounds and returned to her spot.

'Thank you.' He watched his hand intently, hoping to see the skin knit itself together again.

'Where thou find her?' Azare suddenly asked.

He had stopped pacing. There was something unnerving about that steely stare.

'We were both captives of bandits near Crove. The man recovered from the square, the one working with the demons, he was there, and he took her cub. We escaped and travelled here together.'

The elf considered this for a while.

'She is fond of thee,' he said and resumed his back-and-forth march to nowhere.

Meecha looked at the chantress, who was now bathing her cub. They were both so pretty.

'My name's Meecha, in case you were wondering.'

'I was not.'

Meecha rolled his eyes.

A few moments of awkward silence followed before the elf grunted, 'Azare.'

Meecha raised an eyebrow. 'It's a pleasure to make your acquaintance.'

Azare grumbled, 'Thou always so well-mannered?'

'Are you always such a sad sack?'

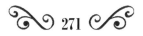

'A what?' the elf grimaced.

'Sour. Grumpy. Petulant.'

Azare's frown deepened, his fists clenching and un-clenching.

Meecha returned a mocking scowl and said in an exceedingly genteel tone, 'In answer to your question, no, I'm not always well-mannered. Especially to those who don't appreciate it.' He glanced at Azare's threatening fists and added, 'And, in case you forgot, she likes me.'

Chione was not following the conversation, but Meecha flashed a smug grin anyway. He still did not know what to make of the elf. He was a rogue. Perhaps his own kin had exiled him for a good reason. New Anvadore could thank him all it wanted, but it would not change the fact that he was not hunting the demon out of the goodness of his heart. He was after what it stole or was simply enjoying the challenge. It must be most tedious for an elf living alongside humans, even at a distance. For all Meecha knew, Azare was after the same thing the demons were.

A cry broke the silence. A woman's wail was coming from somewhere in the castle. A short time later, footsteps approached the door, and a key turned in the lock. The Captain walked in, his face pale and hard.

'His Majesty shall see you both now.'

'It is the Architects I must speak to,' Azare objected.

'The king comes first.'

The Captain stood firm—neither threats nor pleas would sway him.

'Of course,' Meecha piped in as he hopped down from his chair. Upon nearing the human, he decided to try again

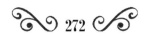

about the jar. 'Delia was attacked by those two men. They were trying to feed her something from a jar. It should still be down there. I was too overwhelmed earlier and forgot all about it.'

The Captain's face tightened. 'Thou knew her Highness by her birth name. Why?'

Meecha hesitated. How much could he say? 'We were friends... briefly. It's a long story.'

'Well,' the man sniffed and stood aside to let him pass into the hallway. 'This is thy chance to tell it all.'

Meecha obeyed, with Chione and the cub plodding after him. The elf followed grudgingly. Once more, they were surrounded by a dozen armed men. The humans' appreciation of Azare's assistance was short-lived indeed.

A rosewood double door emblazoned with the white phoenix was soon before them. The Captain pounded on it three times, and it swung inwards with the help of two guards in white and crimson tunics. Meecha entered a great hall, its marble walls of the purest white, veined with red. There were white columns on either side of the long carpet, this too red and white. Golden vines spiralled up the pillars and in a sequence along each wall. Another of those astonishing chandeliers dangled from the ceiling, a mosaic of a blazing sun spreading out from it to turn into thousands of birds, not only red and white, but every colour imaginable. Meecha lowered his gaze as they approached some steps or a dais—he could not tell, boxed in as he was. They finally stopped, and the Captain dropped to one knee.

'Sire, our visitors.'

The wall of tin soldiers parted to leave Meecha and his companions exposed. His throat tightened at the sight of the man on the throne. A crown of spun white gold embedded with rubies and diamonds rested upon his grey head. Deep-set green eyes simmered above pursed pallid lips. He had already donned the black. He sat straight in his throne, a work of art crafted from gold and crystal, its legs shaped like those of a bird; feathers, talons and all. Two massive curved wings rose behind King Odigan. And in his hands lay Delia's ugly brown shoe—they had taken it from Meecha before locking them up.

'Captain Denna, what art these animals doing here?' he boomed.

Meecha's heart jumped into his mouth.

The old soldier replied, 'They came with the dwarf. The big one helped fight the demon that... We didn't know what to do with them, thy Grace.'

'They won't harm anyone.' Meecha was tempted to address the 'dwarf' error as well, but held his tongue before the king's searching glare, which quickly shifted to Azare, standing proud behind Meecha.

'Why art thou here?' Odigan asked of the elf, his voice dangerously void of emotion.

Azare tried to be evasive. 'I hunt demons.'

'In Anvadore,' was the king's clipped response. 'Why art thou in Anvadore?'

Azare lifted his chin. 'I left my home. My reasons do not in any way concern humans.'

'They do now,' King Odigan snapped and stood from his seat, the shoe flopping to the floor.

Meecha cowered. There were a handful of accounts in the aerieti's pool of knowledge concerning the House of Ayvik. It was Odigan's older brother, Serikan, who had led the human revolution against the elves and was made Grand King after their victory. 'A force of nature' a scholar described him as, unmatched in strength, charisma, and cunning, but one who, sadly, cracked beneath the weight of his crown.

'I shalt ask one last time,' Odigan warned, 'before I have thee dragged to the dungeons. What art thou doing in Anvadore?'

'I am no spy, if that is what concerns thee,' Azare somehow maintained a cool demeanour. 'I have lived in thy forests for cycles without coming near thy cities. But my house was raided by one of those demons, and that is all I am here for. Let me go, and thou shall not see me again.'

'Thou and those things enter my city, and my daughter is murdered,' the king rumbled, trying to blink away tears, but they perched on his eyelids, glistening. 'Thou shalt tell me everything thou know.'

'I know nought about her,' Azare finally flared. 'I am here for reasons of my own. Nothing to do with thee, and I shall not share them. I do not trust thee any more than thou trust me.'

Meecha dreaded the fierceness with which Odigan set his jaw.

'Then thou shalt remain here until thou do,' he declared through gritted teeth. 'Arrest him!'

Swords were out. The cub huddled against its mother, while she bared her fangs at the soldiers closing in on the elf. Meecha shouted for them to stop, but their rising voices and the clanging of their parrying blades surpassed his frail peeps. Neither side was trying to kill the other, but it would not take long for the situation to boil over. No matter how much he screamed, however, Meecha went unheeded. That was until Chione reared onto her hind legs and filled the hall with her roar.

'Please!' Meecha cried again, once everyone had been stunned into silence.

The chantress dropped back onto all fours and looked at him, as if urging him to speak.

He turned to the king. 'May I say my part, your Majesty?'

Odigan hesitated, eager to see Azare in chains, but resentfully accepted Meecha's appeal.

Mustering all the poise and grace he was blessed with, he commenced. 'Your Grace, forgive my brazen friend. Secretive, defensive, conceited he may be, but he's an elf! It comes naturally to them, doesn't it? I don't find it fair imprisoning someone just because they're difficult to get along with, particularly after they saved your city. And, Sire, with respect, can you honestly tell me that your wrath isn't mainly fuelled by his race and not damning facts?'

The king's eyes dropped in shame before he cocked his head.

Meecha lowered his voice to a gentle, sympathetic tone, 'I know what you're doing. You're looking for someone to blame for Delia's death.'

'That is enough!' Odigan barked, fresh tears welling up in his eyes.

'I can't be quiet when you blame the wrong person!'

'How dare thee?'

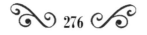

'The demons are gone, far from your reach. If you need to target someone, then here I am!'

Surprise shook the king. 'What dost thou mean?'

Meecha bowed his head, pressed fingers into his own flooding eyes. When he thought himself steady enough, he spoke, voice still cracking. 'We met in Crove before we took a caravan to Anvadore. We... were separated. I—I lost her. I—I was supposed to protect her, but... I should've looked harder.'

His guilt choked him. He shook his head, fighting back curses. He met Odigan's incredulous stare. Azare was watching him too.

'I failed her. Even at the last, I couldn't get to her in time. They hurt her and I couldn't... Your Majesty, I'd wind back time. I'd go to the realm of the dead and never return until I'd found Delia and brought her back. But I can't. I can do nothing to ease your pain. Or mine... But there's one thing I can tell you. This elf's done nothing wrong. He's shown bravery, not just in hunting and battling the demons alongside your men, but in daring to set foot in a human city where he'd be attacked, shackled on sight! If there's anyone who can avenge D—who can avenge Delia and all those who lost their lives tonight, it's him!'

Never had he heard himself so fierce. He shrank under the king's scrutiny, suddenly realising how improperly dressed he was for a royal audience. Rags and filth.

'None dare speak to me so,' Odigan said sternly, a kinder reaction than Meecha had expected. 'None but Delia.'

'I'm truly sorry, your Majesty.'

The king nodded solemnly. 'From what I hear, thou fought bravely too.'

Meecha looked away. 'No. I didn't.'

Odigan stepped down from the dais. 'Who was it then? Who harmed my little girl?'

For a moment, several evil faces crossed Meecha's mind, when he remembered what he himself had referred to. 'The two men found with her. They held her down and fed her something. I couldn't see what it was, but it was in a jar, I think.'

Odigan turned to Captain Denna, 'Hast thou found it?'

The soldier sputtered a bit before replying that they were still searching, all the while avoiding Meecha's pointed sidelong gaze. Denna then departed with most of his men. Their haste jingled their armour like cutlery.

'The one captured hast died of his wounds,' the king divulged.

Meecha groaned. The Scavenger had vital information.

'I suppose I should be consoled by the fact that they were killed in the same manner my daughter was. Thou shalt catch the other two?' Odigan directed that level question at Azare.

'I shall... thy Majesty,' the elf replied, biting the title.

A triple tap on the door drew everyone's attention and an elderly woman in royal blue robes was admitted.

'Mistress Teretta,' Odigan's greeting was amiable yet slightly on edge.

The old human hobbled towards them without a word. She was small and bony, but there was a graceful air of

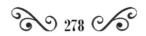

no-nonsense about her. The hair on her head was white and long, braided to the small of her back. She made her leisurely way to the dais, her hands held behind her back. She acknowledged Azare with a bob of her head, smiled at the chantress and the golden eyes peering from under her belly, and halted with a curtsy before the king.

'Sire, forgive my tardiness, but I have received word from the Light. It would like a word with these good people.'

Meecha gaped at her, heart racing.

'Very well,' the king replied. 'Return to me when thou art done. There is much to be discussed.'

The old woman, Teretta, turned her grandmotherly face to Meecha.

'Master Roa I presume? Ni ernath'he Isha?'

Meecha beamed as he exclaimed, 'Diha! Diha ernath'a Isha!' *I always seek the Light.*

And it always seemed to find him.

Chapter 33

A king won over by a moping dwarf. Clever words, a declaration of self-sacrifice, and a stab at the rival race. Like that, Azare was turned from a spy into a favoured guest.

'Are you an agent?' Meecha whispered to Teretta, his voice as clear as if Azare was standing beside him, not twenty feet behind.

The female elder chuckled. 'Oh, no. I am nought but a humble servant. A conduit, if thou wilt.'

Azare frowned. An agent? A conduit? Of what?

Teretta led them through a doorway with a glass mural of the mythical Sun Maiden of the east, a yellow-haired woman holding the sun. They descended a staircase to the inner court, which was tiled underfoot with red granite and decorated with rich flowerbeds and the open sky above. Two vast towers streaked towards the heavens, one near the door they had emerged from and the other direct-

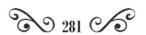

ly opposite, next to the western door. The towers were connected at various levels by long bridges.

'What are they?' Meecha asked their guide.

'That is where the arcanists dwell. There are not many in New Anvadore at present, but after tonight's events more may be summoned from Mecanta.'

'Mecanta?' the dwarf squinted, making Azare question his intellect—or his origin.

Azare and his kin knew this human city well; its Arcane School was built upon the ruins of a thaelil temple destroyed during the Is'mara Grae.

'If thou hast the arcane in thy blood, Mecanta is where thou wouldst go. The greatest human arcanists have studied their craft at its school and delved into its library,' Teretta explained.

'Are you and your brethren not... arcanists?'

'We are, of a fashion. The Divine Architects study the spirit and mechanics, but above all else our order was created for a singular purpose: to defend against evil. Hence we focus on specific forms of magic that are known to harm demons.'

'Light is the bane of darkness. Electrical energy constricts and slows its manifestation. Water is an ally of them both,' Meecha uttered this as if reciting from a book.

Teretta smiled down at him, seeming pleased.

'Precisely,' she said and hobbled up the steps of the western door. This depicted the Silver Archer with the three moons embedded in his bow—one on the tip, one on the end, and one in the middle.

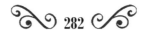

There was no more talking as Azare, Meecha, and the chanters were taken through a number of passages until they reached another door, this one made of wood. They passed into the castle's gardens just as a white peacock was strolling along the path, its plumage spread for all to admire. Chione took her cub in her mouth to stop him from bolting after the bird.

'Not far now,' Teretta said, and followed the path towards the nearest wall of the Second Ring that surrounded the grounds.

Meecha glanced over his shoulder, as if to make sure Azare was still there. He found his contempt for the dwarf swell. When they reached the wall, Azare could see nothing but smooth, grey stone. Teretta tapped its surface four times at various places while muttering under her breath. The bleakness of the stone rippled away to reveal yet another door, this one of metal and inscribed with a number of ancient symbols. A key appeared in the woman's wrinkled hand, a metal thing of the most bizarre design. She inserted it into the keyhole and turned it in a rapid sequence of alternating rotations. Several moments later, the chorus of the door's clattering mechanism came to an end and it swung open. They stepped through and into the grove. The door locked and concealed itself behind them without the priestess's help.

'Welcome to our fair little wood.' Teretta drew a deep breath.

'It's lovely,' Meecha replied.

Azare rolled his eyes at the dwarf's incessant flattery.

'I am glad thou think so, Master Roa. We take great pride in it. These very hands planted the seeds. We have tended it, protected it from despoiling hands. We have watched it grow and now it rewards us with its shade and beauty. 'Tis a shelter, a place of serenity for all who would respect it.'

The noble vijala did not waste time. She stretched her bulk beneath a pine with the cub beside her, its form almost indiscernible against the thick fur of her belly.

'They are welcome to stay out here, if they prefer,' Teretta offered.

'I think they do—but would it be too much to ask for them to be fed and watered? It's been a long journey.'

'Certainly. I shalt have something brought out for them. She has been friendly so far, but... eh... they have nothing to worry about, I hope.'

Meecha smiled at the priestess, his nervous twitch noted only by Azare. 'Oh, of course! If they leave the food at a safe distance, they'll be fine.'

'Good, good,' Teretta said and walked away with Meecha in tow.

Azare did not follow immediately. He turned to the feline and sent out a mental signal to find her consciousness. When he gently probed her mind, Chione opened her eyes and sat up, tail swishing. Her sharp stare bore into him, wary, uncertain, until she accepted his contact. He sent a sense of appreciation and peacefulness through their connection. Her tail halted. He sent her an image of the trees and a feeling of danger about whatever lay beyond them. She responded with an indication of stillness, as if saying that she had no intention of leaving the trees. He showed her his agreement and then informed her of the impending food and water that Meecha had procured for her and her child.

Her ears twitched excitedly, mind thrumming with delight, as well as affection for her red son. *She's adopted him!* Azare's shock leaked through the connection before he could stop himself. Finally, he asked her not to be violent towards the strangers that would come to leave her meal, which she agreed to. He thanked her and gently broke the connection.

He caught up with the others at the channel where the waters from the moat entered the stream through the grove that flowed into a stone courtyard and then under the Beacon. There it was: the Wonder of New Anvadore. The purity of the white and gold lights churning within its lantern was reflected magnificently against the pillar's pale perfection. Azare could see through teary eyes the script etched into the marble, lines of it running all the way to the top.

'Ah! My pride and joy,' Teretta sighed from beside Meecha.

It took Azare and the dwarf a moment to register her words, at which point they both turned to gawk at her.

'*Your* pride and joy!' Meecha cried.

The priestess winked. 'Allow me to introduce myself properly. I am Vorami Teretta, Master Architect—or Lady Mason, as the common folk like to call me.'

'Do thou mean to say that thou built the Beacon?' Azare demanded. A frail old female—a human!—was the genius behind this creation.

'You've done remarkable work here. And please, call me Meecha.' The dwarf bowed.

'Vora.'

'This is Azare.' Meecha pointed a thumb at him.

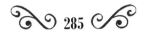

'Well, Azare. With a benevolent guiding hand, yes, I built it. In fact, I designed the whole city under the king's strict supervision. The day his brother left him the crown and ashes for a city, Odigan commanded me to build him a new one, one that no demon would dare enter. It was that dream New Anvadore was built upon; a dream that the Light shared. I was given the tools and their blessing. Four ten-cycles later, here it is. A demon's nightmare.'

'It was not much use tonight,' Azare observed.

Meecha gave him a murderous glare, while Vora dipped her head. She pushed a finger against her lips, a troubled frown adding wrinkles to her face.

'We have not had a chance to test it against a true demon before. As intended, the Beacon alerted us when the first one entered the city and started projecting waves of light and sound to force it out, but when we saw that the demon refused to leave, we had to look for it ourselves. The Beacon can hurt the city as much as it can defend it, so we must be able to depend on it as little as possible. The city did what it was meant to do under the circumstances. 'Twas we that were found wanting.'

'You didn't know what you faced. I'm sure you did all you could.' Meecha's attempt to comfort the human was futile. The depth of her disappointment was clear.

'It was not enough. We must do better next time.'

She climbed the steps of the first building on their left, a square structure with an arched entrance and a blue dome.

'You're an idiot!' Meecha hissed at Azare before he stomped up the steps.

Azare sniffed his disdain and lugged himself into the building, while three priests in white rushed out. The first thing he spotted was the closed white door to a cylindrical room in the middle of the temple. There were altars against the walls covered with blue, white, and gold cloths. Lit candles were melting everywhere, some exuding sweet, earthy smells. Vora and Meecha sat on a bench in a corner and another human stood before them, his back to the door. The stranger's curly ponytail seemed familiar. When he turned, it was Nandil grinning at him.

'Thou live,' Azare said flatly. 'How nice.'

Master Hithe did not look offended. He retorted with a pout, 'Ah, did I hurt thy feelings?' Azare was not impressed. 'I ran straight here, while thou valiantly fought off the enemy. And 'tis a good thing I did. I found the city's first rock!'

Azare grabbed him by the throat.

'Where is it?' he snarled into his face.

Nandil grasped his wrist with more strength than expected, but, instead of fighting back, the merchant calmly pointed at the pair on the bench. Azare met the Lady Mason's disapproving look.

'That would be me.'

Chapter 34

Meecha stood beside the white door while Vora unlocked it for him. The Master Architect pulled it open and inclined her head, kindly motioning him to enter.

'Thou knowest what to do,' she said to Meecha's back as his hesitant steps carried him into the circular room.

The door closed behind him, leaving him alone before a marble pool, elevated to the height of his chest. The white marble at the bottom of the pool created the illusion that it held milk. Still as glass it was, the glistening crystalline water, but it rippled under Meecha's breath when he leant in for a closer inspection. He straightened. Inhaling deeply to steady his nerves, the words came from his lips loud and firm.

'Ernath'a Isha.'

White rays sprang from the waters. A sparkling mist began to rise, swelling and swirling. He watched it take shape—legs, arms, torso, all long and well built. It was

when the wings materialised that he realised. This was not the ghost lady. Meecha dropped to his knees just as the aerieti's luminescent head became complete.

'At'oona ihray tal lita'mae, Atalini Roa,' it said to him in a voice like lightning crackling from the depths of a cavern. Meecha's hair stood on end. *It has been long since we last spoke, Agent Roa.*

It gladdened his heart to know that his Lord even remembered their rare exchanges.

Meecha responded, also in Aerieti, 'I am honoured that you think of me, Master Opheiro.'

'Your name is praised by many grateful souls. It accompanies some of the Light's greatest victories. You see yourself through the eyes of larger beings and undervalue your worth. We have legions of agents with strengths and skills that you lack, but you have surpassed them all. And this you owe to something more powerful than muscle or magic. It's your heart. There's a spark within you that refuses to fade even in the darkest of times. That light you carry is the reason why I recommended you for this mission.'

Meecha looked up at his Lord and was awed once again by his presence. The aerieti's pure skin glowed faintly, blurring much of his facial features. Thick, elaborate coils of a copper-coloured metal covered his body, reaching up his neck and the sides of his head to form a crown of intricately woven antlers, while long hair of the whitest silk tumbled down his back. His wings were nothing but light—Meecha could never tell what they were made of. Emotionless eyes of liquid gold watched him as he spoke.

'You recommended me?'

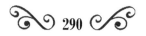

The aerieti Opheiro nodded slowly. 'Indeed. There are warriors aplenty to be found in Itania, but turning to more violence will only help Crantil dig its claws further into this world. What it truly needs is someone that can elude the xalikais' sight and steal their victory from under them. They are already many steps ahead, so you must make haste.

'Your first mission has been to find the thaelil Azare and guide him on his path. The significance of this task has increased tenfold. The demons he hunts are seeking the Key of Crantil.'

'What?' Meecha gasped. 'It's in Itania? Where?'

'We don't know, but Azare is on the trail of the last to have seen it. Go with him. Find the Key before they do.'

'I will, my Lord. I will find the Key, whatever it takes,' Meecha declared and then muttered, 'But...' The aerieti Opheiro inclined his head, fixing him with an expectant stare. 'How was it hidden for so long? How—when did you discover its location?'

Opheiro nodded. 'Fair questions. We always knew it never left Itania, but it was hidden from our sight through ploys and magic. I believe you had just left the city of Crove when the truth was revealed to us.'

'So you have been watching me.' For the first time ever, Meecha was strangely unnerved by this.

The aerieti hummed his affirmation. 'Itania has been... unremarkable since the invasion of Arak Sildrax. Over the years, his abandoned servants were either hunted down or frightened into discretion. Our full attention was no longer required. That changed when you began to investigate. You riled something, a xalikai plan, perhaps, long in the making.

You set off a ripple of dark whispers that drew our interest. Indeed, Agent Roa, we're watching.'

Meecha nibbled his lip to stop his thought from escaping his mouth, but it was determined. 'Delia too?'

Opheiro squinted and a moment later brightened with recognition. 'The human girl. From your visions.'

Meecha could only nod. He was not sure what response he was seeking. His Lord clearly perceived his trepidation.

'Agent, our place isn't to change the course of life but to preserve its balance. You know this. You couldn't prevent her death any more than we could. She's at peace.'

'But,' Meecha sighed. 'She was important. She was supposed to live. I'm certain of it. My visions...'

'May have simply been premonitions.' Opheiro's voice was soft yet stern. 'It's not uncommon for agents to experience mental awakenings. Interdimensional travel can affect the mind in incredible ways. Have you had any more such dreams?'

'No.'

'Then it's possible that your transforming mind accidentally touched upon your future's channel. Not to warn you. Or help change her fate. It simply happened.'

He was right, of course. Meecha's dreams had contained no hints of Parda or the Scavenger or that cursed river. They had been the scantiest jumble of images from his journey.

'Do not lose focus, Agent Roa,' the aerieti instructed. 'And don't depend on prophesies. It's likely that you'll need to make your own luck for this mission.'

With a flash of light, Opheiro's avatar shrank into mist, which then floated back into the waters, smooth and untroubled. The magical rays retreated until Meecha stood alone once more in the silent, spotless room. And yet it echoed in his mind.

They knew. They saw. They let her die.

Chapter 35

'Master Iridan came to me. I cannot recall how many cycles have passed,' Vorami Teretta admitted, tapping her fingers against her blue-draped knees. 'He wished to know about demons. More specifically, about the time when they came into our world. I told him all I knew, but he was not satisfied. He was looking for the means that had allowed the Sildrax, Arak, to cross. I unearthed old texts, journals belonging to some of those who witnessed the carnage, and found an interesting report from a thaelil mage. It made reference to a dagger with a curved blade of amber. An agent of the demons had used it to rip the fabric of our dimension and open a gateway for Arak. And that is when Inan showed me his pendant.'

Puzzlement knotted Nandil's brow, who sat beside her on the bench. 'Quite the secret,' he muttered.

'After Arak was defeated by the dragons, the thaelil took the dagger to keep safe, but it was lost along the way. It must have ended up in the hands of Iridan's forebears. They must have been oblivious to what they were holding. Or, perhaps, not.'

'What happened to Inan after you spoke?' Azare asked.

'He left with the pendant. He said he knew a place where he could hide it.'

'Did he say where?'

The priest looked down at her hands—her fingers were long, nails slightly dirty. 'No.'

Azare's eyes narrowed at the catch in her voice.

'Thou have more to say,' he coaxed with as much civility as he could muster.

Vora studied him sceptically.

'Our causes have linked us, Mistress Teretta,' Azare sighed. 'Demons are risking their lives in search of that blade. This can only mean that they plan to use it. Perhaps they only intend to return from whence they came. But what if they do not?'

Vora pursed his lips. 'Then would it not be wiser to leave it hidden? The demons do not know where it is. Only Inan does, and they cannot find him either.'

'But am I correct in thinking thou have the knowledge they need?'

A boulder would have had more expression than her. She was clearly not giving up her secret. Azare bristled as he pointed at the twenty and seven arrows on his forehead.

'Know what these are? They are demons. All killed by my hand. Thy purpose is to defend against evil. Mine is to hunt it.'

The priestess blinked, and Azare leant closer.

'One of these demons had claws so fine it could reach into thy nerves without thee even knowing. It could inflict such pain as to make thee beg for death. Another could raid thy mind and turn thy fears against thee. Two of my brothers were driven to madness and four maimed themselves while battling their nightmares. The she-demon that infiltrated thy precious city is a shapeshifter. She could take the form of thy king, if she wished. It is but a matter of time before the demons work out that thou know something. And how do thou think thou shall fare when they become desperate?'

He could see the fear in Vora's eyes, but the Master Architect still would not yield. Azare snarled, 'Why can thou not trust me?'

'Answer me this,' she suddenly said, meeting his glare straight on. 'Why art thou not with thy kind? What has driven thee to pursue these demons all this way? Better yet, how do I know that thou art not after the same thing as them? Or that thou art not one of their agents? It would not be the first time for an elf to side with the enemy. Thou hast failed to make thy motives plain, and thou do not strike me as a person who cares about anyone but himself. What is thy true purpose here?'

Azare was taken aback. He was about to pin the scrawny relic to the wall when a voice came from behind him.

'His purpose is his own.'

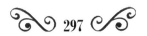

He turned to find Meecha walking towards them. Azare thought there was a new gleam in the little man's eyes. He had entered that room stooped and troubled. He strode now straight and stern to Azare's side.

Meecha spoke to Vora again. 'The Light trusts him.'

The priestess's eyebrows shot up, and she gave Azare an incredulous squint. Still seeming unsure of his value, she frowned at Meecha. 'What did they say?'

'The demons are after the Key of Crantil.'

Vora's reaction was a grim nod.

'The key of what?' Nandil inquired blankly.

'The blade,' the priestess offered.

'What blade?' Meecha wondered in turn.

The Master Architect sighed. 'The Key was crafted into a dagger during the time of Arak Sildrax's invasion. Its blade—the Key itself—was separated from the hilt and turned into a pendant. That pendant, an heirloom, I suppose, of Inan's family, was last in his possession. The demons now seek Inan for the Key.'

'What's Crantil?' Nandil winced.

This time it was Meecha who provided the answer. 'Crantil's the home-world of the demons. What you refer to as the abyss.'

'Oh. And why's it called a key?'

The dwarf took a lengthy breath.

'Imagine that there are doors in the world you can't see. Every world has its own doors and bridges to connect them with other worlds. Inhabitants of some of these worlds crafted keys that would allow them to open their

doors and cross the bridges. Crantil created one such key and used it to enter Itania—that's your world.'

Nandil's mouth dangled open, his eyes wandering, picturing these wondrous doors and bridges.

Azare, on the other hand, was doubtful. 'How thou know this?'

The dwarf guffawed. 'I'd be happy to sit and talk about myself for a cycle, but now we need to find that Key.'

Azare and Nandil directed pointed looks at Vora, who grumbled her surrender. 'Inan left a message for his daughter. He said I must give it only to her, if she came looking for him.'

Azare pressed two fingers against his closed eyelids. 'She is dead. The demons killed her.'

Vora gaped at him for a moment—a flash of doubt. What was she questioning? Rune's death or his innocence of it?

She shook her head solemnly. 'The message was this: I have gone to the diamond in the mountains. Wheel thy way from the nose to the toads. Follow a maid bright. Fly or descend, thou shalt swim.'

An awkward pause followed.

'What was that?' Azare's gritted growl shattered the silence before Nandil muttered, 'The diamond in the mountains,' and Meecha cried, 'A treasure hunt!'

'It makes no sense,' Azare barked.

'It will when we work it out,' Meecha retorted.

'The diamond...' Nandil continued to mumble.

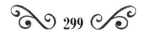

Azare rounded on the imp, 'I came to kill a demon, not indulge some mad thief.'

'So you admit to being a selfish, blood-driven brute,' Meecha spat. 'You don't care about the future of life in this world. You just want another trophy.'

'In the mountains...' whispered Nandil.

Azare bent closer with a low rumble, 'I shall rip your tongue out of your head.'

But Meecha would not back down. 'My tongue saved your neck. And, for the record, if you kill me, I'll come back and haunt you for the rest of your life. How many centuries will I have the pleasure of talking your ear off?'

'The diamond in the mountains...' Nandil repeated, his quizzical scowl suddenly loosening.

The Lady Mason decided to intervene. 'Please, my friends. This is no time to fight.'

'The diamond in the mountains!' Master Hithe gasped.

'I do not need saving!' Azare's roar shook the temple.

'Why? Are you a mighty thaelil who can't be touched by inferior beings? Last I saw, elves were mortal too,' Meecha pointed at the traces of blood on his slashed armour. 'Just like the rest of us.'

'Thaelil *are* superior!'

Nandil shouted something, but was ignored as Meecha let out a frustrated growl and stomped his foot. 'No wonder humans hate you! I'm curious, Azare, what do you think started the Rift War?'

'The humans.'

'And what caused their rebellion?'

'Their hunger for power,' Azare declared with vehemence.

'Wrong,' Meecha stabbed him with the word. 'It was the elves' arrogance. You were so sure of your own supremacy that you took all other races for granted. As just and virtuous as you think you were, you controlled your subjects with an iron fist that belittled and suffocated them and, ultimately, brought them to their breaking point. They had every right to bring down your tyranny. Get off your high horse and grow some compassion in that tiny heart of yours!'

Azare stared at him. It was the second time in his three hundred years that he had heard the thaelil referred to as tyrants. His ancestors had loved Therea and tried their best to maintain its prosperity. But it was also true that their advanced powers urged them into seclusion from the rest of the world. It was possible that they had not recognised the harshness of their ways, since they did not understand the people they ruled.

Nandil's voice emerged from the fragile silence that had fallen, 'I know what the diamond in the mountains is.'

All eyes turned to him. He cleared his throat and continued with a mysterious undertone.

'A couple of years ago, I overheard Inan tell grandpapa about a crystal island he'd found in the mountains along the eastern road. He said it shone like a diamond.'

'Did he give any further details?' Vora asked.

'No. But this message for Rune must be directions to it. All I know is that we start from the eastern road.'

'We?' Azare noted coolly.

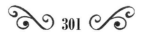

Nandil gave him a defiant nod, 'I'm coming with you. Inan is a good friend to us Hithes. Was... I want to know what happened to him. I also wish to see those monsters gutted. And, if that doesn't suffice, someone has to keep you two from killing each other.'

Vora entwined her hands upon her lap. 'You are set, then. We can request a few soldiers to accompany you.'

Meecha shook his head. 'That might not be wise. The fewer who know about the Key the better. We'll have to deal with the demons ourselves.'

The Master Architect nodded. Nandil stood, stating his need to sort some affairs at the store and prepare himself for the perilous journey. They all joined him on his way out of the temple. Once outside, the merchant agreed to meet them at the eastern gate in the morning and then departed. Azare was escorted by a polite priest to another building on the right side of the Beacon, but Vora kept Meecha behind.

'Items were found where the princess and her attackers fell, as well as on the body of the man thou pointed out. Could thou give thy insight?' the Lady Mason inquired, piquing Meecha's curiosity.

They entered the grandest structure, a fair distance to the Beacon's left. Inside were offices, libraries, and work-spaces for carpentry, alchemy, scribing, calculation, and who knew what else. Vora led him into a room occupied by a central counter, cupboards, and shelves containing books and scrolls. It looked like a storage area. Upon the counter were a number of objects. Meecha immediately recognised the Scavenger's sword. There was his brooch and a bunch of letters, the red ribbon that presumably once held them together forming loops beneath and around them.

'Have you read them?' Meecha asked.

Vora nodded. 'Indeed. They are letters of favour for a Nonar Akeida, but they seem old. Some of the lords and ladies addressing him are long buried.'

The Scavenger was either impersonating this Nonar or using a relative's influence to further his own.

'Does the brooch mean anything to you? A house's emblem, perhaps?' Meecha picked up the trinket and passed a thumb over the fox—or whatever the animal was called in Itania.

The Master Architect, hands on hips, shook her head. ''Tis not familiar to me, but we are searching the archives for its likeness.'

A fine set of dark leather saddlebags lay further down the counter. Meecha approached it, while theorising out loud to Vora.

'This man was making efforts to impress, and King Odigan was his ultimate target.'

'He was?' The priestess frowned. 'Art thou certain?'

'Yes, he admitted it, in a way,' Meecha told Vora as he lifted a saddlebag flap. 'But the more I think about it the more I believe that Akeida's goal was to get himself in the king's good graces. He dressed up as a noble, bore documents to support his claim of lordly descent, and, I think, took Chione's cub as a gift. A white and rare animal for Odigan's collection.'

The bag offered nothing unusual. Smoke and a pipe, a pouch of dried fruit, a comb, and a silk shirt. The other bag bulged tantalisingly. Meecha flipped its flap and gasped. There, crumpled into its confines, was his hat. He yanked

it out, ecstatic, only for his grin to drop. There was a dark stain, a wide dried streak, barely discernible against the hat's black. He brushed it lightly and his finger came up pink. It was blood. Meecha looked up at Vora, his eyes begging for a less horrifying explanation than what he imagined.

'The bags were under the wreckage. The hat must have fallen out in the turmoil. 'Tis thine?' the woman winced.

Meecha continued to stare. 'Whose blood is it?'

Those wrinkled lips pursed. Uncertainty quivered Vora's lashes. Her eyes were pale green, light and sad.

'It could belong to any one of them, Meecha. Do not torment thyself.'

Meecha's throat caught as he gazed down at the hat. He wanted to throw it away. Burn it. But it was dear to him. He found his fingers reluctant to let go of the brim. At the same time, he did not want it on his head. So it dangled by his side, a tainted love.

Vora was talking. 'We should get some rest and leave this horrid business for the morn. Light willing, we shalt find our answers soon enough.'

Those two words rankled Meecha. *Light willing.* He set a searching stare on the Master Architect and for a moment found her a fool, a gullible pawn. *Light willing.* But so was he. At least the priestess did not know better than the aerieti's benevolence. *Light willing.* They willed much.

Chapter 36

He wrung the cloth over the small bowl. The water tinkled sweetly as it fell, a sound too innocent for the blood it mingled with. The hat sat on Meecha's lap, one side sodden. He resumed scrubbing the stain away, making slow but steady progress. His fingers tingled against the cloth's wool, which had formed faint dimples beneath his tips. They were pink. He tried not to think about it too much. *I'm a hardened agent.* In fact, his attempt to convince himself that it was paint, or spilled dye, almost succeeded for a few moments. Then his heart sank again. *An agent true.* The pit in his stomach gaped wider, his anger bubbling up through it. Its sharpness frightened him to a pause. *I chose the mission over her.* He rubbed harder, focused his mind on cleaning the hat. The accusing daggers in his belly were smothered for a time, while the cloth was dipped and wrung and put to work twice more. The bowl was soon more blood than water, yet hints of the stain remained. Like Meecha's nightmare. Just touching the hat now, his soul's shield, his lucky charm, his sole

companion on many a quest, brought back the image of his own hands holding it up as a vessel for Delia's sacrificial blood, she hovering above him in her golden gown. *I sacrificed her.* Meecha's rage surged. *For the mission.* He flung the hat across the room. It gave the wall a harmless *slap* and rolled onto the floor, flat. His guilty hand flopped against his knee, while the other dumped the cloth in the red rippling water. A ragged sigh shook him before Azare's voice made him jump.

'Eat now or starve until noon.'

Azare was on a stool lacing up his boots. He had risen without Meecha even noticing. The elf clipped the three golden rings into his black hair, almost ceremoniously, and stalked out the bedroom. The night's tension left with him. The room, not to mention Azare's bed, had been too small to offer reprieve from their weariness or growing enmity.

Meecha glanced at the plate of fruit, bread, and yellow cheese waiting for him on the table. He stood abruptly and turned his back to it all, preferring the sight of the neatly folded clothes on a chair in the corner. He quickly changed into the child-sized garments: a white woollen shirt, brown trousers, a faded dark green jacket, and a pair of leather ankle boots. His compass fit snugly in a pocket over his heart. There was also a belt that held a sheathed dagger against his right hip. Meecha's old rags lay sprawled over the chair. Scolding himself, he folded them nicely and placed the wrecked sandals on top, their straps barely holding on by their threads. He made for the door, reaching for the handle, but then looked over his shoulder at the hat. It called to him, tugged at his conscience. He could not abandon it. Delia's death was not its doing. *Only mine.* Stiffly, Meecha picked it up from the floor and stormed out of the bedroom, knotted stomach filled only with bile.

Soon he descended the steps of the Residential Quarters, the drying hat hanging from between disgusted fingers. The sky was that misty blue of early morning. It made the priests in the azure robes look regal. The light of the Beacon, looming to the right of the building, radiated a glorious pale yellow. If it did not hurt his eyes, Meecha could have marvelled at it all day. Azare stood on the edge of the precipice beside the Beacon, looking down at the square. Meecha left the elf to his musings and moved in search of Vora. He wished to talk more about New Anvadore, this city blessed by the aerieti.

He made for the Temple across the plaza, where he had encountered Lord Opheiro. It took more than a few steps for the sound to knock on his awareness—an incoherent murmur of voices. He turned to the cliff again. The noise was definitely coming from below, in the direction Azare was staring. Meecha crossed a little bridge mounting the stream and hastened to the other side of the Beacon to peer over the edge. He gasped when he saw the swaying sea of people that had flooded the square around the well. They looked like ants from this height, dotted with faint flickers of candlelight. Their voices rose in a melodious hum, although the splashing waterfall obscured most of it. He still found himself entranced. Their song echoed throughout the Ground District and climbed the cliff to grip Meecha by the soul.

'They loved her so.'

Meecha looked up. He had not heard the Master Architect approach. Failed again by his senses.

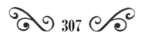

'Delia?' he asked, steeling himself.

The priestess nodded. 'For an Ayvik, she was a bright spirit.'

'Her family isn't popular, I take it.'

Vora frowned with puzzlement. 'They are odd folk. Odigan tries to prove that he is not his brother. And, in all fairness, he has succeeded. He is the founder of this fine city. He is good to his people, and Therea has prospered in his reign. But he is a troubled man. And who can blame him? A lifetime of anger, suspicion, guilt. Of trying to make up for Serikan's betrayal. We are lucky our king is only mistrustful. Unfortunately, his temperament has rubbed off on his children. Except for Delia. Out of all that austerity and gloom she came—a warm girl, compassionate and fearless. The unspoken wish of the people was to see her on the throne one day.'

The old woman may have been one of those people. Her sombre eyes ascended the great column, as if in askance, but when they reached the glowing lantern at the top she smiled sadly and placed a reverent hand on the marble. She turned from the cliff and headed for the trees beyond the plaza.

'Come,' she said.

Meecha followed and Azare strolled after them. They trailed the stream into the grove and then to where they had left the chanters. Chione was under attack by her little one. It hopped from side to side, grinning and yowling. It pounced onto the back of her neck and bit her ear, which she barely seemed to feel as she dozed beneath the trees. There were bones littered across the ground—hopefully none of human origin. A basin of water stood nearby with a fallen leaf floating in it. When Chione's head rose to acknowledge them, the cub slid down to sit astride his mother's shoulders. Vora stopped at a comfortable distance, while Meecha moved closer.

'Hello there,' he smiled.

She got up laboriously and met him halfway. The cub was crouched upon her back, clinging to her fur. Meecha knelt before her, shy as a rabbit. She sniffed his face and suddenly rubbed her head against his poor little noggin, knocking him onto his backside.

'I missed you too,' he chuckled and stroked her cheek.

Her fur was so thick and soft. She nudged his palm, and he scratched her jaw. This had clearly never happened to her before—her eyes widened and then closed into slits. She purred loudly. He moved to the back of her ear, scratching more vigorously. Chione sighed and squirmed with pleasure, tilting her head further into his hand. The cub whined. It reached out and patted Meecha's fingers. It welcomed his touch and nearly flopped off Chione as it melted like butter in his palm.

'This going to take long?' Azare's mordant voice intruded.

Meecha rolled his eyes and set the cub upright.

They all entered the gardens through the same magical door in the wall. They retraced their steps through the castle to the throne room, where they found the king in the company of two new faces, in addition to a dozen guards. One important-looking figure was a young man standing tall and broad-shouldered beside Odigan in his phoenix throne. His hair, waves black as coal, fell to the base of his neck. His sharp eyes were light, but Meecha could not make out their colour from this distance. He wore black, but for the collar of his tunic, which was threaded with white vines and studded with emeralds.

The smaller throne was occupied by the second presence, a flaxen-haired woman in a plain black gown that covered her from neck to toe. The closer Meecha got, the more lines he could discern on her aged face, but her beauty was still with her. A crown of spun white gold and rubies rested upon her head, her hair gathered high to leave her kind yet solemn features unhindered. There was a tenseness to her drawn lips, her deep blue gaze, her hands folded in her lap. Meecha instantly recognised those eyes. Dead pools staring up at the sky—that was his last memory of Delia's.

'Ah, there thou art,' King Odigan's resonant voice brought Meecha back to the present. 'I trust the priests housed you well?'

Meecha reached the bottom of the dais and bowed. 'Yes, your Majesty. We're rested and ready to set off.'

'Good, good. Captain Denna returned with this jar thou mentioned. It has been delivered to thy quarters, Mistress Teretta. All we can tell is that it seems to be blood, but thou may yield more from it.'

'With the help of the Light, I shalt examine it, Sire,' the Lady Mason responded. She then addressed Meecha. 'We may be wiser by the time thou return.'

'Return from where?' a gruff voice inquired.

It was the tall stranger.

'The east, thy Highness.' Vora was gracious yet curt. 'Our friends here shalt hunt down the fiends that attacked us.'

'An elf, a dwarf, a beast, and a cub. We are sending a circus instead of an army?' the man—the prince—demanded of Odigan.

The king patiently indulged his son. 'The army must stay to protect the city.'

'The elf hunts demons for a living,' Vora added. 'The beast's power equals, if not surpasses, the elf's. And Meecha here is a favoured agent of the Light. I can assure thee, thy Highness, there are none better suited for this task.'

The prince was not appeased. 'I shalt go too with our best men and mages.'

'Do not be absurd, Dradan,' the king grumbled.

'I want those monsters that murdered my sister. A larger force ensures their capture.'

'And slow us down,' Azare cut in. Meecha winced.

Prince Dradan turned his harsh eyes on the elf.

'Thou hunt them alone, I suppose. Hast thou been more successful than an army would be?'

Azare's expression darkened as the prince descended a step to look down his nose at Meecha. He had green eyes. *Snake eyes.*

'A favoured agent of the Light,' Dradan mused. 'And what would thy council be, wise one?'

Meecha trusted this human as much as a xalikai.

'Another assault may indeed be upon us, thy Highness,' he replied in his finest diplomatic tone—he could not help but mock the Therean royalties' dialect. 'A second demonic invasion. Thou and thine army art welcome to accompany us, but thy time would be better spent training and preparing for a threat far graver than two lesser fiends. A

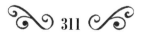

virtuous sovereign knows that some causes require risking the few for the many.' A pang of doubt checked his tongue for a moment. 'Our *circus* can match these foes. You should ready yourselves for the nightmares that come.'

Dradan's lips were a thin line.

A chuckle came from Odigan. 'Thy speech-craft would be invaluable to me, Master Roa. Do return to us in one piece, and thou shalt have a place in my court.'

Meecha bowed again. 'Your Grace honours me. I'll consider your offer once our hunt's concluded.'

'Of course, my friends. One of our finest horses awaits you at the gate, along with a week's provisions. I fear we do not have any more mounts to spare.'

Azare was about to protest, when he whipped round to look at Chione. Their eyes connected before the chantress began to climb the steps towards the woman.

'Get away from her,' the prince barked at the same instant that King Odigan leapt to his feet.

'Wait! Thy Majesty,' the elf hurriedly directed his words at the queen, 'she wishes to speak to thee. I shall interpret.'

Interpret? Meecha wondered.

Chione reached the woman, whose white-knuckled hands gripped the throne's arms. The chantress sat on her haunches, forcing the cub to jump down.

Dradan's blade was halfway out of its scabbard. 'I said—'

'She senses thy pain,' Azare interrupted the prince. 'As a mother, she has felt it too.'

The queen's eyes widened and she seemed to relax a little as she glanced from Chione to Azare and back again. Dradan and his father hesitated. They hunched warily, ready to rush to the queen's defence.

The elf continued with his hooded eyes fixed on the chantress, 'When she was taken from her home in the snow she had a... a litter of five. All she has left is this one. And she almost lost him too.'

The queen leant closer to Chione, her expression that of pained understanding.

'She could smell these strange beasts—demons, I think she speaks of—all through her journey. It is a... a pungent, bitter scent. Her family died because of these demons—I can feel her fury,' Azare shuddered. 'She wants thee to know, as a mother to a mother, that she shall avenge your daughter as she shall her own children.'

The cub suddenly yowled, and Azare laughed softly, a most unusual sound.

'And so shall he.'

The queen's tears escaped their confines and trickled down her pallid cheeks. She pressed her hand against her chest to keep her sobs at bay and whispered, 'Thank thee.'

The chantress picked up the cub in her mouth and padded down the steps. She paused at the bottom to drop him onto his own paws and then trotted towards the doors with the little one running after her.

'Your Majesties.' Meecha bowed once more to the queen and king.

'Bring me the demons' heads, if thou can,' Odigan requested of Azare.

'I shall keep one for myself, if thou do not mind.'

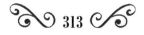

The king smirked.

Meecha reserved a shallow bob of his head for the prince. 'Your Highness.'

He noticed the man's irate scowl before Vora ushered him and Azare out of the throne room. They caught up with the chanters in the hallway outside.

'Is Dradan the heir?' Meecha asked Vora.

The Master Architect's nod was slow and glum.

'The wrong sibling has died,' Azare stated. He had stolen the words from Meecha's mouth.

They walked the rest of the way in silence, exiting through the heavy oak doors they had originally entered by. The gardens were now properly doused in sunshine. Meecha and his companions marched along the stone walkway towards the southeastern gates of the Second Ring. When he glanced around at the vibrant paradise, he spotted two people sitting on a bench along a left-hand path. They were surrounded by shrubbery blooming with pink and red flowers, but he could see that they both had the same black hair as Dradan. One's was long and the other's short. The one with the long hair glanced over a slender shoulder, and Meecha realised that it was a woman. She stood and advanced with such grace that she appeared to be floating along the flora-flanked path. The second person, a man, followed her to the junction where the two paths met. Black was also their choice of dress.

'Are they the other siblings?'

'Yes. Laylin and Ditrik Ayvik. She is now the youngest.'

The prince and princess halted about ten feet from the crossroads. Vora bowed deeply as she passed them by, as

did Meecha. Azare chose to be his defiant self and met their stares—beautiful they were. Her eyes were a lovely blue-green, while he had their mother's doe-eyed blue to soften the angles he had inherited from his father. It was Laylin, however, who put Meecha on edge.

Her face must have been what the queen had looked like in her youth. A pretty pointy nose, small red lips like rose petals, high cheekbones, and flawless skin. Her demure dress did little to hide the perfect curves beneath. For the naive observer she was a dark-haired angel, but Meecha could see a different creature in that sweet puckered smile that barely touched her twinkling, unreadable wolf-eyes. Once outside the castle grounds, Meecha sighed with relief. He felt safer chasing demons than being in the presence of the Ayvik children. He even missed his own family.

The broad streets of the Sky District were flanked by mansions, parks, and smartly dressed humans. He was less distracted than on his initial rush into the castle and noticed that some of the ladies' outfits were somewhat familiar. They possessed qualities similar to the fashion of seventeenth-century Europe, another part of Oparu. Vivid colours, wide sleeves, broad necklines, overskirts pinned back to allow full view of gaudy petticoats. Once more he questioned the commonalities between Oparu and Itania, first the language and now the fashion.

The next thing Meecha realised was the lack of horses. Vora explained that for reasons of cleanliness no large animals were allowed into the city, with a few exceptions. Horses were stabled at the gates, and livestock stayed outside the walls. Small pets were allowed, since they were fairly easier to care for. The multitude of man-drawn carts suddenly made sense.

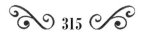

As usual, Chione and her cub, he riding on her back, were drawing too much attention, but the presence of the Lady Mason allowed them untroubled passage. Fortunately, Azare had pulled his hood over his head, and his distinctive pointy ears were not adding to the spectacle they had become.

'Here we are,' Vora announced as they reached the massive gateway—one of the Sentinel's heads could fit through that.

There were two vast structures on either side of the gate, accommodating at least fifty horses each. A number of the animals were roaming the paddocks out front or being fed, groomed, or prepared for their riders. Meecha was surprised to see the creatures do nought but flinch at the sight of Chione.

He looked up at Azare. 'Are you calming the horses?'

'Yes,' the elf responded through a face of stone.

It was a big chestnut stallion with black patches that Vora walked up to, saddled and strapped with bulging bags. It had a beard—short black and brown locks waving from its chin. The stable boy holding its reins handed them to the priestess, who then led the majestic animal back to Meecha and Azare.

'This is Thasha. He was a hardened traveller when his master was alive. I am sure he misses the open road.'

'He certainly hates the city,' Azare stated. 'But thaelil do not ride, and he cannot reach the stirrups.' He indicated Meecha with a brisk tilt of his head, who glared indignantly in return.

'I could use him,' Nandil's jovial voice preceded his cocked stride onto the scene.

A sizeable satchel hung from his shoulders over a long black coat, and a handsome longbow crossed his back, its arrows sticking out of a quiver at his hip. He saluted everyone with nods and smiles.

'He is all thine, Master Hithe,' Vora said, and Thasha's reins changed hands once more.

'Greetings, Thasha. I am Nandil. A fellow explorer, thou might say. Those look heavy.' Nandil looked at the saddlebags.

'They are,' Azare immediately complained.

Nandil quickly unfastened the straps and heaved the bags off the stallion only to shove them into the elf's arms.

'Thou can carry them then, mighty defender of horses.'

Meecha barked a laugh as Nandil leapt into Thasha's saddle and trotted off towards the eastern sun.

'Farewell, New Anvadore,' he hollered, waving the city goodbye. 'Do not weep, for Nandil Hithe shall return anon with tales and treasures for all his good friends.'

Azare hefted the bags and stalked after him.

'Good luck,' Vora clasped Meecha's hands with both of hers.

'Thank you. And good luck to you too... with the Ayviks and all.'

The woman sagged further, sinking into her weary age.

'There's always Light to be found.' Meecha did not permit a hint of doubt to infect his gentle voice.

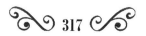

Vora smiled appreciatively. 'I know,' she said. 'It stands before me now.'

A knot constricted Meecha's throat, but he managed to utter a final farewell before his emotions got the better of him. Chione padded up beside him, the cub swaying with the motion. Seeking some support, some comfort, Meecha rested a hand on her shoulder. She purred as the silver walls of New Anvadore became another part of the past. The hat remained by his side. His losses still very much in the present.

Chapter 37

Azare glanced behind him. Thasha trotted at a leisurely pace with Nandil and Meecha on his back. Chione was not in much of a hurry either. She and her son plodded on behind the bearded horse, as if on a stroll instead of a hunt. A day had gone by, and they had progressed half what he would have alone. *Why stay? Is there any use to them?* Perhaps. They had knowledge. And Meecha had the chanters—Chione was a fine fighter. If nothing else, the imp and human could serve as shields. Whether Azare liked it or not, he had companions now. And what company they were.

At first, Meecha and Nandil's entertainment had been to gossip about the royal family. The human had so many outrageous tales it took him most of the morning to unload all regarding Ditrik's love for games and women. Dradan's reputation was darker compared to his little brother's scandalous one. Apparently, the heir of Therea was quite un-

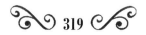

kind towards the small-folk, not to mention suspected of spinning his own schemes in the web of the nobility. Surprisingly, Nandil did not have much to say about Laylin, except to praise her beauty and her singing voice. When Meecha had expressed his concern over the princess's character, Nandil had refused to believe that anything crooked could exist behind her heavenly face. He only reconsidered when Azare asked him if Laylin's innocence felt the same as Delia's. The human had gone quiet as he gradually shed his cloud of gullibility and realised that Laylin Ayvik's sweetness might not be so true after all.

Meecha had then taken Nandil's mind off the matter by suggesting they find a name for the cub. That was the only time Azare felt the weight of the saddlebags on his shoulder. Even after they had made their choice, his encumbrance did not lessen. *Have they forgotten what we're here for?* He searched the horizon for Inan's 'nose', the first clue in the thief's directions to the 'diamond in the mountains'. Rune would have known immediately what her father was referring to, but she was dead. All Azare had was a useless pair of chatterboxes.

'We should make camp soon,' Nandil said.

The sky was darkening, but there was enough daylight left to cover a bit more road.

'Not yet,' Azare grumbled.

A few moments went by, and the human spoke again.

'We must rest. We shall start off again at first light.'

'If thou want to stop, do so,' Azare fired back. 'I shall not.'

'You have the provisions,' Meecha piped in.

'You should have thought of that before you gave them to me.'

Nandil cursed Azare, but Thasha's hooves still clopped after him. The forest on their left was thickening with shadows, but the hills beyond the valley on their other side could still be seen against the fiery sky. *A little further.*

When the night was almost truly upon them, Chione stalked away towards the trees. The cub, now dubbed Adalis, remained with them, but was constantly glancing in the direction of the forest and yowling. Not long after, his mother emerged dragging a big feathered carcass. It looked like a cicho, a long-legged bird native to Therea. Adalis bolted in the direction of his meal.

'Aren't you hungry?' Meecha asked of Azare.

'We do not know how long this hunt shall be. We need to make the food last.'

Then came Nandil's heated remark. 'Do we have a say in the matter, slave driver?'

Azare growled a sigh, 'Fine! We stop now.'

The human slid off Thasha, his bow and arrows bumping awkwardly, and helped Meecha down. He then led the stallion to the side of the road and started looking for something to tether him to. Azare squatted over the bags and inspected their contents, when the dwarf turned to him. 'Could you tell Thasha not to run off?'

Azare grudgingly reached for the horse's consciousness, for having Nandil and Meecha travelling on foot would slow them down considerably. Thasha's mind was calm yet alert. He was tired and hungry, but also excited about this new journey. He was not fond of being so close to the big hunter. He did not mind his two riders though. Azare requested of the stallion not to leave them and then expressed their need of his strength, which Thasha appreciated. The horse responded that he would love to run free again, but the dangers of this land were known to him, and he would prefer to be in the safety of their herd. He would stay.

'It is done.' Azare resumed his exploration of the bags.

The little man spoke to Nandil. 'You can release him.'

The human was doubtful. He expected the stallion to balk as soon as he was free. But he did not. Instead, he lowered his head and grazed. Nandil unsaddled him and still he stayed, munching on grass. Meecha seemed amused by Thasha's compliance, an attitude that wavered as he dropped his hat on the ground. Azare had found it odd that the thing had been in his hand instead of on his head the whole time. Now he perceived a wrongdoing on the hat's part. Meecha had a broken mind, no doubt about it.

By the time a fire was lit and their dinner served—salted pork, bread, and cheese—Chione and Adalis had returned from their feast, white snouts smeared with blood. As they made their way to Meecha, Thasha stepped away nervously. When the chanters sat, he halted on the opposite side of the campfire, behind Azare. The horse's large dark eyes watched them intently, while they licked their lips and purred with contentment.

Nandil sat on his blanket. When he had yanked it out of his bag earlier, a number of items had flown out with it: a book, a fork, a comb, and a tinderbox, the last of which they used to ignite the twigs for the fire. Meecha and Azare had been provided with bedrolls in addition to the food and skins, one containing wine, the other water.

After their meal, Nandil was eager to break into the wineskin, and Meecha was happy to oblige. The human immediately extracted three tin cups from his bag, stating that you should always be prepared for a chance encounter with a good spirit. Azare declined the cup offered him, refusing to drink his senses numb. While they served themselves, Nandil lamented his own small collection of nectars he had to leave behind at the shop. They clinked their cups and drank to things and lives lost.

What do they know of loss? Azare unsheathed his left sword and laid it across his legs before extracting from a pocket a cloth wrapped around a small vial of translucent yellow oil. He sprinkled some of the oil onto the cloth and began to wipe the blade. There was still blood along the edge that had robbed the she-demon of her hand. The rest of her would be quartered soon enough and she would become his twenty and eighth kill. Not a bad count, but not the best either. Brother Akhil's sakairin lined his brow with fifty and three marks. But his age was great. He was older than Azare by almost five centuries. Yet demons still thrived. It forced Azare to question the worth of their efforts. His heart clenched, and he scrubbed the metal harder, its sheen mirroring the fire's blaze.

'What was Serikan Ayvik's betrayal?' Meecha was asking. 'All I know is that he went crazy, set fire to his castle, and disappeared.'

'There are tales aplenty to boggle thy head,' Nandil responded, swallowing the last of his wine. He reached for the skin by his foot. 'But there's an old poem that hints towards the true happenings.'

Master Hithe filled his cup to the rim and handed the skin to Meecha so he could replenish his own. He then took a swig, cleared his throat, and began his recitation. His deep, dramatic voice even drew a sidelong glance from Azare.

'How, oh, how Golden King

Smite thou the elven kin?

How, oh, how the fate of man

Tipped thy mighty hand?

How, oh, how thou forged the city

With heart and voice and majesty?

How, oh, how thou reached for glory

In the claws of ancient history?

Why, oh, why Golden King

Allow the demon in?

Why, oh, why Fallen King

Burn thy loyal kin?'

Nandil rewarded himself with more wine, while his companions brooded in silence. Azare remembered the elders speaking of the time when Anvadore, the first human capital of Therea, had gone up in flames at the hand of the same man who had stolen the kingdom from them. While Azare's kin plotted their return to their rightful place, there were some who wondered what had come to pass. What evil had possessed Serikan that he would turn to ashes all that he had bled to achieve... and all those people who had devoted their lives to him? Speculations came and went, mainly surrounding his power-hungry nature. There were suggestions that he was a fiend himself, but that was all they were—notions born from anger. Azare now found himself considering the implication of a demon whispering in a king's ear.

'How are you so sure this is the truth and not just another rumour?' Meecha asked Nandil.

The human leant closer, eyes twinkling in the firelight.

'I have my sources. And accounts too similar to be coincidence. There has been talk of magical scrolls an' sinister doings in the last few cycles before the fire. Something was amiss, an' the king was involved.'

'Why would demons want to destroy Anvadore? Wouldn't they rather profit from it?'

'Demons are sly, unpredictable in their ways,' Azare offered. 'And they are attracted to all things dark: violence, greed, lust. They must have been drawn to Serikan like bees to honey.'

But why brave such a prominent figure? Risking the sight of man and thaelil alike.

'Do you think what they were trying to do to Delia is connected to what happened to Serikan?' Meecha wondered, dread bending his voice to a mumble.

Nandil gazed at him for a moment before knocking back the rest of his wine, wincing as it flooded his gullet.

'That jar. They said it might be blood, did they not?' Azare said.

'Yes.' The dwarf's apprehension spread to his face, while he waited for Azare to put his thoughts into words.

'It may have been demon blood. If consumed, it can have strange effects on people. It can render one ill, delirious, aggressive. It depends on where the blood came from. But the demons could have also enchanted the blood in the jar towards a specific purpose.' He set his jaw. 'It may well be that they intended to possess the girl.'

'Ah, enough of this,' Nandil suddenly moaned. 'Am goin' a sleep.'

His eyelids were already drooping when he stretched himself upon the blanket. Meecha checked that his hat was still beside his bedroll, gave the cats a scratch goodnight, and curled up, but did not close his eyes for a long while. *An agent of the Light? He probably did come from a circus.*

Only when both swords were clean and gleaming did Azare too lie to rest with the sheathed weapons at his sides. He slept lightly, allowing his consciousness to dip but one foot into slumber's tranquil pool. Its waters tugged at him, inviting him in. There was little he longed for more than to surrender, but he resisted. He had to remain vigilant in case anything crept up on them. He feared as well the dreams that came... It was always the fires that he saw, the gold and the red. Thaelil and trees screaming in the inferno. The horror. The guilt. And then the face, flames licking away porcelain skin to leave sizzling... *Stop!* He emptied his mind of thought and emotion, until there was nothing but a void. In this blank cocoon he remained until morning.

As soon as the glow of the sun's first rays touched the eastern sky, his eyes snapped open. He was far from rested, but his body had recuperated enough to carry him a long way. He roused his companions as he laid out a small breakfast of bread, meat, and two oranges. Meecha settled for three orange slices. Nandil and Azare finished off the remainders, while Chione and Adalis went off to hunt. It did not take long for their party to return to the road. Azare was pleased. They kept their original formation as they spanned the unchanging landscape.

Meecha resumed his typical conversations with Nandil, often focusing on topics concerning Therea's culture. The dwarf turned out to be knowledgeable of the kingdom's affairs, especially during the time of the elves' reign. He even named many thaelil kings and queens in sequential order. Perhaps Meecha was more than he appeared. Whether a divine messenger or a clever spy, he knew things none outside thaelil society should be privy to.

They stayed true to their pace until the hot midday sun forced them to seek shelter amid the trees. Azare was loath to stop, but even he had his limits in this heat. Chione was agitated. Her tail swished back and forth, lifting a film of dust from the ground. Her ears kept twitching backwards, and she could not sit still. Adalis tried to snuggle against her, but the unbearable temperature drove him away every time.

At some point, Meecha mentioned a strange cloud that had followed Chione and him on their way to New Anvadore, providing them with shade and water. Azare recalled some of his Elemental Lore from home and of the water sprites flying their clouds around the world carrying word and comfort. He told the dwarf this, which seemed to amuse him greatly, exclaiming that the sprites must be allied to the aerieti. When Azare and Nandil gave him peculiar looks, he explained that these aerieti creatures were in truth the Divine Architects' so-called Light. And his masters. The little man then plugged his lips with the mouth of the waterskin.

They soon took off again, but this time through the forest and all on foot. The road on their right ran straight and unhindered, until shortly before dusk they found a huge rock lying on the left side of the track.

Meecha was the first to point it out. 'The nose!'

Nandil barked a disbelieving laugh at the rock, which did indeed resemble a nose sticking out of the ground. It even had nostrils.

The human recited Inan's poem, 'Wheel thy way from the nose to the toads.'

Meecha wrinkled his own nose trying to puzzle it out, while Azare drew profound satisfaction from knowing something that he did not. 'The symbol of the North is the Wheel.'

The dwarf lit up with interest. 'Why?'

Azare sighed and explained in a monotone. 'The needle of a compass spins like a wheel when on the exact northern point of the world.'

'Does it? Interesting,' Meecha squinted, while Nandil looked around, seeming to be taking note of landmarks.

The dwarf pulled out a shiny gold compass from his jacket and clicked it open. He frowned at the hand and looked over his shoulder—towards the southeast—just as Nandil pointed at the immense wilderness of Caod before them.

'That way.'

Puzzlement pursed Meecha's lips. Whatever intelligence he had, it seemed, did not include navigation.

Chapter 38

Meecha swiped yet another cobweb from his face. *Thasha's doing it on purpose.* On foot there had been no such problem. He was having a hard time clambering over roots and rocks, though, not to mention climbing out of the holes he would stumble into. Azare would have skewered him, if Nandil had not wisely hoisted him into the stallion's saddle. His feet had not touched the ground since. *We should be stopping for the night soon.*

The positive side of the situation was that he had the chance to study the forest without having to worry about his every step. The first word to pop into his head to describe the forest of Caod was old. It was dense, dark, and eerie. You could barely see the earth through the bed of leaves and jutting roots. Some of the trees had trunks thick as houses. Others were twisted and gnarled. They were all draped in elaborate, shimmering spiderwebs or shrouding

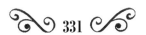

the nests of unseen birds. Apart from their occasional twitter, it was quiet. Very quiet.

Thasha picked his way carefully as he followed Azare, the elf prowling effortlessly through the trees. Nandil trudged along behind the horse, his pack jingling softly, his bow occasionally tapping a branch or a root. The quiver was on his back now. Chione found her own path alongside the rest of them with Adalis on her back—he had been having similar difficulties to Meecha.

But he's growing. He was a little taller than when they first met, and he seemed to have built some muscle. Meecha pictured the young chanter as an adult. He could become greater than his mother. What a sight they would make, the two of them together.

The thought made Meecha smile, although Chione's behaviour was a cause for concern. Her tail had not stopped swishing since they entered the forest. It was that agitated whip-like swish. Her head was still sunk, her ears plastered to her scalp. Those wild golden eyes shifted every which way, pupils dilating to black pits with every sudden sound. The rustle of a leaf. The breath of the breeze. The flutter of wings. Each one had been putting the chantress further and further on edge. When Meecha asked Azare if he knew what was wrong with her, the elf had replied that her thoughts were ambiguous at best. The blame was placed on Caod's thick atmosphere, since even she could not decipher what she smelt.

They continued their trek for perhaps another hour before Azare decided to call a halt. A fly buzzed past Meecha's head as Nandil helped him down from the saddle. He stamped his cramped legs, while the elf lit a modest fire and laid out their dinner. He was not much of a cook—it was the same scraps of pork and bread and cheese. The last two were turning a bit stale as well. Meecha wished he could take a peek into those saddlebags. If they had oranges, who knew what else was in there?

Azare surprised him by yielding some slices of sun-dried tomatoes. He also added the half-empty wineskin to their scanty banquet. The elf had either decided to be generous or was hoping that Nandil and Meecha would promptly drink themselves to sleep. Strangely enough, Chione had not gone off to hunt, so Azare gave her and the cub some meat to chew on. Thasha happily walked around, munching on flowers and foliage. He was unperturbed by the ghostly forest, but the chantress still gazed around as if expecting an attack.

Their evening was not disrupted, however. Nandil shared stories of his time as a travelling tradesman, not just in New Anvadore, but in cities all across Therea and beyond her borders. He told them of Dakrá, a neighbouring union of towns, residing in the wilds of the south. Its mountains and crags were peopled by brave but gruff folk. It was said that it was easier to survive the Dakrá River than a Dakráni's temper. Nandil then boasted of having crossed a dreaded forest called the Sakai Akek, a name that made Azare's head pop up to attention.

'It is Thaelil,' he said. 'Its meaning is Demon's Claws.'

Nandil chuckled nervously before recounting his experience. Trees more like vines bristling with thorns, insects that thirsted for his blood, voices that tried to lure him to madness. The more he described this place, the more Meecha believed its name held some relevance to the claws left behind by the demon Arak. This Sakai Akek would be a good place to look for his hand.

Nandil quickly changed the subject to one that brightened his mood considerably—the Ca'roon Isles, the largest of which was entirely inhabited by women. As the tale went, the first of them to find the island had been running from lives riddled with peril and abuse. The women trained themselves with the bow. The spear and sword too. Men were advised to never tread its shores without the consent of its people. Ilja Island was now an independent community never short of denizens, for even in the present day many disgruntled women sought its refuge, some often with child. They had goats and chickens. They grew vegetables and fished. They even practised their own medicine and mystical crafts. Some of the most notorious female mages were Thorns.

'Thorns?' Meecha asked.

Nandil nodded, 'The Ilja's Thorns. That is what they are known as. And they do not seem to mind.'

'What happens if the pregnant women give birth to sons?'

'They feast on baby stew,' Nandil replied nonchalantly.

Meecha's stomach churned. Both he and Azare gaped at him, until the human burst into roars of laughter. The elf gave Nandil a disgusted look, while he doubled over, cackling like a madman. It took him several moments to collect himself, coughing and teary-eyed.

'Boys an' girls, they keep them all,' he explained sheepishly, failing to keep the occasional chortle under control. 'The few men that do live on Ilja are Thorn-born, brought up as equals to the women. In truth the sons are deeply valued, for when they leave to make their fortune, they bear the Thorns' hope for change.'

'Thou seem to know much about these Thorns. For a man,' Azare noted.

Nandil blushed and reached for the wineskin.

'I... eh... met one,' he mumbled.

A mischievous grin stretched across Meecha's face.

'Met one? Do tell that tale.'

Nandil took a long swig straight from the skin and swallowed gradually, mulling over his coy response. 'Her name was Esierta. She saved my life. She told me of her home while we walked to the nearest town. An' that is all I shall say about her.'

Azare was uninterested in any more particulars. He unfastened the scabbards' straps that crossed his chest.

'What about thee, Meecha?' Nandil retaliated with a sly smirk. 'Is there a special lady dwarf?'

'First of all, I'm not a dwarf. Secondly, there have been many special ladies in my life.' He cocked his head smugly at the human. What he was not about to confess was that most of those luima girls wanted to get close to Jaika or a shoulder to cry on when his brother broke their hearts.

'If not a dwarf, then what are thee?' the elf wanted to know.

'Oh, don't change the subject, Azare.' Meecha was eager to turn the spotlight on someone else. 'It's your turn. How many beauties have you stolen from us plain folk? Hundreds, I bet.'

A deep scowl distorted Azare's face as he set his swords upon his lap.

'More? Less?' Meecha probed.

The elf's discomfort made Nandil join in. The wine had imbued his cheeks and nose with a rosy hue. His elbow poked Meecha a bit too hard. 'I think our friend has had his heart broken.'

'Oh, no! What happened? Which one turned thy majesty's face upside-down?'

Meecha blinked. He heard a faint whistling sound and a yelp. When he opened his eyes again, he found a glimmering steel point hovering before his left eye-socket. Chione was up and growling vehemently at Azare.

'The one who died.' His hoarse voice slid down the blade.

Violent tremors seized Meecha's body. They threatened to make his fear seep down his pants. His jaw was slack, his throat dry. He dared raise his sight from the razor-sharp edge and meet the elf's glare. The sword was still, as if wedged in rock, but Azare's calmness was gone. His lips were curled back into a vicious snarl. His shaking was almost as bad as Meecha's.

'We shall part ways on the morrow,' he rumbled. 'Or I may serve thy head to the Light on the flat of my blade.'

A mist now shrouded his honey eyes. He blinked it away and stormed off through the trees.

Chapter 39

Meecha opened his eyes to a cloud of white. He soon recognised it as fur and the thing pushing against him a stomach bulging and receding with breath. He lifted himself up to his elbows to take in the rest of Chione sleeping soundly beside him. He glanced around for Adalis and found him playing with his hat, the cub's tiny fangs exploring its rim.

'No,' Meecha croaked and scrambled towards the cub.

Adalis pounced away, looking quite perplexed. Meecha snatched the hat from the ground and yanked it down over his head. He glowered at the young chanter standing a few feet away with his head tilted to the side, perhaps wondering what he did wrong. Meecha took a deep breath and smiled at him, stretching out a hand. The cub inched nearer. When he was close enough, Meecha scratched the top of his head, which made him arch his neck and purr. He sprawled himself across Meecha's knees, demanding a full back rub. Meecha obliged, while looking around the camp.

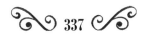

Nandil and Chione were roused by his voice. Thasha rubbed his neck against a tree, his big brown eyes watching Adalis and him. Azare was nowhere to be seen. His bedroll was gone, but the saddlebags were still there.

Meecha could not remember the last time he had felt such fear. The elf had almost killed him. He had seen it in his eyes. Whatever had stayed Azare's hand, Meecha was grateful. But the bitter taste of cowardice and guilt still lingered in the back of his throat. He had been so quick to condemn Azare that he did not take the time to fathom what could have shaped him into the person he was today. A life as a demon-hunter had been sufficient background information. But the death of a woman... That was an unexpected piece to the puzzle, a puzzle Meecha had unknowingly upturned the night before.

He gently moved Adalis from his lap and approached the saddlebags. He rummaged through them, expecting to discover delicacies that the elf had kept to himself, but it did not turn out that way. Other than the usual suspects — a loaf of stale bread, a wheel of cheese, a hunk of salted meat — there were two more oranges, a generous pouch of dried tomatoes, raisins, and nuts. Assuming Azare had lightened the load before leaving, Meecha made the best of their supplies.

He handed Nandil some raisins along with his bread and cheese before cutting one of the oranges into quarters with a knife he found in a pocket. With his hair dishevelled, his clothes all crumpled, and a sour after-wine face, the human looked aged and as awkward as Meecha felt. The elf's absence was noticed, but all Nandil did was frown at his food before cramming it into his mouth.

'Did you,' Meecha wondered, 'know about...?'

Nandil shook his head. And mumbled while chewing, 'I didn't.'

He swallowed and sipped some water.

'What do you think happened to her?' Meecha said.

The human shrugged, 'Demons? It would explain his obsession with them.'

Meecha popped a raisin into his mouth and gnawed on his thoughts.

'It could have something to do with his leaving his people. But... whether he chose to leave or was in fact exiled, if a demon was involved, why would Azare need to go? What if,' his eyes widened and he gasped, 'what if he killed her?'

Nandil scowled at him, but Meecha continued, 'Think about it. Some demons can change form. How do you think he'd react if he found out his lover was actually a demon?'

Nandil shook his head. 'Thou making up stories now. Anyways, would they not forgive his crime once they knew what she was?'

Meecha pursed his lips.

'Azare is a hunter, a soldier to his people.' Nandil's gaze on his bread darkened before he tore a bit off with his teeth and rolled it around while talking. 'We can only guess what he endured. But if there's something we did learn yesterday 'tis that his past is in truth beyond guesswork. An' that one should never discuss a thaelil's personal life.'

They finished their breakfast and gathered their belongings. With the awful stain practically gone, Meecha's hat proved to be less discomfiting to wear, so he reluctantly kept it on his head. Thasha was now given the duty of carrying the saddlebags in addition to Meecha, but no complaint came from the stallion.

'We are still going north, yes?' Nandil asked.

Meecha pulled out the compass. If north was twelve o'clock to the needle's four, then…

'Yes,' he replied as the black pointer looked past his right shoulder. 'And I'd think that Azare will be doing the same. We may catch up to him.'

He put the compass back in his pocket.

'I wouldn't mind if we kept our distance,' Nandil said cagily.

'That's not an option. He's important to this cause. We need him on our side, not against us.'

The human regathered his hair with a leather strap as he took the lead. Chione took the tail. She was calmer today, Meecha was pleased to see. Her step was lighter, and her eyes would now meet his instead of darting in every direction. Perhaps it had been Azare that had made her nervous. Who knows what he had been whispering to her?

Adalis sniffed the air from atop his mother, listening to the chiming of Caod's birds. The forest was far more enchanting during the day with the sun's haze floating through the wizened trees. There was a bit of movement as well, shy creatures skulking in the bushes. The previously invisible cobwebs now glimmered as they floated into the light.

Wheel your way from the nose to the toads. Follow a maid bright. Fly or descend, you shall swim. Inan did not give much away when it came to riddles. Then again, the 'nose' was a nose, albeit a stone one.

They passed the day in peace. Nandil filled their time with song and saga. He was quite the entertainer, more bard than merchant. Despite the man's flair, Meecha found himself appreciating the quiet between acts. Their midday meal was taken on foot—in the saddle for Meecha—while Chione disappeared for a hunt. When she returned with two fat rabbits, the party halted to let the chanters—and Thasha—eat. The horse looked less nervous around the cats as he grazed. Meecha took this chance to stretch his legs and do some exercises to warm up his body, much to Nandil's amusement.

A short time after they had set off again, rain began to fall. It pattered against the canopy of interwoven treetops. It did nothing, however, to stop the moist mist that had built up around the party. The coolness gradually seeped into Meecha and made him shiver, but he sighed despite himself. There were certain things in life he had developed a keen appreciation for. Warm pies, for one. Jazz music. Kind people. And the smell of rain. Coming from a planet as harsh and dry as Durkai, he could not get enough of that sweet, crisp freshness. It filled him with a sense of love and cleanliness. Caod had an exceptionally breathtaking smell. All the maturity of its wood, soil, and flora washed over him as he inhaled deeply. His insides fluttered and he chuckled. Meecha pulled his coat tighter around himself.

The rain stopped by nightfall, but it had already left its mark. Even Meecha had to admit that he was looking forward to a cosy fire and a hot meal. Nandil dumped the pile of wood he had collected and extracted his tinderbox, as well as a small pot, from his bag of wonders. In his eagerness to get a fire started, he forgot poor Meecha on Thasha. Chione trotted past, oblivious to his plight. He studied the ground. It was precariously far from the stallion's back.

He turned again to the human, deciding that it was best to forsake his pride than break his legs. Nandil's lips were pulled thin against his teeth as he struggled to ignite the soggy branches. Meecha called to him, but his voice was drowned out by Chione's hiss.

Her fangs were bared, claws out, hackles high, and eyes trained on something in the air. Adalis cowered behind his mother, the black of his eyes widening as he too followed whatever was flying in erratic circles above their heads. Nandil froze in mid-strike of the tinderbox to stare at the canopy, while Thasha skipped from hoof to hoof, unsettled by the chanters. Meecha clung to the saddle and tried to follow everyone's gaze. Once he caught sight of the tiny black speck dashing from one side to another, a bird swooped down from a tree and took chase of the insect. They zoomed past Meecha and through the trees from whence their party had come. Everyone was still and silent. Chione's guarded stance did not change, but Adalis stepped forward, his ears perked. Meecha's heart had just begun to settle when two sounds were heard: a roar followed by a squawk. His blood curdled.

'I think we should keep going,' he suggested to Nandil without taking his eyes from the direction of the sounds.

Nandil shoved the pot and tinderbox back into his sack. This time it was Meecha and Thasha who led the way at a hurried pace with Nandil and the chanters close behind. *What was that?* Two possible answers existed. A Caod beast. Or a demon. Shaped as a fly. The one Azare was hunting? How long had it been tailing them? What had it heard? Horror gripped Meecha. He tried to remember if they spoke of Vora at all. And of Inan's riddle. *Only the first line.* They had been watching them all this time — since entering Caod! That was when Chione had started to act strangely. It must have been the demon she had smelt, but in its fly form she could not identify it. Not until now. *Azare!* The demon-fly must have gone after the elf. That would explain the chantress's brief respite. What if it caught up with him? What if he ran into a trap? The same trap that Chione had been anticipating the night he left. *I'm his guardian. I'm to keep him safe.*

Meecha spurred Thasha faster, and the stallion complied, as fast as the trap-riddled path would allow his hooves to go. It did not take long for Chione and Adalis to overtake them, she being far more agile than a horse. Nandil held his own. He seemed accustomed to cross-country jogs. Meecha would have offered him the saddle, but it would not have been fair to Thasha. At any rate, there was no sign of pursuit, so maintaining their speedy trot was their only objective for the time being.

After a while, the forest's earthy scent changed. It was slowly infiltrated by faint smoky wisps. They grew muskier the further the party advanced into Caod. It was a contrasting smell, both sweet and pungent. It reminded Meecha of an extinguished match. Soon enough they came upon its origin.

The ground sloped downwards abruptly into what looked like an overgrown crater. There were more trees upon the ridges of the hole than within it, and those within were crooked and leafless, like skeletal fingers broken into contorted angles. The moonlight moved freely in there, but created no magic. It was rather sucked into a thick fog drifting around to manifest swirling white wraiths.

Meecha shivered at the foreboding sight and Thasha agreed with his hunch. The stallion halted at the edge of the crater and would not move further. He had said through Azare that he knew some things of the area's dangers, and Meecha was not about to defy him. His great head turned to the right, and he walked around the mysterious hole. The others tagged along, Nandil looking relieved that they were avoiding the fog. *Did Azare do the same?*

Chapter 40

Meecha looked out over the fog's fluffy white plains just rising past the crater's rim. What could have made that impressive dent in the ground? A meteor? A very small one, otherwise the whole forest would have been destroyed. The smell, however. There was no smoke to pinpoint a fire, but it was not a simple smoky odour, was it? It was sulphurous, sprouting from the middle of a forest to negate all other smells. *Would it even mask a demon's scent from Chione?* He hoped not. But if it did, it would surely work to their advantage too. The demons would have just as hard a time sniffing them out. This was what Meecha chose to believe, while he watched over his sleeping comrades.

They had skirted the crater for several hours before Nandil had declared that he could go no further. So they halted for the rest of the night under the shelter of deeper trees, away from the moon's light that could betray their location. No fire. No cooking. Just a cold snack and sleep with Meecha on watch. It was the least he could do, feeling quite the lord riding the whole way while everyone else walked. Again he cursed his small legs, his feeble being. He tested the point of his dagger on a finger, mocking its usefulness in his hands. What could he do if a demon showed up? Stab its toe? Run around it? Throw raisins at it? *Just keep your eyes and ears open.* And this he did until morning.

The first to stir was Adalis. He stretched from his mother's side, tail arching, and yawned, flashing his teeth. He came groggily to Meecha and nudged his hand with a wet nose, startling him out of his trance. His gaze had been fixed on the rolling fog turning a sandy yellow with the dawn. He must have fallen asleep with his eyes open. It felt like it. He thought he had dreamt of that wonderful sunrise he had seen back home. A forlorn feeling now accompanied his torpor. His head drooped towards the young chanter trying to make his fingers work. With fits and starts, Meecha's brain was set into motion. It sent the command for his hand to move, to glide gently over the cub from head to tail.

Chione woke with a sneeze, her ears back. A lazy grumble escaped her throat as she yawned, her teeth rows of lethal white stalactites bordering a cave that could envelop half of Thasha's head. This same thought must have gone through the stallion's mind. He shied away from the chantress, his clopping hooves rousing Nandil when he passed him by.

The human rubbed his eyes and face, and sat up with a groan. He squinted at his surroundings and mumbled, 'I miss my bed.'

Meecha shared the sentiment but only had the strength to nod. His hand was stuck in a repetitive cycle, stroking Adalis's silky-soft fur again and again. Naturally, the chanter enjoyed every moment of it.

It was Nandil who handed out their breakfast. Chione and Adalis settled for some meat and cheese. To Meecha it all tasted like ash, but he swallowed it anyway. He had a long drink of water, and it occurred to him that he had not brushed his teeth since Crove. It had been a while since he bathed too. HHHe surely reeked worse than the forest. *The demons need only follow my stench.* Soon a miserable Meecha allowed himself to be lifted onto Thasha's back once more.

'Sleep, now, lad,' Nandil told him, and he obeyed gladly.

He lay over the front of the saddle, legs dangling, hands folded beneath his cheek. Trees hovered past as his eyes rolled back into his skull. The stallion's motion quickly rocked him to sleep, and he dipped into blessed emptiness.

When he came to, his left hand hung against Thasha's shoulder and a lock of the horse's mane glistened with drool. Meecha quickly wiped it away with a sleeve and straightened up. He gazed at the forest that was still bearing down on them, his mind clearer and his mood brighter. Nandil was ahead, also staring this way and that, up and down. The chanters were behind. The cub yowled at Meecha when it saw him looking. He waved back.

The smell is stronger. He wrinkled his nose. A branch snapped beneath Thasha's hoof, making Meecha wince. There was no hope of going unheard with this clutter of wood, rocks, and dry leaves underfoot. He hunched over the horse's neck and paid close attention to his surroundings for the rest of the day.

By evening the smell had become toxic. On the one hand, Meecha was positive that they had reached its source.

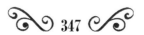

On the other, he put aside the meteor theory. This was more of a chasm, a fissure, a long scar in the earth. He buried his face in his coat, as did Nandil. The animals, however, had no such luxury. Chione and her son kept growling and sneezing. Thasha's ears were fully turned. He tossed his head and snorted.

The fog was thicker here, and as daylight faded, its fiery glow became more and more apparent. At this point, it did look like smoke, grey tendrils drifting up from numerous places. Hissing noises came from the depths of the fissure, infernal roars. Gurgling, burping sounds added to the hellish ambience. Meecha spent some time observing the foul-smelling cloud, expecting to see some movement within—a tail, a horn, a wing—until Thasha stopped abruptly. Nandil had halted in front of him to face the fissure, his teary eyes wide above the muffled half of his face.

'What is it?' Meecha called through his collar.

'What does that sound like?' the human asked in return.

Meecha frowned and stretched his ears. It suddenly dawned on him.

'Toads!'

Nandil's eyes were smiling.

'So, now we must follow a maid bright.' Meecha could barely contain his excitement. 'What's that? The moon? Which one?'

Nandil, looking quite mysterious in his shroud, shook his head.

'As the Wheel is the symbol of the North, the Sun Maiden is the symbol of the East.'

Meecha took out the compass. The needle wobbled. It pointed behind and slightly to the right, more south than east. What it was actually indicating would certainly be worth investigating at a later date. For now, Meecha looked through the eastern trees and met a pair of red eyes.

The demon screeched. Meecha dropped the compass to cover his ears. Chione roared just as the fiend pounced on Meecha. Thasha screamed and reared, hurling both of them from his back. They crashed to the ground and rolled towards the chasm. Meecha balled up his fists and tried punching the demon in the ribs, while its claws ripped his back. A screen of dust lifted in their wake to fill his mouth and nostrils, mingled with the demon's sickly smell. Meecha's heart lurched when he dropped through air and mist. He gave the monster a hard kick, breaking its grip. He heard Nandil and Chione's cries before he hit the bottom hard.

His breath was knocked out of him. The thick sulphuric smell would not let him get it back. The very air was on fire. Meecha lay stunned and blurry-eyed, his lungs aching. The gashes across his back burned, and his limbs were heavy. His body felt broken, disconnected. A grating sound reached him. He turned his head and saw the demon crawling towards him on three paws, its claws scraping the floor of solid earth. *It's missing a hand*, Meecha noted. Blood-red eyes loomed, and a snarling mouth.

'Where is it?' it hissed in the human tongue. 'Where is the Key?'

He did not respond. He forced himself off the ground, shaking and bleeding. He came to a crouch and watched the demon draw near.

'I shall make thee shorter still. Tell me where it is!'

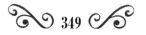

'Come closer and I will.'

This gave it pause. It glared at him from all angles, trying to decide if he was bluffing. It gnashed its fangs and hissed before rushing at him. Meecha threw dirt into its face. It groaned and then shrieked when he plunged his dagger into its side. He gave the blade a twist, pulled it out, and ran for his life.

He dashed through the fog. There was no ghost or monster in his way, but what he did almost trip into was a swirling pool of molten fire. There were dozens of them, crevices spewing smoke shimmering with heat and fumes. He coughed and gagged as he searched for a way out, but he was disoriented. He was leaving a trail of blood behind him too. *I can't outrun it*, Meecha decided and halted.

The demon soon appeared, clutching its ribs, quivering in its wrath. Black blood streamed through its fingers. Cruel eyes bulged from their sockets, and its lips peeled back into a horrid grin.

Spittle bubbled from its jaws as it hissed, 'I shall rip thee open and make thee watch as I eat thee piece by piece. Thy sugary soul shall be a special treat. Are thy Masters watching? Shall they miss their fool?'

'Even if I die, another will replace me. You'll never touch the Key. Nor will Itania ever be yours. You'll lose just like the last time!'

The creature of Crantil cackled. 'The last time has not ended! It was only the beginning!'

Meecha's heart skipped a beat. He rushed around a fiery crevice, but instead of running after him, the demon jumped through the billowing smoke. Its great black form broke through the cloud unscathed and took a swipe at him. He ducked, and his dagger cut into its bicep, but this time the fiend twisted around and backhanded him. He spun through the air, falling just short of another crevice sputtering like a cauldron of boiling soup. His whole head throbbed. There was blood in his mouth. He spat it out as the demon strode towards him. Meecha leapt to his feet and slashed the air to keep his foe at bay. It hesitated, circling and backing away from his advances. It jerked forward, and he retreated a few quick steps. It snarled and did it a second time. Meecha recoiled and then screamed when a column of fiery smoke seared his back. He lunged aside, dropping the dagger, at the same moment that the demon pounced. It missed him, vanishing through the screen of smoke.

Meecha grit his teeth. The pain in his back was unbearable. He turned onto his belly and crawled to where he hoped the fissure's wall might be. He did not find out. A hand hauled him around, slicing his shoulder. He looked up into those horrible red eyes. The demon smiled maliciously and ripped his chest. He cried out as it pulled back for a second strike. And the sky flashed.

The fiend's startled eyes found an actual cloud hovering over the fissure. It rumbled and lit up. The rain began to fall, making the lava in the crevices spit and hiss. Meecha smiled, despite himself. The cool drops soothed his scalded skin. The abyssal creature standing over him troubled him no longer. There was nothing more he could do about his fate. It was only when his blurred gaze rested upon the towering black figure that he realised that the rain was having a much different effect on it.

It growled and batted the air with its claws, as if fighting off bees. It screeched defiantly at the cloud before its head snapped back down to Meecha. He squeezed his eyes shut as it straddled him and punched him in the face. He blacked out, but his ears did catch one last sound. A magnificent sound.

Chione's roar.

Chapter 41

He dreamt of blood. His blood. A pool of it. It was dark as tar, sticky and thick. He was still in the fissure, and so was the demon. Its eyes were ablaze, smouldering like the pits around Meecha. Its claws ripped into him, one hand after the other. He screamed and wailed, but could not move. Paralysed. But he could feel every slash. The demon dug towards his soul.

'Meecha!' Nandil's voice sliced through the dream and yanked him awake, his eyes snapping open to find the man shaking him violently.

Nandil was as breathless as he, and his expression mirrored Meecha's own terror.

'Bless thee, lad! Thou gave me a right fright.'

Meecha gawked at him. He tried to speak, but his throat was raw. He must have been screaming.

He croaked, 'Wa—water.'

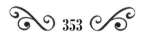

Nandil darted out of sight, while cool air brushed Meecha's front. He lifted his head a little to look. His shirt was gone, but his organs were still inside him. His chest, though, bore four nasty gashes. He let his head drop back when Nandil returned to dribble some water into his mouth. He choked somewhat, but managed to drink, sighing with relief once the skin was taken away.

'How thou feelin'?'

Meecha shook his head, not knowing where to begin.

Nandil spoke instead. 'Chione kept trying to come in after thee, but I think she couldn't bear the smoke. We could hear thee an' that... thing. An' then the cloud appeared! The rain must have cleared the air, for Chione jumped in immediately. I saw the demon change into a bird an' flee before she could grab it. She carried thee back and has been licking thee all night.'

That explained why Meecha did not feel as sore as he had expected. His back still stung and prickled when he moved, and his face felt numb and swollen. But he was alive.

'Thou were crying in thy sleep,' Nandil added. 'It sounded bad.'

Meecha's mouth tightened. He did not wish to discuss it. Nor did he want to go back to sleep. Fortunately, Adalis presented him with a solution. The chanter trotted up beside him and gave his face a gentle sniff and a peck. He sat against his side and started to lick the end of one of his scars. Meecha lifted his right hand—at least one part of him that did not hurt—and rubbed Adalis's ear between his fingers. The cub purred and leant into his palm, so Meecha kept at it, grateful for the distraction. He soon discovered how true it was that cats were the best comfort to the sick. His previous distress was trampled by Adalis's cuteness.

'Where's Chione?'

'Hunting. I've made some stew for us. It's still warm.'

'I'm not hungry.'

Nandil tutted, 'Thou having some.'

He disappeared, leaving him to cuddle Adalis in peace. Meecha traced the muscles around the chanter's shoulder-blades and down his left front leg. He was wiry and strong, even as a cub. And his eyes were like liquid gold, so bright and wild. Not like the red ones. They were plain feral. Malicious. His mind flashed back to the fissure amid smoke and claws, the monster looming over him, muscles long and taut, slick, dark skin enveloped by the lava's blazing glare. It smiled as it cut him...

'Here.' Nandil once again returned him to the present.

The human squatted beside him with a steaming bowl in his hand, and Meecha's hunger suddenly grumbled its presence.

'Would thou rather sit up?'

Meecha nodded, took a deep breath, and pushed himself up. The wounds in his chest hurt, but far less than his burns. He inhaled sharply at every twinge. Nandil put the bowl aside to help him. When he was finally upright, heart beating hard, he let out his breath along with a ragged groan. He slumped and saw that he had been lying on Nandil's blanket. The human put the warm bowl in his hands. It was indeed stew with a large chunk of bread in it, which he proceeded to use as a spoon.

'So thou do have a cloud for a friend,' Nandil remarked and pointed at the sky.

The gallant white cloud hovered above the treetops. *Water sprites.* A smile crept onto Meecha's lips. His appetite reclaimed, he gorged on the thick broth and the bits of pork and bread, until he remembered something important.

'The demon,' he murmured into the bowl. Nandil paused from repacking the food into the saddlebags. 'I mentioned the failure of Arak Sildrax's invasion, and the demon said it didn't end, that it was just the beginning.'

He gulped down the last of the stew and wiped his mouth before glancing up at Nandil. The human looked perplexed. He had a bundle in one hand and a bag held open with the other.

'What does that mean? Their defeat was part of their evil plan? What have they been doing all this time?'

Meecha shrugged as he put the empty bowl aside. 'I shouldn't be surprised. As Azare said, xalikai are cunning. They can fathom schemes that are beyond intricate. The most our petty mortal eyes can hope to see is a glimmer of their plans. Even with aerieti eyes upon them, they can still catch you unawares. It makes you wonder which side's the smartest.'

His vacant stare settled on his hands, callused and scraped.

'Sali-what?' Nandil inquired.

A surge of anger filled Meecha at the man's stupidity. It was not just him. Entire civilisations lived in complete ignorance, many of them tall folk that fancied themselves superior to him. *Deluded fools.* He turned his bland eyes to Nandil and held them there for a few moments before springing to his feet, ignoring the pain that shot through his body.

'We must get going.'

He did not feel sorry for the bluntness in his voice. In fact, he found himself refreshingly emotionless.

'Chione's not back, and thou shouldn't strain thyself.'

'Chione!' Meecha called.

Nandil winced, 'Is that wise?'

'Does it matter? They already know where we are. Chione!'

'Calm thyself.'

'I'm perfectly calm,' Meecha replied matter-of-factly. 'What I should be doing is finding that Key. A brush with death isn't going to stop me. It's not my first time, you know. Chione!'

The chantress appeared through the trees with a bird in her maw. They packed up while she and Adalis ate. Without a word, but with a troubled quirk to his brow, Nandil handed Meecha a fresh shirt along with his hat and compass. Then they kicked off, bound east. Meecha had wanted to walk this time, but Nandil refused. They did not argue long. Having to be carried for yet another day was better than prolonging their stay in that forsaken forest. The sulphurous odours had returned stronger than before, which urged the party into a swift pace. Soon enough they saw light at the end of the trees. The sun was setting and the moons were soaring by the time Meecha was borne out of Caod.

The sudden openness they were faced with made them pause. A grand valley stretched before them. The mountain range was to their left, the road so far to their right they could barely see it. Several days ahead the mountains had formed a curvature that intruded into the dale's smoothness.

'That must be it. The diamond must be in there,' Nandil said in a rather gloomy manner, at which point Meecha declared that he did not need to ride any longer.

The human gave him a flat look but agreed. Meecha thanked him on the way down. He knew he had not been the most likeable of companions that day. He knew his legs would slow them down. But he could not help it. He needed to walk. There was a tension inside him that he had to expel, and some exercise would do him good.

His stride was quick and forceful. The air drifted into his shirt to caress his aching back. It was a strange sensation, a simultaneous prickle and tingle. He wondered if it would leave a mark, a scar that he could carry with pride. He had fought a demon, wounded it even, and survived. Once again he had evaded death. The final sleep had reached for him time and time again, but always left empty-handed. *When will its lucky day be?* The chanters walked alongside him, while Nandil usurped his place upon Thasha's back. The stallion was quite content, following at a leisurely trot, his ears jutting forward and his tail high.

They travelled well into the night before they stopped to make camp. Meecha's exhaustion quickly led him to his bedroll, but not before Chione lathered him with saliva. He could not stomach more than a small chunk of cheese, and even that made him ill. He was restless, not only from his upset stomach. He tossed and turned, trying to force unsettling thoughts from his mind, but they would not give him peace. Xalikai and aerieti, Delia and his family—hers too—filled his skull, his emotions flitting from anger to sadness to numb contemplation. *Gods and elders. Can they really be trusted?*

Dawn was slow to arrive. Plenty of time for seeds of doubt to grow. Dark vines wrapped around his heart and bones. Meecha lay on his side staring up at his cloud, while it gradually changed from a dark grey mass barely outlined by the lunar light to the ethereal white and gold foam that it was now. Actually, it was more like a huge poached egg. He chortled, despite his stomach's displeasure of the imagery.

He was still sprawled across his bedroll when Nandil woke. Meecha turned down breakfast and waited for his companions to finish theirs before finally hauling himself off the ground. He also declined the saddle.

'Thou look terrible,' Nandil told him. 'The vapours have made thee sick. Thou should be resting.'

But Meecha was resolute. *I'm stronger than you think.*

Another day went by with the chanters by his side. Nandil and Thasha would gallop ahead and then circle back. Such grace the stallion had. For his size, his step was elegant and quick. And Nandil seemed in tune with the animal's energy. Even their colours blended nicely—browns, blacks, reds. They might have been destined for each other. Perhaps the aerieti needed a knight for this game of wits. Meecha suddenly felt like a cog. Nandil could be another that he was meant to turn. Azare definitely was. Perhaps even the chanters. How many lives were dragged into the plot? Chione's other children? Were the aerieti their true killers? A knot grew in Meecha's throat. A pinch in his brow deepened into a frown when he pondered the possibility that Chione was procured for him, as counterbalance to his incompetence.

Rage bubbled inside him again, and he wanted to scream at the sky, curse the ever-watching eyes. They were no different from the demons—things agents and innocents battled in their stead. He pressed his shaking hands into his eyes. Flecks of colour danced behind his eyelids, and it almost hurt as his fingers pushed into his sockets. He bit his palms to keep from crying.

'Meecha?'

He abruptly lowered his hands. That was when he realised that not only had he stopped walking, but he was on his knees, quivering. He blinked at Nandil. The human hopped off the horse and fell to one knee before him.

'Thou going back in that saddle.'

Meecha mounted Thasha without complaint. He did not even notice that his hat was missing from his head until he saw Nandil wearing it. What good had it done him anyhow? It could shield his soul no better than the aerieti could his life. Nor he Delia's.

'*Foolish child,*' his father's voice scolded him. '*Look at you. You are no Roa!*'

Indeed, he was not. Nor was he an agent worthy of the title. Then what? What...?

Chapter 42

H e gazed groggily at the plains. They were marvellously flat and wide and so green. The blue of the sky was pale and bright. It stung his eyes. He looked away, and his sight locked upon Thasha's mane swishing with the motion of his trot. Meecha's body was as limp as jelly. He wobbled and swayed in the saddle. It was a miracle he was still on it.

It was almost four days since they had left Caod, and his condition had worsened. His heart hurt. There was a burning sensation in his chest and his stomach was still in turmoil. He had not eaten anything in days, so it was no food poisoning, which left the sulphur as the culprit. He had inhaled a fair amount of it. He hoped it did not cause any permanent damage.

A gust of wind swooped past them, lifting dust and grass in its wake. Meecha gasped when he saw the vague form of the ghost lady float by. One moment she was there smiling at him, and the next she was gone. *Only wind and dust.* He was seeing things. It was usually in the dark that he noticed fiendish forms watching him. The twinkling stars turned into scarlet eyes. He no longer slept. The demons could sneak up on him if he closed his eyes. In his dreams they always did.

'What is it?' Nandil asked from beside Thasha.

Meecha gaped at him. He shook his head slowly and stammered, 'Nothing.'

The human spared him a concerned frown before turning his attention ahead again. Their destination was getting closer. They could be there within a day. He was unsure how ready he was to face whatever lay within those crags. He was now hallucinating during the day. It could not be a good sign.

His wounds, at least, were healing. They barely hurt at all. He was once again grateful to have found Chione. Whether by luck or divine intention, it did not matter. He would not have survived this mission without her—and Adalis, of course. His love for the chanters sweetened the heat inside him and made the journey bearable. He silenced his thoughts, ignored his phantoms, and focused on the mountain before him. They were almost there.

...

It had taken Azare a day to find it, but there it was at last. A hole at the base of the mountain. A cave hidden behind some overgrown hedges. It was narrow and dark and the only way through.

He swept the bushes out of his way and cautiously ducked into the cave. At first, his eyes had enough light from the entrance behind him to see well through the gloom, but once truly plunged into the warren's darkness, his vision reached only a few feet ahead of him. It was rocky and dank, and there were tiny creatures crawling about his feet and over his head.

It would have been amusing to see Meecha in this place. Azare could imagine him crying like a child all the way to the other side. Fortunately, the pest was no longer his concern. He may have gone back to the city to find some other dupe to keep him safe. But Azare somehow doubted that. It was most likely that he tripped into that fissure and made a roast piglet of himself.

Azare shoved away his guilt. *It does not matter. Meecha made his own fate. He does not matter.* Nothing was more important than finding the she-demon and carving his revenge out of her hide.

Chapter 43

'Where are you, Meecha? Where have you gone, my boy?' Namoya asked of her son in Luimari.

His tongue felt thick in his mouth. He could not speak.

'Tell me where you are. Let me come to you. Let me bring you home.'

Meecha's voice was lost. He tried to push words through his open lips, but they would not come.

'I miss you, Meecha. I miss my baby. Where do you go? Don't you love me? Don't you care about my heartache?'

'I'm sorry,' he managed to cry.

'Why have you left us? Where are you going?'

'To fight the demons,' he told her.

She frowned through her scarlet locks. 'How?'

He went numb with fear. He did not know the answer.

'How will you fight them? How can you win? Please, come back to me.'

'I can't, mother. I have to find the Key. I must find it before they do.'

'What key, my son? Where has this futile hunt taken you? Where are you going?'

Meecha suddenly remembered Inan's riddled message, but it appeared before him in jumbled fragments.

'The diamond in the mountains,' he said and slowly started to put the puzzle back together.

'Wheel your way from the nose to the toads...'

His mind utterly dormant, Meecha tried to put the words in order.

'Follow... follow a maid bright...'

His mother's hair rippled in the chill wind. She drew closer, watching him intently, her kind eyes filled with tears. They begged for his trust, for an explanation. Meecha desperately tried to remember the last line of the riddle. It was something about flying and... and water. No, swimming!

'Fly or descend, you shall swim!'

His mother appeared even more hurt.

'Are you toying with me?'

'No! No, mother. It's directions to the place where the Key is hidden. That's where I'm going. I must save this world from the demons. I'll make you proud, mother. You and all. I'll be a true Roa when I return. And I'll tell you everything. Everything. I promise.'

Namoya suddenly gasped. Her eyes bulged, and she started to sob. Her beautiful hair burst into flames. She shrieked into Meecha's face, but her eyes did not show pain. They were angry. They hated him. She reached out with black talons and punched through his ribs. She gripped his heart and squeezed.

His scream echoed in his ears as he bolted from his bedroll. He swirled, sweating and panting. Blind. The night was black, starless, for his cloud had been joined by others. His clammy hands clutched at his chest. He sobbed and touched his face, wanting to gouge his eyes out again. An anxious voice called him, but he kept scratching himself and weeping.

'Meecha,' the voice said again, but it was different. Yet familiar.

His fingers retreated from his eyes as he turned. There was not much light to see by, but the meagre illumination from the campfire's smouldering coals was enough for Meecha to recognise the person before him. His eyes went wide.

'Father?'

Yanga Roa stood beside the fire, his pale eyes piercing the dimness. His form was hunched and threatening.

'Ran away again, did you? Ran from your responsibilities. I always knew I had a coward for a son.'

Meecha's anger flooded his lungs. He had to let it out or erupt. 'I'm no coward. I save lives! I'm a hero! But you don't know. Don't care. You always see me as a failure!'

His father smirked, and the muscles in his right arm flexed. He hefted something. Only then did Meecha notice the hammer in his hand.

'A hero,' Yanga spat. 'Your grandfather is a hero. He has toiled for our name's good standing, and your continued breathing brings it to ruin. We'll all be better off if you don't return this time.'

He advanced, and Meecha was shocked to discover how unsurprised he was by this outcome, being murdered by his own father. Neither did he feel remorse when he prepared to defend himself. *No!* He would not shy away. It was Yanga's turn to fear him.

He howled and rammed into his father. They thudded to the ground and Meecha rained furious punches down upon him. Yanga tried to ward off his attacks, but Meecha straddled him and got a grip on his throat. He snarled like an animal, putting all his strength into choking the life out of his father. He fuelled his muscles with all the rage, fear, and despair he had accumulated through the years. He laughed triumphantly into Yanga Roa's reddening face.

A deafening roar shook Meecha to the core. A demon was crouched near him. He jumped off Yanga and crawled frantically away from the fiery eyes. He whimpered when another fiend joined the first, and together they approached him with tongues and teeth bared. He screamed when the second demon pulled back a clawed fist. And all went black.

...

Azare heaved himself up through the hole and into the morning light. The sun's glare had never been more welcome. The tunnel did have an end after all, and it brought him to the western bank of an empty riverbed. The channel was deep and wide. It must have once contained a torrent.

He slid to the bottom and walked across to the other side, beyond which were huge mounds of rock. This place was less a mountain and more a gigantic mass of earthen spikes and hills. He climbed onto the eastern bank and looked up at the treacherous formations. He picked his way carefully, but made steady progress to the top. As soon as he crested the apex, he paused to gawk. He had found the river.

A massive globe of water sat in the middle of a crater. In truth it was like something had pushed its way *out* of the earth. And that something was an island tipped with a structure that sparkled from the water's murky depths. *Fly or descend, you shall swim.*

There were dark shapes in the water circling the island. Guarding it? For how long a time had this watery barrier been held? Powerful magic was at work here, but whether or not it would keep the demons out remained to be seen. As Azare thought this, another question occurred to him. *How had Inan got in?*

Chapter 44

eecha's head throbbed. He was nauseous and hot. He could hear hooves. He could feel the horse's motion and smell its musk. *Thasha?* With some effort, he forced his eyes open and saw the grassy earth moving below. Muscle and fur pressed against his cheek. He lifted himself a little higher and looked around. Nandil was ahead, leading the stallion by the reins, while Chione and her son were on the right. The mountain towered over them, casting a vast shadow across the plain.

He made to scratch his hairy chin, but his other hand followed the first unbidden. He looked down and found his wrists bound with rope.

'Nandil?' he murmured and lurched precariously when Thasha suddenly stopped.

The human appeared by his side with a split lip and a purple bruise on his left cheek.

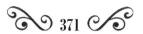

Meecha gasped, 'What... what happened?'

The man tilted his head curiously, 'Thou not remember?'

Meecha shook his head, while he sifted through his memories. 'I... I had a dream. My mother turned into a demon. And then my father attacked me, and I tried to kill him. But then more demons appeared.'

Nandil rested a firm hand on his shoulder. 'I don't know about thy mother, bu' the rest of it was somewhat real. Not as thou remember it, that is.'

Meecha gaped, 'Was it you I attacked?'

'Thou were screaming in thy sleep in another tongue, and even when thou woke, thou continued mumbling an' shouting things. Thou went berserk on me and only stopped at the sight of Chione. I had to knock thee out.'

Meecha was horrified. 'I'm sorry,' he eventually whispered.

'Ah, I've had worse injuries. But I believe I know what's happening to thee.' Nandil appeared simultaneously reluctant and intrigued. 'During thy fight with the demon, did thou swallow any of its blood?'

Meecha's breath caught.

'No. I don't think so. I was unconscious at the end of it, though.'

'When we recovered thee, thy mouth was covered in blood. I thought it was thine, bu' what if the demon fed thee its own? Thou remember what Azare said.'

Meecha was either going to faint or vomit.

'I've been feeling strange,' he muttered. 'And seeing things.'

'And being unusually foul,' Nandil added.

'That too,' Meecha agreed sheepishly. 'What can I do?'

'I can think of only one person who can help thee. And he's in there.' Nandil pointed towards the great wall of stone.

It did not take them long to find a small cave at the base of the mountain. The bushes that had been concealing it were bent out of shape. Azare must have gone that way. Unfortunately, the size of the hole only barely allowed Chione passage, so Thasha was out of the question. Nandil removed Meecha and the bags from the stallion's back. He secured the stirrups against the saddle so they would not bother the animal on its way home. Then he took hold of its great head, running his fingers through its beard and scratching its chin. Thasha pricked his ears and leaned closer, his mouth fussing with Nandil's face and hair. The human laughed, stumbling back.

'Off with thee now,' he chuckled and solemnly patted Thasha's neck.

The human pointed towards the road. 'I shall find thee again in Anvadore. Go home.'

Thasha bumped his forehead into Nandil's chest, drawing a grunt and a sigh from behind his affectionately pursed lips.

'Ah, ya lummox,' he exclaimed and pushed the horse off him.

Thasha did not offer too much resistance to the hand urging him away. He continued on his own in the direction of the road, but kept glancing back at them as he went. Meecha envied the animal. He did not know if he would ever go home. That word again. *Home.*

Nandil heaved another sigh while fashioning a torch out of a branch and some cloth from one of his shirts. Setting it aflame with his tinderbox, he approached the entrance to the cave, when he halted and glanced at Meecha.

'Thou go first. Forgive me, lad, but I don't want thee behind me.'

Meecha guiltily complied with the human's concern. He entered the tunnel with the torch's light illuminating the way. The rock was dark and dry, occasionally poking out of the ground, walls, or ceiling. Roots had broken through as well. They made Nandil jump. Even bent down as he was, he hit his head on the ceiling a number of times. Everything was covered in a thick layer of dust. Beetles and other insects skittered across the floor, while spiders claimed dominion above. None of these dismal things, the gloom and its creatures, bothered Meecha. Surprisingly, it was the light that did.

The flame flickering against the walls irritated his eyes. It made him dizzy, unsteady. It surrounded him with shapes both fiery and abyssal. His heart raced. Cold sweat made his body shiver. His breathing hastened, and he felt nauseous. He stopped.

'Put out the torch,' he pleaded.

'What? Why?' Nandil asked.

Meecha tried to take a breath, 'I can't. I need... Chione.'

The chantress squeezed past Nandil with Adalis on her back. She looked square into Meecha's eyes. *How does Azare do it?* He buried a hand in her fur and spoke to her, trying to externalise his emotions. He hoped that she would sense his fear, his vulnerability.

'I need you to guide me. Show me the way through.'

Her ears twitched. She blinked. Her head briefly brushed against his before she started off down the tunnel. It was not wide enough for them to walk side by side, so he took a gentle hold of her tail and followed. When he felt sure of the pace and the path, he closed his eyes to the shades and let Chione lead him back to the light.

...

Azare reached out a hand to touch the glimmering surface. His fingers dipped effortlessly into the globe. It truly was just water: cold, calm, and blue. There was no current to it. Its denizens swam in any direction they pleased. There were small fish and fat fish and some with little spikes. There were snakes too, slithering swiftly through. If there were other creatures, he could not see them in this vast rippling bubble.

He would have to swim, fast and hard. His lungs could bear the distance. His swords, however, would be useless under water. He pulled out a black-hilted dagger from the back of his belt and clenched it between his teeth. He then removed the three golden clasps from his hair and put them inside a secure pouch at his hip. He inhaled and exhaled thrice before taking a final deep breath and diving into the globe.

It was like swimming in the most tranquil, clear lake. Nothing inhibited his passing. Beams of sunlight streaked down from above, draping the crystal fortress in a brilliant haze. The small fish fled from Azare as he pushed through the water with powerful strokes and kicks. He kept his eyes ahead but still on the lookout for predators. They would be the whole purpose behind the globe's construction—to guard the fortress.

His bite on the blade hardened, pressuring himself to maintain a good pace. His strong body granted him a speedy progress. As long as he remained calm and unhindered, he would reach the diamond quickly enough. Each great ark of his arms brought him closer, and Azare was soon past halfway. His lungs were starting to feel the strain, but they were trained for worse conditions than this. They would not fail him, unless he failed them.

A sudden sting in his right leg made him turn to find one of the spiked fish scurrying away and a faint cloud of blood surrounding his thigh. It did not matter. He could not falter. He turned back ahead and swam towards the fortress. Three-quarters of the way, his breath dangerously close to its limits, and he felt a disturbance in the water. It was like a gust of turbulence rolling over his legs. Another fish trying its luck with him. He should not have allowed the distraction, but he whirled around and nearly dropped the dagger in terror of the giant creature floating before him.

Its body resembled that of a snake's but with two clawed brawny arms and two vast membranous wings—or fins. Its bottom jaw protruded from the rest of its smooth head to close with its upper jaw at a sharp angle. An edged crest began at the top of its skull and ran down the whole of its spine to end at the tail where it turned into a fin similar to its wings. *A dragon. It must be.*

Azare immediately attempted a mental connection, but was interrupted. The creature opened its immense jaws and roared at him, its wail reverberating within the globe. Its wings produced a loud thrumming sound when they beat against the water, and the dragon streaked towards him. Azare barely managed to twist out of its way, spinning against its scales as it swept past. In that brief contact, he noticed that its black skin had an aquamarine iridescence to it. Within moments the thought was gone, for the dragon passed him by and swerved nimbly to rush at him again.

He sent another mental signal to the dragon, but it would not let him in. It responded with its own message instead. Azare's mind filled with a sense of anger towards intruders and a desire to protect. The water pulsed with the dragon's roar and then with another beat of its wings. He could not fight a dragon, especially in this element.

He was more surprised by his reaction to his imminent doom than by the realisation of it. He was afraid. The panic squeezed the last of the air out of his lungs, and he was drowning. He had come so close to his goal only to be rendered helpless. All the power of his blood could not save him now. If he had magic, perhaps he would have stood a chance. But he was a simple warrior. An outcast. A failure. This dragon would do what his people could not bring themselves to. Kill him.

The water finally invaded his mouth and his nose. He thrashed. The dragon opened its maw to blot him out of existence. Its great teeth were closer. He blinked, and light flooded his vision, speckled with little black dots, slowly turning to dark water once more. The dragon had swallowed him. Azare closed his eyes—it was like falling asleep, except that he was floating instead of sinking. As if a giant hand was carrying him away to the resting place of his fathers.

Chapter 45

With a gasp Azare came to, spewing water. He writhed and flipped onto his stomach, racked by a violent cough. His throat was raw, and his nostrils had an itch he could not scratch. His shoulders ached beneath his swords, so he yanked the straps free and let the weapons clatter to the floor. He rested his forehead on the cold surface and squeezed his eyes shut, panting. He had drowned. The dragon had eaten him. But this did not seem like death. He could feel every pain in his body. He remembered his lungs near bursting and the dragon rushing towards him and the light of death and then his eyes dimming. He frowned. How could he still see after death? Unless that light was something else.

He opened his eyes. The marble beneath him was smooth and clear like crystal, yet veined with white and pale blue. He lay in a corridor made entirely of the same marble, but the blue colour gradually changed its hue in various places. There was an archway at the end of the hall and a statue beyond it.

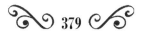

Azare looked behind him. A door stood closed, wreathed in bars and coils of a grey metal. There was nothing remarkable about it, except that there was water on the floor before it. He rose and grasped the crystal pommel. He opened the door and was dumbfounded for the second time that day as he looked out into the sphere's watery world. Fish swam blithely by, but there was no sign of the dragon. Azare was inside the fortress, the water magically barred from entering. It stopped precisely on the lip of the doorframe and not a drop entered. It must have been him who brought some of it in.

Closing the door, he picked up his swords and made for the statue. His footfalls echoed, no matter how silently he tried to walk. He passed through the archway, abandoning any notion of stealth. The crystal statue stood in the centre of a circular chamber, dim and cold. The blue veins in the marble adopted a purplish shade here. They spiralled around the floor and then up the walls like branches. The translucent white that dominated the fortress's interior reminded Azare of the inside of a seashell. The statue, a broad fish of some kind with black opal eyes and pearls running down its spine, was on a marble pedestal. There was a certain grandeur to it that led him to believe that this animal was of some importance to the dwellers of these halls. Its significance, however, was now lost. The majesty that once inhabited the place had vanished along with its people.

Azare strode through the room and into the next corridor, which was wider than the last. He reached a junction with another hallway, but he stayed true. He could tell that there was another chamber at the end of the passage he was in and it had something in its centre as well. Not a statue.

When he stepped into the room, he found its size to be five times that of the previous one. It had an oval shape and a ribbed ceiling, and the object in the middle was a cushioned stool on a dais. The colouring was much the same, except that these walls were veined with a dozen shades of blue. The cushion on the stool was the colour of sapphires, its legs crystal and inlaid with black opals. He made his way towards it.

There was a grand hallway on the far left end of the chamber. That must have been the main entrance to the throne room, if that was indeed what it was. On the right side was a large door embossed with the same fish. He approached it and pushed. The creature cracked in half as the door swung open.

The stale air of closure and decay washed over him — he had to cover his face with his arm. The light from the throne room flooded the darkness. Bones were strewn across the floor. Then, as the opposite wall became clearer, he saw the body. A bearded corpse slumped against the marble with its arms wrapped tightly against its chest. Within its embrace was a box.

...

Tears of awe had welled up in Meecha's eyes the moment he had seen the orb sitting in the centre of the great enclosure. His eyes were still wide and moist when he walked the last few feet towards it. It was like a massive snow-globe, but with fish swirling around the diamond castle instead of white flakes. This may have been the most remarkable spectacle of his life so far.

'How do we get through?' Nandil asked from beside him.

Chione whined at the water. It would be impossible to get her and Adalis to swim all that distance, even if they did stand a chance of survival. There had to be another way.

It came from above. Meecha's cloud swooped down from the mountain's western peaks to hover, thundering, over the orb. The raindrops fell, turning into steam upon contact with his feverish skin. A few moments went by before any change occurred. The water began to churn, slowly creating a whirlpool concentrated on an indentation that was taking shape right in front of Meecha and his friends. It was as if an invisible spear was penetrating the orb's wall and making a hole in the water. The hole grew wider and deeper, until a pathway was formed three Chiones tall and four Chiones wide, leading straight to the castle.

Meecha glanced nervously at Nandil and the chanters before taking the first step onto the watery bridge. When he did not sink into the orb, Chione, Adalis, and the human followed his lead. Everyone was hesitant for the first few feet, but they soon grew accustomed to the experience. Not so much the chanters, who glowered at the tunnel walls that hummed as the water rushed over them.

A short time after that, they all got another surprise, when a huge shadow passed under their feet and came to glide alongside them on the other side of the barrier. Meecha could not make out its features clearly, but he was sure that he could see a head, a long neck, a fin like a sail, and a tail far too long for his liking. The creature droned before abruptly swooping down to the orb's depths. Its reverberating wail was the last they heard of it on their descent to the diamond's intricate metal door.

Chapter 46

The body was preserved. There was no sign of decomposition. The wrinkles and bags under its sunken eyes were intact. Its flaxen hair fell like straw around its face and over its leather-clad chest, over its entwined arms and the box. *Inan?*

Azare passed a large semi-circular table with high-backed chairs arrayed around its exterior curve. This could have been an audience chamber long ago. He kicked a shattered ribcage out of his way. Perhaps Inan had had a companion. Azare preferred not to consider what had happened to him. But why had that body decayed and Inan's had not?

Azare reached the wall, looking warily down at the man. He held the box so tightly that his arms would have to be broken. Azare squatted before him and took hold of the top edges of the box. He tried to pull it free but, as expected, it was firmly caught in the corpse's grip. He grabbed

one wrist to break it, but was taken by surprise when the hand gripped back.

He leapt away, nearly tripping over some bones. The corpse groaned. Its hand returned to the box, but its head began to rise. It looked at Azare through hollow eyes of a washed-out brown. It took a wheezing breath and spoke.

'Who...?'

Azare responded reluctantly but not with an answer to the dead man's question. 'Thou Inan?'

The lifeless eyes rolled back into their aged skull. When they returned, the corpse gave him a limp nod.

'Thou living or dead?' Azare demanded.

Its eyes rolled back again and returned with the answer. 'I... am... neither.'

Inan's every word was accompanied by a lengthy exhalation of air. It made him sound like a snake.

Azare gripped a sword-hilt. 'How?'

'This place has done it.'

Azare did not have time for a discussion. 'I have come for the Key.'

The corpse's eyes widened a little.

'The... Key...' these words came louder than the rest. 'Why?'

'Demons seek it. I wish to protect it.'

If he spoke of his true intentions, of using it to lure the demons to him, Inan would never give it up. Even as a ghoul, he may have retained some of his righteous reasoning for coming all this way to hide it.

'Then thou may have it.'

His joints cracked and groaned as he opened his embrace to let the box tumble to the floor.

'Be gone, accursed thing. Let me die.'

Azare snatched it up, surprised at how easily it was parted from its guardian, and made for the door.

'Hold.'

He glanced back at Inan.

'Thou can't open it without my sight.'

Azare frowned. 'Meaning I must unlock it in thy presence?' He sighed at Inan's nod. 'So be it. How do I open it?'

'Find the way.'

Azare brought the box to the light and studied it. It was a steel container with bolts along the edges and an engraved pattern on the lid. The pattern, three interconnected rings, was surrounded by another etched circle. A movable disk, perhaps, that undid the locking mechanism.

'Thou not know the way?' he complained.

Inan's riddle had been more than enough puzzle-solving.

The ghoul drew a short breath and replied, 'No.'

There was something about it that tugged at Azare's memory. Was it the shape? The design? The pattern? He passed a finger over the rings cut into the metal. And gasped. He then scowled.

'It seems to need a key of sorts,' he said. 'It must be hidden somewhere around here.'

'I believe so.'

'Thou not know what it is?' Azare looked at the cadaverous Inan—he could barely keep his head up.

'No.' The word fluttered through his lips, and Azare slid his right sword out of its scabbard.

'What is this?' Inan wheezed when he saw the gleaming blade pointed at him.

Azare held the box behind his back and declared through gritted teeth, 'Thou are not Inan.'

The ghoul gaped at him and hissed, 'Why would thou think this?'

'Because Inan made this box,' Azare barked. 'He would know exactly what the key is and that it was never hidden here, but with his daughter. Quit the charade, demon. Show thy true face!'

Its shocked expression remained a little longer, but soon melted into a spiteful sneer.

'I thought this would work,' it whined. The fake Inan stood up in one smooth motion. 'I was not aware thou knew him.'

'Thou are ignorant of much. But thy worst mistake was murdering his daughter.' Azare's voice shook and he clenched his jaw.

'That girl kept many secrets,' the creature snarled. 'I should have skinned her instead of burning her. She would have had so much more to say.'

'Be quiet!' Azare's fury coursed through him. Even the blade quivered with emotion, his knuckles white around the hilt.

'Ah,' the fiend said. 'Thou knew her too. Better than her father, yes?'

Azare was about to hack at its face, when something dashed past him. *Meecha!* The little man's growl was wild as he charged at Inan-that-was-not-Inan with startling speed, teeth and nails first.

'Bitch!'

He pounced onto the disguised creature's leg and bit into its thigh. It howled and transformed back into the lean, nightmarish form of the she-demon. Dark blood streamed down her leg from around Meecha's mouth. Her claws would have flayed his back had Azare not wrenched him off her, tossing the box into a corner. He retreated to a safe distance.

'Damn that dragon!' she shrieked at them both. 'It should have rid me of you.'

The fish that wounded me, thought Azare. *It was her.*

She spat at his feet. 'Come then, thaelil scum, this xa-likai flees no more!'

Azare's revenge was again disrupted, this time by Chione. She appeared in the throne room and rushed towards the audience chamber. But she did not notice the winged demon emerge from the wide corridor behind her. He was bloodied and missing his right wing and arms— the dragon's feat, no doubt. Azare sent her a mental warning, and she skidded to a halt. She turned to face the great beast, at which point the she-demon slithered out of the room and around the chantress to join her comrade.

Azare picked up the box from where he had dropped it and shoved it into Meecha's arms.

'It contains the Key. Do not lose it,' he said and strode out to stand by Chione's side.

...

Meecha stared at the metal box with wide-eyed astonishment. *I have it. I have the Key.* He gripped it tightly against his chest and walked timidly out of the room. He stopped behind Azare and Chione, looking across the vast hall at the two demons. The winged one was maimed, which would tip the scales of the fight, this critical battle over possession of the Key of Crantil.

'I suppose asking you for the box would be futile,' the she-demon said in her own language.

'You suppose correctly,' Azare fired back in kind.

Meecha's body shuddered. Her blood was already taking its toll.

'Before we begin, tell me something. Where were you when my claws were exploring your lady's innards?'

A tremor shook Azare. 'Your fate will be far grimmer. Your words will only lengthen your suffering.'

A stabbing pain in Meecha's head made him stagger to the left. He clutched his temples, while tottering to the corner. His blood burned, and his eyesight wavered. He dropped to one knee and retched, the taste of bile and demon blood heavy on his tongue.

'What was the wench's name?' the she-demon taunted. 'Rune, was it? What a fitting name. She was quite the riddle, wasn't she?'

'You know nothing of her!'

Another skewer in Meecha's brain made him lurch to the right. Finding support against the wall, he stumbled towards the small corridor.

'Oh, as a matter of fact, I know more than you,' the she-demon hissed. 'Did she ever entrust you with her family's secret? You see, she knew what her father's amulet was. Can you suspect why?'

Azare was silent. Meecha looked in his direction, but everything was a blur.

'Your beloved Rune was a traitor! She came from a long line of traitors. Her family has been harbouring the Key until we had use for it again. Didn't she tell you?'

Through a single lucid moment, Meecha discerned the ache surfacing on Azare's face, but then another wave of nausea spurred him into motion again.

'You lie!' the elf cried, drawing the other sword to accompany its twin.

'That's not even the best part,' the she-demon's voice overpowered his. 'Even in death Rune couldn't trust you. She's been watching you drown in sorrow, and she has done nothing to ease your suffering.'

Meecha found the edge of the doorway through which he had come. He stepped in front of the opening where there was no support to be had. He wavered. A strange, alien urge pulled him towards the demons.

'No! She... she is gone!' Azare shouted just as something rammed into Meecha, throwing him onto his back.

The box flew from his hand and skidded all the way to the dais in the middle of the room. The she-demon hissed

furiously at Adalis, who stood upon Meecha's chest, nipping his nose.

'Thank you,' Meecha hugged the chanter, his mind clearing.

Nandil skulked out of the corridor to call to Azare, 'She fed Meecha her blood a few days ago.'

The she-demon snarled in Therean, 'And thy mind has yielded many insights, Agent Roa. I would not have found this place without thee. And I would not have known that Rune is thy master. Thou serve a traitor!'

'I didn't know who she was,' Meecha shouted at the ceiling—he could not see Azare. 'But a traitor wouldn't have made it to the aerieti. She sent me to guide you, Azare. I think she knew that her death would lead you to a dark place. She loves you! Don't allow this monster to distort her memory. It's trying to stall the inevitable. Its fate was sealed the moment it killed your lover.'

Azare's voice was a low rumble. 'Rune was my wife.'

A golden glow began to manifest in the room. Both demons retreated a step or two, hissing. When Meecha's eyes finally found Azare, he gasped. The elf was ablaze. The scars on his face had cracked open to reveal a fiery light within. No, it was not like fire. It was the sun. His eyes were liquid gold. Azare abandoned his swords and screamed. The she-demon ran for the box.

Chapter 47

The forest of Arhan. Old as the mountains, its voice deep and vivid. Its sweet breath carried the scent of its skin and its children. Animal and thaelil walked together, even in the city blessed by the sun every morning and put to sleep by the moons each night.

'Magic is alive in Arhan,' Elder Gindira said to him once. 'In the soil, in the air, in the water. Extraordinary things have come to pass in Arhan, the oldest home of thaelil kind.'

This was where he found himself once more. Cizi was on the prowl beside him, the string of his fine bow drawn to his cheek, the arrow nocked and ready to fly. His sakairin was only six marks deep, but his skill told of a promising future. *Brother. Forgive me, brother.*

Azare took the lead, his swords freshly polished and sharpened. His eyes searched the trees for the intruder, the brazen demon that had dared tread the sacred grounds of

Arhan. And there it was. It rose from behind a hedge to snarl at them. It was small—easy prey.

Azare came out of the shadows and stepped into the stream rushing over a waterfall to the lake below. Cizi followed warily, his arrow trained on the demon. The fiend gnashed its fangs, warning them off, but it only drew them nearer. *I was such a fool. I did not see, brother.*

When they were well into the stream, the demon chattered excitedly and a powerful sweep of energy hurled them over the edge. Azare could hear the demon laughing as he fell. He was swallowed by the lake, engulfed by its chill waters.

A flash of golden light and he was facing Cizi, who stood in the waist-deep water holding up an unusual piece of rock. Azare snapped at him to stop playing around. The young thaelil dropped it back into the lake, but golden dust remained on his hands.

Another flash and Cizi was lying in his bed burning up with an unprecedented fever, shouting in his sleep of fire and hell-hounds. His sweat seared holes into his bedclothes and none could touch him without gloves or magic. His little sister stood in a corner staring at the chaos, eyes wide with fear.

Flash... and Azare was telling Gindira of their failed hunt and the rock they had found in the lake. He overheard the Elder discussing with the others a firestorm that had occurred in the area while Azare and his brother hunters had been away on a trail. The rock, they said, must have come from the sun and kept some of its fire. Instead of quenching it, the Arhan lake's waters absorbed it, perhaps altered it. And Cizi's body was rejecting the subsequent fusion.

Flash... Cizi was stumbling down an alley, glowing and weeping. He howled that he was on fire, that he could feel his body coming undone. Azare and many others ran to his aid, but were too late. *Too late to run.* The young warrior burst into flames—years of desolation did not quell his screams, which still echoed in Azare's ears. Cizi erupted, unleashing the sun in all its fury. Golden flames enveloped trees, dwellings, thaelil. They blotted out the moons. Only fire existed for a time undefined, eating away at shrieking Arhan.

The blaze flared brighter, and Azare was trudging through the forest towards its end. He had travelled this far before, but he never imagined himself doing it for the last time. He could never return. He had been able to control the sun in his own blood, yet the risk was too great. He longed to have perished with his brethren. He would have been spared the pain of seeing the same wish mirrored in the eyes of his remaining kin, including Gindira's. But, no, he survived. His wounds were healed, his strength restored so he could live the rest of his life in exile, in shame. He had to abandon his home, bury his grief with the hated humans.

Flash... A dark night. A dank street. And a pair of bright emerald eyes. His world was turned on its head, his wits lost to the power of her gaze. She moved closer, step by step, with a dancer's swagger and a dagger's smile. Her breath brushed against his lips, and his heart lurched. He grimaced, bewildered by his reaction to this creature. Frozen in place, his eyes explored every inch of her beautiful face. He even took in her scent. She smelt of cinnamon, oranges, and the smoke of wood. Her smirk softened. Her eyebrows lifted endearingly, while she shied and blushed under his spellbound glare.

'Thou never seen a woman before?' she chuckled nervously.

He could not keep the edge from his voice as he responded, 'Thou are human.'

It was more of an incredulous statement, an exclamation towards the absurd emotions he was experiencing for an enemy. How charming it was, the way her nose crinkled when she frowned. How the green of her eyes shone like dew-covered grass when they widened to devour his soul. All of a sudden, she tore herself away. Her gawk was the same as all others' who saw thaelil for the first time. But her sneer returned, deeper and more playful than before, and she hefted his pouch with pride.

'How clever am I? I just picked an elf's pocket,' she gave him a coy giggle. 'Can thou get it back, I wonder?'

Flash... and Rune was in his arms. He had retrieved his pouch but not his heart. That belonged to her, then and forever after. She rested against his chest, safe and free from care. Her golden clasps glimmered in her pale curls; frayed silk draped over her slender shoulders. Three blissful cycles shrouded in her love, her touch, her cinnamon smell. He was no longer in exile, but where he had always belonged. With Rune in their little cabin in the woods.

Flash... and the red flames danced on the roof. She was on the ground halfway out the door. He dropped the deer. Tears blinded him as he carried her to safety. Her skin was crimson, swollen, blistered. Her scent was replaced by the odour of seared flesh. Wisps were left of her beautiful hair. But her eyes... her eyes were as dazzling as ever. They clung to him. They begged him to hold her tight. He did so, pleading and howling to the Gods. Sobs seized him while she tried to speak, managing only to rasp and moan, until she gasped for air, shuddered, and sank into his arms. Limp. Lifeless.

His face slackened. He stared at her, deaf to the inferno crackling nearby, blind to his world crumbling around him. For a moment, his breath left him too. A void appeared where his heart once throbbed. That had gone with his wife, so he could find her when he followed. His groan became a growl. His growl became a scream. And that became a roar that caused the trees to shiver and bow. He hacked at them in fury—her killers were beyond his reach. But not for long. He would find them. He would rip them apart, piece by piece. He was a hunter once more.

Flash... and he was still roaring. He filled the throne room with his anguish and rage. He wanted Rune back. He wanted her murderers dead. He wanted to be with her again. The sun could do that for him. It could make everything right. All he had to do was let it go. Let it burn. He could already feel it happening. He flared and the chamber turned hotter. Any moment now he would burst into glorious flames, and it would all be over.

'No, my love!'

His eyes snapped open. Her hair radiated white against his blaze. Her gaze pierced the sun's glow. And her smile...

'Not yet,' she said.

Her hand was cool against his blistering cheek.

'Rune,' he gasped. 'My Rune.'

She stroked his eyes, his nose, his mouth. She wrapped her arms around him and he shivered. His eyes brimmed with tears he had thought spent. He could feel her, soft yet electrifying. There was a fresh, sweet taste to her lips like the waters of New Anvadore. And her smell. It was as if it had never left him.

'I want to come with thee,' he pleaded.

Stars fell from her eyes. 'I know.'

They clung to each other, neither wanting to let the other go.

'Let me join thee,' he whispered in her ear.

'Thou shall, my love.' She buried her face in his neck and gave it a lingering kiss. 'But not yet. Stay thy fire. It's needed elsewhere. Thy time shall come, Azare, an' I shall be there to greet thee.'

She started to pull away, but he held her tighter, shaking his head.

'Thou must let me go. Calm thyself an' let me go. Find solace in my love an' in my promise that we shall be together again. An' it shall be forever.'

He forced his arms to part from around her waist.

'I love thee so much,' he groaned as she drifted away, dissolving into a shimmering cloud of blue light.

He squeezed his eyes shut, tears dripping onto the floor, and took a deep, ragged breath. He drew the heat back into his body. He slowed his pulse and regained control of his senses. When he opened his eyes again, Chione was battling both demons, while Adalis slashed at their legs with his little claws. Meecha was using his fists and teeth. Nandil's bow was finally seeing action—one arrow was sticking out of the she-demon's thigh and three were lodged into her companion's thick hide.

Azare held onto a fragment of sun and charged past Chione. The she-demon failed to react in time while being assailed from multiple fronts. He grabbed both her arms and spread them wide, immobilising her. He then hit her with that tiny portion of sunlight. She screeched and tried to break free, but she was already burning. Her skin bubbled and cracked. Her howl turned shrill just before she combusted and started to disintegrate. He watched her being slowly reduced to ash. The arms, the head, the torso, the legs. A thrill ran through him when he upended his fists and the last of the she-demon floated to the floor.

Chione had already moved on to the other beast. Even with two of his four arms, he was a fearsome opponent. But when his companion crumbled before his eyes, he went truly berserk. He threw the chantress aside and made a headlong run for Azare, whose strength was finally spent. His reflexes failed him and he tripped over one of his swords. The great fiend slowed to a prowl. Batting away Nandil's arrow meant for its eye, it came to tower over Azare, a grotesque grin breaking across its face. Horns and claws were brandished in triumph before it lunged for him.

Out of nowhere, Meecha dove onto Azare's fallen sword. He gripped the hilt with both hands and roared, putting all his might into one ascending swing. The blade whistled upwards, while the demon leant down. Both Meecha and Azare were struck by a deluge of blood from the creature's neck—it was too thick and hard to slice in a single sweep. The demon flailed and gurgled wildly, buckling to the floor and dragging Meecha along, he still attached to the sword. The little man planted a foot on the writhing thing to help pull the blade out. One of the fiend's hands grasped his leg, the other went for his waist, but Meecha brought the sword down a second time. And a third. And a fourth. And the taloned hands finally slackened to the floor, the head rocking on its horns. A frantic laugh escaped Meecha. When he turned on his heels, however, rigid and awkward, he looked terrified.

'How about that?' he said shakily and Azare could not help himself—he cracked a smile.

Nandil appeared, carrying the box. Chione limped up to them and Adalis scampered over and nuzzled her.

'What about this?' Nandil inquired.

'Let us open it.' Azare laid it upon his blood-soaked legs, reached into the pouch at his waist, and pulled out the three clasps.

The others watched him clip one clasp into the other until they made an intertwined shape identical to the one carved into the lid. They fit perfectly. He turned the now unlocked disk and opened the box.

Nestled within was a claw—or a fang or a curved blade made of amber—and about the length of Azare's palm. Its base was wrapped in wire that ended in a little loop, from where Inan must have hung it as a pendant. The Key of Crantil. It looked unremarkable, but the threat it posed made it very special. This was part of an instrument that could open a gate to the abyss. Arak Sildrax and his demons had used it. And they wanted it back. Azare closed the lid and handed the box to Meecha.

'Thou are to be its keeper, no?'

'I suppose so,' the little man replied, holding the container with care.

Azare stood up, stifling a groan, and reclaimed his swords.

Meecha tilted his head. 'How did you know how to open it?'

Azare became grim. He cleared his throat and replied, 'Rune told me that her father was once a box-maker, and when I saw the lock on this one I knew what the key was. She rarely took these clasps off her hair. They were the only thing I had left to remind me of her.'

'I'm sorry for your loss. She's a lovely lady.' Meecha paused. He licked his lips, glancing uncomfortably at his shoes. 'I'm also sorry you were kept in the dark. I don't know how much, if any, of what the demon said is true, but I'm certain she only wanted your wellbeing.'

'And my swords.' His dryness drew a curious flash of anger from Meecha, who hefted the box awkwardly.

Azare took the demon's head by the horn and hoisted it over his shoulder. He then remembered what Nandil had said earlier. 'How thou feeling? With the demon's blood.'

Meecha bit his lip. 'Hallucinations, violent outbursts, upset stomach, general discomfort… All in all, I'm quite all right.'

'Thou been through the worst part. As long as the new blood does not take effect, thou should be getting better. If it does, I look forward to muzzling thee.'

Azare sneered as Meecha stuck out his tongue. They made for the small corridor.

'Azare.'

He turned with a sigh. 'Yes, Meecha?'

'You'll see her again.'

Azare smiled inwardly. 'Yes. Yes, I shall.'

Nandil trotted up to them from the direction of the inner chamber, holding a bulging rag, which he was in the process of knotting at the top. He noticed Meecha's enquiring look and shrugged.

'Inan's bones. What I could find, at least. This is a pretty tomb, but he should be buried right. With Rune, 'haps. They were good people.' He turned a hooded glance at Azare. 'No matter what, their hearts were good.'

Human comfort, Azare mused as he sniffed and made for the exit. *Fragile, self-destructive, inane creatures.* A strange, annoying warmth tingled his heart. He grunted, while his companion's voices echoed behind him.

'Nandil,' Meecha said. 'You wouldn't have my hat, would you? And needle and thread. And a bit of cloth?'

'Aye, I believe I do,' the human replied. 'What for?'

'I can't be carrying this box around,' the little man stated before intoning, 'and I have an idea.'

Chapter 48

N ew Anvadore was draped in black, peasant and noble alike. More banners accompanied the phoenix over the city now. Their black was streaked with cloth of silver to make them glimmer as they wavered in the wind. The priests' robes were dark grey or midnight blue, and even the soldiers had donned black cloaks. *They're still in mourning.*

Princess Delia's funeral had surely come and gone, but she may not have been the only reason for those downcast faces. They feared the meaning behind the demons' attack. They were possibly wondering if history was about to repeat itself. This would be cause enough to question the king. After all, it was his brother who had wrought the destruction of old Anvadore by associating with demons.

Some glum gazes turned to Meecha and his fellows. A few even showed recognition. A grinning boy waved to him, and he tipped his hat in return—Nandil had produced it, slightly crumpled, from the depths of his bag when they had emerged from the diamond and walked the watery bridge back to dry land. It felt right to have it back on his head. Its power, however, had changed its effect on him. It did not protect or heal his soul—his friends did that, and his own endurance. In his eyes it was no longer a mystical shield or lucky charm, but a plain old hat he rather liked, as well as a reminder of why he was an agent.

He made worlds better by guarding the innocent and guiding the worthy. Sometimes he failed. And the faces of the fallen haunted him. But it was for them that he did it all, not the aerieti, his often heartless masters. He did it because he was angry at injustice and corruption and betrayal. He would stamp them out with every life he saved, or gave purpose to, no matter how small. As long as he and all these bright lives persevered, fought back, the evils of the worlds would not win.

Had Rune's family truly been a part of Itania's darkness? Had she? Meecha's heart told him that whatever she used to be was gone, forgiven by the aerieti. Her and her father's actions spoke of a change of heart, a will to keep the Key from the demons' clutches. That is what Meecha would believe unless proven otherwise.

Now, the Key's protection was paramount, and the dismantling of the Crantil plot. Fortunately, the hat found a way to reclaim its honour and increase its importance in this quest. Meecha could feel the extra weight, literal and metaphorical. He hoped the wind would have a harder time stealing the hat, but some additional safety measures would be warranted. A loop of string, perhaps.

Eyes widened at the sight of Chione and Adalis trotting along on either side of him. Nandil relished the attention for simply walking behind him. But it was Azare, his hair neatly gathered in the golden clips, who earned the most awed stares. He had not pulled up his hood, so his ears were visible, drawing the eye as much as his burden did. It was wrapped in a sizeable length of cloth, but not all of it would fit. The elf was still using one of the great horns as a handle. *They know what it is. This should lift their spirits a little.*

By the time they reached the Second Ring's gateway into the castle grounds, a crowd had gathered to escort them. The guards looked baffled, until they too saw Azare's bloody sack. Their jaws dropped.

'Is that one of them?' people shouted.

'Are they dead?'

'Can we mount it on the wall?'

Nandil was more than happy to address them.

'The beasts are dead!' he boldly announced with arms outstretched. 'This is the head of the biggest one. 'Tis our gift to ye, good Anvadorians. Those monsters met the gruesome end they deserved.'

The crowd hooted with joy. They hugged one another and cheered. Nandil basked in the adulation, until Azare grabbed him by the scruff and dragged him into the gardens. The way was barred behind them, and they walked in peace to the castle's oak doors. At the steps leading up to them, they swung open and Vorami Teretta's petite, blue-robed figure strode out to greet them.

'Welcome back, my friends. 'Tis heartening to see you all live. And victorious, no less. When Thasha returned alone, we feared the worst.'

'He made it back?' Nandil cut in, delighted.

'He did, and in good health. Thou may visit him later.'

Meecha was the first to shake the priestess's hand. 'It was quite the trial, Vora. I look forward to scrubbing its memory off me with water and soap.'

Vora chuckled. 'Thou shalt, Meecha. Baths and beds await to soothe the aches of your journey. First, however, I must bring you to the king. You were seen coming before your own eyes even touched our walls. The royal family has gathered in the throne room to shower you with praise.'

The Master Architect led them down the familiar halls.

'The whole family?' Azare asked.

'I fear so.' Her expression suddenly darkened. 'And... they know about the Key.'

Meecha's stomach clenched. 'How?'

Vora wrung her hands as she replied softly, 'After you left, I acquired some additional shadows besides my own. Eventually, I was questioned about thee and thine interest in the demons.'

'They didn't hurt you, did they?'

'Oh, no. It was a civilised discussion, but one I couldn't take lightly. Forgive me, Meecha, but the truth had to come out, if only to avoid unnecessary tension.'

'I understand completely, Vora. Lies and deception will only rile the Ayviks. Sharing important knowledge will keep them happy and cooperative.'

The priestess regarded him with relief. 'I am glad that we have some sensible players on our side. Charging with-

out thought or caution shalt lead to disaster. We need to plan. We must think like our friends in the Light.'

'And like the enemy,' Azare said.

'For we can't always tell whose faces they wear,' Nandil added, drawing a remorseful nod from Meecha.

They finally stood before the phoenix doors, and Vora knocked with a knuckle. The doors opened to reveal the king and queen sitting on their thrones. Dradan and Ditrik stood beside their father, while fair Laylin hovered with poise over her mother's shoulder. The princess wore a splendid violet dress, the collar wide across the shoulders and decorated with black pearls. Her lustrous hair was plaited into a long braid, and a jewel hung upon her brow. Her brothers were in fine tunics, Dradan in red and Ditrik in dark blue. They seemed fully recovered from their grief. Only the queen remained stoically shrouded in black. Even Odigan had traded his attire for a dark shade of green.

Meecha could see the scorn in Ditrik's face when the prince beheld their wretched states. Layers of dirt and blood had caked their skin. Meecha had been somewhat relieved when his nose had ceased to acknowledge their stench. At least he had done his duty and warned Vora that they needed to bathe. Her disregard was to blame for the royals' discomfort.

'Ah, our heroes,' boomed the king.

He got to his feet leisurely, while Meecha, Nandil, and Azare lined up before the dais. Chione sat before them, but Adalis ran straight for the queen. Laylin squeaked and pulled away, while her mother welcomed the chanter with an affectionate smile.

'You have grown,' she exclaimed, watching the cub climb the steps.

Meecha politely interjected, 'We gave him a name, your Grace. It's Adalis.'

'Adalis. Strong, regal.' The queen's smile deepened.

The cub reached her and climbed unhindered onto her lap. He purred when she stroked him—he was getting too fond of cuddles. Laylin watched with a mixture of envy and disdain.

'Welcome back, friends,' Odigan said. 'I see you have not returned empty-handed.'

Azare stepped forward, holding before him the demon's head. His left hand untied the cloth. With a swift flourish he yanked it away and gasps rippled around the room. Laylin covered her wrinkled nose. Dradan's face depicted amazement, while his brother scowled. The queen stopped caressing Adalis—her unblinking gaze was fixed on the monstrous head. The king descended to come and glare into its dead red eyes. He placed his hand upon its snout and smiled spitefully. He then looked up at Azare.

'Hast thou claimed thy trophy?'

'There was nothing left of it to claim.'

King Odigan gave the elf a satisfied nod and turned to acknowledge Nandil.

'Master Hithe, I wast not aware of thy part in this.'

Nandil bowed. 'Thy Majesty, Princess Delia was a dear friend. I wished to help bring her killers to justice. Or worse.'

Meecha caught a derisive twist to Laylin's mouth.

'Thank thee,' Odigan responded. 'It wouldst seem her fondness of thee wast not misplaced. I am certain she would be proud of thee.'

Nandil's head dipped even lower, and the king moved on to Meecha.

'And thou, Master Roa, hast proven my son wrong in the most splendid manner.'

'He did not—I bet the elf did all the work,' Dradan grumbled.

'Truth be told,' Nandil interjected, 'it was Meecha who beheaded the demon.'

All the royals gaped at him. Prince Dradan practically snarled.

'Is that so?' the king marvelled.

Warmth ran up Meecha's neck to his cheeks as he stammered, 'Well, it was more of a lucky strike. Or five. Good timing and all.'

'He saved my life,' Azare told them and sniffed with disdain when Meecha gawked at him.

'Waters open before him,' Nandil added. 'I've seen it.'

'And his words sway kings,' a husky voice cut through the flattery like a saw.

Laylin glided to the edge of the dais. She clasped her hands behind her back, her dazzling eyes fixed on Meecha. Her next words were coated in honey when they emerged from her ruby lips.

'We art all grateful for your service. A feast hast been prepared to celebrate your heroic return. Your names shalt be whispered in awe throughout New Anvadore and it shalt not take long for your exploits to reach the ears of the rest of Therea. Yet there is something troubling that must be addressed. Thou, Agent Roa, neglected to tell us all there is to know about the dangers ahead. Thou misled my father, kept thy true intentions to thyself. Why is that?'

The king did not contradict his daughter. His expression made the same accusations.

Meecha widened his eyes in an innocent fashion and then sighed ruefully. 'I can't deny my mistrust. As an agent of the Light, I've seen many betrayals, even from the most unlikely of sources. My masters are very secretive too. Can you blame them after seeing for yourselves what the enemy is capable of? I was forbidden from divulging my mission to anyone. I'm a soldier like any other, following orders. But those orders were meant for the good of the realm. I swear, your Grace, I'm here to protect, not harm.'

Some uncertain moments went by, until Odigan finally succumbed.

'I understand. I too know much about betrayal. But, now, I need the truth.'

Meecha took a deep breath and acceded, for the sake of the Ayviks' 'happiness and cooperation'.

'My initial mission was to find and recruit Azare in the fight against the demons. Later I was told what the enemy truly sought: the Key of Crantil. It had been used in the first demonic invasion to open a portal between their world and this one. The demons that attacked this city were the ones assigned with its recovery, and that's why I was following them. To stop them or find the Key before they did.'

'Wert thou successful?' the king inquired.

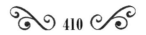

'I believe so. We found an interesting box hidden in some ruins.' *Here goes nothing.* 'We could not open it, but the demons desperately wanted to. I'm certain it contains the Key.'

Laylin descended a step. 'How canst thou be sure if thou cannot open it?'

He mirrored her charm. 'An agent of the Light knows when evil is near.'

The princess pouted and cocked her head haughtily. 'What dost thou intend to do with it?'

'Keep it safe.'

'Would thou consider remaining in New Anvadore? I promised thee a place in my court,' Odigan proposed. 'And there's nowhere safer than the castle vaults.'

Meecha considered this. 'I can't stay, your Grace. I've much to do, and finding the way to access this box is one of them.'

'The open road is no place for such a dangerous artefact,' Dradan protested.

'I agree. Dost thou even know where to go for the knowledge thou seek?' Ditrik joined his voice to his siblings'.

Vora came to Meecha's rescue, 'The library of Mecanta may hold answers.'

'Or my people,' Azare put forward.

'The elves?' Dradan exclaimed. 'Why involve them?'

Azare retorted, 'For one, they would not use the Key for their own gain.'

All three Ayvik children were in an uproar, cursing him and his ilk. The elf was not shy to retaliate. Meecha sighed. *Here we go again.* Azare threw the demon's head at their feet, shouting that they were more like their uncle than their father. His comment cut deep, for both princes went for their swords. Odigan tried to calm his offspring, while Nandil and Meecha did the same with Azare. Only when Laylin suddenly fell silent did everyone else notice the queen standing behind her, her long fingers resting on the girl's shoulder. Adalis trailed her down the steps. She approached Meecha, willowy and delicate.

'This squabbling is pointless. Demeaning,' she stated matter-of-factly, her rich voice surprisingly calm and stable. 'This Key is a vital piece in the grand scheme between Light and Darkness. It must be kept safe and thy path clear of obstacles. Keep it in thy possession and the demons shalt not stop hounding thee. Thou may not wish to part with it, but this castle is the best place for it. If thou wish further reassurance, I shalt place it under my personal protection.'

She halted before him, but Meecha had yet to make up his mind.

'I sensed the danger to the city before the demons appeared. I sensed my grievous future that hast not yet reached its conclusion. It wast I who saw thy return through water and diamonds. In the same way, I shalt know if the box is ever at risk. I give thee my word that I shalt keep it safe. None but my hands shall touch it. Canst thou trust me, Agent Roa?'

Chione acknowledged the queen with a sniff and a gentle rub against her leg. She purred.

'I think I can, your Grace.'

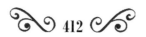

Nandil sullenly extracted the box from his bag. When Meecha had no further use for it, he had given it to the merchant, who eagerly claimed it and what other loose trinkets he could fit in alongside Inan's remains—the bejewelled chair was too heavy, he'd said. Nandil placed the box in the queen's hands. She studied it, hefted it slightly, before looking back up at him, Azare, and finally at Meecha. She glanced up at his hat, and a spark appeared in her eyes. She straightened and filled the room with her radiant voice.

'I, Aisri Ayvik, eldest of the House Deitana, Queen of Therea, and servant of the Light, swear to thee, Meecha Roa, that I shalt protect this box with all my power.'

Her children would have been far more satisfied with the box in their care, but they held their tongues. Everyone, it seemed, had remembered their places.

'Excellent,' the king clapped his hands. 'You must be eager to freshen up before the feast. Your quarters await you. Your every need shalt be provided for. Allow New Anvadore to express its gratitude.'

And so it happened. Meecha, Azare, and Nandil were ushered to the baths, while the chanters were led to the grove to dine on the finest and most succulent steaks, a donation from the best Anvadorian vendors. Nandil sought out Thasha at the stables as soon as he was clean, dressed, and perfumed. They were all given a selection of clothes to pick from. Azare chose a simple outfit of black leather trousers, a black silk shirt, and his own boots, which he at least had the decency to polish before putting back on. The only colour on him was the gold in his hair. His bland attitude towards this fine occasion did not deter the maids from swooning in his presence. Meecha, on the other hand, decided to oblige their hosts by wearing the phoenix tunic that had been purposefully hung at the very front of his wardrobe. It was made of splendid burgundy silk with the white bird emblazoned on the front. He picked some burgundy trousers and a pair of black boots. He thought he looked quite dashing when he looked at himself in the mirror. The hat and dreadlock certainly gave some flair to the whole ensemble. Perhaps he would let the beard grow out too.

During these hours before the feast, a handful of lords and ladies came to fawn over them. Only Azare seemed to fit their expectations. They were all very eager to see Meecha's fearsome pets, but he fell even further in their eyes when he refused to drag the chanters into a room full of people just to entertain them. Their pinched faces would not relent even when he explained that their own safety would be at risk.

The whole of New Anvadore buzzed with jubilant sounds by the time Meecha, Azare, and Nandil were ready to face the masqueraded wolves. They agreed, however, that there was something they had to do first. They got directions from one of the servants and made their way to the gardens, trying to ignore the delicious smells that had begun to fill the halls.

Chapter 49

The gravestone was of white marble moulded into a man-sized phoenix taking flight. An inscription was chiselled into it and filled with red ink so the name of the one buried beneath was clearly legible.

Her Royal Highness of Jherea, Delia Ayvik.

Birth: summer of the Fiftieth Cycle P.R.

Death: summer of the Sixty-sixth Cycle P.R.

'A summer child,' Meecha mused.

Nandil sighed, 'She was only ten an' six. Barely a woman, but wiser than Teretta. An' so kind. No king or Light could stop her helping the poor.'

'I think she took from her mother's side of the family.'

'She did indeed.'

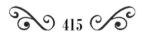

'What does P.R. mean?'

'Post Rift.'

'All the graves are the same,' Azare noted, glancing around the graveyard. 'Only names and soil set them apart. When my people die and are returned to the earth, their graves are marked with a tree or a flower. Princess Delia was an extraordinary human. So young, yet she inspired her people. She deserves better than this.'

The burial ground of the royals was walled off by hedge and fence from the rest of the gardens. Currently, it accommodated the princess and her grandparents, each with their own marble phoenix to stand guard over their bodies. The only difference between them was the recently disturbed earth over Delia's grave.

The elf approached the gravestone and knelt before it. He buried his hands well into the soil and spoke in an unfamiliar tongue, Thaelil most likely, harsh yet strangely pleasing to the ear. Upon a deep, humming voice his words were carried to the earth, until a shoot of grass broke through the dirt between his fingers. Astonished, Nandil and Meecha watched the shoot grow into a golden stem, which then sprouted leaves and finally a white bud. Its petals uncurled. Meecha gasped when he realised that it was the same flower that had grown behind Azare's burned-down cabin. *It was no simple ritual. It was Rune's grave.* The white and golden blossom continued to grow with the help of Azare's voice. He retreated to let it enfold Delia's phoenix. When it stopped, only the top line of the script was visible. All else was hidden behind branches and leaves of gold.

'By the Light,' a voice came from behind them.

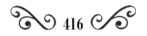

Azare ceased his singing. Queen Aisri stood at the graveyard's entrance. Her eyes were wide and tearful—trembling hands covered her gaping mouth.

'Thy Grace,' Nandil bowed and shied from her path.

She stepped between them, her sight ensnared by Azare's flowers.

'They are Neniti,' he explained softly. 'Flowers of the Lost. Their gold stems become the paths to lead our loved ones to a peaceful place in death.'

Aisri regarded him, her wise features heavy with emotion. 'Thou wouldst do this for my child? A human thou dost not know?'

His brow furrowed. He seemed as perplexed as she. 'I suppose I have come to doubt what I was taught about thy kind. That only the worst can be expected from humans. I never would have imagined that I would marry one.'

Bewilderment flashed across Aisri's face. 'What is her name?'

Meecha spotted a minute crack in Azare's composure. 'Rune. Her name was Rune.'

He scowled at the surrounding hedge, blinking several times. The queen's previous delight vanished, but Azare quickly returned with a fervent gleam in his eyes.

'I saw her.' Meecha and Nandil exchanged looks. 'When I was face to face with her murderer, I almost gave up. My grief overwhelmed me, and I nearly killed us all. But she stopped me. She appeared to me and she was...' His happy chuckle tipped a stray tear from the corner of his eye. He wiped it away. 'She is in a good place, and if Delia was as special as Rune was—and the love she has been given tells me that she was—then she shall go to the same place as my wife. I merely hope to have made her passage brighter.'

The queen's smile resurfaced. 'Thank you, Azare. I know how pain can disguise a person, and I am honoured to have seen the benevolent being that lies beneath thy hard shell. It saddens me that our peoples cannot forget the past. Whether this changes someday or not, thaelil shalt always find an ally in me.' Aisri turned so she could address them all. 'So shalt each and every one of you. You may not know this, but before my father gave me to the king I was studying to become a Divine Architect.'

Nandil would have been the one to know, but, by his shocked expression, this information had eluded him.

'It's good to find another kindred spirit,' Meecha grinned.

'Allow me to sweeten our encounter with a gift. May I borrow thy hat for a moment?'

She knows! His smile sat frozen. Trying to stay calm, he slowly reached up, took off his hat, and gave it to her.

She held the hat before her, her right hand resting on the top. 'I still possess some useful magic.'

She closed her eyes and muttered under her breath. For a few moments her soft mumbling was all that could be heard in the graveyard. Meecha thought he picked up his own name somewhere in the incantation. Then, all of a sudden, his hat glowed. It was engulfed by a bluish-white aura the colour of lightning. And then it was not. Aisri bent down and plopped his hat back onto his head.

''Tis done. Thou art now the absolute master of this hat. Even if thou lose it on the other side of the world, it

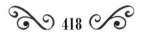

shalt always find its way back to thee. And only thee,' she said pointedly.

'That shall make things easier.' Nandil gave Meecha a sharp look. 'Just make sure it doesn't need to find its way back.'

Meecha's abashed face dropped to his feet.

Nandil patted him on the back. 'Come on, demon slayer. Let us join the feast.'

'Yes, you should,' the queen urged. 'You art heroes now. And this day belongs to you.'

She reminded Meecha of a doe, striding gracefully towards the gate, the hem of her black gown making the grass curtsy. They all followed her out of the graveyard, but he halted just outside the fence to look back at Delia's phoenix.

He had a feeling that the princess was not done fighting. He could just imagine her standing side by side with Rune, watching over their loved ones. His eyes drifted up to the dusk. A few hasty stars had already emerged. Two of the moons had too, pale and majestic.

'We'll make you proud,' Meecha said to the sky. 'Every demon that gets in my way shall be fed my boot. This I promise you. While Agent Roa takes breath, Itania will not fall. Ladies...'

He tipped his hat goodnight.

Epilogue

The white sun on the great, straight tooth is beautiful. Even from here I can see it breaking the darkness above. One of the pale balls is beyond, but less impressive to me. My son has no interest in any of this. Earth flies as he plays, thickening the smells—good smells. Dirt. Plants. Water. We like it here. The air shifts and my hair with it. A pleasant feeling. It makes my eyelids heavy. My chin pressed against the ground. But something comes. Another scent. Human.

I take some more in—mild and sweet it is, not like our feeders. I look towards its source without moving too much. There behind a tree. A two-legs. It is small. A male youngling. Fearful. And curious. It shows its teeth at my son—not for harm. It is like my red son's face of affection. I do not want this one any closer, though. It smells annoying. No, that smell does not belong to it. A taller two-legs approaches the smaller. It is older, male, and bad. It speaks.

'Begone.'

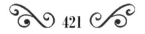

I do not understand the words, but the youngling jumps. It wisely retreats from us, wishing to flee, no doubt, but it stops, its eyes fixed on the other. My boy shies from that one too. Good.

'Thou Ditrik, no? On' of them princes.'

The older two-legs—it is barely of age—looks angrily down at the youngling, like I would a pitiful skittering prey.

'What is that to thee, whelp?'

The youngling's legs shuffle. It is preparing to run again.

'Delia spoke of thee. She show me thy face. All thy faces. An' thou were there. Thou saw.'

Now, it is sad. These two-legs are bothersome. My sigh goes unheard.

'Saw what?'

'Delia bein' taken,' the youngling mewls. 'It was my fault. I cause trouble an' they try to take me. An' she protect me. They took her. And, now…' it sniffles disgustingly. 'Forgive me.'

Bigger two-legs exudes fear, as well as anger. It looms threateningly over the little one, which lifts its eyes and whines again.

'I try to tell the guards, but they wouldn' help. Honest, I try an' they laugh. But thou told them, yes? Then they help. They don' listen to us, dirty folk, Master Father says—'

'Be quiet,' the predator snarls.

My boy hides behind me, but the youngling just cowers. Run, weakling.

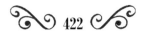

'Thou art making up stories. Lies. I was not there. Do thou hear me?'

The youngling trembles as it backs into a tree. The predator sighs and brings out something shiny from its hairless coat. It clicks into the youngling's paw.

'Here. A gift for thy promise that thou shalt not speak of this again. No more lies.'

The tiny fingers close around the thing before its mouth mumbles, 'But—'

The predator pounces. It grabs the youngling by the neck and pins it to the wood—it yelps and whimpers. My boy edges out from behind me and hisses at the bad two-legs. How surprising. Fine then. I have had enough of them too. I shout for their silence, jolting them both out of their senses. The world now reeks of terror. It is acceptable for a hunt, but not when I am to rest a full stomach.

Dirt and leaves lift at the two-legs' flight. They run in the same direction—away from us—but I am pleased that the youngling is faster. It lived then. Perhaps, it may live even longer. My boy is pleased. Yes, child, your red brother would be happy too.

Acknowledgements

This story and its universe have been a long, solitary work in the making. Yet some people were allowed into my little bubble of fun. Each person added insight and perspective to the shaping of Meecha's journey and my own as a writer.

My most important thanks go to my family for their support when I needed it the most. My mum, in particular, patiently read and reread the manuscript over many years. She brainstormed for titles and ideas as eagerly as I did, while saving the occasional character from their author's cruel schemes.

Next, a big thank you to my editors, Jeni Chappelle and Nick Hodgson. They didn't just help make the manuscript presentable. Their professional voices of reason and encouragement gave me much-needed confidence and direction on the way to self-publication.

At this point, it's an institution I want to give thanks to. My time at the University of East Anglia transformed the

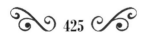

book in several major ways. Inspiring studies and academics opened my eyes to the potential of literature and taught me how to really have fun with writing as an artform.

Finally, I simply wish to pay homage to the authors of my childhood: J.R.R. Tolkien, Robert Jordan, Phillip Pullman, Ursula Le Guin, Terry Pratchett, and many more fantasy geniuses. They filled my world with so much joy, pushing my brain and pen beyond the confines of reality.

Thank you to everyone who embraced my weirdness. My goal of an epic trilogy by the age of 17 may have been delayed somewhat, but its ultimate fulfilment and expansion wouldn't have been possible without your warmth.

About the Author

Electra Nanou is originally from Thessaloniki, Greece. She is now a copywriter, content writer, and literary blogger based in Norwich, UK. She has self-published two short stories: *Familiar* and *Bumba Queen Weave*. *Roa Seeks* is her first novel.